Redhead

IAN COOK

Matador
9 Priory Business Park
Wistow Road
Kibworth Beauchamp
Leicester LE8 0RX, UK
Tel: (+44) 116 279 2299
Fax: (+44) 116 279 2277
Email: books@troubador.co.uk
Web: www.troubador.co.uk/matador

ISBN 978 1848767 652

British Library Cataloguing in Publication Data.
A catalogue record for this book is available from the British Library.

Typeset in 10.5pt Minion Pro by Troubador Publishing Ltd, Leicester, UK

Matador is an imprint of Troubador Publishing Ltd

Printed and bound in the UK by TJ International, Padstow, Cornwall

To Maggie,
with love
and thanks.

"…there is something Pagan in me that I cannot shake off. In short, I deny nothing, but doubt everything."

Lord Byron

ACKNOWLEDGMENTS

This book would not have been written without the generosity of those who read various drafts and gave invaluable help and advice, namely: Jane Alexander, Frances Banyard, Jo Bull, Christopher Clarke, Sandra Clarke, Christopher Cook, Matthew Cook, Yolanda Fernández Caliani, Mary Flannery, Janet Foster, Keith Foster, Paul Freeman, Peter Hawkins, Celia Hinton, Oliver Hinton, Pat Holt, Pete Holt, Michael Hosier, Rosalind Laurie, Heidi Mannan, Vivienne Osborne, Fred Raveney, Colin Rix, Eric Sargeant, Gill Seward, Fiona Stewart, James Stewart, Tom Stewart and Ivan Stipala.

My deepest thanks go to my wife, Maggie, who has been unstinting in her support, whether through constant editing or as a sounding board.

Much of the action in the story relates to real places such as the Standing Stones of Stenness, Ring of Brodgar and Unstan Chambered Tomb in Orkney. I should mention that the Newton Stones also exist, but they are in private grounds.

Whilst researching the book, I visited the Orkney island of Sanday and found everybody I met there both kind and helpful. In that unpleasant, although purely fictitious, events occur in the story on what is recognisably the island of Sanday, out of respect to the inhabitants, I have changed the name to Norstray.

CHAPTER 1

Tunisia, 1921

It was Christmas Eve in Carthage. Two middle-aged men were making their way down Byrsa Hill, trying to keep to the shadows of the ancient streets. Reaching a crossroad, they stopped to draw breath.

A full moon broke through the clouds, bathing the age-old ruins in a cold light. Warm sounds of laughter, snatches of excited conversation and carols sung in French drifted over in waves from the surrounding villas. A child protested as he was put to bed against his will.

In truth, both men would rather have been relaxing and enjoying the festivities than facing the task in hand.

Unnoticed by either of them, a large hawk dived down and landed on top of one of the pillars that stood scattered around the site. It watched the two men intently.

One of the men, Paul Durand, was a minor public official in the French administration service. He shivered, half with cold but half in anticipation of the events ahead. His fingers fumbled as he fastened the top button of his well-cut wool jacket.

His companion, François Attali, wore the uniform of a Tunis police inspector.

Both were amateur archaeologists in their spare time and had rapidly established themselves as experts on Punic Carthage. Together, they had initiated excavations at the necropolis and had established a small museum to display their finds. It was this shared passion that had brought them together on the cold December night. When a number of ancient Carthaginian stelae – carved commemorative stone slabs – had appeared on the black market in the Tunis Medina, their combined amateur and professional interests had propelled them into action to try and track down the source. An informer had put it about that an unauthorised dig was going on near the old harbour in Salammbô. On Christmas Eve, there was a good possibility that the culprits would not expect to be disturbed.

As they passed under a low archway, Attali slipped and stumbled. "*Merde*," he muttered under his breath. Durand ignored him. Trying to regain his balance, Attali stood up and banged his head on the arch, knocking his *képi* sideways. "*Fait chier*," he cursed. For just a moment, his dishevelled hair glinted in the moonlight.

They moved more carefully now, dodging from cover to cover. As they neared the bottom of the hill, they both caught sight of movement that caused them to freeze simultaneously. Quietly, they shrank back, crouching into the shadows. There below, two unkempt-looking men were digging vigorously with spades in a substantial pit.

As Attali and Durand watched, bracing themselves for their next move, one of the men stopped digging and reached down to free something from the soil. He held up a two-handled urn, studied it and put it to one side. Then he immediately picked up another. Attali nudged his colleague, and they slowly stood up together.

"*Allons-y!*" Attali shouted, like a cry to battle, as they sprang from their cover.

The diggers swung round, startled. In a panic, they scrambled up the side of the pit, one clawing his way up with a single hand, his other hand clutching an urn. Faced with a choice between hanging on to the urn or escaping, he looked back defiantly and threw it back into the pit. The *crack* as the urn smashed echoed into the night.

The Frenchmen reached the pit, gasping for breath.

"Let them go," said Attali. "This is more important." They watched as the thieves vanished into the darkness. Durand anxiously looked down into the pit for the broken urn. He slithered down the side of the hole and started gathering up the shards. At that moment, he noticed the contents that had spilt out. He picked up a blackened object and rubbed it with his hands to reveal a small skull. Expressions of shock, then disbelief, and finally fascination played over his face. He held the skull up for Attali to see.

"Can't be human, can it?" he said. "Too small. A monkey perhaps?"

"Or a small child," the inspector replied.

Durand instinctively rejected this suggestion, the implications being too great to contemplate. Instead, he looked around the pit. More urns could be seen in the bottom and sides; it was as if someone had methodically stacked them there. He reached down, prised another from the soil and gently lifted it above his head to inspect it in the moonlight. The glaze lit up a glowing red and faded as the moon disappeared behind clouds.

Durand lowered the urn, turned it upside down and apprehensively shook out the contents. There was a soft thud as another small skull hit the ground and rolled a short distance.

Excitedly, Durand started brushing the soil away from the side of the pit to reveal more and more urns. He turned round to beckon Attali, but his friend was absorbed in brushing the dirt away from a newly-excavated stone stele.

After clearing the last clump of soil away from the stone, Attali studied it carefully. In the dim light, the scene displayed in the carving on the stele was disturbing. It showed a man wearing what seemed to be a long robe, perhaps translucent, as his legs could plainly be seen, and a hat shaped like a modern fez. His right hand was raised in a gesture of worship, but in the crook of his left arm he was holding the unmistakable figure of an infant child.

Attali looked down and confirmed what Durand already suspected.

"There's something a bit nasty about all this," he said. "This man – he's not the father. He's a *kohanim* – a priest. And what we've got here must be the *tophet*, the place where they used to sacrifice babies."

Attali's mind was now racing. Tophet was the place outside Jerusalem, mentioned in the Old Testament, where child sacrifices had regularly been performed – a custom found throughout the ancient Middle East. Aware now of the importance of the moment, he instinctively seized the chance to dramatise.

"I wonder if they used Moloch?" he said, realising that this terrible form of sacrifice by fire could well have been carried out in this very place.

As if in response, the moon broke from the clouds again, illuminating the urns so that the men seemed to be surrounded by red lights. They both looked around, alarmed.

"Quite bright out here tonight," Durand said, trying to maintain a professional cool.

Attali took off his *képi* and smoothed down his hair as he gazed upwards. "Well, it's full moon," he said, attempting to match his friend's composure.

"Even so, I don't remember seeing moonlight this strong before," replied Durand, as he watched the glow behind the fleeting clouds. Refocusing his attention on their historic discoveries, Durand shook the urn again to make sure it was empty.

High above them, still keeping guard from the pillar, the hawk leaned forwards in their direction, shifting its weight from claw to claw and silently flapping its wings.

It was Attali who heard the sound of children crying, at first only faintly. As it grew louder, he started and stared around him. Durand was absorbed in sifting through the ashes shaken from the urn. The crying grew louder; almost unbearable now, so that Attali clapped his hands over his ears. He was about to shout out when it abruptly stopped. "Did you hear that?" he said quietly.

Durand looked up. "What? Did I hear what?"

Attali tried to keep his voice under control. "Babies – crying."

Durand glanced at his companion, shrugged his shoulders, and turned back to the contents of the urn. "I heard nothing. Probably a cat."

"That was not a cat," Attali muttered to himself. He listened hard, hands ready near his ears, seeking some sort of explanation. But the noise had gone, and he gradually lowered his arms.

Without warning, Attali's *képi* was sent flying, as the silent hawk swooped down on the two Frenchmen, talons outstretched. It landed with a thump on Attali's head, tearing out tufts of his hair. He screamed in pain, his arms flailing as he tried to beat it off, but already the bird's cruel beak was gouging deeply into his face.

CHAPTER 2

London, present

The Tower at Canary Wharf stood out brightly against a cold, miserable winter sky, the beacon on its pinnacle blinking defiantly at the gathering darkness.

On the twelfth floor, the newsroom of the *Metropolitan* was engaged in its usual frantic early evening activity.

Rebecca Burns jumped up from a desk and waved to a girl who walked through the main door. All male eyes instantly looked over towards Rebecca, as if drawn to a magnet. She knew that she attracted attention. It was difficult to miss her flame-coloured, wavy, shoulder-length hair, artfully highlighted by her lime green jacket and black pencil-tight skirt.

Now twenty-three, Rebecca had decided to abandon the security of a salaried position on a Scottish newspaper and take her chances as a freelance feature-writer based in London. To her delight, the *Metropolitan* had liked her portfolio and now took regular pieces from her.

Syreeta Dasgupta walked over to her. If Rebecca aspired to the image of a single, smartly-dressed female professional, Syreeta could not be more different. A young reporter of Indian origin, who had been on the paper for nearly three years, Syreeta exuded flamboyance with her long legs, short denim skirt, gamine hairstyle and broad Birmingham accent.

Syreeta flopped down in a chair, turning her back on senior reporter Geoff Evans, who was sitting nearby typing into his laptop and clearly irritated by the two women about to start chatting.

Rebecca and Syreeta had soon become friends, and it was to Syreeta alone that Rebecca had confided the main reason which had brought her to London. Six months previously, Rebecca's parents had been killed in an air crash while on holiday in Peru. She was their only child and had therefore borne the sole responsibility of dealing with the aftermath of their deaths.

Rebecca had had the undeniable urge to start afresh; to seek a new life in a busy city, which had also led to her breaking up with her boyfriend, a reporter on the same Scottish newspaper.

Once settled into her own studio flat, Rebecca found her new freedom brought with it a strong desire to travel, to get away for a while. She hoped that Syreeta would like to join her.

Syreeta listened to Rebecca chatter away before replying. "I'm really sorry, Becky. I love the idea, but I just don't have any holiday left. Isn't there anybody else who'd like to go?"

"I can't find anybody," replied Rebecca, in her soft Scottish accent. "Nobody's up for North Africa at this time of year. Miserable lot. These last few months have all been a bit too much – and now finishing with Hamish, on top of it all."

As Syreeta put her arm around her, Geoff Evans glanced over at them.

"It's all been a bit stressful," Rebecca said quietly. "I really need to get away somewhere different. Maybe only for a few days. Just to get some sunshine and sort my mind out."

"I know!" said Syreeta. "Why don't you see if anyone wants a story doing there? At least you'd get to meet some locals. And you wouldn't have to be on your own all the time."

Rebecca brightened. "Any ideas?"

"You could try Charles. He covers North Africa."

Geoff Evans had been eavesdropping as usual. "Why don't you just go to the Costa Brava like anybody else?" he said, in his strong Welsh accent.

Syreeta turned around slowly to face him. "You never did manage to crawl out of your valley did you, Evans? Why don't you get a life?"

They glared at each other while Rebecca raised her hands to

avoid becoming involved. The stand-off was interrupted by Mike, a computer engineer, attempting to push past Rebecca with a trolley laden with equipment.

"'Scuse me, Ginge," he said cheerfully.

Rebecca was about to answer back, when her mobile rang. Glancing at the number, she flushed slightly, and went over to the window for privacy.

"I wish you wouldn't keep phoning me," she whispered tersely into the phone. She listened for a while. "Look. It's over, Hamish. Finished. It just didn't work out for us, did it? Now I'm in London. I've got a new job and a new life. Sorry." She listened again. "No, I can't. Please stop phoning me here. Look, I've got to go. Got a meeting. Bye."

Her eyes were moist with tears as she gazed out of the window over the myriad lights of Docklands. A small bird landed on the windowsill and fluttered away. Then, for some reason, it turned back and, to her dismay, flew straight into the window with a muffled thump. She looked anxiously out of the window to see if it was all right. Seconds later, she saw a dark speck fly away and disappear into the blackness.

Reassured, she smiled to herself, but then frowned when she caught sight of her reflection in the glass. She had always hated her freckles. Her mother had called them angels' kisses. Her mother had always known what to say.

Her mind flashed back to when she was ten or eleven. She had been a lonely child, lacking in confidence. One boy in particular at school had taunted her for weeks. "Carrots, Carrots…" he had called her, making the other children laugh.

Her mother had been a fighter. An independent-minded artist and musician, she had taught her daughter how to stick up for herself and answer back.

Her father, a sociable, laid-back travel writer, had said she should put herself above comments like that and ignore them. It was his interest in places and people that had inspired her to be a journalist. And now they were both gone.

She looked at her reflection one more time and then, self-consciously trying to smooth down her bouncing hair, made her way to one of the glass cubicles that surrounded the open-plan office. It had the name 'Charles Wright: Foreign Editor' on the door.

Nearing sixty, Charles had the patrician looks of a senior diplomat. Rebecca was aware of his reputation for always acting cool, like the successful journalist he was; confident and unflappable. Yet, as she walked in, he slammed down the phone and threw his hands in the air.

"Why can't people understand that a deadline is a deadline?"

As she stood there, wondering if she had chosen a good moment, he quickly regained his composure, his face relaxing into a friendly smile.

"Rebecca. And what brings me this pleasure?" He fingered the top of his open-necked shirt to straighten the tie that was no longer there.

She already knew it was always best to get straight to the point with Charles.

"I'm thinking of going to North Africa. Just for a short break. I wondered if you needed anything doing? Since I'm going to be there."

Charles looked interested and smoothed back his silver hair. "Thinking of anywhere in particular in North Africa?"

Rebecca sensed an opportunity. "I'm not sure yet. I might look at some Roman ruins. Can you recommend anywhere?"

Charles pushed the phone away and gestured for her to sit down. She noticed that he was looking at her hair.

"If you fancy going to Tunisia, there's been an intriguing incident down in Carthage. Could make a good little piece. It seems some workers were doing some repairs at an ancient sacrificial site. Apparently a couple of them saw visions of children being sacrificed, and now they refuse to go anywhere near the place."

"Sounds a bit grim."

Charles looked her straight in the eyes. "The odd thing is – the workers who saw the visions both had red hair."

"Redheads – in North Africa?"

"Sure," said Charles. "They're not that uncommon. Quite a few Berbers have red hair. Tell you what – we've got an excellent contact in Tunis. A friend of mine, Ali Benzarti – writes mostly for *Le Soir*. Good man – does some work for us occasionally. He mentioned the story to me when I spoke to him a couple of days ago. It's not really his sort of thing – he's a political correspondent. You could be just the person, if you get my drift. You might spot things other people wouldn't. Mind you, you might have to tread carefully. Don't want you running any personal risk or anything."

A look of concern flitted over Rebecca's face.

He laughed. "It's okay. I'll get Ali to meet you at the airport. He'll look after you."

Rebecca made her decision instantly. "Okay. Done. I'll sort out flights."

"Have fun," said Charles, getting up to escort her to the door.

She went straight to Syreeta's desk, ignoring Evans' enquiring look. "I need a coffee," she said.

"I'll come with you," Syreeta said, taking the hint. "So? What did Charles say?" she asked, as soon as they were out of Evans' range. When Rebecca told her about Charles' proposal, she grimaced.

"I thought he might get you to do a nice little travel piece. But 'children being sacrificed' – yuk. Don't let it spoil your holiday."

CHAPTER 3

As she exited customs in Tunis Carthage airport, Rebecca was relieved to see a smart, middle-aged Tunisian approaching her. He was tastefully dressed in a pale grey checked sports jacket, a quiet blue tie and a cream silk shirt, and he exuded an old world courtesy. The scent of an expensive aftershave wafted around him.

He took off a pair of tinted glasses as he stepped over to greet her. "Miss Burns? My name is Ali Benzarti."

"How did you recognise me?" she said, immediately regretting her decision to travel in jeans.

"I spoke to Charles on the phone. He gave me a very good description of you."

"Did he indeed!"

"He was actually very complimentary," said Ali.

When he politely took her trolley, Rebecca quickly warmed to him. Walking to the exit, they were accosted by numerous men, loudly touting taxi services. Ali politely declined them all in Arabic, until they drifted away.

Emerging from the terminal into the brilliant sunshine, Rebecca put on her newly purchased designer sunglasses. The warmth enveloped her, and she felt a growing sense of happiness and well-being.

Ali headed towards the car park. "You know, Charles and I were both Paris correspondents when we were young. Different newspapers, of course," he explained. "We're still good friends, you know. He is in good health?"

"He seems fine. Actually, I don't know him that well. I haven't been working with the *Metropolitan* that long. I think he's very well respected."

"I'm not surprised. He always got better stories than me."

He opened the passenger door of an old white Mercedes for

her, before placing her suitcase in the boot, making sure it was firmly locked.

The car purred towards the barrier. Once they had cleared the precincts of the airport, he turned towards her.

"First of all, we shall go to your hotel. Tonight, we shall go out for a meal and I shall tell you what I know." He shook his head. "I can tell you now, it is a very strange business."

Almost straight away, she caught sight of a large expanse of smooth water in the distance.

"That is Lac Tunis," said Ali. "And beyond it is the Mediterranean Sea."

The sunlight glinting on the water abruptly disappeared, and a drop of water fell on the windscreen. Ali switched on the wipers.

"It's only a light shower," he said. "We get lots at this time of year. It will soon stop. See the rainbow?"

A rainbow had formed high over the lake, the colours vivid and distinct. But a minute later the sky cleared, and the rainbow faded away, as rapidly as it had appeared.

Rebecca's hotel was in a quiet street off a broad, French colonial style, tree-lined avenue. Small and intimate, the hotel retained the Art Deco look of the 1930s, creating an air of refined decadence. Rebecca guessed that Ali had chosen it carefully.

Ali picked her up at eight o'clock sharp, as promised. He looked immaculate in a cream suit, lilac shirt and silver silk tie.

"You like French food?" he asked.

"Very much," replied Rebecca, liking the idea of any food.

"Then we shall go to my favourite restaurant. It is not far. But first, we shall have an aperitif on avenue Habib Thameur. We can sit outside and watch the world go by for a while."

Ali's world was clearly exotic. He was greeted effusively by numerous men, and one elegant woman in particular. She was sitting at an adjacent table with two Pekinese dogs and caught Rebecca's attention. Rebecca instinctively noticed that the woman's hands and feet were peculiarly large.

"*Ça va, Pierre?*" Ali greeted her. Startled, Rebecca looked at the woman again, trying hard not to stare. Despite heavy make-up, the woman definitely had the shadow of a beard.

Smiling, Ali directed his attention back to Rebecca. "Now, we must celebrate your visit. I propose we have a Kir Royale." Rebecca willingly assented.

When the cocktails arrived, Ali raised his glass with a well manicured hand. "*A votre santé.*"

Rebecca raised her glass and returned the toast.

"First, I shall tell you what I've managed to find out," he said. "Then we can relax for the evening."

"I like that idea," replied Rebecca, ignoring the attentions of one of the Pekinese dogs.

"Well, you will know that Carthage is not far from here. Just a few kilometres up the coast. Have you heard about the *tophet*?"

"Is that the place where sacrifices were carried out?" she asked, remembering her chat with Charles.

"That's right. Sacrifice by fire. Terrible. They used to burn their victims. The site was excavated in the 1920s by the French. That's when they found many urns containing human remains. Some were babies."

"Charles mentioned children being sacrificed."

Ali nodded. "They also found stelae. Some of these are in the Bardo Museum here in Tunis."

He stopped and bid "*Bonsoir, Alain*" to a good-looking young man passing by on the pavement.

"Recently, the authorities have put new railings around the site. The old ones were rusting away, and they were worried about things being stolen. There are some carved stones there, just lying around the place. Not particularly interesting, but worth quite a lot."

Rebecca took out her notebook and pen, placing them on the table.

Ali smiled. "You are going to quote me?"

"I just want to remember all this," said Rebecca. "At least I haven't brought my tape-recorder."

"Thank God – I can't stand those things," he said. "Well, a group of workers was asked to do some overtime in the evening, to finish the job of painting the rails. There were five workers – two had red hair. They were Berbers, probably related. It was just getting dark when they started to pack up."

Rebecca took a large sip of her drink.

"First of all, both the Berbers suddenly heard the sound of babies crying. Soon, the sound got louder, and there was the noise of drumming and children screaming. They say they saw the ghostly faces of the children as well. The men were terribly upset. But the odd thing is, the other three workers did not see or hear anything at all. They thought the Berbers were mad. The Berbers ran away as quickly as they could. The most remarkable thing is that all the children had red hair."

"Oh, Charles didn't tell me that," she said. "Do we know what happened to the two Berbers?"

"They're all right. But they absolutely refuse to go anywhere near the *tophet*."

"Do we know where they are?"

"They've moved on to another excavation at the Punic ports in Carthage. There is a British archaeologist there."

"Could we talk to them?"

"I've already arranged for us to go over there tomorrow morning. We can take the commuter train to Carthage. It takes only half an hour."

"Sounds good."

"There's something else I should tell you about." She looked at him expectantly. "The day after we did the story, I got a phone call. It was from a Madame Bourguiba."

He leant towards Rebecca. "Madame Bourguiba is French, but she married a Tunisian and stayed on after Independence when most of the French left. She is a widow now, her husband died a

14

few years ago. He must have been quite well-off, because she still lives in an expensive part of the Medina. Recently, she told me a story about her father, a certain François Attali and his friend Paul Durand..."

Ali proceeded to recount the extraordinary incident which had occurred in Carthage in 1921.

He picked up his glass of Kir Royale, took a sip and put it back on the table. "One more thing I must tell you," he said. "Monsieur Attali had red hair."

Rebecca looked anxious for a moment. "What happened to him? Was he badly hurt?"

"He survived, but his face was always badly scarred. He died some years ago."

"How sad. How reliable is this Madame Bourguiba, do you think?"

"I checked the archives. The story is true, exactly as she said. But there was something else, too, according to some other reports."

Rebecca opened her notebook.

"Both Attali and Durand said that the moonlight was quite unusual that night. It was extremely bright – so bright that they could see the red colour of the funeral urns they had found. I personally went through the news articles from that time, and people were reporting many other strange things. Some fishermen commented on the strong moonlight as well, and also on a glow in the sky that kept changing colours. Two of them reported that their compasses had inexplicably malfunctioned, with the compass needle spinning round and round, apparently out of control. Then the needle began to point south, instead of north. It was as if the North and South Poles had switched over.

Nothing like that had ever happened before, but the phenomenon did not last more than half an hour, and it later appeared it was just a local incident. I couldn't find any other reports of similar occurrences outside Tunis. In the end, the meteorologists put it down to a local atmospheric disturbance."

"Are you saying that the events at the *tophet* could have been related to the abnormal meteorlogical conditions? That Attali heard babies crying and was attacked by a bird because of unusual weather? If I put that in a news story, it might raise a few eyebrows."

"I agree with you. It does sound bizarre," said Ali. "But the two sets of events definitely coincided with each other."

As Rebecca scribbled in her notebook, Ali placed a sheaf of papers on the table. "I have made some copies of the articles for you," he said. "They are in French, naturally, but I think you will find them very useful for your work here."

She glanced at them. "This is very kind. I'll read them tonight – I do know some French." She put them in her handbag. "Do you think we could see this Madame Bourguiba?"

"It is already organised. I am sorry I shall not be able to come with you, but I have to cover a student protest at the university tomorrow afternoon.

"What's it about?" asked Rebecca.

"They are protesting about the large amount of foreign investment here. They think we are giving away the right to control our own country, that foreigners are taking over again. I hope it doesn't get nasty. Last time, they were throwing Molotov cocktails. Anyway, I've arranged for you to meet Madame Bourguiba at her house at four. She seems well-educated – her English is very good. And you will have the chance to visit the Medina."

"One thing," Rebecca said. "I'd like to ask your advice. As you see, I have red hair myself. Do you think I should cover it up when I go into the Medina?"

"Not at all," he said. "It's very attractive. You certainly should not cover it up. Oddly enough, I was called a ginger once – by a Cockney in a London pub. I don't know why, because my hair is dark." He smiled knowingly at her. "And now, would you like to eat?"

Neither of them had noticed the tall, well-built man who had arrived a few minutes earlier and had seated himself a couple of tables away. His features were distinctly Middle Eastern with black hair, olive skin and a prominent nose. He exuded a cosmopolitan smoothness. Even in such a colourful environment, however, it was his eyes which immediately commanded the attention of those seated nearest to him. His eyes were not brown as expected, but an unusually bright green.

CHAPTER 4

The TGM, a little metro-type train, left Tunis and rattled its way along the causeway over Lac Tunis. It soon reached the Mediterranean coast at La Goulette and trundled up towards Carthage.

In the morning, heading out of town, the train was quiet. Rebecca studied the station names on the map of the line in the carriage. They read like a lesson in ancient history: Carthage Salammbô, Carthage Byrsa, Carthage Hannibal, Carthage Amilcar... Her appreciation of the romance of Carthage easily persuaded Ali to offer to show her around the ruins.

They were the only two people to get off at Carthage Hannibal, named after probably the city's most famous inhabitant. She wasn't quite sure what to expect and was agreeably surprised to find that, despite its ancient name, the whole area looked more like a smart suburban estate; green and pleasant with spacious villas surrounded by large, mature gardens. Clearly popular with the wealthier Tunisians, these luxury villas were set back from roads lined with orange trees.

As they climbed to the top of Byrsa Hill, Ali detailed the colourful and cruel history of Carthage: the founding of the once mighty city by the Phoenicians, its sacking and then rebuilding by the Romans.

Reaching the summit, she was delighted to see only a handful of tourists around at this time of year. Surveying the ruins with the Mediterranean hazy in the distance, her imagination ran riot, fed by Ali's descriptions. Only when he gently reminded her that they were there to do a job did they head back to the train and the few stops to Carthage Salammbô.

"We can walk to the Punic ports," said Ali, as they emerged

from the station. "They're not far." He stopped as they reached a crossroad. "We can see the *tophet* if you want," he suggested, a little hesitantly.

"I'd love to," said Rebecca. "As long as you think it's quite safe. I don't want to be attacked by an evil bird, you know," she added, with an ironic smile.

Ali chuckled. "I'm sure you'll be all right. It's daylight and the sun is shining. And there'll be other tourists around." He was right. The other tourists included a group of voluble French.

"To be honest, there's not a lot to see," explained Ali, as they walked around. "There are a few good votive monuments dedicated to Tanit, though. This sort of thing." He patted a large stone with the sign of Tanit, like a stylised keyhole with arms carved on it.

"Remind me," said Rebecca. "Who's Tanit?"

"She was a lunar goddess, the consort of Baal Hammon, the supreme god of the Carthaginians." He walked ahead. "Over there, there's a sort of stone cavern with some more stelae in it." He led her into a shadowy vault. It was empty apart from scattered stones, some of them labelled.

Out of the sunlight, it was cold and dank, and the nasty stories associated with the place crowded into Rebecca's mind, making her feel uneasy. As she turned to leave, she thought she detected a movement among the shadows. She was trying to discern if anything was there when Ali touched her elbow, making her jump.

"Shall we go now?" he said, smiling. "There's nothing much more to see here. Let's go on to the Punic ports."

Rebecca was about to follow him, when she smelled something pungent. "Did you say people were burnt to death here?" she asked. The smell seemed to get stronger and more acrid.

"That's right. Sacrificed to Tanit and Baal Hammon."

"Can't you smell burning?"

He sniffed the air and then laughed. A Frenchman puffing on a Gaulois cigarette emerged out of the gloom at the end of the vault. "*Bonjour*," he said, exhaling a cloud of smoke, and went off to join his friends.

Laughing together, they didn't notice another figure in the shadows of the far corner; a man bent over a carved stone which he was studying closely. As Ali and Rebecca turned to leave the vault to go back into the sunlight, he straightened up, his eyes following their departure. There was a sharp *click* as a flick-knife sprang open. Impassively, he cleaned his fingernails.

Ali could see that Rebecca was disappointed by the sight of the Punic ports. After all, they looked like nothing more than two big ponds.

"But, can you imagine," said Ali, "this is where the Carthaginian naval and merchant fleets were based." He spread his arms wide. "They traded from here all over the Mediterranean. They explored far and wide and set new limits to the known world. They even got as far as Cameroon. Amazing people. And it was from here that they fought all their naval battles. They were slaughtered in the end, by the Romans. And now, this is all that remains. It's so sad."

He brightened as he looked over the water. "I think our friends are over there."

Rebecca could see that an excavation site had been fenced off near the Oceanographic Museum. A number of workers, supervised by a Tunisian, were carefully scraping soil away from the foundations of a building. She noticed that two of the workers had noticeably dark red hair.

Ali called over to the supervisor, took him to one side and spoke quietly to him. The supervisor nodded and beckoned to one of the red-haired men. Ali took him to one side and conversed with him in rapid Arabic. He then got out his wallet and gave him a few notes.

"It's okay. They have agreed to talk to us," he said, as he returned to Rebecca. "But they are not very happy about it. They are worried that people will think they are mad and will laugh at them. So they don't want any photos taken, and they don't want to be named. I said that was all right."

"Why don't we just ask them what happened and let them do the talking?" suggested Rebecca.

"Okay," Ali said. "Let me introduce you." He spoke again in Arabic. Looking a little sheepish, the two men shook hands with her.

"Ask about the crying babies," said Rebecca.

Ali addressed them once more. One started telling the story, calmly at first and then with some animation. The other one joined in, occasionally nodding in agreement but obviously disputing some points.

"What are they saying?" asked Rebecca impatiently.

Ali held up his hands to them. They stopped talking and looked at her.

"Just as I told you. They say it was barely dark when they heard the sound of crying. When it got louder, they stopped working. Then they saw the faces of the poor children. They were scared stiff and wanted to leave. The other men said they couldn't hear or see anything and laughed at them. But just as they were about to leave, they saw something else."

"What was that?" asked Rebecca.

"I was just going to ask," said Ali, and turned back to them. One man spoke quietly while the other listened and nodded. He stopped talking and waited for Ali to interpret. "This is something new. I hadn't heard about this before," he said. "They say they saw a man dressed in white robes. They recognised him as a *kohanim*, a Punic priest. According to them, he walked straight across the *tophet* and disappeared through a solid brick wall. He was carrying a baby." Ali looked a little uncomfortable. "The baby had red hair as well."

Rebecca felt a tingling sensation run down her spine.

"They probably told us about this only because you are here," said Ali.

As they thanked the two men, Rebecca caught sight of a man who she felt sure could only be English. He was ambling nonchalantly over to them from the direction of the museum, clasping what she assumed was a large mug of tea.

Tall, gangly, loose-limbed and well-tanned, his dark brown hair was slightly unkempt, betraying an obvious lack of concern with style and custom. It was just possible to discern the logo of a London scuba-diving club on his faded T-shirt. Not quite thirty, he could have been mistaken for an athlete, but for his ill-judged, too heavy, black-rimmed spectacles.

"What have we got here then?" he asked, beaming with enthusiasm, as the supervisor handed him a shard of pottery. He took out a coloured handkerchief from a trouser pocket, removed his spectacles and polished them. Without them, Rebecca was instantly struck by his good looks, though she got the impression that he was unaware of them, or at least indifferent.

He pushed his hair back and wiped his brow with his handkerchief. "Looks Punic to me. Not really my field, though," he said, rubbing away the soil. Then he turned to Ali, with a twinkle in his eyes. "Checking out all those rumours of spooks and ghosts again then, Ali?"

"Well, Dr Cavendish," said Ali, almost imperceptibly fluttering his eyelashes, "these *rumours*, as you call them, are interesting enough to bring the *Metropolitan* newspaper all the way from London. May I introduce Rebecca Burns?"

Rebecca couldn't help feeling slightly embarrassed as, smiling, he firmly shook her hand.

Her professional side quickly took over. "Nice to meet you. Do you know anything about the visions these men say they've had, Dr Cavendish?

"Jim – please," he said. "'fraid not. I've just called in for a few days on my way back to Cambridge from Egypt. In fact, I have to leave in few minutes to get a plane. I've got a lecture to give tomorrow. And somebody actually wants to meet me to talk about funding. Can't miss that." He caught the eye of the supervisor and tapped his watch. "Okay, Mohammed?"

"Okay, Jim," the supervisor replied. "I'll get the car." He went off in the direction of the museum.

"What were you doing in Egypt, Jim?" Rebecca asked.

"Looking at temples dedicated to the sun. Actually, I'm a scientist – solar physics. But anything to do with the sun interests me. That's what brought me to Carthage. Heliolithic cultures were often associated with the Phoenicians."

Rebecca looked blank. "Heliolithic cultures?" she asked.

"You know – cultures associated with sun worship. Sea-faring peoples like the Phoenicians helped to spread them. That's why I called in here. I like to keep up to date with the excavations." He gestured to the works. "But this building here really isn't that interesting. It was probably just a warehouse."

Rebecca decided to ask a direct question. "Did the Carthaginians really sacrifice children with red hair?"

"They probably did sacrifice children," Jim answered. "Don't know about the red hair, though." He paused. "But they certainly sacrificed redheads in ancient Egypt. Probably to ensure a good harvest, because the ripe corn was red." Rebecca noticed that he glanced at her hair with just a hint of a smile. "You know that women with red hair were picked on in witch-hunts in the West until a couple of hundred years ago?" he said. "Funnily enough, there are stories about people with red hair in most cultures, and in some of the most amazing places."

"Really? Like where?" asked Rebecca, just as the car pulled up alongside them.

"Easter Island in the Pacific, for example. In fact, I shall be heading out there myself soon. I'll be working with Larry Burton on a dig there. Now there's somebody you should meet. He's a specialist in the ancient Near East – one of the best in the business." Mohammed got out of the car and opened the door for him. "Look, sorry about this, but I have to go now. Tell you what – give me a bell in the UK. I'll tell you what I can and maybe arrange for you to meet Larry. Have you got your notebook?" He jotted down a number and passed it back to her.

Waving goodbye to everybody on the site, he clambered into the car, and in a few seconds was gone. Rebecca glanced at the phone number, feeling very happy with the way things were going.

As they walked back up the hill, Ali turned to her, smiling mischievously. "Dr Cavendish seems very pleasant?"

Rebecca flushed slightly. "He could be a very good contact for background to this story."

"People here say that he is a member of your aristocracy, a lord even."

"I really don't know," said Rebecca.

Ali smiled again. "There is something else I should tell you – something that Madame Bourguiba told me. It was François Attali and his companion Paul Durand who found the famous 'Priest Stele' in the *tophet*. It shows a carving of a priest carrying a baby, and it's here in Tunis, in the Bardo Museum."

"Can we see it?" asked Rebecca.

Ali looked at his watch. "We can go right now if we catch a taxi and go straight there. I need to be at the university by three o'clock, and you have an appointment with Madame Bourguiba at four."

Ahead of them, a man was getting into a taxi.

CHAPTER 5

Ali took pleasure in sharing his knowledge of Tunis. In the taxi, he told Rebecca that the Bardo Museum was housed in the former royal palace of the Bey, in the west of Tunis. Proudly, he explained that as well as its Punic remains, it was renowned worldwide for its collection of Roman mosaics.

He took Rebecca straight to the Priest Stele, which stood close to the entrance, enclosed in a glass case. He enthusiastically showed it to her and stood back so that she could study it.

"We're lucky the French didn't take it back to the Louvre," he said.

Rebecca was rather underwhelmed, until she looked at it more closely. Through the reflected light of the glass case, she could gradually make out the figure of a priest holding a very small child. The horror of what it represented began to dawn on her.

"It is quite something, isn't it?" said Ali. "Let's get some baguettes and take them to the garden."

The beautiful gardens of the Bardo were covered with Punic and Roman stones, placed tastefully among tree-shaded benches, inviting relaxation after the effort of visiting the museum.

Ali wiped invisible dust from a stone bench with his handkerchief and politely motioned Rebecca to sit down, offering her a filled baguette.

"What would you like to do?" he asked. "You can either stay here for a couple of hours, or I can drop you off at the entrance to the Medina. You could look around the Medina before you meet Madame Bourguiba."

"That sounds fun," she answered. "Is it easy to find her house?"

"I've got a map for you. She lives in a very smart quarter of the northern Medina. Here – I'll show you." He unfolded a map, took out a gold pen from his inside pocket and studied the map for a second. "She lives here, rue du Pasha, number 42." He marked it on the map. "I will drop you here at place de la Victoire. This is the main entrance to the Medina, near to the old British Embassy. There are so many places to see – mosques, tombs, palaces. But if you see nothing else, you should visit the Jemaa Zitouna – the Great Mosque. And if you want to do some shopping, there are souks all around that area."

"Is it safe?" asked Rebecca, suddenly feeling the need for reassurance.

"Oh, yes, quite safe enough in the daylight. Just keep an eye on your handbag, that's all."

His expression became serious. "But make sure you leave before sunset. I wouldn't advise being stuck in the Medina after dark – it can be dangerous. When you've finished with Madame Bourguiba, you can get a taxi back to your hotel. If you have difficulty getting one, go back to the place de la Victoire. You'll always get one there. If you get lost, here's Madame Bourguiba's number, and you already have mine."

He jotted down Madame Bourguiba's phone number on the map and glanced at his watch. "We need to go now."

As he got up, he looked over Rebecca's shoulder. "Do you know anyone here in Tunis?" he asked.

"No, nobody except you. Why?"

"There was a man there just now. He was looking at you, as if he recognised you. He's gone now."

She looked around. There was nobody to be seen apart from a young family. "What did he look like?"

"Not a typical Tunisian I would say. Large nose. Middle Eastern, perhaps. Middle-aged, with slick black hair. Very smartly dressed, nice suit. Something a little strange about his eyes. They were green. Perhaps not exactly the sort of person you would want as a friend. Something a little sinister about him."

"I don't think there's anybody around here who would know me," said Rebecca. "And certainly not somebody who looks like that." She decided to put her uneasiness to the back of her mind. "Shall we get a taxi? You don't want to miss that protest."

As the taxi pulled up in the place de la Victoire, Ali got out and opened the door for Rebecca. "See you this evening, then. I'll be at your hotel at eight. Remember – any problem – just call me."

He got back into the taxi, opened the window as it drove off, and waved to her. As the clamour and bustle of downtown Tunis closed in around her, she felt a surge of excitement.

CHAPTER 6

Rebecca stood at the roadside for a while and then dodged through the crowd to the side of the entrance to the Medina. She got out the map and worked out a route to rue du Pasha. It seemed straightforward enough.

As she folded up the map, a small boy approached her. "You want good guide? I know Medina very well. You want buy carpet, gold bracelet?"

"No, thank you," Rebecca replied. Then, slinging her handbag over her shoulder and pinning it hard to her side, she plunged into the Medina.

Overwhelmed by the jostling throng, she edged along the narrow street, determined to get to the Great Mosque without being sidetracked by the over-eager stall-holders who called over to her in English. "Look here, Madame. Fine jewellery. Real silk. Very nice. Very cheap."

How the hell do they know I'm English? Why not German or Scandinavian? she thought. "*Merci, non,*" she kept saying with a fixed smile, as she pushed forwards running a gauntlet of traders.

Yet, as she approached the Great Mosque, she could not resist stopping at a colourful open-fronted shop, crammed with the most beautiful soft leather handbags. A bag in a delicate shade of beige caught her eye. She had seen a designer bag almost identical in Covent Garden, but the price tag had been well over five hundred pounds. Way outside her limit. She could not resist asking the price, trying not to sound too enthusiastic.

"One hundred dinars, Madame. Very good price. Very best leather. Feel it."

She did a quick calculation in her head. Less than fifty pounds, and that was just the starting price. Ten minutes later, she had haggled the price down to seventy-five dinars – just thirty-six pounds. Feeling pleased with herself, she slipped her own bag from her shoulder, found her purse, and paid the shopkeeper.

It all happened very fast. Just as she dropped her purse back into her bag, she felt a pull on the strap. There was a flash of light on the knife as it sliced though the strap, and a small hand appeared from nowhere to grab the bag as it fell. Rebecca caught sight of a boy, no more than eight years old, dodging into the crowd and disappearing. The angry shopkeeper yelled out something in Arabic. A few people turned around, but it was too late. He had gone.

"That's all I bloody well need," she groaned to herself, quickly realising her money, her credit cards and her mobile had all gone. She thanked God that she had left her plane ticket and passport in the hotel safe.

The shopkeeper got out his phone and phoned the police. "They say you should go to the police station," he said, after a short conversation. "I can show you how to get there."

Rebecca looked around forlornly, but the few interested witnesses had moved on. She checked the time on her watch. It was already three-thirty. Closing her eyes for a moment, she took a deep breath and made a decision.

"Can you just write down the address for me. I'll go there later. I have to get to rue du Pasha first."

He went into the back of the shop, came back with a sheet of paper and wrote down the address of the police station. Still in shock and disorientated, she found it difficult to concentrate as he explained, writing a few notes, how to get there as well as to rue du Pasha. As she slipped the new bag over her shoulder, the shopkeeper looked at her with a friendly smile of sympathy.

She had no problem finding her way to the northern part of the Medina. The few notes were precise. Only when she reached the deserted end of a street did it dawn on her that she was not in the right place. Instinctively, she reached to get her phone out of her bag and check with Ali or Madame Bourghiba, but stopped short and swore to herself.

She looked around for somebody to ask for directions, but there was only a group of boys kicking a ball around. Taking out the sheet of paper, she started walking over to the boys. They stopped playing and stared at her. All of a sudden, one picked up the ball and kicked it as hard as he could straight at her, catching her on the shoulder.

"Why did you do that?" she said, bewildered.

The boy pointed at her hair and laughed. "Witch, witch, witch, witch," he chanted. The others joined in, one after another.

Then they all started closing in on her and pointing at her hair. She turned and started to walk away back down the street, but they followed her, chanting "Witch" together.

She walked faster, trying to get away from them without losing her cool. When, one by one, they broke into a run, she had no choice but to do the same, cursing that she was wearing a skirt and praying that somebody would come to her help.

Stumbling around a corner at the end of the street, she almost knocked over an old man with a cane. He pulled back, startled.

"Pardon – *excusez-moi* – I'm so sorry," she exclaimed, with a mixture of relief and embarrassment.

As the boys rushed around the corner, he took in the situation instantly, raised his cane and shouted something in Arabic at them. One boy defiantly pointed at Rebecca, yelled "Witch" a final time and retreated after his departing friends.

"Are you all right? Can I help you?" the old man said in perfect English, and with an old-fashioned courtesy. Upright, with a white, trimmed, military moustache, he was wearing a red felt *chechiá*, the Tunisian version of the fez.

"Thank you, thank you," she said, flushed and still shaken. "I don't know what would have happened if you hadn't been here."

"Next time I see them, I'll hit them around the head with this," he said, waving his cane in the air.

She got her breath back and tried to speak calmly. "I was trying to find rue du Pasha – number 42 – Madame Bourguiba. I'm supposed to meet her there."

The old man smiled. "But it's just here. Round the corner. Come, I'll show you."

They walked no more than fifty yards and turned a corner. He pointed his cane. "There it is. Number 42," he said.

"Thank you so much," she replied, feeling rather stupid.

"Just press the bell, it's at the side of the door." He waited until she stood in front of the house, waved his cane to her and walked back slowly round the corner.

CHAPTER 7

Rebecca rang the bell at the side of the huge blue panelled door. There was no response. Stepping back, she looked up at the windows and caught a glimpse of a face peering down at her. She tried ringing again, and several seconds later the door slowly opened. The face of an old lady appeared.

"*Oui?*"

"Madame Bourguiba? I am Rebecca Burns."

"*Ah, un petit moment, s'il vous plaît.*"

The door opened fully, and Rebecca stepped in. As it closed behind her, she turned around to see an elegantly dressed lady standing there.

Beautifully coiffed, she epitomised classic French chic. Her hair, delicately tinted, was cut in a bob, revealing small diamond earrings. She was wearing a cream blouse under a navy tricot, with a matching slim, calf-length skirt. Around her neck hung a thin gold chain, complemented by a gold bracelet.

"I'm sorry I'm late," said Rebecca.

"No matter. I am not going anywhere. I'm pleased you came here. Mohammed is out shopping at the moment, so I have prepared tea myself. You like tea?"

"Yes, please," said Rebecca, looking around.

Behind the door lay a traditional Tunisian courtyard. In the centre, a small fountain played quietly in a stone basin set on a pedestal. The floor was laid with decorated tiles to the edges of a raised terrace, beyond which she could see open doors screened by bead curtains. Palm trees were planted around the courtyard perimeter, from which were strung lights for the evening. Cacti grew in large, cobalt blue ceramic pots placed around the terrace, and purple bougainvillaea covered an entire wall.

Madame Bourguiba led Rebecca across the courtyard to two cushioned cane chairs with a low table set between them. A tray was laid for tea with a Tunisian silver teapot and two tall glasses, filled with green leaves, in silver holders.

"Please, sit down." Madame Bourguiba waited until Rebecca was seated before she sat down herself. "I am sorry I do not have English tea. I hope you like mint tea?"

"I love it," said Rebecca, starting to relax again with the sheer serenity and beauty of the place. "It's very peaceful here."

"Yes. I will never move now," Madame Bourguiba replied. "Since my husband died I sometimes like to have company, and I have plenty of old friends here in the Medina. But in this house it is always quiet, and Mohammed looks after me well."

She poured the tea and passed a glass to Rebecca. "I understand you would like to hear about my father's experience at Carthage?"

"It does sound dreadful. Ali Benzarti told me about it, but I was wondering if I could ask you a few more questions?"

"But what happened to my father happened ninety years ago. I only heard about it when I asked my mother about my father's scars."

"Ali told me that your family are French."

"Yes, but I am the only one left here now. They all went back to Toulouse in 1956 at Independence. I should have gone back as well – the French were not liked. But I was married to a Tunisian, so I stayed, of course. It is normal. My husband was a well-respected surgeon, and I was teaching English and French at the university. I love English. Sometimes we used to visit London and go to the theatre there. My husband died quite young. He was only just sixty." She fell silent.

"And your father – did he go back to France?" asked Rebecca.

"No, he died here in 1939. He looked a little bit like you. He had red hair as well, perhaps a little bit more blonde, but still red. His family came from Normandy. The children here were terrible. They used to call my father all sorts of names because of his red hair and because of his scarred face. The scars were very bad. He was just '*Papa*' to me. I inherited my mother's dark hair, so I had no problems. Sometimes I think he really must have suffered."

"That doesn't surprise me. Just now, a gang of boys chased me. I'm sure it was because of my hair."

"I am so sorry. The children here are a little wild. You know, you should leave the Medina before nightfall. It can be quite dangerous after dark, especially for strangers. Even my father was attacked once in the Medina. By a man with a knife."

"Was he all right?"

"Oh, yes. My father was very strong. He fought the man. But it was very unpleasant."

While Madame Bourguiba topped up Rebecca's glass with more tea, Rebecca surreptitiously checked to see how low the sun was. It was still some way from setting, but she couldn't help feeling anxious.

"Do you know what happened to Paul Durand?" asked Rebecca, deciding to change the subject.

"It was difficult for him. He never heard the crying himself, so he could not confirm my father's story. But the attack by the bird was real enough for him. He was very proud to have discovered the *tophet*, but after that, the professional archaeologists took over. He died too, not long after my father."

She smiled kindly at Rebecca. "Now, you must tell me what you have managed to find out."

"Something to do with red hair," said Rebecca. "I must tell you what the workers who heard the babies crying told us this morning. Something that wasn't reported." She proceeded to tell Madame Bourguiba about the ghostly priest carrying the red-haired baby.

"I wish my husband were still alive to hear about this," said Madame Bourguiba. "He was a very educated man. He knew about the whole history of Carthage, and its strange gods and sacrifices. I miss him so much."

Madame Bourguiba rested her hand lightly on Rebecca's knee.

"I know I'm just an inquisitive old lady, but you seem a little sad. Has something happened to you?"

Feeling vulnerable and caught unawares, Rebecca began to pour out her problems. First, she told Madame Bourguiba about her handbag being stolen, but soon found herself telling her about her own mother and father.

"My parents were killed in a plane crash a little while ago." She went on to tell how her father had been researching a lost city in the Amazon. Her mother had joined him for a holiday in Peru, when their plane went down over the Andes.

Madame Bourguiba's eyes reflected deep concern and understanding. "I am so sorry," she said. "I felt that something was making you sad."

"Thank you," said Rebecca. "It doesn't hurt quite so much now." She went quiet for a moment. Then she jumped as the doorbell rang.

"Don't worry, that will just be Mohammed back with the shopping. He must have forgotten his key. Would you open the door for him, please."

Rebecca crossed the courtyard to the door, lifted the heavy cast-iron latch and started to pull the door open. She only just had time to catch sight of a bottle sailing into the courtyard. It smashed on the edge of the fountain and burst into flames.

"*Mon Dieu*," cried Madame Bourghiba, pushing the table as she instinctively shrank back. A glass fell to the ground and smashed.

Madame Bourguiba was shaking as Rebecca rushed back, put her arm around her and helped her into the house.

The fire soon burned itself out, leaving only broken glass and a few scorched tiles. Rebecca went over and closed the heavy door again.

Madame Bourguiba looked at the scene from a doorway and shook her head defiantly. "They do not frighten me. They did not throw me out at Independence, and they are not going to make me leave now."

The door to the courtyard opened again and a short, elderly man walked in, laden with bulging plastic bags.

"Thank God," said Madame Bourguiba. "Mohammed is back."

Looking bewildered, Mohammed put down the bags, sniffed the air and inspected the burnt tiles. Even as Madame Bourghiba explained what had happened and asked him to call a taxi for Rebecca, he eyed Rebecca with suspicion.

CHAPTER 8

That evening, in a room of a small hotel just off avenue Habib Thameur, the green-eyed man took off his jacket and tie and placed them over the back of a chair.

He retrieved a small packet of twisted paper from a jacket pocket and untwisted the paper. Very carefully, he tapped the brown powder contents into a glass of water and stirred the dark liquid with a spoon. Next, he placed a small stone carving on the bedside table. It was a bird with folded wings and a curved beak.

Sitting on the bed, he studied the carving for a minute, as if building up the courage to drink the foul-looking contents of the glass. Grimacing, he grabbed the glass and downed the contents in one.

For a while, he sat with his head between his knees, as beads of sweat formed on his forehead. Suddenly, he put his hand to his mouth, dived into the bathroom and retched into the basin. Shaking, he went back to the bed, stretched himself out on it and shut his eyes. Two minutes later, his eyes flickered behind the closed lids.

He found himself pushing open a huge wooden door and emerging into the brilliant Egyptian morning sunlight, which flooded into the colonnaded courtyard of the Temple of Edfu in Upper Egypt. But this was the Upper Egypt of over two thousand years ago. His clothes, too, were those of a High Priest of the Temple of Edfu of that time.

Smoothing down the gleaming white cotton of his tunic, he strode towards the massive gateway through which the temple traffic entered the temple complex. Looking up at the boundary wall, he noted the freshly carved reliefs that had not been there when he was last in the temple. They illustrated the victory of the god Horus over his arch-enemy, Seth.

Striding out beyond the gateway, he ignored the greetings and shouts of recognition, as people prostrated themselves at the sight of him, and walked down to the banks of the Nile.

Nothing had changed since his departure. The dull green river flowed towards the Great Sea, and the dhows slowly navigated the waters as they had always done. Reassured, he turned round and shielded his eyes against the sun as he gazed out at the desert, stretching away into the distance. Deciding he was now ready to face his master, he walked back purposefully through the gateway and across the courtyard.

The entrance to the Great Hall was guarded by two, ten foot high, granite statues of Horus, here represented as a falcon. Entering the Great Hall, he paused to let his eyes adjust to the dim light and then moved on to the second hall. Attendants preparing ointments and perfumes in the adjacent laboratory stopped working and bowed their heads towards him. As he went through the smaller offering hall and the vestibule, he slowed down, dreading the ordeal he knew was to come.

At last, deep inside the temple, he reached the inner sanctuary. Coming to a stop at the entrance, he fell down and kissed the ground. At the far end of the sanctuary stood a block of hollowed-out granite. It was the naos, the shrine of the all-powerful god Horus. The priest got to his feet, walked slowly into the sanctuary and stood before Horus, with his head bowed.

Horus was standing inside the shrine. In his form as a peregrine falcon, he was over seven foot tall, and dressed in his daytime regalia. He towered over the priest. Draped over his shoulders was a crimson cloth, underneath which could be seen similar cloths of eau-de-nil green and pure white. Clasped to his body and tucked under his wing, he held his royal regalia: the crook, the flail and the sceptre. On his head he wore the Pschent; the Double Crown, representing power over all of Egypt. At his feet, just above his talons, he wore gold anklets, and around his neck, a jewelled collar which sparkled with coloured lights whenever he moved his head.

Imperious and impassive, the god looked straight ahead. Then the beady eyes flickered downwards. The beak opened. "Speak, Neferatu," he ordered, the voice deep and rasping.

The priest looked up. "O my God, I am at your command," he intoned.

Horus became visibly agitated, a wing spreading away from his body, until it touched the side of the naos. "You have failed. You allowed her to escape." His voice trailed off into a hiss.

Neferatu hung his head. "It isn't that easy. There were people everywhere. She was never alone. The stele dedicated to me was not powerful enough, and I had to use the *ayahuasca* drug to get back here. It made me sick. I don't like using drugs."

Horus glared at him, unblinking. "Then find more effective icons. You must do whatever is necessary to finish the task. Get her to come to you, to your territory. The temple guards and the Moloch are at your disposal – the sun is strong enough now to get them through to the right dimension. The redheads must be stopped. Kill the queen, and the nest will die."

Neferatu shrank back. "And Seth, your uncle? Has he found out what we are planning to do to his people? He is your sworn enemy and will do anything to protect those with red hair."

"It will be too late when he finds out," said Horus, ruffling his feathers. He lifted a claw, and the gold anklet glinted in the light. "Let me remind you, today is the Feast of the Beautiful Meeting. It is the one night I am allowed to spend with my wife, Hathor. She is already on the barque coming down from Dendera. And your role is to officiate at the ritual."

Neferatu took a deep breath and bent his head downwards. "Your wish…"

"I want to celebrate in style," Horus cut in. "We have a few of Seth's supporters to sacrifice later on. You will need to prepare for the ceremony." He lifted a wing and pointed it to the exit.

Neferatu prostrated himself once again, stood up and walked respectfully backwards out of the sanctuary. Once out of sight, he walked back through the temple and into the courtyard, hunched and bristling with a foul temper.

The bright sunshine could not dispel the ominous atmosphere. Piles of dried rushes were being brought in through the gateway and stacked into a pyre, ready to burn the bodies after the sacrifices.

Only when he reached the end of the courtyard did the priest's mood lift, as he noticed a group of twenty or so men and women shackled together and guarded by a small group of soldiers. Obviously from all ranks of life, some of the men were rough-looking peasants wearing simple loincloths. Others, both men and women, were richly attired in full-length white tunics, their jewellery flashing in the sunlight. The one thing they had in common was their red hair.

CHAPTER 9

On the pavement of Great Russell Street, close to the entrance of the British Museum, a clown entertained passers-by. He concentrated on the children, and his appearance immediately caught their attention: the enormous shoes, the baggy trousers and the huge, droopy, yellow chrysanthemum in his button-hole. His lugubrious white face was topped with a bright ginger wig under a mini bowler hat, with a green feather sticking out of it. He stepped up to the children as they passed, put his hand up to their ears and magically produced ten pence pieces, which he gave to them. Parents reluctantly stopped, and he rapidly built up a little group of about twenty boys and girls. He started juggling, and the parents resigned themselves to hanging around for a while.

Inside the museum, a young Japanese couple inspected a display cabinet in the Egyptian room. They barely noticed the small bronze statue of Horus of Pe. When the girl's mobile phone rang, she eagerly started talking in voluble Japanese. She stopped abruptly, obviously waiting for a response. Then she looked hard at the screen and tapped it, before finally trying to call back.

It was while her companion was looking at the display that a man appeared behind them, studying the same group of exhibits over their shoulders. He would have been instantly recognisable to anyone who had met him. It was Neferatu. But he was now dressed as immaculately as any smart visitor to London, in a dark suit, white shirt and quiet tie. In short, he didn't attract a second glance as he checked his reflection in the glass of the cabinet, straightened his tie, turned and walked towards the exit.

By this time the Japanese girl had managed to get through to her caller again and, still puzzled by the sudden interruption, took up the conversation where she had left off.

Neferatu had already walked down the stairs to the ground floor and was making his way to the main exit. He stood at the top of the steps and looked around as if to get his bearings. Then he strode slowly and decisively down the steps and across the museum courtyard.

A small boy was feeding pigeons in the middle of the courtyard. The number of pigeons had rapidly built up into a small flock and more were flapping in. They were directly in line with the main gate as Neferatu walked towards it. With a thin smile of sadistic pleasure on his face, he marched straight through the gathered birds and, nonchalantly but effectively, kicked one that had been too slow to get out of the way high into the air. The boy's eyes opened in disbelief, and his face crumpled into tears as he rushed towards his mother.

Reaching the gate, Neferatu turned left towards the small crowd that had gathered around the clown, the children standing and sitting in front of the row of rather unimpressed adults. The clown was now riding a unicycle as he juggled coloured balls. His bowler hat was on the ground and contained a small amount of money.

Neferatu stopped for an instant, brusquely pushed his way through the crowd, picked up the bowler hat, pocketed the contents in a single movement and threw the hat back on the ground. Before anybody could react, he shoved his way out of the crowd and strode off down Great Russell Street. The children responded first, shouting to alert the unsuspecting clown, who was focused on the trickiest part of his juggling act.

But it was too late. Neferatu had already hailed a taxi, instructing the driver to take him to King's Cross Station.

CHAPTER 10

Neferatu stood looking up at the Eagle of St John, which surmounted New Court Gate to St John's College, Cambridge.

He straightened his jacket, buttoned it and walked east towards the Bridge of Sighs. As he walked over it, he ignored the fine views of the River Cam, glistening beneath the setting sun. Crossing the Third Court, he passed under the Shrewsbury Tower and into the Second Court, where Dr James Cavendish, a Fellow of the College, had his rooms on the first floor.

Jim was expecting him and had set out a tray for tea and buttered crumpets. He welcomed his guest, who introduced himself as Dr Neferatu, into the sparsely furnished sitting room, where he had just finished tidying up numerous books and papers into neat piles in a corner. At the last minute, he had noticed on his desk the letter from the EU, rejecting his latest grant application, and had tucked it into a pile of papers.

He offered his guest the elderly Chesterfield armchair to sit in, having previously turned the cushion over to avoid displaying the tear in it. Dr Neferatu appeared grateful for the offer of tea and crumpets, and they exchanged pleasantries while Jim prepared them. Meanwhile, the visitor was peering with interest at the screensaver on Jim's computer.

"Ah, Stonehenge," he said. "I know it well."

"You've been there?" asked Jim.

"Several times in fact. But this time, I'm here in Britain for a different reason."

"So, how can I help you?" asked Jim.

Dr Neferatu took a sip of tea and stared without blinking at Jim. "I was rather hoping we could help each other," he said, after a long pause. He took a bite of crumpet and chewed for a while. "Very nice. I always seem to burn mine."

The springs in the chair creaked alarmingly as he leaned back. "First of all, I must give you some background." Jim nodded, and Dr Neferatu settled back in the armchair, wincing at the spring digging into his backside. "My main business is dealing in antiques. I have been lucky in the trade and, shall we say, I am not a poor man."

He took another sip of tea. "But I have other interests. My doctorate is from the University of Alexandria. The subject of the research for my thesis was hieroglyphics relating to the Egyptian sun gods and the temples dedicated to them. I am very interested in solar mythology: how it started, how it spread, the forms it has taken, the gods, the goddesses, where and how sun-worship is still practised today. Anything to do with the sun. I can give you more information later, but let's say that it has taken me all over the world."

Dr Neferatu shifted in the armchair. "Now we come to you." Jim looked uneasy, shuffling a little on his chair. "You are an expert on the science of solar phenomena. I know very little about that. I have read some of your papers and, as far as I am qualified to judge, I can see you know your subject. And I know your reputation is first class."

"Thanks," said Jim.

"My problem is that I can't do everything that I want to do by myself." Dr Neferatu leaned forward towards Jim. "I am thinking of setting up a solar studies research unit. It would be a research team to study all activities relating to the sun: physical, astronomical, historical, astrological, mythological. I want it all pulled together in a cross-disciplinary way."

He took another bite of crumpet and chewed for a while. "Obviously, Egypt would be the ideal place for me, but the science resource is not strong enough. Your department is well known, and you have links all over the world." He finished his tea. "Are you interested?"

"Of course. But why do you want to set up a research unit? It's a major investment. I mean, anything to do with the sun fascinates me. But it's my job as well. I don't get paid much, but I do get paid something. And I get somewhere to live."

"With me, the study of the sun is an obsession. You must understand how one can get deeply intrigued by things. Well, now I have made enough money to indulge myself. It's as simple as that."

"Would you like me to introduce you to the university authorities?"

"I haven't time for that. I would just get over-involved in university politics. Now, to start with, I would like a simple, historical survey of sun-worship in this country. It would cover solar observatories like Stonehenge and other important stone circles which may have been observatories. Also, some mention of the movements that are founded in sun-worship.

Then, I would also like a summary of the main scientific research interests around the world that relate to the sun. That's all I need at present. Ten pages at most. That will enable me to develop a full proposal that I can put to you and the authorities." He looked at Jim. "You are still interested in principle?"

"This is very unorthodox, you know," said Jim.

Dr Neferatu shrugged his shoulders. "But what harm can it do? I'm not asking for anything contentious."

"You are asking for quite a hefty piece of work," Jim said.

Dr Neferatu winced again as the spring dug into him. "The problem is, I need it quickly."

"But I'm going to Orkney tomorrow, and to Easter Island in a couple of days' time," protested Jim.

"Do it tonight then," said Dr Neferatu. He fetched out a chequebook. "Would £10,000 for the university make it worthwhile?"

Jim knew that Dr Neferatu's proposal was unorthodox, but he couldn't see anything fundamentally wrong with it. Any grant would help his reputation within the university, and perhaps some of it would filter through to his department. It always annoyed him that so much of his time had to be spent looking for grants.

"It's not exactly the way we usually do things," he said.

"I am aware of how valuable your time is. As is mine, also."

He wrote out a cheque and handed it to Jim. "By the way, I would like you to mention any places of sun-worship that are of particular interest to you, personally."

Jim took the cheque and casually glanced at it, trying to look unfazed. It was drawn on the Bank of Cairo. "Do you want me to email or fax the report to you?"

"Neither. I'm afraid I am not very good with modern communications. I would prefer for you to leave it in the Porters' Lodge by first thing tomorrow morning.

He got up and made for the door.

"Don't worry. I'll find my own way out. I want to look around while I'm here."

Jim felt a strange tingle as he shook Dr Neferatu's hand, but put it down to his own excitement. Even before Dr Neferatu had closed the door, Jim was already pulling out various books from his shelves.

Meanwhile, Dr Neferatu made his way to the Gate Tower, the main entrance to the college. As he emerged, he looked up and studied the statue of St John the Evangelist which stood above the gateway. The saint held a chalice, from which a serpent emerged. At his feet nestled a carved eagle.

CHAPTER 11

The lift pinged and opened at the twelfth floor of the Canary Wharf Tower. Rebecca walked towards the newsroom, wondering how much news of her trip had reached the paper ahead of her.

Veronica, the receptionist, didn't seem to have picked up much. "Hi, Becky. Had a nice holiday?" she said.

Rebecca made straight for Syreeta. Walter King, the drama critic, looked up as she passed.

"Sounds like you've been having fun," he said. Otherwise, it was almost as if she had never been away.

As soon as Syreeta saw her, she jumped up and hugged her. "Oh, Becky, I've been worried sick. Charles said you've had a few adventures, like nearly being set on fire in Tunis. He said you'd got caught up in a student demo or something. Is that right? Are you okay? It sounds terrible."

"It was pretty nasty," said Rebecca, and found herself blurting out the details of the fire-bombing. She was telling Syreeta about the theft of her handbag and the threatening young boys when Geoff Evans looked up from his laptop.

The short, dark Welshman from the valleys was the archetypal tea boy made good. Having progressed steadily through the ranks, he was immensely proud of his position on a national daily. But he still missed the buzz and intimacy of Fleet Street and couldn't accept that the 'Golden Age' of newspapers had moved on. He particularly resented this influx of confident young women journalists, who didn't know shorthand and were painfully ignorant of traditional newspaper practice and law.

"I told you that you should have gone to Benidorm," he said, expressionless.

Syreeta swung round to face him. "Yes, yes, we all know you never go anywhere but Bournemouth," she scowled.

Even for Rebecca, the events of the past few days were quickly becoming too unreal, like a bad dream.

"To tell the truth, it's all been a bit bizarre," she said. "But the odd thing is that I'm still feeling quite nervous. I know it sounds pathetic – even here, though, I still feel nervous."

Syreeta didn't hesitate. "Listen, come and have dinner tonight at my place. You can tell me all about it. Why not stay the night?"

"Really? I'm all right. Just shaken up a bit, that's all."

"Collect your stuff and come straight over," Syreeta said. "Look, we'll talk later. Charles is coming over."

Charles looked very concerned. "Welcome back, Rebecca. Have you got a minute?"

She followed him back to his office and sat down as he closed the door.

"What happened to you? I've had Ali on the phone saying you were fire-bombed in Tunis. What on earth has been going on?"

Rebecca smiled and shrugged. "It all got a bit dramatic and unreal," she said, and started to tell him what had happened.

"Well," he said, "it was a good piece you filed from Tunisia. I'm sure we'll be able to use it." He picked up a pile of computer print-outs, went through them, selected six and passed them to Rebecca. "Look at these. Odd reports about ritual murders. All over the place."

"Has it got anything to do with my story?"

"Have a look. Not much detail, except that all the reports say the murders happened in ruined temples that were linked to sun-worship. But the point is, some of the victims had red hair. It's a bit odd."

Rebecca glanced at the print-outs. "Where's this been going on?"

"The Middle East – Syria and Lebanon. Couple in the South Pacific. And another one yesterday, in Egypt."

"Do you think it's worth following up?"

"Could be interesting."

"If there's a sun-worship link, I know somebody who might be able to give me some information. Somebody at Cambridge University. What do you think?"

Charles nodded. "Good idea. See what you can get hold of. There might be something in this. And if there is, we'll almost certainly run with it."

Rebecca went back to Syreeta's desk and told her about the conversation.

"What are you going to do?" asked Syreeta.

"I'm going to call up Jim Cavendish. He should be back by now."

"Don't overdo it," Syreeta said. "It's incredible what happened to you, you know. I want to hear all about it tonight."

As Rebecca sat down at an adjacent empty desk, Syreeta gazed at her laptop, as if trying to collect her thoughts. She stifled a yawn, started to type and then stopped. Pushing the laptop away, she gazed around the newsroom.

A man smiled at her. He was leaning back in his seat, with his hands behind his head, in one of the glass cubicles. Edward Hargreaves was the features editor, known to all as 'Eddie'. Aged thirty-five, he looked older, his face already florid from too much lunchtime drinking in the Docklands bars. His smile was friendly, with only the faintest hint of a leer. Syreeta smiled back and gave a little wave.

Rebecca, however, had already unintentionally intercepted Eddie's gaze. Suspecting at once what was going on, she turned to Syreeta.

"What's all that about then? He's not your sort, is he?" she said.

"He's all right – when you get to know him," replied Syreeta.

She looked coy, and Rebecca couldn't resist probing further. "You're being very secretive. Isn't he married?"

Syreeta grinned. "He's fun. And he's got good contacts." With a smile, she went off in the direction of Eddie Hargreaves' office.

"No accounting for taste," said Evans in a stage whisper.

Rebecca ignored him and typed into the keyboard of a computer. A minute later, she located Jim – Dr James Cavendish – on the University of Cambridge website. She discovered that, not only was he a Fellow of St John's College, but that he was also a Senior Research Fellow in the Astrophysics Group at, to her surprise, the Cavendish Laboratory.

She quickly established that it was named after Henry Cavendish, the grandson of the 2nd Duke of Devonshire, and that Cavendish was in fact the family name of the Dukes of Devonshire, whose seat was at Chatsworth in Derbyshire.

Intrigued, she clicked on to *Burke's Peerage and Gentry* website, but could find no reference to a Jim or James Cavendish who fitted the bill. It was the same with *Who's Who*.

Slightly puzzled, Rebecca thought for a minute, made a decision and picked up the phone. She groaned to herself on hearing the voicemail and left a brief message. Then, taking her coat, she headed for the exit.

CHAPTER 12

Rebecca rang the bell of the ground floor flat in West Kensington. Syreeta opened the door, smiling and standing behind a large ginger cat, which immediately wrapped itself around Rebecca's leg.

"And how's Tom?" said Rebecca, bending down to pick it up.

"Fat and lazy. He should go out more. Come in," Syreeta said, and headed for the kitchen. "I'm trying to cook. Bit of a joke, really."

Syreeta's flat reflected her character. She had obviously just tidied up the place. There were photographs of friends everywhere: framed, arranged into collages and even stuck on the fridge. On the wall there were bright, colourful holiday posters and some paintings, mostly picked up on holidays abroad.

Rebecca, recognising one of the paintings, couldn't resist a closer inspection. She had painted it herself, a postcard-sized water colour she'd done on a weekend break in Dorset. She'd sent it to Syreeta, who had framed it and given it the place of honour on the mantelpiece. Rebecca put it down again, wondering if she could ever have made it as an artist. She quickly dismissed the thought. *Not good enough*. Her mother had had more talent, and even she had struggled to make it pay by painting the occasional commissioned portrait.

In one corner of Syreeta's living room there was a bar full of bottles of liqueurs of every shape and colour from different parts of the world, and in the kitchen the wine rack was fully stocked.

"I think we should have some nice wine to welcome you back," she said. "Eddie brought a few bottles of Chablis around last week. I don't think we drank them all." She checked the wine rack, pulled out a bottle and handed it to Rebecca. "Will you open it? What sort of music do you want?"

"Do you have any new jazz?"

"Not really. How about African?"

"Sounds good."

The sound of South African township music floated through the flat.

"Are you still playing the sax?" asked Syreeta.

"No – no time. Get to a jazz club occasionally, but that's it. I try to practise, but I don't think it goes down too well with the neighbours."

"Sod them. You've got a life to lead as well," said Syreeta. "Lucky for them it's jazz sax and not the drums. If I had a talent like yours, I'd really flaunt it." She poured the wine and handed a glass to Rebecca. "Welcome back, safe and sound."

Syreeta drained the glass in one and picked up the bottle again. "Drop more?"

Rebecca had taken just one sip. "No thanks. It's lovely, though."

"God, call yourself a journo," Syreeta laughed. "You'll have to knock it back a bit faster if you're going to keep up with the *Metropolitan* boozers."

"All right for them," said Rebecca. "But one glass is enough for me. Any more and I go to pieces."

Syreeta fetched out a wok from a cupboard. "Chinese stir-fry okay with you?"

"Love it."

Tom the cat followed them around and generally got in the way while they prepared the meal together.

As she described the events of the past couple of days over dinner to an incredulous Syreeta, Rebecca finally began to relax.

"Have you contacted this guy Jim Cavendish yet?" asked Syreeta.

"I couldn't get through. Charles thinks there might be a story there. I know there is."

"Sounds to me like you're more interested in Jim Cavendish."

"Not my type. He's just a scientist, for God's sake. Quite boring really."

52

"Uhmm, I've heard that one before," said Syreeta.

She made a herbal tea for Rebecca, a coffee for herself, and they continued chatting; Syreeta updating Rebecca on the newspaper gossip she had missed, until they both started to yawn.

"Thanks so much for this, Sy. I'm beginning to feel normal again. Do you mind if I lie in for a bit tomorrow? I'm completely done in," said Rebecca, as Syreeta showed her the spare room, quickly taking some of her own clothes off the bed.

"Of course not. Sleep as long as you like. I won't wake you. Make yourself some breakfast."

"Thanks, Sy. I've never felt so tired."

Putting on a pair of pyjamas, Rebecca got ready for bed and sat down in front of the dressing-table mirror. She made a face as she unpinned her hair, so that it hung down over her shoulders.

Looking at herself in the mirror, she brushed her hair slowly and sensuously and found herself thinking about Jim Cavendish once again. He was good-looking, certainly, and he gave the impression of being very self-confident. Yet she sensed, without any real evidence, that beneath the professional veneer, there was a more sensitive soul waiting to be discovered. Then, to her shame, she realised that she had put any thoughts of Hamish completely to the back of her mind.

Setting down the brush, she went over to the window and opened it for fresh air. Closing the curtains again, she deliberately left the door slightly ajar, needing the sense of Syreeta's presence. She gratefully climbed in between the sheets and, within minutes, drifted into a deep sleep.

Not long afterwards, the door creaked open, and Tom's head appeared. He crept silently into the room and, without disturbing Rebecca, leapt on to the bottom of her bed, where he curled up.

A few hours later, in the dead of the night, there was a rustle of bird-wings. Then silence. Tom opened one eye and then the other. The curtains parted, and a large, fearsome-looking, mottled-brown hawk edged its way on to the windowsill, its yellow eyes staring at

Rebecca. Tom raised his head and hissed loudly. The bird ignored the cat and continued to look at Rebecca, before moving back behind the curtains and disappearing. The slow, leisurely flap of wings as it took flight was almost indiscernible.

Rebecca turned over. Half asleep, she noticed Tom, who was settling down once more at the bottom of her bed. "Hello, Tom. Keeping an eye on me, then?" she said drowsily, as she turned over to go back to sleep again.

CHAPTER 13

It was just after eight o'clock when she woke up. Tom was now fast asleep in an armchair, but woke immediately and went to his empty food bowl. Rebecca got out of bed and followed him. "Doesn't Syreeta feed you then?" she mocked. She found half a tin of cat food in the fridge, put the contents into Tom's bowl and made herself a coffee.

After writing a thank you to Syreeta, mentioning her intention to seek out Jim Cavendish, she made another coffee and picked up her mobile.

It rang for a while before he answered. "Jim? It's Rebecca Burns from the *Metropolitan*. We met in Carthage, remember? You said I could contact you. Can you talk?"

Jim Cavendish was leaning against the rail of a boat, looking at a grey sea. A fresh breeze was blowing in his face, and the engine noise made it difficult for him to hear.

"Hang on a minute," he yelled, and made his way under cover at the back of the boat. "Okay, that's better now," he said. "Yes, of course I remember. Thanks for your voicemail – I was going to get back to you. How are you?"

"Things got a bit hairy after I left you, but I'm all right now," she replied. "I'd like to talk to you – about people with red hair."

"Listen, I'm on a boat near Orkney at the moment. I'm taking a bit of time off. I want to check out some stone circles before I go to Easter Island. Can't it wait?"

"I really have to talk to you," she persisted. "There've been some ritual murders going on – all over the place. Syria, Lebanon, Egypt, and now the South Pacific as well. And guess what? Some of the victims had red hair. Maybe they all did. The details are still coming in."

"It could be just a coincidence," he replied, without enthusiasm. "Whereabouts in the South Pacific?"

"Don't know yet, but I can find out." She waited a second before continuing. "But listen to this. The funny thing is, all the killings apparently happened in places connected to sun-worship."

There was a silence as he took this in, so she continued, "I need to find out – why redheads? And what has it all got to do with sun-worship?"

"I don't know what it all means," Jim said.

"Perhaps we could meet up?"

"Sure. Of course, I'll be pleased to see you…"

Rebecca made a snap decision. Jim didn't get another word in.

"Then will you meet me at the Kirkwall airport, around lunchtime? I'm just off to Heathrow now. I'll let you know what time I'm arriving."

"What!" exclaimed Jim, but she had rung off. He took the phone away from his ear, looked at it and slowly put it back to his ear. "Okay," he said to himself, and chuckled, shaking his head in disbelief.

Slipping his phone back into his rucksack, he went back on deck to watch the land getting closer.

CHAPTER 14

Feeling apprehensive that she may have been too bold in her approach, Rebecca had decided to meet Jim as one professional seeking help from another. In the event, she was relieved that he had seemed pleased to see her again, and had quickly offered to take her to the places he had intended to visit.

It rapidly became evident that Jim knew Orkney well, and his enthusiasm for the islands was catching. He explained that the Stone Age sites were world-famous, and new ones were constantly being found and excavated.

Orkney, he told her, consisted of fourteen large islands, which were linked by ferry, and many more smaller ones. The capital, Kirkwall, was on the largest island called Mainland. The Ring of Brodgar on Mainland would be their first port of call.

The monument dominated a hillside, from where it had overlooked Loch Harray for 5000 years; vast and impressive in its Neolithic splendour.

Of the sixty original standing stones, hewn from local sandstone, only twenty-seven remained, still arranged in a perfect circle of over one hundred yards wide. The stones themselves, several of them reaching twice the height of a tall man, stretched towards the sky, some like guillotine blades, others like triangular-topped lozenges. A wide ditch ran around the outside of the circle, broken by two entrance causeways, set diametrically opposite each other. Outside the ditch, about one hundred yards to the southeast, was one large solitary slab of rock, known as the Comet Stone.

The pale, northern, winter sunlight seemed to drain the colours of any brightness. The loch was a light blue, and the green grass around it contrasted with the dark brownish-green of the heather that grew wild inside the Ring. Even the pillar-box red of Jim's hired car seemed to fade and blend with the landscape. The feeling of wide open sea and sky, the isolation and the remoteness of the place, seemed worlds away from Rebecca's recent experiences. Only a bird wheeled in circles, high in the sky above them.

Rebecca and Jim crouched down to examine faint inscriptions carved into the stump of one of the stones. They resembled a child's matchstick drawing of a tree without leaves.

She outlined the inscription with her finger. "What does it mean, Jim?"

"It's a Norse tree rune. Graffiti, by the looks of it. Hang on, I'll work it out – it's quite easy to decipher." He got out a pen and notebook and made some annotations. "It seems to be 'Biorn'," he pronounced. "It's quite a common Scandinavian name. It must have been carved by a Norse invader." He smirked. "Biorn again."

Rebecca groaned. "And probably a redhead," she said.

"It's possible," agreed Jim. "The Norsemen settled here. A lot of people around here have Norse blood running through their veins." He stood up and looked around the Ring. "But this place was here long before the Norsemen. It was once the ceremonial centre of a huge Neolithic empire, and it was actually built before the Pyramids. Just down the road they are doing a dig, and they think they've found a temple complex. You can't see much, though. It's all been covered up for the winter."

"Getting back to the subject of redheads," Rebecca said. "What do you think it is about us that makes people react the way they do?"

"Put it this way," said Jim. "Redheads have always been different. They have always been either admired or disliked, ridiculed or persecuted, and occasionally sacrificed. But never ignored. Wasn't Lord Byron a redhead, even if he oiled his hair to disguise the colour? 'Mad, bad and dangerous to know', people said. And you must know that painting in the Tate Gallery by Millais – Jesus painted as a red-haired boy, in his father's workshop?

Wasn't Charles Dickens very sarcastic about that?"

"Yes, I know the one you mean. I've always loved the Pre-Raphaelite painters. There you are – they actually *adored* redheads. But I think Dickens called the Jesus in the painting a hideous, blubbering red-headed boy, or something like that."

Jim looked impressed with her knowledge. "Well, all over the world, you hear tales about people with red hair. They're always marked out as different from other people. Sometimes they're even seen as evil."

Rebecca chose not to react, keen for Jim to continue. "In India, there are red-haired demons called *rakshasas*. Japan has its red-haired demon, too, called Aka-oni."

"You seem to know an awful lot about it, Jim."

He smiled. "Sorry. I'm hardly being diplomatic. But if you study solar religions around the world, as I do, it's strange, but you find the subject keeps coming up."

Rebecca made a few notes. Then she noticed another group of stones glinting in the sunlight in the distance.

"What are those over there?"

"They're the Standing Stones of Stenness," Jim replied. "That circle is known as the Temple of the Moon, while this one here is the Temple of the Sun. Some people think the whole complex might have been one massive observatory. Then again, if you listen to the New Age nutters, they are supposed to be centres of earth forces. Ley lines, electromagnetic fields – that sort of thing. Shall we go and have a look at Stenness?"

They wandered back to the car, breathing in the tranquillity of the scene. It only took a couple of minutes to drive over the causeway, leading to the Standing Stones of Stenness.

Rebecca noticed a man standing in front of one of the Stones and felt a twinge of disappointment that she and Jim would not be alone. But, as they approached, he walked away to inspect a large stone slab, embedded in the ground.

The four immense remaining megaliths towered over Rebecca

and Jim, jutting up towards the blue sky, as if trying to connect heaven and earth.

"There used to be at least eleven of them in a circle," explained Jim, as Rebecca took a photo. "The really interesting one has gone now. It was called the Odin Stone."

"As in Odin, the Norse god?"

"That's right. Sometimes called Woden or Wotan. In Northern Europe, Wotan was known as a storm god. The Christians made him synonymous with the Devil. There are even places named after him in Orkney – like Odiness on the island of Stronsay. Oddly enough, there's a ruined kirk on Norstray, where there are six deep grooves in one of the building stones. They're known as the Devil's Clawmarks – but they're just the result of rain erosion, of course."

"How do you know all this?"

"Sorry. I must come across as a boring academic."

"Oh, no, no. I'm really interested."

He pointed towards the north. "The Odin Stone used to stand outside the circle over there, but some idiot farmer knocked it down in the nineteenth century."

"Unbelievable," said Rebecca, shaking her head.

"Well, that's not all," said Jim. "The same farmer then smashed up some of the other Stones and used them for building. The locals were pretty mad, though. For a lot of people here, Odin's Stone had a special magical significance."

"What kind of magic?"

"Originally, it could have been an ancestor stone. It was there long before the Norsemen arrived. We know that it had a large hole in it. Hearsay is that on the night of a full moon, the bones of an ancestor were passed through the hole. That was supposed to bring the ancestor back to life. You often come across that sort of thing in primitive societies." He laughed. "Lucky we weren't here at the time of the Beltane festival. They might have burnt you alive in a wicker cage." Rebecca raised her eyebrows. "Being a nice young girl, I mean," he said. "Nasty pagan fertility ceremony."

"Sounds like you are trying to wind me up," said Rebecca.

"Sorry," he said, smiling. "But Orkney is like that, full of superstitions and ghost stories. It's all very nice when the sun is shining, like now, but imagine this place in the dead of winter, with the mist swirling around. Still, Odin's Stone did have some nicer associations."

"Pleased to hear it."

"Around New Year, they used to hold a five day party where young people could meet. Every year, at least four or five couples used to slip away and plight their troth. The girl used to pray here to Woden. Then they'd go to the Ring of Brodgar, and the boy would kneel in front of the girl and pray. Finally, they'd come back here and grasp each other's right hand through the hole – which meant they were well and truly hitched."

"It sounds quite romantic."

"Yes. It was called 'Romancing the Stone', and it was really and truly binding. You'd have the whole of society down on you, if you tried to get out of it. Same with any other oath, if it was made here by shaking right hands through the hole and reciting Odin's Oath."

"What's Odin's Oath?"

"Well, no one's quite sure any more. The actual words were lost long ago."

Looking around, Rebecca was the first to spot a thin, waving dotted line coming towards them, high in the sky from the northern horizon. At first glance, it looked like nothing more than a black thread being drawn by a celestial hand. As the vanguard of the dark line approached directly overhead, she pointed it out to Jim. But as he gazed upwards through squinted eyes, the front of the line suddenly came to a stop, as if it were coming up against an invisible wall in the sky. Birds veered away in all directions. A dense black ball formed as the birds grouped together, and it slowly grew in size as the line continued forward and melted into it. Even as they watched, the ball became a dark cloud, only to change shape, condensing and expanding like a demented amoeba. Inside it, black specks whirled around, trapped in their own mini-constellations.

Then, without any clear signal, a line of birds left the cloud and started to turn back northwards. The cloud thinned, like a ball of wool being unravelled, until it had completely disappeared.

"Starlings," said a voice from behind Jim and Rebecca. "Migrating down from the north of Scandinavia and Russia, to spend the rest of the winter here."

They turned round to see a fresh-faced, middle-aged man standing there, shielding his eyes with his hand as he gazed at the, now empty, northern horizon. Rebecca immediately noticed his light coloured red hair.

"What were they doing? Why did they suddenly stop and go back?" she asked. "It's as if they lost their sense of direction."

The man pointed to the bird still hovering in the distance, over the Ring of Brodgar. "There's the real reason. Looks like a sea-eagle to me, a visitor most likely. The starlings must have taken fright. Funny, though – never seen anything like that before. Amazing." He watched the bird for a while longer and then turned, smiling, to Jim and Rebecca. "Sorry, I didn't mean to disturb you, but that was a very unusual sight. I fish these parts, and it's very rare that you see a sea-eagle around here, I can tell you."

Jim looked again at the bird. "Yes, I guess we're very lucky," he said. "The effect it had on those starlings was distinctly odd, though. I'm wondering whether something else made them change direction." He looked at his watch. "Perhaps you'll know?" he asked the man. "When can we get over to the Brough of Birsay next?"

"If you go right now, you'll make it fine. The tide will be out for the next couple of hours."

"Thanks," said Jim, and he turned to Rebecca. "The Brough of Birsay is a small island not too far from here. We could have a quick look at a really interesting symbol stone there – before we get the plane back. The Norsemen had a settlement on it, but the Picts were there before that. A really excellent job has been done with the excavations there."

The man's eyes lit up. "Archaeology's my hobby. I help out on the digs whenever I can. Like the one just up the road at Brodgar. All this on our doorstep, and no one really knows what our prehistoric ancestors were up to."

Jim nodded in agreement.

"If you're interested in archaeology, you should come up to Norstray where I live," continued the man. "There's a whole unexcavated, prehistoric burial site there."

"Oh, I've heard about that," said Jim enthusiastically, "but I've never been there."

"Well," the man said, "if you ever get to Norstray, just ask for Sandy Lewis, and I'll show you around. Everybody knows me there. And if I'm not around, ask for my brother, Jock. He probably knows more about Norstray than me."

"I might just take you up on that," said Jim.

The man swung a bag over his shoulder. "I'd better get going as well. Jock's been fixing my boat. It'll be done now." He strode off towards the exit gate. "Enjoy Birsay," he called back.

"Let's go, Rebecca," said Jim. "The last time I tried to cross over this causeway, the tide was in and I couldn't make it. We should be lucky this time, if we get a move on."

Rebecca followed him, stumbling over the tussocks of grass. Reaching the exit gate first, Jim realised that she was not keeping up with his fast pace. He stopped to wait for her to catch up and held open the gate for her to pass through in front of him.

CHAPTER 15

Rebecca and Jim walked together to the parked car.

"Your work is important to you, isn't it?" she ventured.

"Keeps me busy," replied Jim, as she got into the car.

"It's just that, I was thinking about doing an article on choosing science as a career," she said. "What about you? What made you go in for science? Did you always know that was what you wanted to do? You seem very dedicated."

Jim shrugged his shoulders. "That's what it's all about, isn't it? What makes the world tick? The search for the truth ultimately, I suppose. Meanwhile, though, I'll happily accept a better understanding of how things work."

"Even so, not many of my friends went in for science," said Rebecca. "And most of those who did, left and went into law or finance instead."

"And I can see why," he said. "The money's rubbish, and I spend half my time trying to conjure up grants."

"You must have gone to a good school if they taught science well? So many find it impossible to get good science teachers."

"Yes, I was lucky. We had a really good physics teacher."

"Was that a public school?"

"No, no. Just the local comprehensive. I was the family misfit."

"Misfit?"

"My brothers went to public school like my father. They're both bankers now."

"I don't see you as a banker."

"At least I escaped that fate," said Jim, and he laughed. "I was due to go to Eton as well, but my father lost the family fortune on the stock market. Ironic really, because he had just been given a knighthood for 'Services to the City of London'. Anyway, I was sent to the local comprehensive." He watched her expression, as if judging her reaction.

"Well, it was the same with me – state school in Edinburgh," she said. "But it was good enough to get me into Glasgow University."

"To do what?" asked Jim.

"My degree's in Spanish and French."

"Lucky you. Languages weren't my thing. Much preferred physics. That's what got me started on astronomy. We built a telescope after classes at school. Mother always seemed to be out, anyway – too busy with her social life to bother with me."

Rebecca smiled encouragingly.

"At Cambridge, I did astrophysics. Then a PhD on solar phenomena at Oxford. And now I'm back at Cambridge as a physics lecturer. Not much money, but plenty of time to do field research. Suits me."

"Do you have time for much else?"

"What else? A social life? Not really. I travel too much. A bit of tennis and a bit of scuba diving when I can."

"Is your wife in the same line?" she asked, as casually as possible.

"My wife?" Jim said, looking somewhat taken aback. "Yes. When I had a wife, she was a scientist too, at Cambridge. She was American – liked the idea of marrying into what she thought was the English upper class. My family lived in a manor house, near Chellaston in Derbyshire."

"Well, Cavendish is a very aristocratic name."

"I believe we are related to the aristocratic Cavendishes, but very distantly. Anyway, she soon found life with me was not as grand as she expected. So we divorced."

"I'm so sorry," said Rebecca, "I didn't mean to…'

"That's all right. We were too young, I guess. Not a good time. Suppose I've got used to being on my own now."

"Is that what you prefer? To be on your own?"

"It suits me fine for the moment," said Jim. He started the car, slipped it into gear and began to drive towards Birsay.

Almost immediately, Rebecca noticed an enormous dome-shaped, grass-covered mound in the distance. "What's that over there?" she asked, keen to open up the conversation again.

"Now, that is *really* interesting," said Jim. "That's Maeshowe. It's actually a Neolithic tomb. They're found all over the islands – a lot of them in isolated places and virtually unvisited. But this is the biggest and best known in Orkney. And, you know, something quite fascinating is happening in there at the moment."

He checked the date on his watch. "In a couple of weeks, it will be the winter solstice – December 21st. For a short time, leading up to the solstice, the rays of the setting sun shine right down the entrance passage into the very centre of the tomb. For the ancient Orcadians, the winter solstice was obviously very significant."

CHAPTER 16

The small car park overlooking the Brough of Birsay was deserted. Jim parked the car facing towards the sea. The prediction was correct; the causeway was exposed. Getting his rucksack out of the boot, he slammed the door shut, not even bothering to lock the car in this isolated spot. They made their way easily over to the island, Rebecca pleased to see that no one else was there.

The evidence of once thriving communities was everywhere: a Pictish well, the ruins of Norse dwellings, a small monastery and a kirk. Now it was all abandoned to the elements.

Rebecca was the first to notice the stone slab. Rectangular and nearly two metres high, it was covered with strange carvings. "What's this, Jim?" she called over to him.

He walked over to inspect it. "That's it! The Pictish symbol stone. Or at least a copy – the original's in a museum in Edinburgh."

He pointed to the carvings. "These are very typical. See here – a mirror and a crescent. And this symbol that looks like an upside-down pair of compasses – that's called a V-rod. Under it, that thing that looks a bit like a lion – that's the so-called Pictish Beast. And look, there's a really fine eagle symbol as well. Those three men at the bottom are probably Pictish warriors. See the shields and spears?"

Rebecca could barely make out the details, but she took Jim's word for it.

As the wind gusted around them, they were too engrossed in exploring the ruins to notice the time passing. They were even too absorbed to notice that there were no birds, not even seagulls, to be seen.

Jim was reading a description of the settlement on a noticeboard, when he straightened up and looked around. The sea was already beginning to lap gently over the causeway. "Hey! I think we'd better get going. The tide's coming in fast." He checked his watch. "And it'll be getting dark soon. I didn't realise it was so late."

The eagle swooped quite suddenly. Neither of them saw it coming, and as it swept past them, the outstretched talons caught the edge of Rebecca's coat, throwing her off-balance.

"Jim!" she screamed.

The bird soared upwards into the sky, wheeled and hovered for a few seconds, high above the car park. Then it plummeted down again, aiming straight for them.

Terrified, Rebecca fell to her knees and covered her head with her hands. She daren't even look.

Jim whipped his small rucksack off his back, grabbed the handles and whirled it around his head. As the bird closed in on them, he hurled his rucksack at it and ducked. It caught the bird on the wing, so that it veered sideways. Flapping wildly, it managed to regain its balance and soared skywards once more. Yet, still, it was not scared away. High above them, it continued to hover menacingly.

Rebecca peaked out from behind her hands. "What is it? What's it trying to do?" she gasped.

"Let's just get out of here," Jim said. "Once the tide's in, we'll be stuck. And that bloody bird's still up there." It seemed poised to attack again. Jim grabbed his rucksack. "Okay, let's go," he shouted.

They clambered over the rocks to the causeway and began to splash their way along it. When they were about halfway over, Jim stopped and glanced around. The bird was already swooping down towards them, but, at the last moment, it abruptly veered away, as if wary of Jim.

The water was now lapping around their ankles. The eagle glided past slowly, but at a distance, then climbed into the sky and drifted around in circles above them.

At last, they reached the end of the causeway and clambered up the steps towards the car park. Jim stretched out his hand to help Rebecca and virtually pulled her up. At the top of the steps, he looked distraught.

"Where's the bloody car?" he cried. The car park was empty.

CHAPTER 17

Jim pointed along the coastal path. "There's a place along there where we can shelter. Come on." They started to run, the bird gliding along effortlessly at the same pace, swooping from side to side a few yards in front, as if taunting them.

Rounding a curve in the path, Jim stopped and indicated downwards to a small building covered in grass.

"Make for the hut. It's the best we can do for now." He leapt down to it and shoved at the door. It creaked open and they fell into the dark interior. Jim slammed the door shut behind them and stood with his back against it.

Rebecca pressed herself to the wall alongside a small dirty window at the back of the hut, so that she could not be seen from the outside.

"I don't think I can take much more of this," she said, shaking.

"It's just an eagle. But I've never heard of one attacking humans," Jim said. "Perhaps it's got young around here." Rebecca did not look convinced. He rubbed the dirt off the window. There was no sign of the bird outside the back of the hut. "Where the hell is it?" He went to the door, cautiously opened it a few inches and peered outside.

Rebecca felt nervous. "Maybe we should wait a bit longer?" Jim ignored her and warily glanced around.

The eagle was barely twenty feet away, sitting on top of a stone cairn and staring at him, its yellow eyes standing out in the twilight gloom.

He closed the door quickly. "Still there. We'd better phone the police." He fetched out his phone from the rucksack, only to find that the screen was blank. He stabbed at the keys. "Damn thing's not working. I must have bust it when I chucked my bag at the bird. Try yours."

Rebecca switched on hers and keyed 999. She listened for a while, then frowned. "It's just crackling."

"Give it to me," Jim said, and put it to his ear. He listened. "There's probably no signal here. We'll just have to stay here in this place for a while. Most likely it'll get bored soon." He looked around. The hut was empty apart from a wooden bench. He beckoned Rebecca to sit down, and joined her.

As they sat there, the sky outside darkened rapidly, throwing the inside of the hut into blackness.

"Looks like bad weather brewing," said Jim. He got up and slowly opened the door again. He could still see the outline of the bird, its glowing eyes staring at him. He eased the door closed and sat down again.

They were still sitting there in uneasy silence, when a soft, flickering glow began to illuminate the inside of the hut, until soon, green and red light was pouring in through the window. They got up and pressed their faces to it in astonishment. The whole night sky was ablaze with flaming colour; a glowing green curtain hung there, fringed with deep red at the bottom, rippling as if it were being gently blown by a heavenly wind.

"You're seeing the Northern Lights," Jim said. "We're a long way north here, and getting quite close to the Arctic. In fact, in terms of latitude, we are just about halfway up Norway."

He went to the door and opened it an inch. As Rebecca apprehensively joined him, he opened the door further. The bird had gone. Rebecca was overwhelmed with relief. As they stepped outside, she was entranced by the brilliant lights. Beneath the display, just above the horizon, hung a full moon. The reflected moonlight and sparkling many-coloured lights mingled and glittered on the calm, mirror-like sea.

Rebecca gazed upwards. "It's just beautiful. I've never seen anything like this."

She was admiring the changing patterns of light, when Jim broke the silence. "Maybe it was electrical disturbances caused by the aurora that affected your mobile."

It was just then that the eagle glided down from the roof of the hut and landed back on the cairn. As it turned to face them, they both dived back inside.

Jim groaned and sat down again on the bench. "It's got to go sometime. It can't stay here for ever."

Rebecca didn't reply, but just sat there silently beside him. After a minute, she was still silent and had become completely still. Her expression was blank, as if she had gone into a trance.

"Rebecca!" Jim exclaimed.

She didn't respond. He waved his hand in front of her face, but her eyes didn't even flicker.

Suddenly a brilliant flash of lightning lit up the inside of the hut. Almost simultaneously, a long clap of deafening thunder shook the hut so forcefully that the door rattled. Jim looked out of the window. The storm had blown up out of nowhere, and the blaze of colour had vanished, as if it had never been there. The sky was now black and featureless, and rain was drenching down, driven by the wind against the window. He got up, edged the door open again and looked out. The wind and rain blew in, soaking him in seconds. He could still dimly make out the eagle, but it suddenly spread its wings, swooped off and disappeared into the darkness.

Jim waited for a few seconds more, closed the door and sat down again beside Rebecca. He gently shook her shoulder. "Rebecca, Rebecca. It's okay, it's gone," he whispered.

She stirred very slowly, as if she were surfacing from a deep sleep, and turned towards him. She stretched out her hand, slipped it under his jacket and rested her head on his shoulder. Jim coughed, but she ignored him and, undoing a button on his shirt, put her hand on his chest. He gently removed her hand and freed himself.

In an instant, Rebecca seemed to fully awaken. Apparently totally unaware of her previous actions, she sharply pulled away from him and rushed to the door.

Outside, the noise of the storm was fading as quickly as it had begun. The clouds had vanished, and once again the full moon hung over the sea. No trace now, though, of the aurora, the Northern Lights.

"Doesn't the moon look magical?" she said.

"I prefer the sun myself. I like the warmth," he responded.

They stood there for several minutes, but there was no sign of the eagle.

"Okay, let's go," Jim said, taking her elbow.

When they reached the deserted car park, Jim shook his head. "We'll have to get help. There's a phone box by the Earl's Palace down the road – let's try it."

They had almost reached the gaunt ruins of the once stately home, when they saw a solitary car, neatly parked at the side of the road. It was Jim's. He stopped and put a hand to his forehead. When he tried the driver's door, it was open.

Jim bristled with rage. "Someone must have pushed it here for fun. What a bloody stupid trick. Joyriders, I suppose. They're probably still here, but there's no more damn time to mess around." He checked his watch. "We need to shift, or we won't get back to London tonight. I have to get ready to go to Easter Island the day after tomorrow."

A look of disappointment flitted over Rebecca's face.

CHAPTER 18

As they drove back to the airport at Kirkwall, Jim's mind was in a whirl. The events of the day had disturbed him; the incident with the bird didn't seem right somehow. He had heard of birds attacking humans, but normally for a good reason, because their territory was threatened, or whatever. *And then that line of birds changing direction – that was truly weird. Could a sea-eagle really have had that effect on them? Or could it have been for some other reason?* He knew that birds guided themselves by using the Earth's magnetic field. *Was it possible that something had happened to the magnetic field – maybe just a blip? That would also explain the aurora borealis.* He made a decision to check with his colleagues when he got back to Cambridge.

But what had really thrown him was Rebecca's apparent trance in the hut, and her unconscious display of affection. That had really shaken him. It briefly entered his mind that it was more than a coincidence that her strange behaviour had coincided with the other bizarre events. But then he quickly dismissed the thought. The lingering sensation of her touch on his body had awakened a need he had suppressed too long.

He was aware that he had immersed himself in his work to help get over the trauma of the divorce. *Perhaps it's time to get more of a life,* he thought. *Maybe I'm ready for another relationship.* Compared to his wife, and the rare, occasional dates he been on since his divorce, Rebecca was very different; lively and *very* attractive.

He shifted in his seat so that he could catch sight of his reflection in the driver's mirror, and tried to imagine how he could appeal to someone like her.

His thoughts were interrupted by Rebecca. "How long are you going to Easter Island for?"

"Only about a week. I have to get back to present a paper with Larry Burton at an archaeological conference in Aberdeen. It's a real opportunity to work on a dig with Larry – and on Easter Island as well."

"Is that the one you said I should meet – the Near East expert?"

"Yes – Professor Burton."

"Perhaps you could do me a favour?"

"What's that?"

"Would you try and get me some info on the redhead murders that have been going on in the South Pacific?"

"Well, I'm not sure. I'm no reporter. Might be a better idea to go there yourself, if you can."

Rebecca's face instantly brightened.

CHAPTER 19

Rebecca excitedly showed her Carthage story to Syreeta. It was tucked away in the Foreign News section, but it was there.

"You certainly went through enough for it," said Syreeta.

Rebecca looked up from reading the paper. "It wasn't exactly uneventful in Orkney, either."

"You know, I'm getting quite worried about you. Wherever you go, there seems to be trouble," said Syreeta. "Are you going to follow up on the story?"

"Of course," said Rebecca.

"How about your friend, Jim?" said Syreeta, her eyes twinkling. "Did he come up with much?"

Rebecca didn't rise to the bait. "He does seem to know an incredible amount about anything to do with the sun. And the odd thing is, there does seem to be a red hair connection with the sun as well. What's really useful, he has contacts in lots of places where there have been redhead murders."

"So what happens now?" Syreeta persisted.

"Jim's just off to Easter Island. He's going to check out the murders in the South Pacific and let me know."

"Oh no! Don't tell me. Now you're thinking of going to Easter Island?"

"Why not, if that's where it's all happening?" Rebecca replied.

"Yes, but how much is all this travelling going to cost you? It's quite an investment you're making. What happens if there isn't a story? Say nobody takes it?"

"I'll check with Charles first."

"But won't it be dangerous? With your red hair, I mean? Why don't you wear a wig?"

"You're joking. I'll just have to be careful, won't I. Anyway, there are bound to be some tourists around with red hair, as well as me."

She sat down in front of her computer to check her emails. She skimmed through them and jumped when she saw one headed 'Easter Island':

Hi Rebecca,

Yes, you're right about the redhead murders on Easter Island. Four here, and now more in other parts of the South Pacific. Three on the island of Tanna in Vanuatu and three in Tahiti. Dig going well. Fascinating place. You'd like it. See you in Aberdeen?

Jim.

Rebecca grabbed the newspaper with her story in it and strode purposefully to Charles' office. He looked slightly taken aback when she rapped on the glass and walked straight in.

"Yes, well done," he said, seeing the paper. "Nice piece. The editor's very pleased. He wants you to follow up the redhead angle." He reached for a print-out and handed it to her. "There've been two more murders in Egypt – near Edfu. Redheads again, they were stabbed through the heart. Can you get on to it?"

"You mean go there?" said Rebecca.

"Up to you, but the editor's very keen on this story."

"I've just had an email in from Dr Cavendish on Easter Island. There've been four more murders there – and some on other islands, too."

Charles sat back abruptly. "Easter Island! You're not thinking of going there, are you? That's a bit off the map for our readers."

"The point is, I've got a very good contact there. Someone who could help me get a really good story."

Charles looked doubtful, but Rebecca looked very determined. He picked up a pile of papers, and leafed through them until he found what he wanted.

"Here you are. Report on murders of redheads in Easter Island

– from Juan Perez, our stringer in Santiago."

He handed it to her, got up and went to a map on the wall. His finger moved over the vast expanse of the Pacific Ocean and stopped. "Easter Island, also known as Rapa Nui. It's a long way away."

"Just one thing," said Rebecca. "These murder victims – are they Westerners?"

"No – locals. There are lots of redheaded people in the Pacific." He turned away from the map. "Isn't there a famous painting by Gauguin of a redhead in Tahiti or somewhere?"

"I didn't realise we got around so much," said Rebecca.

"Just about everywhere by now, I should think. But if you're thinking of going to Easter Island, you'd better take care. They're having quite a bad time. Four murdered over the past year – two just last week. And nobody seems to know why. At least, nobody's talking. It could be a local vendetta. Come to think of it, Easter Island's got a history of tribal warfare."

"How about the stringer in Santiago – Juan Perez? Could I use him?"

"I think Perez has got his own contact on Easter Island, a local man. See if he could help."

"Okay. I'll speak to Perez," Rebecca said, walking to the door.

Charles looked after her. "I'm not at all sure we should be letting you go," he said. "Perez could easily handle it."

"Not as well as me, if you see what I mean. Anyway, I'm big enough to look after myself. As long as there aren't any snakes."

As she left his office, she tossed her hair. "As they say, better red than dead."

CHAPTER 20

The garden of the Hotel Vinapu in Hanga-roa, the capital of Easter Island, was the pride and joy of its proprietor, Señor Pakarati. A keen gardener, he was acutely aware of the destruction of the island's natural flora over the years, largely by sheep-grazing, which had left wide expanses of rough grass and the now ubiquitous Eucalyptus trees.

Partly as a feature for his guests, but mostly for his own interest, he had collected many plant species native to the island and distributed these among the more common and attractive garden plants. The indigenous plants were all carefully labelled with their botanical and common names in the local language of Rapa Nui, as well as in Spanish and English, too, if they had an English name.

Rebecca's attention had been drawn to several banana trees growing along one side of the garden. Señor Pakarati had planted different varieties of banana to act as conversation pieces; bunches of small red bananas competed for attention with green plantains and tempting, large yellow varieties.

Jim was examining an unusual, yellow-flowered shrub. The flowers resembled tiny yellow chicks, bursting out of egg-like buds.

"See here, Rebecca," he called out, as he read the label. "It's a toromiro tree." Rebecca joined him, and he handed her a flower. "This used to grow only on Easter Island. Even today, it's only found in a few botanical gardens around the world."

When Jim had met Rebecca at the airport, he had seemed surprised, even slightly shocked, to hear that she had been prepared to travel so far for a story. But, despite the misgivings he had expressed about a redhead visiting the island under the present circumstances, he had seemed delighted to see her. Tired from the final leg of the journey from Chile, and disorientated by a completely different culture, she now found Jim's presence comforting and reassuring.

Alone in the garden, they sat down in deep wicker chairs at a table where Jim had left his beer. Rebecca took a sip of freshly-squeezed orange juice and leaned back to enjoy the warmth of the evening sun.

"Are you sure you wouldn't like something a bit stronger?" asked Jim. "A glass of wine?"

"No thanks," she said. "I don't really drink."

At first, they discussed Rebecca's forthcoming programme. She had arranged to meet Pablo Rapu the next day and start her investigations.

Jim found himself consciously suppressing a natural urge to overwhelm her with facts and figures about the island and its history.

According to her guidebook, the air here was said to be filled with certain mystical vibrations. So whether it was due to this, or merely the inclination of travellers in unfamiliar places to seek common ground, their conversation drifted, quite naturally, to talking about themselves.

As Rebecca told him about the loss of her parents, he listened attentively, and she quickly found herself going on to tell him about her break-up with Hamish. She had the impression that Jim, whilst sympathising with her, was quite pleased that she was not yet in a new relationship. She suspected he was naturally reticent about his personal life, and yet, before she knew it, he was telling her about his failed marriage and the pain it had caused him.

As they sat there, Rebecca conscious that they were beginning to sound like two sad, lost souls, a sweet scent drifted over towards them.

Jim nodded towards the white, trumpet-shaped flowers, hanging down among the leaves of a tall shrub. "Datura," he said.

"Otherwise known as 'Angels' Trumpets'. They contain hallucinogenic chemicals. They were supposed to have been used in witches' brews. Love potions, as well."

Hesitantly, he reached out and touched her hand. "I'm glad you came," he said, almost blurting out the words. "I didn't really think you'd make it."

Rebecca, taken by surprise, was wondering how she should react, when an elderly couple wandered into the garden, dispelling the quiet moment.

Jim looked up at the darkening sky, took his hand away and checked his watch. "Oh dear," he said. "You're going to have to excuse me. Larry's up at the dig by himself. I'd better get back there – he'll be wondering what's happened to me."

"Yes, I'm supposed to be here to do a job, myself," Rebecca said, smiling. "I still have to make final plans for tomorrow."

"I'm so pleased you're here," he said.

As they both stood up, he put his arm around her and kissed her lightly on the cheek. "I'll see you tomorrow. Why not get your colleague to bring you up to the dig? It's at Orongo. Larry will be able to give you lots of information about Easter Island – and redheads, too. He knows the history of this place inside out."

With that, he took his arm away and, with a wave, disappeared into the hotel. A minute later, she heard a car start and drive away.

As she sat down again, the scent of Angels' Trumpets engulfed her. Different emotions spun around in her head, and she felt intoxicated and out of control. Maybe the guidebook was right. It was almost as if the island did indeed have mysterious powers. And it felt as if they were taking over her life.

CHAPTER 21

Of course, she had read all about them, and seen them in photographs and documentaries. And yet nothing had prepared Rebecca for the sheer wonder of standing, dwarfed, before these four strange Easter Island statues towering over twenty feet into the sky.

She gazed up at their heads, each one capped with a huge red-coloured stone cylinder. Their sightless eyes stared over her, far into the distance. White, puffy clouds sped over the sky, so that the statues seemed to be moving, like a ship on the ocean.

She felt happy and, buoyed by her blossoming relationship with Jim, she found the imminent prospect of covering a series of murder cases more and more exciting. This was something she could never have hoped to attempt back in the UK; at the *Metropolitan*, the story would have automatically been covered by Bill Green, the chief crime correspondent. If she managed it well, this story could get her a good by-line, perhaps with a photo.

Pablo Rapu had met her at the hotel as arranged, and she had actually enjoyed riding pillion on his small Japanese motorbike. Pablo was proud of his Easter Island heritage. Like Rebecca, he was in his mid-twenties, and his dark good looks added to his South Seas warmth. Although his main job was with the Tourist Office, he was occasionally called on to help out Juan Perez with local stories.

Rebecca, impressed by the sheer size of the giant statues and to be standing so close to them, was happy to play the tourist asking the usual questions.

"They're amazing, Pablo. Who do you think made them? I've heard all sorts of theories."

Pablo took obvious pleasure in showing off his knowledge and his English. "Our ancestors made them. The statues are called *moai*, and the platform they stand on is called an *ahu*. You can see that the *moai* look inland – they protect us. They are representations of our ancient chiefs – the *ariki*." He pointed to the carved hands. "Look at their long nails. This is a sign that the *ariki* didn't do any physical work." He pointed upwards. "One group here used to stretch their ears, as you can see on the statue. They were called the long-ears. The others were the short-ears."

"Were they actually from different tribes or races?" Rebecca asked.

"It is not certain," Pablo replied. "One legend says that two kings came from the east, and there's only South America to the east. The first king was called Machaa. Then there was Hotu Matua – he was the first king of the long-ears. Later, there was Tuu-ko-ihu, but he was from the west – that's Polynesia. But there are many legends."

Pablo checked the position of the sun and pointed in a general westerly direction. "Tuu-ko-ihu was a short-ear. The long-ears ruled the short-ears, and they forced them to build the *moai*."

"I've heard that they were carved out of solid rock in a quarry, and dragged across the island," said Rebecca.

"Yeah, maybe that's why the short-ears got fed-up. There was a terrible war, just before your Captain Cook arrived. Most of the long-ears were killed by the short-ears." He dropped his voice. "People say there was even some cannibalism."

"What about the blocks on top of their heads?" asked Rebecca.

Pablo looked uncertain. "They are called *pukao*. But nobody really knows what they are."

Then Rebecca asked the question she had been holding back since she saw the stone blocks.

"Why are they red?"

Pablo thought for a bit. "Perhaps because red is a sacred colour in Polynesia. We also have gods with red skins, who wear hats made out of red feathers. They are very powerful gods." He smirked a little. "They say here that the colour red is very sexy." Rebecca ignored the comment and turned away. Pablo quickly stopped smiling.

"Some people say that the long-ear chiefs had red hair, and that the *pukao* are like top-knots. That was the way we used to do our hair."

Rebecca turned back to him. "Listen, Pablo. That's really why I'm here – red hair. What's going on here? Four people with red hair murdered in a year." Rebecca guessed what he was thinking. "Do you think it's safe for me here?"

"Sure. Just stay with me," he said.

Then his expression changed. "You know, I do find it a bit scary. It's just like the tribal wars are starting again." He started to walk to his motorbike. "Come on. I should take you to see the Chief of Police next. He can tell you what's been going on."

"Do you know him?" asked Rebecca.

"Everybody here knows everybody," said Pablo. "*Vamos.*"

He got on his bike and started it up. Rebecca clambered on behind him, with as much dignity as she could muster in the pencil slim skirt, which she thought appropriate before she knew that she would be travelling by motorbike. Pablo let the clutch out quickly and revved the engine so that the front wheel lifted off the ground. Rebecca could only stop herself falling off by lightly placing her arms around his waist.

As they raced away, a large brown bird silently flew down, perched on top of the highest statue and watched them as they sped towards Hanga-roa.

The bird was a hawk.

CHAPTER 22

Diego Garcia, Chief of Police, was in his small office, busily occupied with a pile of papers on his desk. More papers and buff-coloured files were heaped on every available surface: filing cabinets, on top of two fragile-looking chairs and even on the floor against the walls, from which the paint was peeling. A fan above him creaked slowly round, lifting the papers on his desk a little with each revolution.

He was in his mid-forties, and his thinning hair, for which he compensated with a thick black moustache, was swept back to his neck. There it formed ringlets, wet with sweat, just above the collar of his limp white shirt. He was a decent man who valued his normal, quiet, controlled existence. But now his life had been thrown into disarray by unwanted attention.

When Pablo walked into his office accompanied by Rebecca, he jumped to his feet.

"*Hola, Pablo. ¿Que tal?*" he said, with a slightly forced smile, as he took in the sight of Rebecca.

Pablo drew himself up and smiled broadly. "*Buen dia*, Señor Garcia. May I introduce Señorita Burns from the *Metropolitan* newspaper in London. Our problems are making us famous. She asks to know all about the murders."

Garcia rapidly cleared the papers from a chair and beckoned Rebecca to sit down. "*Encantado, señorita*. Welcome to Rapa Nui. It would be more pleasant if you had come in better times. This sort of thing does not exactly help our tourist trade, and without that we certainly do not have much else." He stood up. "One moment, please."

Putting his hand on Pablo's arm, he gently but firmly manoeuvred him to one side. Garcia turned his face away from

Rebecca and spoke to Pablo in rapid Spanish, with obvious frustration.

Pablo looked put out for a moment. "*No sabía que fuera pelirroja.*" He then smiled enquiringly, raising his eyebrows. "*¿Pero, es muy linda, no?*"

Garcia looked unimpressed for a moment, then noticeably relaxed. They didn't appreciate that Rebecca had understood every word they had said. Garcia was clearly exasperated with Pablo for turning up with an inquisitive, red-haired foreigner. Pablo had tried to defuse the situation by jokingly drawing attention to Rebecca's good looks, despite her being a potential liability.

She blushed, partly with embarrassment, partly with irritation.

Garcia turned to her, smiling. "I'm sorry señorita. We were just discussing the best way to help you."

Don't lie, thought Rebecca. "*Gracias, no quisiera causarles ninguna molestia.* I wouldn't want to cause you any trouble, but if you want to help me, you could start by telling me what's been going on."

Garcia glanced at Pablo as if to say, *why didn't you tell me*? Pablo shrugged his shoulders almost imperceptibly.

Garcia lowered his head. "I'm sorry. Not many of our tourists speak Spanish," he said. "Normally it is very quiet in Rapa Nui. Usually people behave well. Sometimes there's a little bit of pilfering, or maybe a fight when someone gets drunk, but nothing much. That's why the murders are so shocking for us."

"But four of them? In a year?"

His face fell. "Five, I'm afraid. We've just had another one reported."

Rebecca knew the answer already, but asked anyway. "Redhead?"

Garcia nodded and raised his hands in a gesture of helplessness.

"But why redheads? What's the motive?"

Garcia looked genuinely bewildered. "That's the odd thing. If you had asked me two hundred and fifty years ago, I would have put it down to tribal feuding. Short-ears murdering long-ears."

"Because long-ears had red hair?" Rebecca prompted.

Garcia seemed relieved to share his burden a little. "Or just because they were different. At that time, most of the long-ears were killed. Only very few, direct descendants remain."

"Are they the people being killed?" she asked.

"There are lots of people here with reddish hair. Even the short-ears and long-ears had relationships. The strange thing is, the people being murdered are those with the reddest hair. So far, anyway." He glanced at Rebecca's striking hair, before quickly looking away.

Rebecca asked a question she didn't really want to ask. "How were they killed?"

The answer was not what she wanted to hear.

"Nasty. They were all knifed in the chest. And all the bodies have been found near *moai.*"

Rebecca turned to Pablo. "*Moai.* Aren't they the statues we were looking at, Pablo?"

"That's right," said Pablo. "Our ancestors used to make sacrifices by them," he added, to Garcia's irritation.

"Sacrifices?" queried Rebecca.

As Pablo opened his mouth to comment, Garcia answered quickly. "*Si.* But that was all over two hundred years ago. There's no reason I can think of why it should start again."

"Are there any witnesses?" asked Rebecca.

"Well, if there are, they're not coming forward."

"The problem is," Pablo interjected, "the island is covered in caves, so people can hide and wait for their chance. After, they can quickly disappear again. Sometimes a cave is known only to one family, maybe only to one person. They used to put dead bodies in them. They're still used for storing *moai maea.*"

"*Moai* what? Sorry…" Rebecca interrupted.

"Carved stones of animal-like figures," Garcia explained. "They are household idols used by the families. Sometimes they have been owned by a single family for hundreds of years."

"It's all making our red-haired people very nervous. They are frightened to go out," said Pablo. "When they do go out, they go around in groups."

Garcia ended the interview abruptly. "Pablo says you have a friend working with Professor Burton on the archaeological dig at Orongo. Professor Burton knows a lot about Rapa Nui, probably more than me. Perhaps you should talk to him."

He stood up and showed them to the door. "But, please señorita – ¡*Tenga cuidad!* – Take care!" With that, he turned back to his pile of papers.

CHAPTER 23

The deserted village of Orongo lay at the highest point on the island. It consisted of a group of ancient abandoned stone huts, some of which were still intact and inhabitable. Built so that they were set into the rocks, and with low roofs, they would have provided protection against the worst extremes of weather. Close by, there were some rocks covered in strange, sculpted markings.

The village itself was perched to one side on the rim of an extinct volcano, Rano Kao, its gigantic bowl-shaped crater stretching over a mile across. One step too far towards the crater and one would have plunged helplessly to the bottom. Pools of water, lit up by the sunlight and scattered among patches of vegetation stretching to the far side, concealed a treacherous quagmire.

Walking a short distance in the opposite direction to the crater, one reached the edge of the cliffs, which dropped vertically a thousand feet to the crashing sea below.

Rebecca was grateful to dismount from the pillion of Pablo's motorbike, the novelty value long since replaced by discomfort and a constant fear of an accident.

Pablo beckoned her to admire the view. She followed him, although she was now growing impatient to see Jim again.

The view inland revealed the town of Hanga-roa, laid out below them in its entirety. Beyond, they could see virtually the whole island, stretching out to the blue-hazed horizon. At Pablo's insistence, she crept to the very brink of the cliffs. The vastness of the Pacific Ocean shimmered under an azure-domed heaven. The wind gusted lightly and, shivering with a mixture of elation and vertigo, she stumbled back to rest against the firmness of a large boulder.

A short distance away, the few tents of the archaeological

camp were pitched in the shadow of the stone huts. A trestle-table had been set up and was littered with pieces of flat rock of various sizes. A small team of local workers was cleaning some large rocks. Three of the workers, who looked like a father and two sons, were instantly distinguishable from their colleagues by their reddish hair. Rebecca noticed them immediately.

Patches of soil had been removed at the base of several of the boulders which had carvings on them, and on the bare rock beneath, one could already make out the faint patterns still to be cleaned up.

A sound of scraping came from within one of the huts. It stopped, and a man emerged from the low entrance, knees-bent and clutching a large slab of stone.

Professor Laurence Burton, known to his friends and colleagues as Larry, carefully carried the slab to the table. He studied it for a few seconds and gently and quickly began to remove the grime with a brush. That completed, he examined it closely, his clear blue eyes gleaming with interest.

At sixty-four, with a full head of almost white hair, he was still upright, slim and moved like a fit man. Even in his khaki work trousers, dirty and well-worn at the knees, and an old denim shirt frayed at the collar, he still had the air of a distinguished academic.

Seeing Larry's find, Jim stopped scraping soil away from a boulder and bounded over to see what he had discovered.

"Another bird-man petroglyph. And what a beauty!" he exclaimed. "Dammit, where did I leave my camera?" He thought for a second and went into one of the stone huts.

Catching sight of the visitors arriving, Larry tore himself away from the find. "It's that man from the Tourist Office again, with a visitor," he called out to Jim. "I'd better find out what they want."

Pablo held out his hand. "Good afternoon, Professor. Please meet Señorita Burns from the *Metropolitan* in London. She is here to write about the murders. We were hoping that perhaps you could help us."

Rebecca cringed and cut in quickly. "Hello. You must be Professor Burton. I'm Rebecca Burns. A friend of Jim Cavendish? He might have mentioned I was coming?"

"Ah, yes, so he did," he said, shaking hands with her. "Larry Burton. Yes, it's a nasty business – bit of a mystery. But, er, to be perfectly candid, it's nothing to do with what we're doing here. We try to keep out of that sort of thing, you know. It's a small place. And people here don't really bother us." He turned towards the hut. "Jim!"

As he emerged from the hut and caught sight of Rebecca, Jim's face broke into a broad smile.

"Rebecca! Welcome to Orongo!" He hugged her, warmly shook Pablo's hand and turned to Larry. "Larry, time for a tea-break, don't you think?"

"Well… okay," Larry replied.

Jim disappeared into a tent and produced a battered Thermos flask and four mugs. He pointed to some low rocks towards the cliff-edge, high over the sea, where they could sit. Larry poured out the tea silently and passed the cups around. The tea looked evil; dark brown and over-brewed. Rebecca took a sip. It tasted as bad as it looked. She continued to drink but noticed that Pablo had quickly put his mug to one side.

"So, how can we help you?" Larry asked, stirring his tea.

"I'd be interested to know what you are doing here?"

"We're looking for petroglyphs," Larry said.

"Petroglyphs?" Rebecca fumbled to find her notebook.

"Carvings on rocks. There are thousands of these all over the island," Larry said, now visibly relaxing at the thought of talking about a favourite subject. "Ancestor figures, weird mythical creatures. You name it."

"Most people don't know much about these. They are only interested in the statues," said Pablo.

"The carvings have attracted far less attention, but are just as fascinating," interjected Jim. "We're really looking for the older ones, which have been covered up for years."

Larry took a gulp of tea and stood up. "Come over here," he said, and led the way to a large rock. It was about the height of a man and almost completely covered in carvings. Because of the lichen, it took Rebecca a while to spot the strange figure that only became evident when Larry outlined it with his finger.

It was half-man, half-bird. A large eye was carved on the head, and an enormous curved beak protruded in front of it. The body, though, bore little resemblance to that of a bird. It had crude human legs and a long spindly arm with a large hand, holding what appeared to be an egg.

"This figure here. He's a bird-man," Larry said, stroking the rock. "According to the people here, the bird-man is the representative on Earth of Make-Make, the god of creation. This place, Orongo, used to be a ceremonial village dedicated to the bird-man cult."

Larry pointed out to sea in the direction of a small rocky island about a quarter of a mile away. "You see that island there? It's called Moto Nui."

The sea was high, and powerful waves were crashing well up the cliffs at the island's edge.

"Look at those waves!" Larry exclaimed. "And yet, once a year, each clan on Easter Island chooses somebody to take part in the traditional race to Moto Nui. They have to climb down these cliffs, brave the rough sea and swim to the island. Then they have to find the egg of a sea-gull and bring it back here. First one back means that the chief of his clan gets to be bird-man for the next year. And it's a great privilege to be bird-man."

"This happens every year as part of our festival," Pablo cut in.

But Jim took over. "The winner's clan is known as the *Ao*. *Ao* is also the name of a special, ceremonial canoe paddle. It is double-headed with a strange face painted on each end."

Larry pointed towards the huts. "The funny thing is, yesterday we found a stone with the same face painted on it. It was in one of the ceremonial houses. I'll show it to you later. Anyway, in the end, the bird-man cult took over from the worship of the statues of the ancestors – the *moai*."

"Does this have anything to do with the redhead murders?" asked Rebecca, trying to steer the conversation back to her main interest.

Larry gazed out over the vastness of the ocean, as if collecting his thoughts together. If he had looked upwards, he might have seen a stationary dot, high in the sky above them. A sudden gust of wind blew his hair over his forehead. Brushing his hair back, he turned round again to face Rebecca.

"When the first Europeans arrived here – a Dutch boat in 1722 – they noted that there were a lot of red-haired natives. Then, more recently, Thor Heyerdahl – the Kon Tiki man – had this theory that a redheaded race had travelled to Easter Island from Egypt and the Middle East, via South America." He paused. "Almost as if they were being driven out of whatever place they landed in."

"What do you think? Do you believe Heyerdahl was right?" asked Rebecca.

"Heyerdahl's a bit out of fashion now," said Jim, before Larry could answer. "From the latest DNA analysis, it looks as if the islanders originally came from Polynesia."

"But no one has proven anything yet," Larry said emphatically.

"So it is possible that the redheads could have sailed here from South America?" asked Rebecca.

"Yes, it is possible, I suppose," said Jim. "And all these places have a history of sun-worship, too. The extraordinary thing is that, with all the great distance between Easter Island and Egypt, they both had the same word for the sun – *Ra*. Same goes for monoliths – stone structures like the Egyptian obelisks – and these *moai* statues here. They're found all over the world where sun-worship was practised. And they are often about commemorating the dead – a form of ancestor worship. You remember the standing stones we saw at Stenness and Brodgar? Well, some people believe that they, too, are representations of important ancestors."

"You could say it was the sun that brought Jim to Easter Island," Larry said. "The site here at Orongo was once an ancient sun observatory."

Jim laughed. "Rebecca must have the impression I think about nothing else."

As he stood by the sculpted rock, the sunlight shone through his brown hair. *His hair is exactly the same colour as his eyes,* thought Rebecca.

"I suppose it's partly true that the sun brought me here," he said, smiling at her. "But it was just as much in the hope of finding something new, something unexpected." He unconsciously ran his hand over the curved surface of the rock, as if caressing it.

Rebecca smiled back, and for a moment he seemed to lose his thread.

"The whole site here at Orongo is aligned to the sun," he then went on. "We think it was built to mark the solstices and the equinoxes. There's another site on the island that's aligned to the moon, as well as the sun. These places could have been used to mark the seasons of the year. The right time to plant crops, that sort of thing."

"Or quite possibly something more sinister," said Larry. "I'm afraid sun-worship was often associated with blood-thirsty sacrifices."

Larry glanced at the local men, who had now stopped working and were sitting down. "Listen. I'm sorry, but we have to press on right now. Why not join us for a meal tonight?" He nodded in the direction of the three redheaded men who were talking together. "Señor Nata and his family over there are cooking a meal for us. We could talk more then."

"Thank you, Professor Burton. I'd like that." Rebecca turned to her new colleague. "What about you, Pablo?"

Pablo looked happy. "Sure. At your service, Rebecca."

"Just one more thing, Professor," she said. "You were going to show me the strange painted face you found yesterday."

"Call me Larry," he said. "Come and have a look. These are actually ceremonial houses."

He led them over towards the stone huts. They were squat and made of flat, closely inter-fitting stones, with a flat roof covered in grass.

Jim turned to Rebecca. "You know, it's a funny thing, but there are some prehistoric houses in Orkney remarkably like these, quite near where we were. It makes you wonder who built them. Some people say the Phoenicians were there too, a long time ago."

"Phoenicians? In Scotland?"

"Well, it seems incredible, but they did get around," said Jim. "They were brilliant sea-farers. Even the ancient Egyptians employed them for their long distance exploration journeys. Red hair link as well, Rebecca."

"Really?"

"Sure," said Jim. "The Phoenicians originally came from what is now Lebanon. And that is perhaps how redheaded people spread throughout the world, because Lebanon, even now, has one of the highest percentages of red-haired people in the world. The Phoenicians are well known for the trail of red-haired descendants they left behind wherever they travelled."

"So are you saying the Phoenicians could have taken red hair to Scotland?" asked Rebecca.

"You never know," said Jim.

"But I thought red hair in Scotland came from invading Vikings?"

"Perhaps the Phoenicians – or even their ancestors – went to Scandinavia as well."

Larry stopped outside a hut. "This is the one, but you will have to crawl in on your knees – the entrance is very low."

Inside, there were no windows and the only light inside came through the doorway. It took a while for Rebecca's eyes to adjust to the gloom.

Larry switched on a torch and shone the beam over the wall. "Just take a look," he said, lighting up a painting.

It was difficult to decipher at first, a cross between a Stone Age cave-painting and a piece of modern abstract art. She was able to pick out the eyes on the face first, then the eyebrows and finally the hair, which was represented by a few vertical lines.

"Funny hair-style," she said.

"It's probably stylised feathers," said Larry. "It's rather like the headdresses the Incas used to wear. And the Sea Peoples as well – the Peleset. The Sea Peoples date back to even before the Phoenicians in the Levant, and could be the original long-distance seafarers."

"This is just mind-boggling," said Rebecca.

Larry looked pleased. "If you like all this, you should come to Aberdeen next week. We'll be doing a whole presentation on it there."

"I'd love that. Will you let me have the details?"

Outside the hut, Larry took a pen and notebook from his shirt pocket and wrote down a website address. He also added his email address and mobile number.

"Thanks," said Rebecca. "Perhaps you could tell me all about it at the dinner?"

"Yes, and you will be able to meet Dr Neferatu as well. He's a bit of a mystery. Apparently he arrived a couple of days ago – but we haven't seen him yet. Jim says he knows him, and that he could be a good source of funding. I hear he's an expert on sun-worship, but I've never come across him myself."

Jim smiled at Rebecca. "He could be very useful to you with your story." He walked with Rebecca and Pablo to the motorbike. "See you tonight then. It should be fun."

CHAPTER 24

Rebecca swung her bag on to her back and checked her watch as Pablo got on his motorbike. It was just gone four o'clock.

"Pablo – would you mind taking me back to the statues we saw this morning? I've got my watercolours with me, and we've got a couple of hours to spare. I'd quite like to do a quick painting."

"You paint?" he said, surprised.

"Nothing very ambitious – just small postcards, really. They don't take too long."

"Why not take a photo instead?"

"I do that as well, of course. But I like to send paintings to friends. When you paint, it sort of fixes the scene in your mind, better than a photo. It's something my mother taught me – she was a real artist."

"I'm not sure I should be leaving you alone," he said.

"There'll probably be some more tourists there. Anyway, I can always get you on your phone."

Pablo didn't look happy. "Okay. I need to go to the Tourist Office, but I could drop you off and pick you up later?"

"Lovely."

His motorbike spluttered into life. She clambered on to the pillion and waved goodbye to Jim and Larry.

Pablo drove carefully down the slope, trying to avoid the worst of the rocky bumps. They pulled up a short time later by the statues. By this time, it was late afternoon and only a group of four tourists remained.

"Are you sure you will be okay on your own here?" he asked. "Is there anything you need?"

"No thanks. I've got my paints and my water, that's all I need."

"What time should I come back for you?"

"About six o'clock will be fine."

As the sound of the motorbike faded into the distance, Rebecca walked around the statues looking for the best perspective. In the golden sunlight, they seemed friendly and protective rather than mysterious. She saw them now as guardians of the island.

The clunk of a car door disturbed her thoughts, and she saw a car with the four tourists head off in the same direction as Pablo.

The whole area was now completely deserted. Sitting down on a rock, she looked out to sea. A few seagulls wheeled around, their urgent cries piercing the air, and then even they flew away, leaving only the sound of the waves breaking gently on the shore.

She decided the best view would be had by walking a little further inland and painting the statues with the sea behind them, to show their faces. Walking across the rough grass, she selected a rock, sat down and leaned against it.

Now on her own and enjoying the peace and quiet, she put aside Pablo's concerns and decided to concentrate on her painting. She took out her small tin of watercolours and opened it. She then poured some of her mineral water into a plastic bottle cut in half and set it down beside her. Taking out a blank card and her pen, she started to draw in the outlines of the painting in black waterproof ink.

The outlines completed, she chose to paint in the sea first. It took several attempts to find the right blue. Absorbed, she mixed colours fastidiously until, to her eye, she had achieved a perfect match with a delicate shade of aquamarine. She then washed in the colour of the sea behind the drawings of the statues.

Satisfied and weary, she leaned back against the rock again, gazed over the open sea and let her mind drift over the events of the day.

The image of a little raft appeared from nowhere on the horizon. She watched it dreamily, as it floated slowly over the sea towards her, until she could just make out the tiny figures perched under a single sail, swollen by the wind.

The cry of a seagull made her start, and she realised that the sun, although still above the horizon, was beginning to set. But there was no longer any sign of the little sailing craft.

She quickly mixed up golds, browns and reds to paint in the statues, highlighting the eyes in white, with black pupils. Using a chrome green, she washed in the grass in front of the statues and finished the painting by stippling in patches of darker green, to denote the larger tussocks of grass.

By now, the sun was hanging just above the horizon, staining the sea blood-red and forming long shadows behind the statues. She shivered as the air chilled slightly.

With her pen, she scribbled her initials in the corner of the painting, dated it and carefully slipped it between the remaining blank cards for safekeeping.

She checked her watch; Pablo was already half an hour late. But as she wandered back to the road she could make out the sound of a motorbike, and in a few seconds, Pablo drew up in a cloud of dust.

"I was beginning to think that you had forgotten me," she said, half frowning.

"Sorry," he said brightly. "A couple of Germans needed a hotel for the night. It took me a while to find one."

He parked the bike and walked over to the statues. "You know, I love this place. It's so peaceful," he said, looking out to sea. "Can I see your painting?"

"It's not very good," said Rebecca, reluctantly pulling it out of the pack and handing it over.

Pablo studied it carefully. "The little raft is interesting."

"What little raft?"

"Here," said Pablo, touching the card.

Rebecca took it back. He was right. It was there, painted on the sea between two of the statues; a tiny raft with a white sail and three tiny figures on it, one of them waving.

"I was just thinking about a little raft on the water when I was looking out to sea. I remember that quite clearly, but I'm sure I didn't paint it. It must have been all those stories I've been hearing today, playing tricks on my mind. I must be going mad."

Pablo laughed. "Well, if it wasn't you, I don't know who did it. One thing's for sure – it wasn't me. Listen, we should leave now. They are expecting us around eight o'clock and I know what you English people are like about punctuality."

Rebecca climbed on behind him. "Home, James," she said, laughing.

CHAPTER 25

The stars of the Southern Sky shone brightly over Orongo, and the sea glittered under a large silver moon. In the crater of Rano Kao, pools of water sparkled far below with reflected light. The wind had dropped and the air hung heavy and warm.

Larry and Jim had worked hard to make the archaeological site look as attractive as possible for the dinner. The digging equipment had all been carefully tidied away, and a few choice stone carvings had been put on display.

The table was already laid for the dinner, a sheet serving as a tablecloth and mugs supplementing the few glasses they possessed. The cutlery was mainly odds and ends but adequate, Jim having set himself a sheath-knife. Gas lamps were slung over the table, and moths of every description were flitting blindly around them. Larry and Jim were leaning back in camp chairs, pleased with the day's work and relaxing, drinks in hand, while they waited for their guests.

In the background, among the tents, a meal was being prepared. Señor Nata crouched and took something steaming from a shallow hole in the ground. In the gas-light, it was possible to see that he was fine-featured, with high cheekbones and kind, smiling eyes. His skin was weather-beaten and lined, and his dark red hair was flecked with grey. Though he moved like a much younger man, he was clearly middle-aged. Nearby, his mother, an old, white-haired lady, was preparing vegetables. Her wizened features revealed a close resemblance to those of Señor Nata. The two younger red-haired men, now wearing brightly-patterned loose shirts, were collecting plates and implements for carving and serving.

When Pablo and Rebecca drew up noisily on the motorbike,

Jim jumped up and went over to greet them. He put his arm around Rebecca and shook hands with Pablo. "Glad you made it all right. Come and join us."

Rebecca, in skin-tight jeans, slid from the pillion seat with some difficulty. She noticed straight away that Jim had put on a clean shirt, but that one of the buttons was about to fall off.

Larry got up, strode over to them and shook hands, offering each of them a glass of red wine. They sat down, Pablo seating himself next to Rebecca.

"You know, we're in for a real treat tonight," Larry said, joining them at the head of the table. "Señor Nata and his family are cooking us a local speciality – suckling pig and sweet potatoes wrapped in banana leaves, all baked in the ground."

"Did you know it's also a food offering to keep the *aku-aku* happy?" said Pablo. "They'll certainly put some by for them."

Rebecca laughed. "Pablo, what on earth are the *aku-aku*?"

"The ancestral spirits, of course," he replied, and waved his arms around theatrically. "They're everywhere. Some are good – some are bad. There are people here who believe that they can take human form. Sometimes they even live as part of the family."

"Really?" said Rebecca, laughing again. "Did you invite them, personally?"

Pablo ignored her. "Some people are supposed to be able to communicate with the *aku-aku*," he went on mysteriously. "They call themselves *ivi-atua*." He looked meaningfully over at the old lady. "Señor Nata's mother, for instance."

As he spoke, Rebecca thought she detected a movement in the darkness behind the old lady. It seemed to hover for a few seconds, and then a dark figure emerged out of the gloom.

"Looks like the other guest has arrived," said Pablo. "Funny, I didn't hear a car."

Dr Neferatu strode over to them. He was well-dressed in a light suit that emphasised his powerful build. However, his smart appearance seemed out of place on an archaeological site.

Rebecca took an instinctive dislike to him; *greaseball*, she decided, in an instant judgment.

Jim, though, welcomed him warmly. "Ah, Dr Neferatu, pleased to see you again. It seems Easter Island is a popular place to visit. May I offer you a glass of wine?"

"Thank you – white," he answered slowly, in a deep gravelly voice, calmly looking around and taking in the scene.

"I think it's chilled enough now," Jim said, fishing a bottle out of an old bucket. "Let me introduce you. This is Rebecca Burns from the *Metropolitan* newspaper in London. Rebecca's here to cover the spate of murders on the island."

He turned to Pablo. "This is Pablo Rapu, who is lucky enough to live here. And you, Dr Neferatu? I suppose that it's your antiques business that's brought you here?"

"Yes, indeed," replied Dr Neferatu, expressionless.

Ignoring Pablo, Dr Neferatu grasped Rebecca's hand. As he did so, she felt a sharp stab of pain and, glancing down, was startled to find that one of his nails was digging into the side of her hand.

"*Enchanté, mademoiselle.*" He dragged the words out, still holding her hand.

"The pleasure's mine, *monsieur*," replied Rebecca, trying not to wince. Then he dug his nail in even further. A sudden tiredness almost overwhelmed her, and she felt her body starting to sag.

"You have travelled a long way. You must be feeling quite drained," he drawled, emphasising the word 'drained' almost comically. "With jet-lag, I mean," he added, continuing to hold her hand and staring at her with his green eyes.

"Tired – yes, just a little, but Pablo's helping me with the story," she said, making an effort to stand up straight, whilst trying to extricate herself from his iron grip.

"He helps everybody here," Larry said, obviously blind to Rebecca's discomfort.

"I also work for the tourist board," Pablo explained.

Slowly, Dr Neferatu released Rebecca's hand and briefly shook Pablo's outstretched hand.

"When did you arrive, Dr Neferatu?" Pablo asked.

"Wednesday. Two days ago."

"Two days ago?" said Pablo. "I didn't know they were doing flights on a Wednesday."

Dr Neferatu sighed. "It might have been Tuesday. I travel so much, I never know which day it is."

Pablo gestured around the site. "Do you have a special interest in all this too?"

Dr Neferatu looked around and shrugged his shoulders, as if he could scarcely be bothered with pleasantries.

"Not exactly. I'm in import-export, and you have some very nice antiquities here. The petroglyphs, for instance. Also, some of the carvings."

Pablo looked put out. "Perhaps we shouldn't be letting all these things go out of the country. It is our heritage, after all."

Dr Neferatu looked down his long nose at Pablo. "That may be so, but I have to tell you, your authorities have already agreed to sell certain things. I operate entirely above board, I always obtain all the necessary papers, and I pay a fair price."

He turned away, made for Jim who was setting out the plates on the table and took him to one side, out of earshot of Rebecca. "Dr Cavendish – the report you did is excellent. I think we shall be able to work together. We shall talk further."

"If you want to hear about the work we're doing here," Jim replied, "we'll be presenting in Aberdeen next week. You would be very welcome. It would also be a good opportunity to talk some more about funding."

"I shall be there," intoned Dr Neferatu, and he went over to look at the stone carvings.

Rebecca was still nursing her hand, when she became aware of Pablo staring at her. "You know, it's not everyday I get to work with such a beautiful girl," he said, in a low voice.

Rebecca groaned inwardly. "Thank you, Pablo. You really have been very helpful. I'd have been lost without you."

"Perhaps we can take a walk after the meal. You must see the view from the cliff top at night."

She gave him a sunny smile. "What I really want to do is get as much information as possible, while we've got the opportunity. That's why I'm here."

"Of course," said Pablo, appearing to take the hint. "It's just that it's not everyday that I meet somebody like you. A real professional."

Rebecca turned away and was raising her eyes to the sky, just as Larry called out that the meal was about to be served. Larry took the head of the table, and Rebecca ended up opposite Dr Neferatu and Jim, with Pablo beside her.

The meal was served on a large platter by Señor Nata. The suckling pig had been carved into pieces and placed in the centre of the plate, with the vegetables arranged attractively around them.

Dr Neferatu held up his hand as soon as a small portion had been placed on his plate, politely declining the second serving Señor Nata offered him. Rebecca, on the other hand, was ravenous, and gratefully accepted a double helping.

Dr Neferatu was not the easiest dinner guest, making only perfunctory comments whenever attempts were made to draw him into the conversation. He seemed to prefer simply observing the other guests.

The talk soon switched to the purpose of the dig and the findings. Larry and Jim's enthusiasm for their work was catching, and Rebecca found it easier to chat to them, rather than attempting to force a one-sided conversation with Dr Neferatu.

As the glasses were being refilled, she became aware that Dr Neferatu had not eaten a single thing. He had carefully moved the portion of pork from one side of his plate to the other, and had covered it with a banana leaf. Pork of any kind was clearly a dish he did not wish to eat, and yet it was only Rebecca who seemed to notice.

She decided to try and find out more about the antiques he

was hoping to find on Easter Island. "Have you got your eye on anything special here you'd like to buy?" she asked.

Dr Neferatu looked up from his plate. "Not really. There's nothing much new here that I haven't seen before. But that carving over there – that looks rather interesting."

He was looking in the direction of Señor Nata's mother, who was holding a carved wooden figure in front of her and staring at it. As he pointed to the figure, Rebecca noticed that the nail on his index finger was about half an inch long.

"It's called a *moai kava-kava* – an ancestor figure. That's the sort of thing I am most interested in. You see the long ears. The old lady is perhaps a long-ear descendant."

Rebecca could make out some of the figure's features, but certainly not the detail of the ears. The carving was about a foot high and appeared to be an image of a decaying male corpse. The rib-cage stood out clearly over a sunken stomach, and she could just about make out the eyes, but only because they were set with black and white inlays.

"How on earth can you see the ears from here?" she asked.

"Oh, you see, I have very good eyesight," was all he offered in way of explanation.

"It looks like a dead body to me," said Rebecca.

As Dr Neferatu picked up his glass and took a sip of wine, it was clear that the fingernails on both his index fingers were long. She wondered how he stopped them from breaking.

"The islanders used to put their dead on platforms to rot," he said, in a low oily voice that made Rebecca feel distinctly uneasy. "After that, they collected the bones together for safekeeping."

"And why did they stretch their ears?"

Dr Neferatu looked thoughtful. "I suppose it is just tribal practice. The tribe of the Buddha is the most famous for this. Think of the images of Buddha."

She was about to ask whether the tribes could be related, when the urgent sound of a drumbeat came out of nowhere.

CHAPTER 26

Rebecca had not noticed that as soon as the islanders had served the meal, they had disappeared from sight. They had now returned and were sitting in a group some distance away by the side of the carved rocks. On their heads they wore crowns made of leaves threaded together, not unlike laurel wreaths. One of the younger men was playing a drum placed between his crossed legs. As the drumbeat became louder and more complex, Señor Nata and the other younger man got to their feet, started swaying to the rhythm and shuffled around in a circle.

Suddenly, the sound of a high-pitched wail floated above the drumbeat, and it took a moment for Rebecca to realise that it was coming from the old lady, who was still seated. She was holding the wooden figure straight in front of her and chanting directly at it.

Rebecca turned to Pablo. "What's that about?"

Pablo's face was serious, and his eyes glistened with emotion. "It's a traditional song. It's only rarely that you hear this. They are singing to Make-Make to bring good luck to the dig."

Conversation lapsed while the diners watched.

As the two men stopped dancing and sat down, the drumbeat became louder and more urgent. The old lady held the carving closer to her face and began to shake it.

From behind a rock, a young girl appeared. If she had been present before, nobody had noticed. Her long red hair was striking, redder than that of the others, and down to her shoulders. She was barefoot, wore a loose green dress and could have been no more than twelve or thirteen.

She seemed oblivious to any onlookers and, as if in a world of her own, she started to turn around on the spot, slowly at first and then rapidly faster and more wildly, arms held high in the air.

Completely absorbed in watching this, Rebecca began to feel dazed as the insistent drumbeat got inside her head. She seemed to be losing her inhibitions in some strange way and was seized by an almost uncontrollable urge to join the girl in the dance.

A surge of deep excitement flowed through her, until her skin glistened with perspiration. Unconsciously and against all usual rational thinking, she could not stop herself from slipping her hand under the table and placing it on Pablo's thigh. Pablo, taken aback at first, and then pleasantly surprised, lightly placed his hand on hers. Feeling her hand trapped and realising what she had done, Rebecca snatched it away, coming quickly to her senses and shocked by her own actions and instincts. Pablo now looked totally confused.

Then, a few seconds later, a look of sheer terror came over Rebecca's face, as her eyes seemed to fix on something in the distance.

Her long scream jolted the whole scene. Pablo instantly placed both his hands on the table. The drumming stopped abruptly, and the dancing girl ran back behind the rocks.

Everybody looked at Rebecca in astonishment. She seemed to be staring, petrified, at the rocks behind which the girl had disappeared. A skeletal figure was emerging from behind the rocks and starting to walk straight towards her. Yet nobody else seemed to see it.

At first, it looked like an emaciated corpse. Then she realised the horrific being was nothing less than the living, full-sized embodiment of the grisly wooden figure that the old lady had been holding. Its bones were held together by mahogany coloured skin, which was peeling away in places and hanging loose. There was no nose, only a deep black hole beneath which yellow and brown rotting teeth were bared in a ghoulish grin. The eyes were viscous white spheres, with jet black pupils. A wispy red beard was stuck beneath the jaw-bone, and long earlobes hung down on either side of the face.

As it came closer, she noticed something alive and moving in the base of the rib-cage. She was overwhelmed with revulsion; its stomach was crawling with maggots.

It advanced slowly, but as it came to a halt barely a couple of feet in front of her, still grinning, it stretched out a bony arm towards her, its fingers reaching out to touch her face.

Rebecca screamed again, backing away in terror, and fell sideways, tipping over her chair in a desperate attempt to escape the bony fingers.

Looking around her, she was amazed to find that no one else was affected by the terrible apparition. They were not even looking at it. Instead they were all simply looking at her with a mixture of concern and amazement. Jim leapt to his feet to help her up.

"Rebecca – what's wrong? What's going on?"

She looked up at him, her face contorted with fear. It took her a few more seconds to notice that the apparition had disappeared. The islanders were sitting there quietly, as if nothing had happened. Even the old lady sat completely expressionless, with the carving in her lap.

Rebecca looked around, bewildered and visibly trembling. "That horrible thing – what was it? Just hideous! Revolting! So…" she searched for the right word, "vile!" Her face was white. "Where did it go?" she whispered.

Jim grasped her arm, trying to stop her shaking. "What on earth's the matter, Rebecca? What happened to you?"

"Didn't you see it? It was right in front of you!" She looked anxiously in turn from Jim to Larry. "A rotten corpse – but it was walking, and full of maggots!" She stared at them, but neither of them looked at all shocked. Just a bit baffled. "But it came right up to me. You must have seen it! It almost touched me. It was right here. Just where you're standing."

Then, again, Rebecca's eyes widened in horror. Looking over Larry's shoulder towards the rock, she could now see another figure approaching. A man, this time, naked apart from a white loincloth and a headdress of bright red feathers.

Again she began to shriek and tremble. Larry and Jim both grabbed her now, their eyes swiftly scanning the scene for any clue as to what she was looking at.

The new figure walked slowly in front of the islanders, and without stopping or turning, walked silently away into the darkness.

Again, no one else but Rebecca seemed to notice it. Once more, she looked expectantly and questioningly at Jim and Larry.

"There! You must have seen that one? It came out from behind the rock. It was walking right in front of us, and then it just disappeared."

Jim looked anxiously at Rebecca, turned to Pablo who was shaking his head and then back to Rebecca.

"For God's sake, you must have seen that one! He walked right past us," she said, pointing to the other side of the table.

"Who was it, Rebecca?" asked Jim. "What are you talking about? We didn't see anything. What was it like? Can you tell us what it was like?" He took her hand. "Come and sit down. You look as if you've seen a ghost. But there's nothing to worry about, I promise you."

"It was definitely a real person," Rebecca said quietly. "Someone just wearing a loincloth, and a headdress with red feathers."

It was at this point that her eyes were drawn upwards to the sky.

CHAPTER 27

The heavens over Orongo were glowing with light. Rainbow shades of red and violet were spreading out over half the night sky, breaking into brilliant greens and blues at the edges. The light pulsated, growing stronger, fading slightly and then brightening again.

But this time everyone else was looking too, gazing upwards in silence at the spectacular sky.

Jim looked faintly relieved. "This is okay," he said reassuringly. "It's the Southern Lights – the aurora australis. The same sort of thing as the Northern Lights we saw in Orkney. We've seen them here a couple of times this week, but nowhere near as dramatic as this. It's rather beautiful, isn't it?"

"Oh, just fantastic," groaned Rebecca, still shaking with fear.

"There's a lot of solar radiation going on at the moment," said Jim. "That's why we can see the Southern Lights, even though we're so far from the Antarctic. It's extraordinary. But, honestly, nothing to worry about. The Earth's magnetic field protects us."

"Never mind about the bloody lights," said Rebecca. "What about the horrible walking corpse, and the naked man with the headdress?" But it was rapidly dawning on her that Larry and Jim had simply not seen them. Nor, it seemed, had anyone else.

"You look as if you've had enough for one night. What about a cup of tea?" asked Larry.

"No thanks," replied Rebecca, deflated. "I think I'd rather get back to the hotel and lie down. Maybe it's just me. Too much travelling perhaps. It must be catching up on me."

Larry looked very concerned. "But are you sure you're all right? Something happened – do you want to tell us again?"

Rebecca shook her head. "No, I'm okay. Really."

"I can take you back to your hotel, if you want," said Pablo.

"Thanks," Rebecca replied gratefully.

It was only then that she noticed Dr Neferatu was no longer there. "I see Dr Neferatu's gone."

"When you got upset he went off without saying a word," said Pablo. "He was going towards the track. The funny thing is, I don't know how he was planning to get back to where he's staying."

"Perhaps he'd arranged for someone to pick him up," suggested Jim.

"I don't even know where he's staying, otherwise I could check," said Pablo. "We'll look out for him on the way back."

Jim took Rebecca to one side. "Are you really sure you're okay? Let me take you back to the hotel."

She thought for a moment. "No, I'd better go back with Pablo. It's his job to help me, and I wouldn't want to upset him."

"It could be because of all this travelling – and this place can be a bit of a culture shock," Jim said, as he walked with Rebecca to Pablo's bike. "Could it be something you ate? It's not the most hygienic place in the world. If you come back tomorrow, you could speak to Señor Nata and his family. They might be able to help. Larry won't mind if I take a couple of hours off. If you like, I could show you where they carved the *moai*."

He held her close as Pablo got on his bike and waited. "Don't worry," Jim said. "A good night's sleep, and you'll be fine."

Pablo rode the bike back to the hotel as carefully as he could. He checked everybody they passed, but Dr Neferatu was nowhere to be seen. Parking the bike, Pablo went into the hotel with Rebecca.

As she collected her key from the smiling receptionist, Rebecca turned to Pablo. "I just know everything I saw was for real. And I know it had nothing to do with bad food, or whatever. I know I saw a walking corpse, and I know I actually saw the man with the feather headdress."

She hoped Pablo, who knew this place better than anyone,

could offer some sort of explanation. Instead, his expression simply glazed over.

"Not now. You need to rest," was all he said.

She moved towards the stairs, but stopped again. "And another thing. There's something very odd about that Dr Neferatu. I don't like him at all. He was really weird."

"What do you mean?" asked Pablo.

"He wouldn't let go of my hand when Larry introduced me to him. Then he dug his nail right into my hand. It was horrible. And it was after that, that I began to feel so light-headed and weary. It was a bit like having some blood-sucking insect drain your blood."

Pablo nodded his head. "Odd character. He didn't even seem to know which day he had arrived. Tuesday or Wednesday, he said."

"Perhaps he was jet-lagged, too," replied Rebecca.

"No, not that. What I mean is, there are no LAN flights here on Wednesdays, and the flight on Tuesday was cancelled because of a strike in Santiago."

Rebecca now felt even more bewildered by the night's events, and she began to wonder if she was in fact living in a bad dream.

"Tomorrow, we'll go and talk to Señor Nata and his family," said Pablo. "I'll pick you up around nine. Meanwhile, get some rest."

With that, he shook her hand and strode out of the hotel.

CHAPTER 28

After Rebecca and Pablo had left Orongo, Señor Nata and his family had cleared the place up and disappeared quietly into the night.

A deep silence fell over the camp and a warm breeze stirred, making the gas lamps flicker. Larry looked up at the sky. No trace remained of the aurora, but the moon, now smaller, still shone brightly. He pushed his chair back and put his feet up on the table.

Jim joined him with half a bottle of wine. "I hope Rebecca's going to be all right," he said. "I'm beginning to worry about her. I think she was genuinely scared out of her wits by something. What do you think could have happened?"

"I don't know. I think she really believed she had seen something real, and that something was pretty unpleasant. But no one else seemed to see anything. So why her?"

Jim topped up Larry's glass and poured one for himself. "It seems obvious to me that she was having some sort of hallucination," he said.

Larry looked doubtful and didn't respond.

"Funnily enough," continued Jim, "I was just reading the other day that the blinding light St. Paul saw on the road to Damascus could have been due to an attack of temporal lobe epilepsy."

Larry had known Jim for some time and knew him to be a cool and analytical scientist. But this was a step too far.

"Oh no. Surely not," he said. "I don't buy that. That didn't seem anything like an epileptic fit to me. Anyway, who knows? Perhaps Paul really did see a blinding light. It could be Rebecca did actually see something that we couldn't. Maybe there really was something paranormal happening around us."

"But nobody else witnessed it, as far as I could see," responded

Jim. "Surely you're not suggesting she was seeing the spirits of the dead? More likely somebody put something in her drink. Pablo, perhaps... or Dr Neferatu..."

"Oh, come on! Pablo is the model of decorum. And why on earth would Dr Neferatu...?"

"I know, I know. But those weird things she said she had seen could only have been inside her own mind. A figment of her imagination. There is no other logical explanation."

Larry looked at Jim. It was clear to him that something was going on between Jim and Rebecca. And yet, for some reason, Jim now seemed to be unsympathetic and was distancing himself from her.

Larry shook his head. "All I know is she was genuinely not just petrified, but revolted by something. I tell you, Jim, there's something about Easter Island, especially Orongo. The sense of the supernatural is everywhere. I'm surprised you don't feel it. Personally, I wouldn't rule out the possibility that she could have seen – perceived if you like – things that perhaps actually were there in some form. Only none of us could see them for some reason."

"Okay, so would a camera have picked them up, do you think?" asked Jim.

"Don't know. Nobody was taking photos."

"So..." said Jim. "We have no proof there was anything there at all."

Larry was feeling mellow with the wine but was beginning to find Jim's comments more and more dogmatic and irritating. During the many times they had worked together, he had grown to like and respect Jim. Now, though, Jim's attitude seemed deliberately harsh and out of character. He wondered what was troubling him.

Larry took his feet off the table and leaned towards Jim. "One shouldn't rule anything out until it's proven impossible," he said firmly. "Anyway, I'm no scientist, but it strikes me that the universe is not only stranger than we imagine, but stranger than we are *capable* of imagining."

Jim merely yawned. "I don't think we're going to get very far with this one tonight," he said. "She'll probably be okay tomorrow."

Larry decided to back off. "Tomorrow, she might see it all a bit more clearly herself."

Jim nodded and changed the subject to Dr Neferatu. They soon established that neither of them had ever heard of him before he had approached Jim in Cambridge, and that his intention to get hold of Easter Island antiquities did not seem to ring true.

When Jim detailed Dr Neferatu's grant proposal, Larry felt perplexed.

"Shouldn't you at least check him out?"

"I suppose I should. It's just that it seemed a bit of a gift. I always seem to be applying for grants, and I'm supposed to be a scientist, not a fundraiser."

Larry smiled in sympathy. "But even so..." he said, before deciding it was too late to pursue the subject further.

They chatted idly about the plans for the next day, until Jim sleepily rubbed his eyes. Making his apologies, he got up and walked a little unsteadily towards his tent. "Don't let the nasties get you in the night," he said, as he unzipped the flap.

Larry sat for a while, deep in thought, before gulping down the last of his wine, stretching his arms and making his way to his own tent.

As he prepared his camp bed, he whistled, slightly out of tune, the opening bars of the aria 'Nessum Dorma'.

"What are you trying to do?" he heard Jim say in a muffled voice. "Wake the dead all over again?"

CHAPTER 29

As he lay on his camp bed with his hands under his head, thoughts about everything that had happened that evening tumbled through Larry's mind. For one thing, he was still worried about the sudden apparent change in Jim's manner and his seeming lack of sympathy for Rebecca. He had always known Jim to be open-minded and generous in nature, and it appeared to him that this evening, Jim had not been at all like the Jim he knew.

And another thing – was it just by chance that Rebecca's extraordinary experiences should coincide with the unprecedented appearance here of the Southern Lights? Perhaps they had affected Jim as well? Could that explain his odd behaviour? But in that case, why wasn't I affected myself? Or was I? Then there was Dr Neferatu. What a bizarre name. Sounds like something out of Dracula. He looks like something out of Dracula, too.

There was something about the way Dr Neferatu had latched on to Jim that Larry did not trust. And there was something very odd about the way he had mysteriously turned up on Easter Island at this particular moment of time.

Furthermore, Larry was more preoccupied than he had admitted by the murders. Until now, he had not felt personally involved. But with the arrival of Rebecca, things were now different, and he could not help feeling, however unreasonable it might seem, in some way responsible for her safety. She did not appear to be an unusually nervous or hysterical sort of girl, and yet the look of terror in her face had been very real, and very disturbing. He tried to tell himself that it was really none of his business and that, in any case, her safety was not really under his control. Eventually, knowing he could do no more that night, he drifted into a troubled sleep.

It was not long before he was tossing and turning, for some reason reliving the terrible event in his life that had occurred so many years ago.

It had happened in Turkey, when he had been driving a Land Rover with his wife, Moira, a fellow archaeologist, beside him. Twenty-seven years old, with long dark hair parted in the middle, dark brown eyes and an attractive tan from four weeks in the Turkish sun, she exuded life and fun. Their two daughters, Kate, who was six and a half years old, and Clea, just five, were playing 'I Spy' in the seat behind them and singing along to 'Puff the Magic Dragon', which blasted out from Radio Cyprus.

Moira, who had been busy balancing motherhood with part-time work as a demonstrator at University College, London, had brought the girls out to join Larry for the long summer break. He was working on the excavations at Aphrodisia in southern Turkey, happy in the knowledge that he was privileged to be involved in such an important dig.

On that fateful day, they were driving to Antalya for the weekend. He knew the road well and was driving cautiously, taking no chances. A few yards in front of him, a pick-up truck was trundling along, transporting a single cow to market. Clearly agitated by the bumpy journey along the rough road, the animal was repeatedly, but unsuccessfully, trying to turn round in the very limited space. Larry did not even notice that the animal was not roped.

Then, quite suddenly, it reared up on its hind legs. Somehow, in the space of a few seconds, it managed to get its front feet on to the tail-gate and was struggling frantically to get itself over. In a split second, it overbalanced and fell from the back of the lorry, straight into Larry's path.

In his dream, his mind desperately tried to stop the next sequence of events, but it was impossible.

For a fraction of a second, he hesitated, unsure whether to swerve out into the road and the oncoming traffic, or to swerve into the deep ditch running along the side of the road. In the event, he opted to wrench the wheel to the right, towards the ditch. But even then he could not avoid catching the side of the cow with the front wheel. The Land Rover reared, tipped over and skidded on its side into the ditch. He lay there for a while, dimly conscious of a wheel spinning slowly, until it came to a halt. All went quiet. Then he became aware of Moira lying beneath him. He could not see her head. A child's moan broke the silence.

He woke from his sleep, shaking and sweating. This dream had tormented him at various intervals over twenty years, fading only gradually with the passing of time. But now it had returned, more vividly than ever.

Moira had died of her head injuries, three days after the accident. Kate had been killed outright, catapulted against the windscreen. Clea had been concussed, but had recovered quickly. He himself had survived, with just a few scratches.

It was only Clea who had kept him going over the intervening years. Larry's sister had helped to bring her up, as he had never re-married, throwing himself instead into his daughter's welfare and his own career.

Clea was now middle-aged, had her own family of a husband and two boys, and lived in Kings Lynn. He was always invited to stay over at Christmas, but he was too proud to risk imposing on them.

Yet in quiet moments, when he was alone, he dreaded the thought of retirement and the loneliness it would inevitably bring. Now, meeting Rebecca, he could not help thinking of his own lost daughter, Kate, and wondering how she would have grown up had she not been taken from him that day.

CHAPTER 30

At three o'clock in the morning, the yacht *Mana* was beating down from the north on a light breeze. It would make good time and reach port at daybreak about three hours later, at Hanga-roa on Easter Island.

The captain, Sean Brady, was on watch and sitting back admiring the night sky. His boat had been chartered in Barbados by Bill and Sue Gibson; they were newly retired and now keen for a new life of adventure, after years of daily grind. Their daughter lived in Australia, and so they had decided to visit her in style, by sailing across the Pacific. Sean had hired his crew of three in Barbados, and it included Dave, the tough and experienced Australian who had crewed with him on and off for five years.

The trip had gone exactly to plan. They had passed through the Panama Canal and sailed south to moor off the Galapagos Islands, joining a tour group to see the wildlife. From the Galapagos, they had sailed on without incident, planning to stay on Easter Island for a few days, before enjoying a leisurely island-hop en route to New Zealand and finally Australia. Now Bill, Sue and the crew were asleep below, after watching the dazzling Southern Lights display earlier in the evening.

The lights had begun to fade at around eleven o'clock, and Sean had been alone at the wheel for about four hours, content to have the occasional cigarette and admire the stars in the clear sky. The coast of Easter Island emerged from the darkness. With just the occasional light on the port side, it was reassuring after over a week without seeing land.

Then, out of nowhere, a huge dark cloud filled the southern horizon, blotting out the stars. It was worrying, as he was sure the night sky had been completely clear before he had nipped below to fetch a fresh pack of cigarettes. He was used to fast changes in the weather during his many years sailing the Pacific, but this one was somehow too sudden, even for these parts. He felt just a fleeting flash of fear, instinctively gripping the wheel hard as the cloud continued to grow, sweeping ominously towards the boat.

A many-forked flash of lightning was followed immediately by a crash of thunder that made the whole boat shudder. The crew began to appear on deck one after another, each one blinking sleepily and gazing around in disbelief.

"Reef the bloody sails. Now!" Sean screamed at them. "Jeez," he muttered under his breath, increasingly alarmed at the swelling sea. He tried to regain his composure, as Bill and Sue stuck their heads up out of the hatch.

"Looks like a bad one coming up," he yelled at them. "There was just no warning." He noticed that they were still wearing dressing gowns. "Get dressed and get waterproofs and life jackets on."

"What's going on?" Bill called up.

"Sudden tropical storm. Now, please, just do as I say."

They disappeared below. Within minutes, the crew were frantically whirling winches, until the sails flapped down to be quickly secured.

"Okay, full gear on, you lot. This could be nasty," Sean bellowed above the wind. The crew groped their way to the steps one after another and fell below.

Now clad in orange waterproofs, Bill hauled himself on deck and looked around in amazement. Above him, torn clouds were rushing over the sky. He caught a glimpse of the moon just before the clouds closed up, engulfing the boat in darkness. A burst of spray hit him full on and his face blanched with fear. He blinked furiously and grasped the rail as a wave hit the side of the boat with a dull thud that sent a glass flying down the steps to smash at the bottom.

"Are we going to be all right?" he shouted at Sean.

"We're only a few miles from port, but I can't take her in – coast's too rocky and visibility's crap. I'm going to have to take her further out to sea for safety. We'll just have to sit it out. Don't worry. It'll blow over soon."

A gust of wind hit the boat like a kick from a giant. Sean steadied himself and reached to press a button on the Global Positioning System to take a reading. Nothing. He pressed the button again. Disturbingly, the screen stayed blank.

"Damn, damn," he said to himself. "GPS's down," he bawled at Bill. "It's okay, I'll use the compass." He closed his eyes and prayed to himself as he went to start the engine. There was an instant roar from below, and he sighed with relief.

There was a moment's respite before a piercing shriek of wind sliced through the rigging, and the boat rolled violently to starboard. The sea broke over the deck and water poured down the steps into the cabins. Coming back upright, the boat steadied herself and the boiling sea spilled back over the sides.

Sean grabbed his chance; he darted quickly to the compass and managed to take a reading. Then he swung the wheel to face the boat due west and towards the open sea.

The only light came from the boat itself. Sean peered ahead into the deepening gloom and checked the compass again for reassurance. The storm was worsening, but he noted with grim relief that everyone was now wearing a life jacket.

"Take the wheel! Keep her due west!" he ordered Dave, and dived below to find his own waterproofs and life jacket.

Coming back up, he was met by a great howl of wind and the clamour and fury of the full storm. Taking the wheel from Dave, he expertly kept the boat turned so that she rode up with the waves, paused for an instant on the crests and plunged down into the troughs to rise up yet again.

The others were crouching in the cockpit, gripping the sides with white-knuckled hands. Bill put a comforting arm around his wife's shoulder as she gasped with fear. The foam on the waves seethed with an unearthly white phosphorescence, as the wind whipped the spray horizontally and so forcefully that it cut their faces.

Nevertheless, Sean had been through many such storms and had total confidence in his boat. He never doubted that they could ride it out. Yet, when a massive crested roller came in like a wall from the port side, he had a flash of intuition that this was it. He was faced with something totally outside his control. Never before had he been struck by such a premonition – that this was where his luck finally ran out.

The towering wave hovered for an instant over the boat, like a cliff of shining, ebony black glass, and then came slowly crashing down. The *Mana* keeled over and was swept along on her side in the foaming sea. The whole boat groaned as it hit the rocks, and there was a shattering report as the keel broke away. Then the sea rushed in through the gaping hole in the hull.

CHAPTER 31

At precisely the same moment that the *Mana* was being smashed on to the rocks near Hanga-roa, Rebecca's room lit up. She sat bolt upright in bed, as thunder rattled the window.

She hadn't slept a wink, unable to rid her mind of images of young girls with grinning skulls and red-haired corpses that danced repeatedly in front of her closed eyes. Her brain would not stop going over all the details, again and again. *Those things did not come out of my imagination. I know they were real, I saw them. But where did they come from? Why didn't anyone else see them? Is there something wrong with me? Is there something weird about this place?*

Wearily, she got out of bed, drew the curtains and looked out of the window. The wind was howling and rain was battering the windowpanes. She could hear rubbish bins rolling backwards and forwards in the street below. Another flash lit up the whole town for a moment, and she caught a glimpse of white crests on the waves in the bay. The ear-splitting thunder that followed seemed to shake the whole building. She yanked the curtains closed again and crawled back into bed, her eyes smarting with tiredness.

It was dawn before the storm subsided, and she fell asleep from sheer exhaustion. At seven-thirty in the morning, she turned off her alarm, planning to doze for just another five minutes, only to awake shortly before nine. Late, flustered and badly in need of coffee, she rushed downstairs to the reception.

Pablo was talking to the receptionist, who seemed to turn away deliberately as Rebecca approached. Rebecca looked at her quizzically and then at Pablo.

"Sorry I'm late," she said.

His response was totally unexpected. Instead of his usual warm smile, he looked at her coldly.

123

What the hell is up with you? she thought. She smiled at him enquiringly. "It was quite a storm last night. It kept me awake."

"You're lucky it only kept you awake," said Pablo. "A boat was wrecked on the rocks near Hanga-roa last night. Five people drowned. They were battered to death on the rocks. Only the captain survived."

Rebecca was stunned. "I'm so sorry. I didn't know."

"They think two of the bodies they found were a British couple. The captain is still in a state of shock – he is still not fit enough to identify them."

"If it is a British couple, I ought to check it out straight away. Can I talk to the captain?"

"I really don't think he's well enough."

"But can we try?"

Pablo sighed heavily. Rebecca smiled weakly, but he merely gestured towards the hotel entrance and his waiting motorbike.

Putting aside her acute need for coffee, she followed Pablo and clambered on to the bike behind him. Without even checking that she was seated, he shoved the bike into gear and took off fast enough to skid the rear wheel, going straight through a large puddle.

It was not an easy ride, and she was relieved when they pulled up outside Hanga-roa hospital. Pablo talked to the man at the desk. "Follow me," Pablo said. "He's in a room off the main ward."

Sean Brady was in a bad way. His head was heavily bandaged, and his face was cut and bruised. A nurse was putting a bandage on his wrist. Pablo spoke to her in what must have been Rapa Nui, the local language. The nurse nodded and left the room.

"Be quick. I promised we'd only be a couple of minutes," said Pablo.

Rebecca leaned over Sean Brady. "I'm very sorry about last night," she said quietly. "I'm Rebecca Burns – I'm a journalist from London. I just happen to be here doing a story. Is there anything I can do for you? Would you like me to contact anybody?"

He seemed not to hear her. There was a look of disbelief in his eyes, and he repeatedly shook his head slowly from side to side.

After a long hesitation, he whispered, "I thought we were going to make it. I was under full power. We should have been heading out to sea, but it turned out we were heading in the opposite direction. We were going straight for the rocks. At full speed! How could that be?"

He turned his head towards the window and looked at the grey sky for a while, before slowly turning back to face Rebecca. "The GPS was down, so I had to use the compass. I've never known a compass to play up before. And then that wave. In all my years at sea, I have never, ever seen anything like that wave."

Rebecca put a hand on his shoulder. He stared into her eyes, his face distraught. "They said I'm the only one to survive. Everybody else drowned. Is that true? I was in charge – I was the one they depended on for their safety. I just don't understand how it happened. Something bloody strange about that storm." Then he turned his head away from her.

"I think it is time to go," said Pablo.

Rebecca nodded, squeezed Sean Brady's shoulder and followed Pablo out of the room. She knew she had a duty to follow up on the story.

"Is there anyone else we can talk to – the coastguard, or Señor Garcia, or anyone else? I must try to get the names of the couple," she said, as they went down the corridor.

"Can we talk about it later?" said Pablo.

For Christ's sake, what's happened to Pablo? she thought. *He was charming yesterday. It's like he's a different person today. What is it about this bloody creepy place?*

"Why not now?" she asked.

"We said we would see Professor Burton this morning."

"Well, okay," she replied. "But listen, Pablo, I'm going to have to get some facts on this story – and I may need your help."

She suddenly felt a desperate need for a friendly face and a bit of reassurance. *At least I'm going to see Jim*, she thought.

CHAPTER 32

Pablo's change of mood made for an exceptionally uncomfortable and bumpy ride.

"Thank God," Rebecca said under her breath when they finally reached the Orongo site and she saw the welcoming figure of Larry striding towards her, followed at a short distance by Jim.

"How are you?" Larry said, looking concerned as she eased herself painfully from the pillion. "What a storm! I thought we were going to get washed away."

Rebecca felt a surge of relief. *At least Larry is acting normally.* Jim, on the other hand, simply stood there, staring at her rather coldly. *No welcome there. Perhaps he's had a bad night, too*, she thought.

"A boat got wrecked last night," she said. "Five people drowned, two of them Brits. We've just been to see the captain, he's the only survivor."

There was a shocked silence. Pablo took over and told the others what Sean Brady had said.

"At a guess, the wind and the currents were too strong for the engine," Jim said. "It was one hell of a storm."

"But even so," said Larry, "it sounds as if the captain was confident that he was heading out to sea, so it's a bit odd that they hit the rocks. He was using a compass, after all. And he was very experienced."

Pablo cut in sharply. "We don't know what happened. There'll have to be an investigation." He lowered his head and wandered off to look half-heartedly at some of the finds, seemingly lost in his own thoughts.

"I don't know why, but for some reason, Pablo doesn't seem very keen for me to get involved in this story," Rebecca said quietly to the others.

But Larry was still looking puzzled. "There's something that doesn't quite hang together. Could the compass have gone wrong? If so, why?"

Nobody commented, and he offered Rebecca a coffee. Accepting it gratefully, she felt she should try to explain about the night before.

"By the way, I'm truly sorry about last night. I didn't want to make a scene, but what I saw was very scary."

"You were probably a bit over-tired, that's all," said Jim. "A bit hypersensitive. You'd had a long journey."

Rebecca's heart sank. "No, no, Jim, listen. You've got this wrong. I was perfectly all right until I saw those horrible things. They were *real* you know, and I've never had anything like that happen to me before."

No one answered. Larry and Jim looked awkward and embarrassed.

"Do you honestly mean neither of you saw any of it?" she said, looking from one to the other.

Larry threw a mild warning sideways glance at Jim. "What *exactly* did you see, Rebecca?" he asked.

To Rebecca, it was unbearable that they didn't seem to believe her, but as she attempted to recall the events and relate exactly what happened, the full feeling of horror came flooding back, and she began to feel quite sick.

"It was just disgusting. You remember the old lady's carving? It was just like that, but it was alive. It was real, I know it was real. I saw it, it was moving." She looked at Jim, appealing for some sign of support and belief.

"And what did this living thing actually do?" he asked.

"It was walking towards me. And grinning in such a horrible, grotesque way. Then it disappeared." She shuddered. "And after that, there was another one. A man with a headdress of red feathers."

But even as she spoke, she began to realise how ridiculous she sounded.

Pablo looked up from studying a stone carving. "Maybe it was a Red Indian," he called over.

"It was nothing at all like a Red Indian," she said, irritated that Pablo was not even trying to take her seriously. "But then he didn't look like a typical Easter Islander either."

"Maybe it's all connected with Señor Nata's mother. Perhaps she really was doing something funny with that carving," Jim said. "Pablo was saying last night that she communicates with the spirits. Well, you never know." He grinned sardonically.

Rebecca tried not to get angry. "Okay," she said, "can I talk to her?"

"She's not here yet. Probably with her family," Larry said. "She could be in the family cave along the coast." He pointed along the coastal path. "They often stay there when they're working on the site. It's more convenient."

"Thanks, Larry," she said, still feeling bruised at Jim's indifference and wondering what had caused his apparent change of attitude towards her.

She walked over to Pablo. "Will you come with me, Pablo?"

He picked up a carving and pointedly studied it. "I don't think you need me," he said.

"Why not? What's the matter? Of course I need you. What's bugging you today, Pablo?"

"Well, I suppose I don't know what to make of you any more. One moment, you seemed quite normal. The next moment you started screaming and saying that you could see *things* that nobody else could see."

"Look! I was well and truly petrified last night. Something very strange happened during that dinner. I don't know what it was exactly. Maybe it was to do with the old lady – or the girl – or the drumming. Maybe it's just this place."

"Perhaps you shouldn't have been drinking."

"Listen, I had one glass of wine, and I was *not* overtired. I thought someone was having some sort of horrible joke," said Rebecca.

"Then why was everybody else okay?"

"How should I know? How could I know why nobody else could see what I saw?" She suddenly lost patience. "Listen. You're supposed to be helping me – that's what you're paid to do. Everything was okay until last night. We were getting on fine, weren't we? I felt we were starting to get a really good story together. So what's changed? Have I done something to upset you, or offend you? If you simply don't want to help me, you can go. I expect I can manage by myself."

He glowered at her. "Maybe you should not have come here at all. All this questioning people, being nosy. Why? It's really none of your business."

Yet there was something about his sullen look that gave her the distinct feeling he was holding something back.

"Listen, Pablo. You are supposed to be assisting me, but if you don't want to, you don't have to. I'm really not bothered one way or the other."

Pablo did not reply. His sullen silence bordered on rudeness.

Rebecca gave up. Turning her back on him, she walked over to Larry and Jim. "I'm going for a stroll," she said, and strode off towards the coastal path. She glanced back over her shoulder towards Pablo.

"Bloody useless creep," she muttered, as she heard his bike start up and the noise fade into the distance.

Now alone, her anger rapidly faded and she felt lost and betrayed. *What's going on?* she thought. *Why the change in Pablo? And why the sudden change in Jim? Is it my fault? Everything was going so well – it's as if I've upset everyone. But surely I'm not to blame, just because I saw those hideous things last night?*

CHAPTER 33

As she walked along the craggy clifftop, Rebecca became increasingly conscious of the strangeness of the ancient island culture that clearly still continued to exist beneath the veneer of modern civilisation. It made her feel increasingly alone and uneasy.

Far below her, the waves broke against the rocks and seagulls circled around her. No trace remained of the previous night's storm and the sky had cleared. The sun was now high and she found its warmth relaxing, enabling her to think clearly for the first time. She made a decision there and then that she had to do this story, whatever it cost her.

"Hello! *¡Hola!*" she called out, hoping Señor Nata or one of his family would respond, but the only reply was the piercing shrieks of the gulls.

She rounded a promontory, cutting off all sight of Orongo, and was surprised to see a solitary statue standing on a low stone platform. This one looked a bit forlorn and was slightly tipped over. It was smaller than the other statues she had seen, and the red stone headdress, if it had ever had one, had long since disappeared. She stopped and looked around the barren landscape for any sign of life. But there was nothing.

Wondering where to go next, she sat down on the platform under the statue and looked out over the sea. The sunlight glinting on the gentle swell had an almost hypnotic effect on her, and she was soon deeply absorbed in going over in her mind all that had happened.

She had the distinct feeling that people were becoming unfriendly towards her. Was it really because of her hysterical reaction to the events of the night before? The receptionist, friendly enough before, now completely ignored her. Pablo, who had been charming, now seemed surly and disagreeable. Okay, he had flirted with her and she had tactfully rejected his advances, but he didn't seem particularly upset at the time. Now, though, he seemed to be annoyed by her and to blame her for all that had happened. Even Jim, who had, till now, been so warm and lovely towards her, seemed distinctly cool. Only Larry seemed openly friendly and sympathetic.

Reflecting on this, she suddenly became aware of a presence and, swinging round, she recognised the lone figure of Señor Nata. *Where on earth could he have sprung from?* Then, behind her, she noticed an entrance to a cave, semi-concealed in the rocks. She smiled at him, but he did not return her smile. He looked distinctly nervous and unsure of what to do.

"I was looking for you. Please, could I talk to you for a moment?" she asked.

He didn't respond immediately, but continued looking at her, as if making up his mind. Then he nodded and beckoned her to follow him into the cave.

The entrance was tall enough for her not to have to bend, and just wide enough for two people to go in together. Inside, although it was dark, there was a feeling of space. As her eyes became accustomed to the gloom, she quickly picked out the figures of the old lady and the two young men, sitting around a battered hurricane lamp. The light illuminated the walls, but it was clear from the deep blackness beyond that the cave continued further than she could see.

As she took in the scene, Rebecca caught a glimpse of the young girl, barely discernible towards the back of the cave. Yet, as if startled by the appearance of Rebecca, the girl quickly turned and melted back into the darkness.

Once in his own territory, Señor Nata appeared to relax a little and gestured towards the others, who were smiling at her. "These are my mother and my sons. My daughter is very shy," he said, glancing towards the back of the cave. "We are very sorry you were frightened last night".

131

For the first time, Rebecca felt intensely relieved. At last, here was someone who would acknowledge that something had happened.

"You speak English?" she asked.

"A little. We sometimes take tourists into our home. Many Americans come."

"Señor Nata, can I ask you what happened last night? I know I saw those things, but nobody else seemed to see them."

Señor Nata didn't hesitate. "We saw them also." He went to the side of the cave and came back with a camp chair, which he placed near the lamp. He patted the chair, inviting her to sit down, and looked at the old lady.

"Only my mother used to see things. She is an *ivi-atua*. She can communicate with the *aku-aku* – the spirits." He waited a moment, before continuing. "She was the only one in the family. But now we can all see." The old lady smiled and drew her shawl around her shoulders.

"But how was it that I could see them?" Rebecca asked.

"I cannot tell you," replied Señor Nata. "But see, you, too, have red hair like us. Maybe that is why – it is a sign. But it was really you that they wanted to communicate with. Maybe you are special to them."

"Why would I be special?" asked Rebecca, worried.

"I do not know," said Señor Nata. "But the spirits seemed anxious to meet you."

"But I don't understand. Why me? I've only just arrived here."

"Perhaps they are trying to warn you," said Señor Nata. There was fear in his eyes. "Something is happening. Something foul. We feel it."

Rebecca chilled inside and tried to pull herself together. "How long have you been able to see these things?"

"Only from one year ago. That's when it started. But that was also the time when the murders started." The family all nodded. "The wonderful thing is that our powers of vision are getting stronger all the time. The *moai kava-kava* is our ancestor, you know. This is why we have the carving. Like you, we could all see him, all of us."

Rebecca noticed the mother was clutching the *moai kava-kava* close to her body.

Then Señor Nata frowned. "But this man with the red feathers is quite new. We have not seen him before."

"Have you ever seen anyone like that before?" asked Rebecca.

Señor Nata shook his head. "No, never. Yet we believe that, perhaps, he is also one of ours."

One of his sons, who seemed to be the eldest, was becoming restless and agitated. "But this is not good for us," he said. "It is very dangerous. This is why we are hated. The others know we see things. They think the spirits help us." He looked angry. "People know we are descended from the long-ears. Our hair is red and we look different to the short-ears. For many centuries they have not liked us. They remember we used to rule this island. They know we were the powerful ones who built the *moai*."

The father looked at his son with patient understanding and spoke quietly. "Once, this island was a paradise. It was covered in trees." His look darkened. "First the Europeans arrived and brought terrible diseases with them. Then the short-ears began to kill us. They still blame us for everything. It is because they know we can see spirits. That is why they are killing us now…"

He suddenly fell silent, and Rebecca saw his face change to an expression of pure fear. As she followed his gaze, she too started in horror as, silhouetted against the entrance to the cave, she caught sight of the huge, beaked head of a bird.

She found it hard to believe what she was seeing. The gigantic, human sized head, with its long and evil-looking curved beak, would not have been out of place in some carnival fantasy. But it seemed totally out of place here on this sunny morning.

Everybody fell silent as the outsized head turned slowly towards them, peering into the cave with its yellow, unblinking eyes.

The only sound in the cave was the defiant chanting of the old lady, who seemed utterly oblivious to the menacing bird. She was holding out the *moai kava-kava* in front of her and staring at it. The sound of her voice echoed around the walls of the cave with increased intensity, reverberating in Rebecca's brain.

Yet as she watched, transfixed, a second bird's head appeared on the opposite side of the entrance, rapidly followed by two more. She looked towards Señor Nata for reassurance, but felt a surge of panic as she saw the expression of sheer terror on his face and on those of his sons. They seemed to shrink back into the cave. Only the old lady seemed calm and accepting, as she continued to chant.

The giant bird stepped into the cave. It seemed to have the body of a man, a very well-built man. A man who was naked apart from a white loincloth. His hairless body and rippling muscles gleamed in the dim light.

Silently, he surveyed the scene in the cave. Then, half turning, he beckoned the others to follow. As he came into the darkness, eight more bird-men appeared from the entrance to join him. For a moment, they stood there, menacingly.

There was no chance for the family to escape. The bird-men went for the men first, easily overpowering them and pinning their arms behind their backs. Señor Nata's mother stopped chanting and clasped the *moai kava-kava* figure to her chest. An iron grip on her elbow forced her up and dragged her towards the entrance. When two bird-men edged towards Rebecca, half terrified, half furious, she sprang up and faced them.

"Don't you dare come near me!"

As she struggled violently, it took both bird-men to get her under control. Yet she, too, was forced to follow the others, screaming and carried with her feet off the ground.

"Get your bloody hands off me! Let me go!" she yelled, kicking at her captors' legs.

It made no difference. The huge bird-men forced their captives out of the cave and into the brilliant sunshine. Only the young girl had escaped them. Somehow, she had disappeared completely into the fathomless depths of the cave.

Kicking and struggling still, the group was dragged along the path, until they reached the front of the solitary stone monument.

The leader of the bird-men stepped forward, his eyes staring coldly at his prisoners. His head was larger and more resplendent than the others. His orange beak was curled cruelly like that of an eagle, and his rich brown feathers ruffled in the breeze. Now the captives all fell silent, Rebecca staring helplessly at the captors in disbelief.

The leader of the bird-men moved first. Stepping forward, he grabbed the carving from the old lady. The bizarre figure studied the carving, before placing it carefully to one side on a rock. His head swivelled around backwards, the body barely moving, and he nodded to the bird-men behind him.

Two of them instantly tightened their grip on Señor Nata's arms, the remaining bird-men surrounding the others and hemming them in. Señor Nata's face was rigid with fear. As they locked their arms under his armpits, the bird-men dragged him to the statue and lifted him on to the flat, stone platform underneath it. Panic-stricken, he tried to struggle free, but the bird-men easily pinioned him down.

For the first time, Rebecca felt their fate was inevitable. There seemed no way out of this. Yet in her mind, she couldn't help thinking, *this is like some ancient Inca sacrifice – with the chief bird-man as the priest.*

She was now starting to shake with terror, unable to control herself. At last she found the voice to scream. "Oh, my God! Jim – Larry – help, help. Help me! Help us!"

The priest reached down and tore Señor Nata's shirt open with both hands. Rebecca could see that his bare chest was covered in red hair. The priest held his hand out as a bird-man passed him a long knife. The blade was curved and caught the light as he raised it up to the sun with both hands, and the beak opened, seeming to utter a silent prayer. The priest then plunged the knife down and deep into Señor Nata's chest.

Rebecca could not look. Closing her eyes, she turned her head away. There was a long, unearthly shriek followed by wails and the sounds of sobbing. When she opened her eyes again, she began to vomit uncontrollably. The priest was holding up the heart of Señor Nata. It was still pumping blood.

CHAPTER 34

The four bird-men closed in on Rebecca and pounced simultaneously. She lashed out at them with almost super-human force, but they were well-built and completely lifted her off the ground. She writhed desperately as they carried her to the *moai*. Heaving her on to the stone platform, they pinned her down by her shoulders and legs. She tried to scream, but, as if in a nightmare, no sound came.

The priest-figure moved quickly, and with one movement ripped her blouse open to the waist. Her mind froze in dread and revulsion. *This is not happening to me. I can't die like this. For nothing.*

The bird-eyes of the priest bored into her with sadistic hostility. "Now the girl," he rasped, and held his hand out for the knife, still covered in blood.

Rebecca started to sob. "Stop this! I haven't done anything! I'm just a writer. People are looking for me. They're not far away." Again, she tried to shout for help, yet she did not recognise her own weak voice, strangled and contorted by fear.

The priest, oblivious to her pleas, started to raise his arm again, more slowly this time, as if he were savouring a great pleasure.

A sudden commotion behind him made him hesitate and then whip round. The eldest son had managed to escape from the group. He dived towards the carved figure on the rock, grabbed it and shook it violently. "¡Venga! ¡Venga!" he shouted.

One of the bird-men tore the carving from his hands and threw it along the path, before bundling him back with the others. Two bird-men held him there, pinning his hands behind his back.

Angrily, the priest turned back to Rebecca and swiftly raised the knife to strike again. For a second he closed his eyes. But, as he paused, a cold, hard, bony hand curled itself, like a handcuff, around his wrist. The priest swung around, his eyes glinting with fury. It was the *moai kava-kava* man, who now stared at him, his teeth bared in the same repulsive grin.

Rebecca, demented with fear, couldn't believe what she was seeing. Though wizened and emaciated, the living corpse seemed to have an unearthly strength. Forcing the priest's arm down with a final wrench, he smashed the priest's hand on to the stone platform. The huge knife clattered to the ground.

The rest of the bird-men froze for a second, before turning on their heels and making for the rocks as fast as they could. There, they simply disappeared.

The *moai kava-kava* man, still grinning hideously, slowly released his iron grasp on the priest's wrist and stood back. His bony face twisted into a monstrous grimace.

The priest glared down at Rebecca and across to the huddled group of victims, who were still too terrified to budge. Then he turned again to look at the *moai kava-kava* man, before walking away and breaking into a run as he, too, made for the rocks and disappeared.

Rebecca found herself lying there on the stone slab as if paralysed, staring at her unlikely saviour. Now expressionless, the *moai kava-kava* man turned away and walked stiffly towards the cave entrance. There, he stopped and looked over his shoulder. The face broke into a revolting, deathly smile. Then, abruptly, he vanished into the cave.

Rebecca, still half-frozen with fear, weakly tried to heave herself up from the stone slab. Her macabre rescuer had disappeared before she could even utter any thanks. Turning around, to her sheer horror, she caught sight of Señor Nata's mutilated corpse. The blood seemed to rush back to her weakened limbs, and she started to scream at the top of her voice. And she kept on screaming.

CHAPTER 35

Along the coast, Larry and Jim were absorbed in carefully brushing down a petroglyph on a wall inside one of the stone houses.

Larry took out a magnifying glass from his linen jacket to study it more closely, while Jim stood back and admired it with mounting excitement.

"The abstract face with stylised feathers again," Jim said.

"But wasn't it someone wearing a headdress – red feathers – that Rebecca saw?" said Larry. "Where is she, anyway? She ought to see this – where did she go?"

He was interrupted by an urgent shout from one of the workers, who came rushing to the house.

"Professor! Professor! Quick! Come quick! The girl – the girl – we heard screams."

As Larry and Jim crawled out of the house, more terrible screams could be heard in the distance. The voice was unmistakeably Rebecca's.

The screaming stopped as the young, red-haired native girl ran up to them, wild-eyed. "Come, come! They are killing them. It's a sacrifice," she cried.

"What the bloody hell!" said Jim, breaking into a run towards the cliff path. Larry stumbled after him as fast as he could, the others following.

Moments later, Jim, Larry and the girl stopped in their tracks, aghast at the horror of the scene.

The old lady was kneeling beside the mutilated corpse of her son, moaning softly. Her grandsons were standing silently besides her, paralysed with shock.

Blood covered the stone platform and dripped to the ground.

Rebecca sat on the platform, shaking and clutching together the remains of her blouse.

Larry put his jacket around her, and she fell into his arms, sobbing. "The young girl told us," he said quietly. He gently lifted up Rebecca's head and looked at her. "I think it's about time you left Easter Island."

CHAPTER 36

Charles sat there shaking his head in disbelief.

"We just had no idea all this was going on. You should never have gone there – we shouldn't have let you go. Of course, it's a bit remote out there – but I never imagined – I mean who would have thought things like that could happen anywhere."

He continued to look perplexed. "We were all a bit worried, you know. We didn't hear any news of you for quite a while. I spoke to Juan Perez in Santiago. His man, what's his name – Pablo – said some out of the ordinary things had been happening, but we didn't have any details. He certainly didn't say you'd witnessed a murder like that – or that there had been an attempt on your life. Sounds like they've deliberately shut the story down." He looked hard at her. "Look, Rebecca, why don't you take a few days off."

Rebecca frowned.

"Don't argue," Charles said. "Take the rest of the week off. We'll use what you've filed. Write up the whole story in detail at home, and let me have it later this week."

"But I'm perfectly okay now. I've already had time to recover."

"You look done in. Go home!"

Rebecca ignored him. "Have there been any more ritual murders?"

"Yes, there have been – one or two. Details are still coming in. But I don't want you anywhere near this story now. You'd be asking for trouble."

"And where were they?"

Charles put a hand to his forehead. "The Middle East again. One in Egypt – we've just heard. Don't know yet if it's another redhead."

141

"I don't suppose there's been anything about people having visions? Redheads, I mean?"

Charles shifted in his seat. "Couple of reports from Scotland, that's all. They've had a red-haired man disappear as well. But then Scotland isn't exactly short of redheads, is it – and the Scots are known to like a dram or two."

"Professor Burton suggested I should go to Aberdeen, to hear the paper they're giving at a conference. It's the sort of background I need. I know this story's going to get bigger."

Charles looked at her and shook his head in disbelief. "I suppose Scotland's safe enough. But to be honest, we'd much rather you switched to something else. It's too dangerous for you to do it."

"Okay, I get the message," said Rebecca. "But you are interested in this story, aren't you?"

"Yes – but not at the risk of your life."

She left his office and made her way over to Syreeta, who was working on a local government corruption story.

"What did Charles say?" Syreeta asked.

"He thinks I should drop the story. Take some time off."

"Sounds sensible. You know we've all been very worried about you."

"Time off is just about the last thing I want. I can't stop now – I'm far too involved in it. You can understand that, can't you, Sy?"

Syreeta looked dubious. "So, what do you do next?"

"Off to Aberdeen to hear Larry and Jim's paper about their work in Easter Island."

"Oh well, you should be all right there," said Syreeta.

Rebecca sat down at a computer and searched 'Larry Burton archaeologist'. She soon tracked down his academic details: Professor Laurence Burton: University of London, worked all over the Middle East, long string of publications, including two books on archaeological findings in Anatolia.

Before she left the office, she went over to Syreeta. "Please don't worry. Nothing very dramatic is going to happen in Aberdeen."

Seeing Rebecca leave, Charles emerged from his office and beckoned to Syreeta. "Syreeta, have you got a moment, please."

Syreeta remained at her work-space for a second or two and then walked into his office.

Charles seemed embarrassed. "Close the door," he said. Evidently something was wrong. She pushed it shut.

Charles took a deep breath. "I've been thinking things over – and I've decided to put you on to Rebecca's story. Putting it frankly, she's been too shaken up by recent events to be able to handle all this properly."

Syreeta protested immediately. "But this is Rebecca's thing."

"Listen, I didn't go into any detail with Rebecca, but it seems all sorts of weird things are happening to people with red hair."

"What sort of things?" asked Syreeta.

"The story hasn't really broken yet, but Rebecca's not the only one. Just odd reports are coming in – from around the world. Redheads having strange visions and psychological crises – personality changes – that sort of thing. And it's getting quite serious. There's been another redhead murder, maybe two. I didn't exactly tell Rebecca, but we just can't take the risk. She's been through enough already – and I'm taking it as a warning."

"To be honest, it's not that easy," Syreeta said.

"Look, this story is simply too big for one person. We may have to get a team on to it. And we can't afford to wait either. Go through what Rebecca has filed and the recent reports. I need two thousand words by Thursday – you've got a couple of days."

"You really expect me to take over her story?"

"If you don't want to do it, say so, and I'll put someone else on it."

There was a look of consternation on her face.

"Okay, okay," he said. "Go and see Rebecca and write it together if you like. But get something to me by Thursday."

"But what do I say to Rebecca?"

"You'll think of something," said Charles, picking up a phone.

Syreeta reluctantly nodded agreement and left his office.

CHAPTER 37

For once it was not raining, and the wintry Aberdeenshire countryside looked stunning. A few hardy sheep grazed the stone-walled fields, and in the distance the hills were hung with mist. The roads were quiet, and Jim was enjoying the drive while Rebecca studied a map.

The shock of the sacrifice of Señor Nata and the attempt on Rebecca's life seemed to have shaken Jim out of the coolness he had shown towards her on Easter Island.

He and Larry had decided to get her away from the island as quickly as possible. Pablo had become unavailable to help. Diego Garcia, as Chief of Police, had seemed quite happy just to take a few brief statements and gave the distinct impression that he would prefer it if all visitors to the island would simply pack their bags and leave.

When he arrived back in the UK, Jim immediately phoned Rebecca and offered to meet her at Aberdeen airport. Seeing him there, she couldn't help feeling relieved that he was once again affectionate and concerned about her.

Jim rested his hand on hers. "Have you managed to recover from all that business?"

"Oh, I'm getting over it. To be honest, though, I'm still having nightmares."

"Rebecca…" he said. He fell silent, put his hand back on the steering wheel and looked straight ahead.

She glanced over at him, sensing that he was trying to find the right words to say something important.

"Rebecca – I'm really sorry if I seemed, you know, a little distant after that dinner on Easter Island."

"That's okay. I thought you might have suddenly gone off me."

He reached over and squeezed her hand. "Far from it."

"Funnily enough, Pablo acted, you know, a bit out of character, as well. He behaved so differently towards me the next day. Quite cold."

"I've been thinking about it," said Jim. "There *was* something very odd about that place. Whatever happened to you that night coincided with the appearance of the Southern Lights. Seeing them in the middle of the Pacific was very unusual."

"Oh well, as long as everything's okay here," she said.

Jim turned to her. "Look, I know it's none of my business, but wouldn't it be better if you just dropped this redheads story?"

"I can't. I've invested too much in it now. Time, as well as my money. That's the trouble with being freelance. Anyway, I think it's going to get a lot bigger." She decided to change the subject. "I still can't find the Newton Stones on the map," she said, as they drove into the small town of Insch.

"Well, we're not missing any interesting papers at the conference today," Jim said. "And I've always wanted to see the Newton Stones. They're supposed to have very mysterious inscriptions." He glanced over at the map. "It can't be that difficult to find them. I remember Larry telling us to look out for a stream called the Gadie Burn. I bet he's already there."

"Do you and Larry have a lot in common?" asked Rebecca.

Jim's eyes lit up. "Yes, I'm very lucky. He's the best. He's a professor at the London School of Ancient Civilisations, as well as Visiting Professor here at the University of the East of Scotland. He's quite an expert on the ancient Near East, especially Anatolia."

"I think he's a very kind man," said Rebecca.

"He's a man of principle. Typical of the sort who witnessed the last of the British Empire, I guess." He looked at her as if wondering whether she would appreciate what he was talking about. "You know, the old style of academic who really looks after his students. He's very modest and completely unmaterialistic, you know. He just lives in a small flat near the British Museum. Though he's rarely there."

"Has he got a family?" asked Rebecca.

"His wife and daughter were killed in a car crash, years ago – in Turkey. He was driving, and it almost destroyed him at the time. Since then he's just thrown himself into his work. He never remarried."

"That's terribly sad," said Rebecca. "It's awful when you lose family like that." Before Jim could comment, her phone rang. She put it to her ear.

"Hi, Sy," she said brightly, her mood changing instantly.

Syreeta sounded anxious. "Becky, I need to talk to you – it's about work. I've been putting off speaking to you about it. It's not my fault. The thing is, I don't know what to do."

"What's the problem, Sy?"

"I need to meet you."

"Why? What's wrong?" Rebecca asked.

"It's about your story. Charles wants a two thousand word piece by Thursday. He asked me to look at what you sent him. He says he wants us to work on it together."

"Why, for crying out loud? What's he playing at? And what's the great hurry, anyway? He told me to take a break. Anyway, I don't actually think I need help."

"Of course not, I know. Could we just meet up and talk about it?"

"Can't we talk about it on the phone? I'm up near Aberdeen with Jim. We're taking a break from the conference."

"This story is getting too big. Charles is worried someone else will do it. If we don't do it, he's going to put someone else on it. It's a bit of a mess – I'm really sorry."

"It's a bit over the top."

"Well, it's got to be written up now. I thought it would be easier if I flew up to meet you."

"Oh well, I suppose so," said Rebecca. "Tomorrow I'll be in Aberdeen."

"Okay. I'll catch you in your hotel tomorrow. You're at the Curzon, aren't you?"

"Yes. But I'll be at the conference all day with my phone switched off. You can text me when you arrive. Sorry, I have to go. Bye for now." She ended the call, feeling irritated at the unwelcome interruption.

"Everything okay?" said Jim, glancing sideways.

"Just work catching up on me. I thought I was entitled to a break."

She looked at the map again. "Perhaps we should ask?"

"Good idea. Let's try here," suggested Jim, and he pulled up outside what appeared to be a general store.

CHAPTER 38

A bell jingled as they entered the shop, and at first glance the place appeared to be empty. Then they noticed the shopkeeper kneeling down, stacking packets of cereals, half-hidden by a display. In the dim light at the back of the shop, an old lady, who could have been his mother, was making sandwiches, presumably for sale in the shop. The shopkeeper got up and went to the counter.

"Can you help us, please?" Jim said. "We're looking for the Newton Stones."

"Oh, you're very close," replied the shopkeeper, looking through the window and noting the direction their car was facing. "Just go back the way you came towards Inverurie. You'll see a lane on the left going over a bridge. The Stones are about a quarter of a mile down the lane in a clump of trees."

At that moment, a sleek black cat leaped up on to the counter from behind the shopkeeper and started to sniff a box of fruit pastilles.

"Now, Tam, you know you shouldn't be here," he said, gently picking up the cat and placing it on the floor. The cat ran to the back of the shop.

"Sorry," said the shopkeeper. "Now where was I? Oh, yes. Look for the rooks. There's a rookery there."

"Much appreciated," Jim said, and turned to leave the shop.

But the front page headlines in the morning papers, on display on the counter, had caught Rebecca's eye. The one on the front page of the *Hibernian* stood out:

'MORE REDHEADS MISSING'

She picked it up and started to read. *Damn, damn, damn,* she thought. *That's it – everybody'll be on to my story soon.* Then she checked the front pages of every daily paper in the shop. The story about the missing redheads was in all the Scottish dailies, but it was not in the nationals. And the big story – the murders – hadn't broken. She gathered together copies of all the Scottish dailies.

"I'll take these, please," she said, paying the shopkeeper. She pointed to the headline in the *Hibernian*. "Have you heard anything about this?"

The shopkeeper and the old lady exchanged uneasy glances. "There's something very funny going on, that's for sure," the shopkeeper said. "All these red-haired people going missing." Rebecca looked at him enquiringly. "Well, you know – the first one was in Shetland. A mother out walking with her baby in a pram. They never came home. No sign of them – just the empty pram." Rebecca paled slightly. "Then two brothers up near Inverness – out hill-walking. Never returned – the search party never found them."

"Did they all have red hair?" asked Rebecca.

"Every one of them. Weird, isn't it? But the worst case was yesterday – a whole family. Right here in Insch. Mum, dad and two children out for a stroll. Only thing they found was a scarf belonging to one of the children. Apart from that – nothing."

The old lady had finished filling the rolls and came up to Rebecca. "You'd better take care yourself, lassie," she said, looking at Rebecca's hair.

"Oh, I shall. Thank you," Rebecca replied. But she felt a sudden chill go through her whole body.

"Any people with red hair should be careful around here," the old lady went on.

Rebecca held up the newspaper. "But why do you think it's happening?"

"Oh, there are a lot of old superstitions around here," the old lady answered.

Rebecca wanted to hear more, but Jim was standing by the shop door. "Come on, Rebecca. Larry will be wondering where we are." He waved to the shopkeeper as he opened the door. "Sorry to rush off, but we're supposed to be meeting somebody there."

Rebecca reluctantly joined him, calling her thanks over her shoulder.

They left Insch and followed the instructions they had been given. The main road to Inverurie ran parallel to a small river, signposted as the Gadie Burn where it ran under the road. After making the left turn, they crossed a small white bridge spanning the river and started to drive down a narrow lane. A clump of trees could be seen in the distance, small black specks circling in the sky above it.

Rebecca was quiet and preoccupied, thinking about the conversation in the shop.

"Do you think I should dye my hair a different colour?" she asked Jim. "Blonde, perhaps, or dark brown?"

"Up to you. If you want a good story, maybe you should leave it as it is," replied Jim. "Depends how brave you're feeling."

She thought his comment sounded rather harsh. "Thanks a lot – really helpful. Perhaps I should just cover it with a headscarf, or get myself a beanie hat."

But Jim was no longer listening. They had reached the clump of trees. "This could be it," he said, seeing Larry's car and parking next to it.

They couldn't see the Stones at first, but a pathway led into the trees. The rookery was very active and the air was filled with the sound of incessant cawing. Thin sunlight filtered through the last of the autumn leaves, so that the ground was dappled with light and shadows. They followed the path through the trees to a small clearing.

The two Newton Stones were about six foot tall, roughly hewn, weathered and covered in lichen. They stood a few feet apart, one leaning slightly forwards, the other slightly backwards, like an ancient couple who were brooding and sulking after a tiff. The inscriptions on them were still clear.

Larry was standing in front of one of the Stones, notebook in hand, closely inspecting what appeared to be a script down one side. Hearing them arrive, he turned round and beckoned them over.

"Hello, you two. Come and see this. Ogham script – ancient Celtic. I'll bet it's a memorial stone of some sort."

But Jim had become quickly engrossed in some writing at the top of the Stone. There were six lines written in a strange script carved into the rock. He pointed them out to Larry. "Any idea what this is?" Rebecca joined them to see what Jim was studying.

"Plenty of people have tried to decipher it, but nobody's managed it yet, as far as I know," said Larry. He pointed to a symbol in the middle of the inscription. "This is what attracts a lot of attention. It looks like a swastika – a sun-sign. It was an ancient symbol of the sun crossing the sky. Of course, that was long before the Nazis adopted it for their own evil purposes. But this isn't really the same as the German swastika. See the end of this one arm – it's bent upwards."

Rebecca went over to the other Stone. "What about this one?"

"Much more straight forward. It's another Pictish symbol stone," Jim said, walking over to it.

He ran his finger over the various features carved into the surface. "Look here – a double disc. And here – a serpent crossed by a Z-rod. See this large Z shape carved over the serpent. They could be symbols of the afterlife. Nobody really knows." He looked at his watch. "Larry, I don't want to rush you, but it's the conference dinner tonight, and time's getting on."

Larry reluctantly moved away from the Stones and checked his own watch. "Heavens! I suppose we'd better be going. I would've liked to have taken some decent photos, though. I'll have to come back another time. Can't be late for the Christmas dinner bash, can we? Are you coming, Rebecca?"

Rebecca looked taken aback. "Nobody told me about any dinner. I haven't got anything suitable to wear." Larry and Jim looked at each other sheepishly.

A minute later, car doors slammed, followed by the noise of cars starting and driving away. For a moment, back at the Stones, all was quiet and still apart from the harsh cries of the rooks. Then, even they stopped.

From behind one of the Stones, the one with the 'sun-sign', a dark but striking figure emerged. It was Dr Neferatu. But this time, he looked quite different.

CHAPTER 39

Unpacking in the hotel room, Rebecca critically examined her clothes. "Why didn't they warn me there was going to be a dinner?" she grumbled to herself, though she knew she really should have packed for more eventualities.

She had brought two dresses, each of them selected for an intimate dinner, but both eminently unsuitable for an official event. She tried on the green one, which was far too short, then the black with the plunging neckline, then the green again, before finally deciding on the black, after all. It might just about do with black tights. Yet the five inch high heels, her only option, risked not only a nasty accident, but serious academic disapproval.

She liberally doused herself in perfume, and after a final brush of her hair and quick check in the mirror, teetered to the lift and went down to reception, where Larry and Jim were waiting for her. While Larry smiled indulgently when he saw her, Jim looked decidedly embarrassed.

"I'll drive," he said quickly.

By tradition, the event was strictly formal. Jim had managed to borrow a tie, which he hadn't managed to knot successfully. Larry was wearing the only formal suit he possessed.

At the conference centre, they passed into the dining room, an annexe to the main conference hall. At the far end of the room, equipment for a band was set up on a small stage. Separate large round tables were arranged over the room, leaving a small dance area in front of the stage. Most people were already gathered around the bar.

After taking in the scene, Jim turned to Rebecca. "What would you like to drink?"

"Vodka, please – Stolichnaya – if they've got it."

Jim looked taken aback. "I didn't think you drank?"

"Oh, I don't know," she said. "I just fancy enjoying myself tonight."

Jim turned to Larry.

"A pint of bitter for me, thanks, Jim."

Rebecca looked around the gathering, took her vodka from Jim and drained it in one. Jim raised his eyebrows.

"At least that obnoxious Dr Neferatu isn't going to be here," she said. "If there's one person who gives me the creeps…"

Jim put his hand to his forehead. "I don't like to tell you this – but he's – er – definitely here. Here in Aberdeen, I mean."

Rebecca looked puzzled. "What do you mean – here?"

"He's here at the conference in Aberdeen – for our paper. He says he wants to work with me."

"What! Why the hell didn't you tell me?"

"I didn't think it was that important. Anyway, it doesn't really have anything to do with you."

She banged her empty glass down on a table and glared at him. "My God, that's all I need. Why on earth should he want to work with you?"

With obvious reluctance, Jim explained Dr Neferatu's visit and proposal, managing to avoid mentioning the £10,000 grant, until the very end.

"You don't actually believe all that crap, do you?"

Jim looked defiant. "Look, if he wants to fund a new department or whatever, it's my duty, my professional duty, to encourage him. He's entirely serious. You may not know that he has got a doctorate from the University of Alexandria. And all he wanted from me was a background document. In fact, I knocked it off in a couple of hours."

"Doesn't it strike you that it's all a bit bizarre? It wouldn't surprise me if he gave you a dud cheque."

Jim frowned. "Why would he give me a dud cheque?"

Rebecca looked at him as if he had lost his mind. "How can

you even think of working with such a repulsive person?"

"What on earth have you got against him? He might be a bit odd, but he's done nothing bad as far as I know. And it's the easiest ten thousand I've ever earned."

"That man is trouble. Have you looked at his eyes? Pure evil. Has the university tried paying in the cheque yet?"

"No – they won't have had time. It'll probably be in the New Year now."

"You'll see – it'll bounce right out of the window. I bet you didn't even check out his credentials."

Jim was silent as Rebecca glared at him, but at that moment, Larry, looking over her shoulder, raised his hand to stop her continuing.

"Might be better to change the subject. Guess who's here! At least, I think it's him. He looks different somehow. And he's making his way over here."

Dr Neferatu was elbowing his way steadily through the throng towards them. Standing in front of Larry and Jim, he studiously ignored Rebecca.

He seemed much older than before, when they had seen him last on Easter Island. There were grey streaks in his hair and his face was now deeply lined. His eyes seemed duller, although still noticeably green. He looked perhaps ten years older, an effect accentuated by his slightly threadbare double-breasted dinner jacket, the lapels of which curled up at the edges.

"*Buenas tardes*," he said, turning his back on Rebecca.

"Good evening," said Larry, shaking Dr Neferatu's proffered hand. "Jim told me you would be here. But I am a little surprised, to say the least. It's a long way to come."

"Not at all, Professor Burton. Your work on Easter Island fascinates me."

Larry glanced at Dr Neferatu's hair. "Are you all right? Did anything happen to you on Easter Island?"

Dr Neferatu's expression remained impassive. "I haven't exactly been taking the sun here, if that's what you mean."

"The weather can be far worse than this, in this part of the world," observed Larry.

Dr Neferatu ignored him. "Now – I must let you get back to your colleagues," he said. Without so much as a 'see you later' or 'goodbye', he turned on his heel and quickly disappeared into the crowd.

Larry looked intrigued. "Imagine him coming all this way. Did you see how old he looked? His hair has gone quite grey."

"Maybe he's just run out of hair dye," said Jim, still rattled by Rebecca's comments.

Rebecca didn't smile. "Well, he's not going to spoil my evening. Would anybody like another drink?"

Larry and Jim politely declined, and Rebecca made for the bar.

"Do you think she's okay?" said Jim. "She's barely touched a drop whenever I've been with her."

"She went through a lot on Easter Island, you know," said Larry. "And seeing Dr Neferatu here must bring it all back."

Jim nodded in agreement. "Even so, it's a side of her character I haven't seen before. We'll have to keep an eye on her." He caught sight of a Cambridge colleague, and they were soon both engaged in lively, academic discussion.

A largely male crowd was trying to catch the attention of the student bar staff. Irritated at being ignored, Rebecca waved her arms around in a vain attempt to catch the eye of a barman. Frustrated, she stepped back and waved a ten pound note in the air. "I was here first. Stolichnaya – and make it a double," she yelled. Surprised heads turned and the crowd parted to let her through.

Taking a large gulp of vodka, she made towards the stage, where five musicians were getting ready. The line-up was electric piano, sax, trumpet, double-bass and drums. They swung into their first number unobtrusively, knowing their job was to provide suitable background music. For a while, Rebecca watched them from the side of the room, tapping her foot to the beat. After a short time, she returned to the bar to demand another Stolichnaya.

With the call from the conference organiser to "Be seated", Jim broke off from his conversation with an associate from Reading University and looked around for Rebecca. She was wandering aimlessly around the room. He went over to her, grabbed her elbow and, catching sight of Larry's hand waving to him, escorted her to Larry's table. As the two of them sat down, the table was full apart from one seat.

The wine was just being poured when they were joined, as if from nowhere, by Dr Neferatu. "May I join you?" he asked.

"Bugger off," Rebecca said, under her breath.

"Of course," Jim answered. But Dr Neferatu had already seated himself next to Jim and opposite Rebecca. Rebecca glowered and downed a glass of red wine in one go. She held out her empty glass towards the bottle, until a genial old historian between Larry and herself obligingly filled it up.

"Do you think you should be drinking quite so much?" Jim whispered to her.

"I'm fine. Just having fun," she said, swaying.

Without warning, she leaned forward over the table towards Dr Neferatu, knocking over the historian's glass of water and soaking the tablecloth. The historian made to refill his glass but, catching sight of her cleavage, spilled more water than he put in the glass.

"Dr Neferatu," said Rebecca, very slightly slurring the words. "So tell me – what do you really think was happening on Easter Island when we last met? What was going on when Señor Nata was murdered? It was like some ancient sacrifice. You know it nearly happened to me?"

Just for one split second, Dr Neferatu looked taken aback. Quickly regaining his composure, his features settled into a hard, almost menacing expression.

"I'm afraid you managed to get yourself mixed up in some local conflict. Very nasty, I agree, but then you must understand that these things can happen in small, isolated communities. Conflicts and feuds can fester for years, or even for centuries."

"But why did I see such horrific things at the dinner there? Things nobody else said they saw. Do you think I was just imagining them?"

"Oh, I think perhaps you must have been rather tired. You must work very hard." He turned away and began to address the young archaeologist on his right.

Rebecca watched him for a while in silence, poured herself another glass of wine and sat there sullenly, ignoring the polite attempts of the other diners to engage her in conversation.

Jim occasionally moved the wine bottle out of her reach, but another diner would always politely refill her glass. Rebecca continued to drink steadily throughout the meal, contributing little to the general conversation at the table.

The band played all through the dinner, sticking mainly to a repertoire of standards from Cole Porter and Rogers and Hart. As coffee and liqueurs were served, the pianist announced a short break while the musicians disappeared off-stage.

Standing up, the President of the Society of Archaeologists introduced the guest speaker; a well-known authority on ancient Persia, who used the occasion largely to bemoan government interference in his fieldwork and the lack of funding for important digs.

Meanwhile, Rebecca had persuaded the waiter to bring her a double brandy.

CHAPTER 40

As the band drifted back on stage, Rebecca's eyes fixed on the musicians. Then, without saying a word, she unexpectedly stood up, almost knocking over her chair, and made her way unsteadily towards the band. Without pausing, she climbed the steps to the stage, stumbling slightly on the top step, and approached the saxophonist, apparently engaging him in urgent conversation.

The saxophonist looked surprised, but after looking around at the other members of the band, who were laughing indulgently, handed over his sax. Rebecca made her way over to the piano player, almost catching her foot in the microphone lead. Alarmed, the trumpet player leaped over to steady it before it fell.

Saxophone in hand, she put her hand on the piano player's shoulder and whispered in his ear. He nodded and called over something to the band.

Jim leant towards Larry. "What the hell's up with her? Have you seen how much she's knocked back? She's legless."

Larry looked concerned. "It must be all she's been through catching up with her."

Clutching the sax, Rebecca was stumbling around the stage, trying to find space for herself. As she did so, word seemed to spread like wildfire around the room. Diners nudged each other and fell silent, heads turning towards the stage.

By now Jim was looking tense and grim; but the other diners were looking on with amusement and curiosity.

Rebecca swayed slightly, righted herself and nodded to the pianist. The pianist started to play the opening chords of 'My Favourite Things'. As the bass came in, Rebecca stood still with her head slightly lowered.

Jim studied his fork, as if he were wishing he were a thousand miles away from the place.

Then, with faultless precision, Rebecca raised the instrument to her lips and hit the first note bang on time. She played on, developing the rich melody effortlessly and with perfect cool. The musicians were now smiling, clearly enjoying the break from routine, while the atmosphere in the room relaxed once more and conversations resumed.

Larry caught Jim's eye. "Did you know she could play the sax?"

"Nothing surprises me now," Jim commented.

"She's almost as good as Eric Dolphy. Almost," said Larry.

"Who on earth is Eric Dolphy?" replied Jim.

As the band finished, the pianist waved Rebecca forward to take a bow. The room burst into applause and Rebecca looked elated. She presented the sax back to its owner and left the stage, none too steadily, slowly weaving her way back to the table. Larry immediately sprang to his feet and pulled out the chair for her. She sat down to smiles and general comments of congratulation, apart from Dr Neferatu, who appeared noticeably indifferent.

"That was a bit of a surprise," beamed Larry. "Well done, Rebecca." Jim was still looking bemused.

"Thanks," replied Rebecca, before gently slumping back into her seat, her eyes closing and her head rolling to one side.

Larry and Jim looked at each other. "She's passing out," said Jim. "I'd better take her back to her hotel."

He helped Rebecca to her feet and guided her, unprotesting, towards the exit. "I'm taking you back to the hotel," he said firmly.

"All right," she said, taking his arm.

Jim managed to steer Rebecca out of the building and into his car, putting his arm around her to stop her falling over. She fell into the passenger seat.

"How are you feeling?" he asked.

"Fine," she lied, trying to get closer to him. He gently eased her away so that he could drive.

The receptionist in the hotel gave Jim a hard look when he asked for Rebecca's room key. He got her into the lift and almost carried her to her room. As he opened the door, she tottered unsteadily inside and half-collapsed on to the bed.

Lying back, she patted the bed by her side. He caught the scent of her perfume. "Come and sit down, Jim," she slurred.

"I'd love to, but you need to sleep. There's a lot on tomorrow."

"Oh, come on. Please, Jim."

Putting her hand on his arm, she tugged at his sleeve, until he sat down on the edge of the bed. She snuggled up to him. Jim kissed her lightly on the forehead and tried to get up, but she wrapped her arm around his neck and pulled him on top of her.

With some difficulty, he hauled himself back upright. "Rebecca," he whispered, running his hand through her hair, "You need to rest." He showed her the time on his watch and kissed her tenderly but briefly on the lips. "It's late and we have an early start tomorrow. I'll see you at breakfast. Okay?"

She put her hand on his arm and squeezed it. "Jim, do you remember that lovely moment in the hotel garden in Hanga-roa, when you gave me that little yellow flower?"

"Ah yes, the flower of the toromiro tree," he said.

"And do you remember the beautiful scent of the Angels' Trumpets?"

"It must be one of the most powerful scents in the world," he said. "Unforgettable."

"I'll never forget that moment, Jim. Do you have to go? Couldn't you stay a little longer?"

"You know Larry is presenting tomorrow, and I'm the co-author. I have to be on the ball for questions."

Rebecca nodded and took her hand away.

Jim kissed her again, stood up and tucked in his shirt.

As he left, closing the door quietly behind him, she lay back contentedly on the bed and passed out.

CHAPTER 41

The University of the East of Scotland lay on the outskirts of Aberdeen in the grounds of a former stately home, now used as the administration centre. Built in the 1960s during a flush of expansion of higher education, the buildings were now decidedly run down, shabby and in need of renovation. Buildings that housed the various faculties were dotted around the campus and served by the university library and the conference centre.

The main lecture room in the conference centre was light and airy, 60's style, but spartanly furnished to the extent that delegates were obliged to sit on bare wooden chairs. After a three hour session, the twitching of bodies trying to find a comfortable position was noticeable and increasing.

The conference in progress was entitled 'Ancient civilisations and migration patterns: the archaeological evidence'. Larry's own paper was listed in the programme as 'Recent advances in the understanding of monumental architecture on Rapa Nui'. His presentation, the last before lunch, was well attended.

Larry was an accomplished speaker. He did not use notes, preferring to speak with the help of slides. He was now drawing to a close and was in the process of summarising.

Jim, as co-author, was seated in the front row. Rebecca was seated behind him, notebook in hand, looking noticeably bleary-eyed.

In the middle of the audience, in a smart business suit and tie, sat Dr Neferatu. If anything, he looked even older and more haggard than the day before, and yet his keen interest in Larry's presentation was clearly evident as he stared at the screen. His hand, clutching a pen, was poised over a large white pad.

On the screen was a map of the world, with dotted lines

indicating migration routes across the oceans. Larry stepped back from the screen, put his pointer down and went up to the lectern.

"In conclusion, our findings strongly endorse the migration theories of Dr Heyerdahl. These are supported by the striking similarities in monumental architecture stretching from the Indus Valley, across islands in the Indian Ocean, to Mesopotamia and the Middle East. Then over Europe, across the Atlantic to Central America, down to Lake Titicaca in Peru and hence over the Pacific Ocean, to Easter Island. Heyerdahl, of course, makes reference to one racial feature in particular, which is found in all these places – people with red hair."

Larry swept his eyes over his audience before delivering his concluding words. "Genetic evidence may support the alternative theory of a migration to Easter Island from Polynesia, but even the geneticists themselves are very careful not to jump to conclusions. Ladies and Gentlemen, the jury is still out."

The session chairman strode over to the lectern. "Provocative as ever, Professor Burton. I'm sure there are going to be some questions. Yes, sir." He pointed over to Dr Neferatu, who had immediately put his hand up.

Dr Neferatu ignored the proffered microphone, stood up and cleared his throat to speak. "Do you see connections between people with red hair on Easter Island and here in Scotland?"

"It's a bit beyond my field, Dr Neferatu," answered Larry, "but red hair was always associated with the Phoenicians, and certainly the Phoenicians were adventurous sailors. They are recorded as going right around Africa. The Carthaginians – who were of the same stock, incidentally – themselves sailed to Cornwall where they bought locally mined tin. And here's a strange thing. Yesterday I crossed a river – the Gadie Burn – at Insch. Gadir, very similar, was the name of a Phoenician settlement in southwest Spain, better known nowadays, of course, as Cadiz. So you see, there could be even more connections than those we know about."

The chairman stepped in quickly, hoping to move on to

something less speculative and closer to the subject of the lecture. The next question was on architectural comparisons between buildings on the Marquesas Islands and those of Easter Island.

But Dr Neferatu was writing fast and furiously in his notebook. His elaborate notes and artistic flourishes caught the attention of a young student seated next to him. They were written in Egyptian hieroglyphics.

CHAPTER 42

In the afternoon, Jim sat on the bed in his hotel room, studying the notes he had taken during the morning presentations and typing intermittently into his laptop. There was a gentle knock on the door.

It was Rebecca standing there, looking forlorn and sorry for herself.

"Hello," he said, "you're the last person I'd have expected. Thought you'd still be sleeping it off."

"Sorry I didn't make breakfast or lunch."

"I didn't even see you in the coffee break."

"I know, but I did make it for the paper. It was really useful. I'm still thinking about everything Larry said. Can I come in, please?"

"Sure," he said, and opened the door wider.

She entered apprehensively, perched on an uncomfortable looking chair and smiled apologetically.

"Jim – I'm really sorry to be so much trouble."

"What do you mean?"

"Last night. I don't usually drink so much."

"I was a bit surprised," he said. "I didn't think you were a drinker. Anyway, I always thought journos could take their booze. All part of the job, so to speak."

"I told you, I don't normally drink. You know what I've been through. It must have all caught up with me."

"Well, I do admit the sax was something else. That was the big surprise. You were amazing. Really. Nobody was expecting that."

"I was terribly drunk. I can't even remember exactly what happened. Just remember you helping me back to my room. I'm really sorry. I think all this red hair business is beginning to get to me. Sometimes I feel I'm not like other people – like part of an entirely different race."

"I can understand that. But people who stand out tend to be picked on."

Rebecca felt upset at first. Somehow she was not getting the sympathy she had expected. Then she flared.

"Picked on! It's a bit more than being picked on, you know. We're being murdered! People are disappearing, in case you hadn't noticed. Right here too!"

Jim appeared unmoved. "No bodies, though. And anyway, whoever disappears around here, there's a good possibility they'll have red hair." He ignored her look of incredulity. "I'm sorry, but it's a national feature, isn't? Look around. More than ten percent of Scots have red hair. And even if they aren't redheads themselves, there's an excellent chance their children will have red hair. It's all down to a recessive gene. Red hair isn't that special, you know."

Rebecca flushed. "Crap! And you're a scientist! Look at the facts! Can't you see how many cases there are now? Not just in Scotland." She counted on her fingers. "Six murders on Easter Island, including poor Señor Nata. You haven't forgotten him have you? And more in the South Pacific. Eight *disappearances* in Scotland – that's what they said in the shop. God only knows what's going on in the Middle East."

"Oh, come on," Jim interrupted. "That doesn't exactly make it a global epidemic."

Rebecca stood up and made for the door. "Give me the car keys for an hour, will you? I'm going out to ask some more questions."

Jim looked at her in surprise, hesitating a moment before passing her the keys. "What, now? Can't you stop nosing around and just mind your own business for five minutes?"

She spun round. "Look, Jim, it's my job, finding out things. I'm a journalist. And it bloody well is my business now, in case you haven't noticed. My hair's the wrong colour and I'm scared. I thought you liked me. I thought you were on my side. Now I'm not so sure."

"What do you mean? Where are you going?"

Rebecca looked at him dismissively. "To do some more 'nosing around' as you put it so charmingly," she said, slamming the door behind her.

She had just started down the corridor when her phone rang.

"Hi, Sy." She listened briefly and then cut in. "Yeah, fine. Tell you what – can I see you a bit later? I've just got to go out for a minute. I'll be back soon." She shoved her phone back in her handbag and made her way out to the car park.

CHAPTER 43

Jim looked at the closed door and then shrugged his shoulders. *I'm not quite sure I need this*, he said to himself.

Trying to collect his thoughts together, he sat down again at his laptop. He had barely started typing, when there was another knock at the door. "Jesus," he muttered in irritation.

Half-expecting to see an apologetic Rebecca again, he opened the door to see instead an attractive girl with classic Indian good looks, dark brown hair and large brown eyes.

"Jim Cavendish?" she smiled. "I'm Syreeta Dasgupta. You don't know me. I'm a friend of Rebecca – from the *Metropolitan*."

He half-smiled back. "Yes?"

"Could I talk to you for a minute? I'm a bit worried about her. I was wondering if she's all right." Jim's expression gave little away. "Can I come in?" asked Syreeta.

"Sure, sure – come on in. Why not?" said Jim, standing back and holding the door open.

Syreeta entered and put her large Prada handbag down on a table next to his laptop.

"Well, funnily enough, I did think she was a bit on edge this evening," he offered. "But didn't you just see her? She's only just left here a minute ago."

"Do you know where she was going?"

"No, she didn't say. I think she's nosing around some place. Don't ask me where."

"Well, that's what she's here for."

"I know, I know – it's your job, going into everything, following everything up. But sometimes I think you lot just blow everything out of proportion and get yourselves, and everyone else, into a mess. Anyway, I just wish she'd give it a break for a while."

Syreeta smiled again. "Do you mind if I sit down?" she said, edging towards a chair.

"Please," he said, with an air of tired resignation.

At that point his mobile rang.

"Greg Ryan here, Jim. How yer keepin'?"

A broad grin spread over Jim's face. He mouthed "Sorry" to Syreeta. Greg was a friend and colleague from the Space Weather Prediction Center in Boulder, Colorado.

"Fine, Greg. Thanks for phoning back. Something I wanted to check with you. I saw the Northern Lights a couple of weeks ago. They were suddenly visible as far south as Scotland. And then, a few days ago, we were on Easter Island, and lo and behold, we could see the Southern Lights from there – and that's a long way north of the Antarctic. What do you reckon is happening? I checked in our department, and they're saying the Earth's magnetic field might be getting weaker – in some places at least. Including Scotland, funnily enough. But they're still looking into it and don't want to make any announcements until they get a better idea of what's going on. It's the sort of thing that could lead to a media panic. I said I'd have a word with you."

"No, they're right," said Greg. "There is something funny going on. We've had a report in from Hawaii. They picked the weakening up there – and a few other places in the South Pacific. I'm not surprised you saw the lights in Easter Island. We're monitoring these events all very closely. Let's hope it's just a blip."

"Let's hope. I mean, if there's a big rise in solar radiation getting through, it could cause all sorts of problems. Skin cancers might be just the least of it."

"Not only that," said Greg. "You know what happened the last time the field weakened, don't you? In a big way, I mean?"

"In a big way? You mean like the last time, when the Earth's magnetic field completely switched over? A pole reversal. Surely you don't think that's likely?"

"Of course, you know the Earth's magnetic field's been getting weaker for the last two thousand years? Since the time of Julius Caesar, in fact," said Greg. "We could be due for another switch."

"I'm beginning to see what you're getting at," said Jim. He paused for a moment. "I mean, compasses will all be pointing the wrong way to the South Pole instead of the North Pole – that sort of thing. Chaotic for planes and shipping. Animal migration patterns would be affected, of course." He paused again. "Oddly enough, I think I might have witnessed that – with some birds in Orkney. They suddenly changed direction, mid-flight. I couldn't be sure, though – they may have been scared by an eagle."

"The other thing is the possible effects on humans," said Greg. "We just don't know how much this could affect people and their lives."

"You mean the magnetic change could affect people's personalities, or something like that?"

"Who can tell? Who knows how far it could go? It's all unknown territory. We'll just have to wait and see. No panic yet, but I'll keep you posted."

"Well, thanks for the warning," Jim said. "I'm actually in Scotland at the moment, giving a paper."

"Keep me posted about what is happening over there," said Greg, and he rang off.

"That sounded like an interesting conversation," said Syreeta.

CHAPTER 44

It was raining heavily by the time Rebecca got to Insch. She parked the car in front of the village shop and ran to the door. The shopkeeper was tidying the magazines in a rack, and Rebecca noticed the old lady was there, stacking tins at the back of the shop.

The shopkeeper looked up and recognised her immediately. "Hello, Miss. Did you find the Newton Stones all right?"

"Yes, thanks. No problem," she answered.

"How can I help you?"

"Before we rushed off yesterday, you mentioned certain superstitions around here, about people with red hair?"

He looked wary. "Oh, I'm sorry, Miss. Nothing personal, you know."

"I was hoping you could tell me a bit more," said Rebecca.

"Well, I don't really know what to say," said the shopkeeper. "There are quite a few Scottish traditions concerning redheads. You probably know about some of them. 'First footing' at Hogmanay, for instance. It's really bad luck if a man with red hair is the first person to cross the threshold of your house in the New Year. Probably comes from the time the Vikings were invading. Could even go back to Biblical times."

"Biblical times?"

"Well, Judas Iscariot had red hair, and he was definitely bad luck. Vampires too. They say redheaded women don't die – they become vampires. It's just myths, you know." He opened a box of cigarette packets and started putting them on a shelf. "Anyway, you look healthy enough. What did you think of the Newton Stones?"

"I didn't have much time to look at them, to be honest.

Apparently there's an inscription on one that's never been deciphered?"

"True enough. They've been trying for at least two hundred years. One Stone is supposed to represent the sun – it's known as the Sun-Stone. The other is the Moon-Stone – the one with the serpent on it."

The old lady's voice floated from the back of the shop with quiet authority. "Dr Waddell managed to decipher it."

"What's that, Mother?" the shopkeeper called back to her.

She came up to them. "Dr Waddell," she repeated. "He came here to look at the Stones years ago, when I was a little girl. Nice man, a real scholar. He said the inscription must have been carved by a Phoenician who came and settled here. I think he said his name was Ikar."

"Did Dr Waddell say exactly what the inscription meant?" asked Rebecca.

The old lady looked vague. "Oh, no. I can't remember that. Too long ago."

Rebecca made a decision. "Perhaps I'll go and have another look. I could take some photos."

The shopkeeper looked concerned. "Better be smartish – it'll be dark soon."

The old lady came up close to Rebecca. "If I were you, Miss, I wouldn't go anywhere near the place. People say it's not safe. Some people have seen the *sidhe* there, especially when it's getting dark."

"What are the *sidhe*?"

"You know, they're like the *banshee* in Ireland. They guard the Stones. Not that I believe in any of that, of course. But some people say they've seen them."

"What do they look like?"

"Shortish, and really ugly. They have been known to attack people."

The shopkeeper sighed. "Don't tell her those old stories. It's all old wives' tales, Mother."

"I'm just saying she shouldn't go there, that's all."

"I was only going to have a quick look," said Rebecca. She couldn't help wishing she wasn't on her own. And yet she was intrigued and determined to go back.

"Well, don't stay long," said the old lady. "And make sure you call in here on your way back. Just to let us know you're okay."

"I'll do that, thank you. But don't worry – I'll be all right. See you later." She opened the door, letting in the next customer.

CHAPTER 45

The car lurched and bumped down the pot-holed lane, as Rebecca drove through pools of water towards the copse. Parking the car, she was grateful that the rain had just stopped. Although the rooks were cawing, they seemed subdued, and a deep gloom pervaded the scene. Water dripped loudly from the trees and there were puddles everywhere. Rebecca ducked as she wove her way down the path to the clearing, trying to avoid brushing against the wet bushes.

She stopped abruptly when she caught sight of the Stones. They looked different now. In the evening light, they seemed even more imposing and mysterious, as if they were guarding long lost secrets.

Walking slowly over to the Sun-Stone, the old lady's warning played on Rebecca's mind and she felt very alone. Examining the inscriptions on the Stone, she couldn't help envisaging Dr Waddell looking at them decades previously.

Stepping back, she turned her attention to the Moon-Stone and found she could easily make out the various signs: the Z-rod, the mirror and the serpent twining its way through the other symbols.

She felt a sudden urge to trace along the line of the serpent with her finger, and then did it again, wondering who had carved it and what it signified. She wondered if she were imagining a faint tingling sensation in her finger. Deep in thought, she didn't notice that the rooks had become silent.

The sound of soft footsteps and rustling branches behind her brought her abruptly back to reality. She swung round and stiffened with fear.

What she saw made her quickly back up against the Moon-

Stone in terror. Breaking out of the bushes about twenty feet away, what appeared to be a savage-looking caveman stopped and gazed in her direction.

He was quite short, but very stocky. His large head seemed too big for his body, and his protruding eyebrows overhung blue, intelligent eyes. It reminded her of a cartoon she had once seen of Charles Darwin, caricatured as an ape. But this was no ape standing there before her. This was definitely some form of human, and he was wearing animal skins, crudely stitched together, covering most of his body. Only the forearms and legs below the knees were visible; and these, like his head and face, were covered in red hair.

He continued to stare at her, as if taking in the scene, and then started to lurch clumsily in her direction.

Rebecca froze against the Moon-Stone, but as the creature slowly approached, she noticed that his eyes were not on her at all. He did not even seem to notice her presence there but, looking straight ahead, lumbered past and crashed into the undergrowth behind the Stones.

Then, total silence again, apart from the sound of dripping leaves. Still taut with fear, Rebecca inched away from the Moon-Stone and peered apprehensively behind it, dreading what she might see.

A rustle in the foliage made her leap back. It was a sleek russet-haired fox. *How long has that been there? Why didn't the caveman disturb it?* Now, startled by Rebecca, it darted off through the undergrowth, showering down droplets of water, only to stop about twenty yards away, almost hidden by the foliage. There, it eyed her, with what seemed keen interest. It cocked its head to one side, like a friendly dog, then quite casually turned back and slipped away out of sight.

Shaken and nervous, Rebecca felt instinctively that she was treading on someone else's hallowed ground. Pulling herself together, she went to grab her bag and get away as quickly as possible.

It was at that moment that there was a sudden sound of flapping wings. Looking up, she saw a large, hawk-like bird land heavily on top of the Sun-Stone. The sight of it instantly chilled her to the marrow. It seemed to eye her coldly, its head jerking from side to side. Hesitantly, she backed away and turned round to run.

She glanced back over her shoulder, fearing the bird would attack her, but found it had disappeared without a sound. But to her horror, she saw Dr Neferatu stepping out from behind the Sun-Stone.

No, no, not again, flashed through her mind. Then, mesmerised, she found herself turning back to face him. He was still dressed as he was at the conference, his dark suit completely out of place in the wet woodland clearing.

As a slow smile spread over his face, she immediately noticed something different about his appearance; his eyes had changed. Previously green, they were now a deep brown.

"Are you all right, Miss Burns?" he sneered.

Without warning, he lunged towards her and tried to grab her hand. She fell backward, but he lunged again and caught hold of it in a vice-like grip.

"Let go, will you," she demanded, attempting to free herself.

But, smirking, he continued to hold her hand, his finger-nail digging in deeply. "Such bad manners."

He looked over her shoulder, as if in anticipation. "Ah, good – Ikar has arrived," he said, and calmly let go of her hand.

She nervously turned to look behind her and froze again. A huge man was standing there.

His appearance was extraordinary. On top of his head, his black hair was covered by a cone-shaped cap. At the back of his neck, his hair hung down in braids almost to his shoulders, and his beard was meticulously arranged in rows of small, tight curls. He was dressed in a skirt of white cotton, slit up the sides for ease of movement, and a tight-fitting, short-sleeved white tunic. A mantle of rich blue and red was slung over his left shoulder, and his muscular brown arms were decorated with simple silver amulets.

He stood, legs apart, gazing at Rebecca with cruel, dark eyes. Pushing his mantle to one side, he rested his hand lightly on the hilt of a sword. His face, as if set in stone, betrayed no emotion. She stared at the figure in disbelief. *I don't think I can stand it. I'm having a vision. He's not real.*

But he was real enough when Dr Neferatu nodded to him. Without a word, the man stepped towards her and grabbed her by the shoulders. Pushing her backwards so that she almost fell over, he forced her back to the Sun-Stone. As he roughly pinned her shoulders against the cold, wet rock, she tried to cry out for help, but the breath had already been knocked out of her. Gasping, she fought for air. "Leave me alone," was all she could whimper.

Dr Neferatu spoke from behind his accomplice. "We are indeed quite alone, I'm afraid."

Ikar leaned forward, putting his full weight against Rebecca's shoulders, completely immobilising her. She tried in vain to struggle, feeling the hardness of the stone against her back.

Dr Neferatu came forward, grabbed her hand again and held it tightly. As if he were draining the very life-energy out of her, she felt herself slowly losing her strength. Her knees started to buckle and her body sagged against the Stone.

She was on the point of passing out, when she noticed a flicker in Dr Neferatu's eyes. They were changing from brown back to green.

At last, he pulled his hand away. Barely conscious now, Rebecca saw him draw out what appeared to be a length of red silk cord from his pocket.

He gestured to Ikar to leave him space, wrapped the cord around his hands and stretched it taut. Quickly, he passed it over her head and twisted it around her neck. As he braced himself to draw it tight, the red thread stood out like veins over his white knuckles.

Dr Neferatu was now so close that Rebecca, struggling feebly, could smell his peculiar odour. It reminded her of a church. It was the unmistakably sweet, pungent smell of incense. She slowly started to drift into unconsciousness.

She barely heard the stranger's voice. It barked from the direction of the Moon-Stone, like a powerful command in some unknown tongue.

The sadistic smile disappeared off Dr Neferatu's face and was replaced by a look of pure incredulity. He closed his eyes and mouthed a silent curse. His hands still at Rebecca's neck, he turned slowly to face an imposing figure emerging from behind the Moon-Stone.

The figure held a short, bronze sword and, like Ikar, he had the appearance of a man from Mediterranean antiquity. Dressed in a kind of light armour, he wore a quilted cuirass, with leather thongs that hung down over a short white tunic. His hair, in ringlets, was sandy-coloured red. Tall and upright, he had the presence and authority of a high-ranking warrior.

Seeing him, Ikar sprang away from Rebecca, who, barely conscious, slumped heavily to the ground as Dr Neferatu let go of the cord.

The jolt shook her back to life and, through half-opened eyes, she tried to make sense of the scene before her. *Is this really happening in present-day Scotland?* She lay there, trembling.

Dr Neferatu stepped back, scowling as he recognised the exotic figure. "Ptolemy!" he spat out. Then he added "Soter" in a sarcastic tone.

Ikar immediately drew his sword and faced his adversary, raising the sword upright in front of him. Dr Neferatu discreetly stepped aside.

Ptolemy, his face impassive, slowly and deliberately brandished his sword in front of Ikar, as if challenging him to do battle.

The two opponents circled each other, before Ikar made the first move. Ptolemy parried the thrust almost casually.

Instantaneously, his expression changed. His eyes flashed with anger, and he leapt forward to take a swipe at Ikar's body. Ikar leapt backwards, the hissing blade slicing through his tunic.

The fight was bitter, the clang of striking metal echoing incongruously through the Scottish clearing. But it quickly became evident that Ptolemy was the superior fighter. As Ptolemy lunged forward with his sword, Ikar jumped sideways to avoid the blow and slipped on some mud. In an instant, Ptolemy brought his blade down, knocking Ikar's weapon from his hand.

Pulling his sword back to deliver the fatal blow, Ptolemy failed to notice a blur of movement at the side of his head.

The talons of a hawk ripped through his hair as it attacked him. He swung at the bird with his sword, missing it by inches. The bird soared upwards, turned and swooped again, keeping just out of range of his wild swipes.

Seizing his opportunity, Ikar rolled to one side, quickly retrieved his sword and retreated behind the Sun-Stone. The bird flew up again, circled once and calmly flew away.

Barely conscious, Rebecca lay at the foot of the Sun-Stone, frantically fearing what would happen next. She waited, frozen still, but there was no movement anywhere, not even a sound. Apprehensively, she edged herself up the Stone. Daring to take a fleeting look to one side, she nearly fainted again.

Ptolemy was leaning nonchalantly back against the Moon-Stone, his sword dangling from his hand. As her eyes widened, he stood upright and bowed his head towards her. With just a hint of a smile, he slid his sword back into its scabbard. Then he slipped silently behind the Moon-Stone and out of sight.

Rebecca closed her eyes and stood there, numb, fearful even to twitch. There was a complete silence around her. Only when it was broken by the caw of a rook, quickly followed by others, did she dare to open her eyes. The clearing seemed to come alive, as if nature itself sensed it could relax again. She nervously looked around, retrieved her bag and crept away from the Stones, very slowly turning round to look behind them. Dr Neferatu and the two adversaries, who had been physically fighting with swords just a minute previously, seemed to have completely disappeared.

She made her way unsteadily towards the path through the trees. There she halted, terrified her attackers could still be lying in wait in the undergrowth. Desperate to reach the safety of the car, she hesitated for a few seconds, her heart pounding, wondering what to do next.

Slowly it dawned on her that she was, indeed, entirely alone. It was almost as if the whole thing she had just witnessed had never happened, as if it had all been a horribly realistic nightmare. But the fierce pain in her shoulders where she had been held so brutally reminded her that, once again, it was only due to some kind of other-worldly protector that she had escaped with her life.

CHAPTER 46

Darkness was falling by the time Rebecca reached the shop. Bedraggled, she ran up to the front door and hammered on the doorbell, ignoring the 'Closed' sign.

The shopkeeper was still there doing the accounts, and quickly opened the door. "Come in, come in. What's happened? You look terrible, Miss. What's the matter?"

She fell into the shop, still shaking. "Someone just tried to kill me," she blurted out. "Someone I've met before. He really wanted to kill me, but I don't know why. I nearly died. I only got away because an amazing man with a sword came and rescued me. Then they all just disappeared, but I didn't know if they'd really gone…"

"Come and sit down," said the shopkeeper, taking her by the arm. He led her through to the back of the shop into an old-fashioned sitting-room, warmed by a roaring fire.

"Here now. Sit right down," he said, pulling up a chair. "Mother," he called out. "The girl's back, she's been attacked." He waited until she was seated. "Now, tell me again what happened. What do you mean – somebody tried to kill you?"

Before Rebecca could answer, the old lady came in, took one look, went up to Rebecca and held her hands. "You poor thing. I knew it wasn't a good idea to go to the Stones at this time of night." She held Rebecca by the hand and guided her to a comfortable armchair in front of the fire. "Now, you warm yourself up, and I'll make some tea."

"We should call the police," the shopkeeper said.

"No, no. Don't do that," said Rebecca. "It's all been a bit weird, and I don't think they would believe me. Just let me stay here a bit, if that's okay. I'll be fine in a few minutes."

The old lady turned around at the door. "Don't even think about going anywhere. You're staying here the night, you're safe in this house. Let me get the tea and you can tell us exactly what happened. Tomorrow, we can decide what to do."

"Thank you. That's kind. I'm probably not in a fit state to drive, anyway." She began to relax as she sat by the fire. Here she felt safe and secure, even though the couple were almost total strangers.

"Do you mind if I make a couple of phone calls?" she asked.

"Of course not," said the shopkeeper. "We'll leave you to it." He left the room and headed for the kitchen.

Rebecca got through to Syreeta immediately. "Sy – it's happened again."

"What do you mean? Are you all right?"

"Neferatu tried to kill me. Just now. You know, the slimy-looking man who was on Easter Island. He's right here in Scotland. He was at the conference. Then, when I went to see these old stones, he suddenly appeared out of nowhere and tried to strangle me."

"Where are you? I'll come right over."

"No, no. I'm okay now – really. I'm with a kind couple in Insch. They're looking after me – they're insisting I stay the night. I just wanted to tell you about it. Don't worry, I'll be okay. See you tomorrow."

"But now I am worried about you. He may still be hanging around there. If someone tried to kill you, he could try again."

"It's okay. I'm safe now. But there's something horrible happening here. Can't tell you now, but that weirdo Neferatu wants me dead."

There was a long silence at Syreeta's end.

"You think I'm making all this up, don't you?" said Rebecca.

"No, of course I don't. I just don't know what to do."

"I told you, I'll be all right," said Rebecca, and she ended the call.

Shaken, Syreeta was staring at her phone, when it rang again.

"Syreeta? Charles here. How's the redheads story going?"

"I've just been speaking to Rebecca. She's been attacked again. Here, in Scotland! Somebody just tried to kill her again – to strangle her."

"Is she okay? I think it's time she came right off this story."

"She says she's safe now. She's staying with a couple in Insch for the night. They're looking after her."

"What the hell is going on up there? I didn't think she could get into trouble in Aberdeen, of all places. And what on earth are you doing there? But listen – listen carefully. Something much bigger is blowing up now. The Earth's magnetic field is changing…"

"I know. I heard about it from Rebecca's scientist contact here."

"Well, we're forming a team to handle it. Mick Green, the science correspondent, is heading it up for the time being. I'm on it, with my contacts. And you're on it, as well. Put something together on what you got from Rebecca's contact, and get it to me tonight. Like, pronto!"

"But what about Rebecca?"

"This is a big story!" Charles said, and put the phone down.

Syreeta got through to Jim immediately.

"Jim – it's Syreeta. Rebecca's been attacked again. I've just spoken to her. Someone tried to kill her, strangle her. Some pervert called Neferatu, or something like that."

"What? You're kidding! Why would he do that? How did she sound when you spoke to her?"

"Very upset. I'm really worried, Jim. Something very peculiar is going on, and it's getting much too dangerous. She may not be so lucky next time." She explained that Rebecca was being looked after by the couple in Insch.

"I'll give her a bell," said Jim.

While the old lady made the tea, Rebecca received three calls in quick succession. Charles was concerned as well, but wary. She had the feeling that he was beginning to doubt her mental stability, that he could even drop her from her story.

Jim wanted to know exactly what had happened, but he sounded distant, somehow. Not really troubled. She had hoped he would rush straight over, but instead he said he would meet her at the Newton Stones, first thing the next morning.

Larry, on the other hand, had sounded genuinely worried. Satisfied that she was in good hands, he had promised to come along with Jim.

Now, while his mother poured the tea, the shopkeeper sat himself opposite her. "You sound as if you're from Edinburgh?" he said.

"That's right – Rebecca Burns. But I work in London. I'm a journalist."

"Keith MacGregor. And this is my mother, Mary. Now, tell us – what happened to you today?"

"Don't push her, Keith," said Mrs MacGregor. "She's in shock, aren't you? You can tell us in your own time." She rummaged in a cupboard and came back with a large tin of biscuits. "Listen, dear," she said. "Can I ask you a rather strange question? Did you happen to see a caveman at the Stones?"

"Well – yes. Yes I did. But how could you know that?"

"Oh, you're not the first one. It's always people with red hair who see him. Quite often they see a fox as well."

Rebecca was stunned. "Yes, there was a fox as well. It seemed almost friendly. Actually, the caveman turned out to be quite harmless, though he looked a bit scary. I didn't get the feeling he wanted to hurt me. It was the other two who tried to kill me. They tried to strangle me."

After telling them what had happened, she sank back into the armchair. "I don't think it will do any good at all to involve the police. They'll just think I'm mad."

"That's up to you, Rebecca," said Keith. "But we're very happy you're staying here tonight."

A black cat appeared at the door and jumped up on to his lap.

"Tam here will keep an eye on you. Won't you, Tam?" He stroked the cat until it settled down, purring loudly.

"It's raw outside. Right now, I'm going to make us all some broth. Then you can have some dinner with us," announced Mrs MacGregor.

Over dinner Rebecca found herself recounting to the astonished couple the whole series of events that had led to her horrific encounter earlier that evening. By the time they had finished eating, Rebecca felt that she was in the company of long-term friends.

When the grandfather clock chimed ten, Mrs MacGregor stoked the embers of the dying fire. After disappearing for a few minutes, she returned holding a towel and a nightie. "I've prepared your room," she said. "It's nice and cosy."

Rebecca hugged them both. Closing her bedroom door firmly, she parted the curtains and looked out through the window. It was jet black outside. Carefully checking that all the windows were firmly shut, she closed the curtains again.

Downstairs, Keith MacGregor opened the back door of the house. Tam looked outside and, encouraged by a nudge from Keith's foot, reluctantly made his way across the garden lawn, as the door closed behind him.

He was about halfway across the lawn, when a great swooping bird plunged down and seized him by the head. It flew off into the darkness of the night, gripping the cat between its talons.

CHAPTER 47

The trees surrounding the Newton Stones swayed gently in the light breeze, and a weak morning sun was slowly driving away the chill of the night.

Larry and Jim were waiting for Rebecca. She was already ten minutes late. Larry rubbed his hands together for warmth and listened as Jim explained the scientific background to the threatened pole switch.

"You are supposed to get this weakening in the magnetic field just before the poles switch over. But since the last time the poles switched was 780 million years ago, you could say we're long overdue for another flip. It happens on average, if you can talk about averages, every 500 million years, but when it does flip, things can happen extremely fast. Apparently, huge magnetic changes have occurred in just a few weeks."

He checked the time on his watch. "Where on earth has she got to? Shall I give her a bell?"

"Give her a few more minutes," said Larry. "But do you really think there's going to be a switchover? It seems a bit catastrophic. What about all the incredible disruption it would cause?"

"Well, there's also the possibility of partial flips – what they call geomagnetic excursions," said Jim. "Sometimes the flip is major, but not quite total, in which case the North Pole will move a long way from its original position. The last one like that was only 30,000 years ago. They called it the Mungo excursion, because it was first identified in rocks at Lake Mungo, in Australia. Since then, it's been detected in rocks all over the world. Geologically speaking, it was just a blip, and it only lasted a few thousand years."

"You do seem to be up to speed on it all," said Larry.

"I know all this because I was up at six this morning looking it all up," replied Jim.

"It sounds like a bit of a potential disaster. Shouldn't the government be doing something about it? At least warning people about the chaos that could to hit us? Giving us a bit of advice?"

"Not wishing to belittle their intelligence at all, but the government isn't too good at science," said Jim. "It prefers to manipulate the truth, until it becomes self-evident. They don't get it, and by the time they do begin to get it, it's too late. It's the same with global warming. Half the cabinet would be in denial if a switch happened, hoping it would go away."

He was looking at his watch again, when they heard a car draw up. "About bloody time," he said.

Rebecca rushed up, out of breath and flustered. "I'm sorry I'm late. We were looking for the MacGregors' cat. It's disappeared."

"Did you find it?" asked Larry.

"No. It's probably stuck up some tree."

It took a moment for Rebecca to take in the scene, now lit by sunshine and peopled with familiar faces.

Larry immediately took her arm. "You poor thing," he said.

But Jim still seemed cool. "Okay. Let's hear what happened again," he said.

What the hell is up with you? she thought.

She became agitated as she recalled the events of the night before. "You know it was that weirdo, Neferatu – your friend," she said angrily. "I couldn't believe it. He actually tried to strangle me, with the help of his really nasty accomplice – a guy dressed like somebody out of the Bible – complete with sword. Neferatu called him Ikar – I remember that. Mrs MacGregor thought that was who the Sun-Stone commemorated."

"Hang on a sec," said Jim. "Neferatu? Are you kidding? He hardly knows you."

"I know it was him. For Christ's sake, I was close enough to him. He had his horrible hands round my neck!"

"And why, of all the people on this planet, do you think you qualify for the special attention of Dr Neferatu?"

"Jim…" Larry interjected.

"Listen to me," said Rebecca. "I have done absolutely nothing to provoke all this. I've hardly met the man. But I know one thing – he's spooky. He's revolting, he smells disgusting, and I want nothing to do with him. But he's stalking me, and for some reason he wants me dead. And he's damn well nearly succeeded. *Twice.* That bird-man priest on Easter Island was him, I know it. It's unbelievable, but there it is."

"Then what happened?" said Larry, before Jim could comment.

Rebecca hesitated. "I don't know how to tell you this. You probably won't believe me – you'll think I've been having a fit or something. Anyway, just as Neferatu was about to do me in, another man appeared. He was dressed like some sort of ancient warrior, somebody very powerful. And I don't mean fancy dress. He was old, as in antique. And very strong – he had huge arms and shoulders. Neferatu called him Ptolemy. Then he added 'Soter', whatever that means."

"What!" cut in Larry. "Did you say Ptolemy Soter? He was one of Alexander the Great's right-hand men. God, he was the Ptolemy who founded the Ptolemaic dynasty in Egypt. 'Soter' means 'saviour.'"

"I don't know who he was," said Rebecca, "but he definitely acted like somebody very important. Anyhow, he saved me – Neferatu backed off just like that. Ptolemy wasn't the least bit afraid of Neferatu – or his foul friend. After that, I just about passed out. But when I came to – you have to believe me – Ptolemy and the Ikar guy were having a really serious swordfight. All over the place. Not Neferatu, though – he just stood well back from it all."

"A swordfight? Ptolemy Soter?" Jim cut in mockingly. "And now I bet you're going to tell us this Ptolemy Soter won and saved you? You've been dreaming, woman."

"I'm sorry, but this was real," snapped Rebecca. "Real swordfight. Real swords. And it happened right here – yesterday evening."

Larry walked around the muddy, churned-up grass and crouched down to study it. "Well, something has definitely been going on here recently," he said.

"That's probably us, this morning," said Jim dismissively.

"It's not where we were standing," said Larry. "And look here – somebody's been skidding around all over the place. We weren't crashing around like this." He drew no response from Jim, other than a shrug. "What about the two who had a swordfight? What did they look like?" Larry continued.

"The one who saved me? He was dressed like a sort of ancient warrior. Like a Greek warrior, I suppose. Except that he didn't have a helmet. I could see his hair – sort of sandy-coloured red."

"What about the other one?" asked Jim.

"The one called Ikar? He had the same sort of clothes. White, sort of Mediterranean style as well, with bare arms and legs and a short cloak. He was wearing a hat – more like a cap I suppose – white, and pointed on top. He had black hair. And he had a beard as well – it was done in rows of neat curls."

"So Ptolemy Soter won the fight and saved you," said Larry. "What happened after that?"

"The good guy, Ptolemy, was just about to kill the bad guy. Then the bird attacked him."

"What bird?" said Jim.

"Where did the bird come from, Rebecca?" asked Larry.

She pointed to the Sun-Stone. "It flew in and landed on that Stone. It was a bit like a hawk. Smaller than the eagle that attacked Jim and me in Orkney, but really evil-looking, if you can say that about a bird. It just sat there, staring at me. Scared me silly." She wondered again why Jim was so unsympathetic. But at least Larry was kind and understanding.

"How did Neferatu come to be there?" asked Larry.

"Well, that's it, I'm not sure. I never heard him coming. He seemed to just appear, all of a sudden."

"You didn't hear a car?" asked Jim.

"Oh no, nothing. One second there was no one about at all. The next moment, there he was."

Jim raised his eyes in disbelief. "This is all a bit difficult to take. You make it sound as if he just arrived by magic."

Rebecca flushed. "Look. I'm not trying to make it look weirder than it was. All I know is that Neferatu wasn't there – and then he was. And the very next moment he was trying to strangle me with a piece of cord. Dammit, my shoulders are still hurting from the other man pinning me to the Stone."

"What happened to the bird?" asked Larry.

"I don't know. It flew away, I suppose."

"We should call the police," Larry said.

"Oh yes, you really think the police are going to believe any of this?" said Rebecca.

"Dead right," said Jim.

"Was there anything else, Rebecca?" said Larry.

"Yes – so many weird things. I almost forgot about him. Before all this happened, right at the beginning, there was some sort of caveman-like figure, who came out of nowhere and walked right past me. Look, I'm really not kidding. This really happened. I saw him."

"So what did he look like? Red hair again, I suppose?" said Jim.

Rebecca gave him a sick smile. "Actually, yes. As a matter of fact, he did, all over his body as far as I could see. He was wearing some sort of animal skin. He was quite stocky, and he had big bushy eyebrows and a big wide nose. Incredibly strong-looking."

"So now we've got Neanderthals in Scotland, have we?" said Jim.

Larry frowned at him. "What happened to him, Rebecca?"

Rebecca touched the Moon-Stone. "He went behind the Stone.

I know this sounds funny, but he just seemed to disappear. When I looked behind the Stone, he had gone, but there was a fox there. Mrs MacGregor said people with red hair sometimes see the caveman and the fox. She had warned me not to come here."

Larry looked intrigued. "I wonder…"

"You wonder what?" said Jim.

"It's just that, if red-haired prehistoric man had a totemic animal, then the fox would make an excellent candidate."

Jim shook his head impatiently. "And what happened to the others?" he said.

"I just don't know. The one who rescued me disappeared behind this Stone as well. The other guy seemed to vanish, too."

"And Dr Neferatu?" asked Larry.

"He just disappeared as well."

"What happened after that?"

"Nothing else. That was enough," replied Rebecca.

"Were you still feeling ill?" asked Jim. "You have been under quite a lot of strain."

Rebecca suddenly lost patience. "I might have had the remains of a hangover, if that's what you're trying to say, but I was certainly not dreaming all this. It was definitely Neferatu – no doubt about that. And he was definitely trying to strangle me. You don't make mistakes about things like that, you know. Neferatu is truly nasty, and I'm petrified of what he might do next. Okay?"

She glared at Jim. "And another thing. His eyes have always been green, right? Well, last night they were brown. But here's the weirdest thing of all – when he grabbed my hand and wouldn't let go, they changed back to green again. That's when I just about passed out. I almost had the feeling he was recharging his own energy by holding my hand."

"I've never noticed his eyes change colour," said Jim.

"Oh, come off it, Jim," said Larry. "Remember the conference dinner? Maybe his eyes weren't brown, but they were positively dull. He looked years older. You even commented on it yourself."

"So he was knackered," said Jim. "He travels all over the world."

Larry ignored him. "Rebecca – has anything like this happened to you before? Before Easter Island, for example?"

"No – never!" replied Rebecca emphatically. "It's all getting completely out of hand, and it's bloody terrifying if you want to know."

"So it seems a lot of your apparitions had red hair. What about the rotting man?" said Jim.

"He did actually have a little red beard, now you mention it," Rebecca said.

"You do accept that, so far, no one else has witnessed any of these things you're talking about," Jim persisted.

"For God's sake, I *did* see those things. And Señor Nata and his family saw the same things as me on Easter Island. They told me. Before Señor Nata was murdered." Tears of exasperation welled up in her eyes.

"Listen, Rebecca, this is no slur on you, but you did seem to go into a sort of trance that evening on Easter Island," said Larry sympathetically. "Do you remember what happened before you saw those things at the dinner?"

"I think I was looking at the carving the old lady was holding. I felt quite mesmerised by it. Then there was all the drumming…"

"I think that old lady on Easter Island could have been a shaman," declared Jim. "People do believe that shamans can enter the spirit world. It's pure superstition, of course. It's just that they are able to put themselves into a trance and have visions."

"Are you saying I'm a shaman?" said Rebecca.

Jim ignored the question. "And what about this time?" he asked. "What were you doing here at the Stones before you saw these visions, or whatever they were?"

Rebecca went over to the Moon-Stone and touched the serpent. "I was looking at the Stone. Especially the serpent – I was completely absorbed in it, drawn into it. Wondering who on earth could have carved it. And what it means."

"Look, Rebecca," said Jim, "if you want to know the truth, I think that, somehow, you've been going into trances and seeing things. Drumbeats, hypnotic music, fixing your concentration on certain symbols – they are all classic devices for inducing trances. Tell me, do you use drugs?"

Rebecca felt like screaming at him. "No, I do not," she retorted. "Nor do I eat magic mushrooms. I'm just a normal person, trying to live a normal life. Okay?"

Jim deliberated for a moment. "Maybe, just maybe…" he said. "I'm wondering if there's some sort of connection between all of this and these recent changes in the Earth's magnetic field."

"Now what are you talking about?" said Rebecca, unsure whether to take him seriously.

"Larry and I were talking about it before you arrived here this morning. It so happens that, at this moment, the Earth's magnetic field is weakening in odd places and letting through a lot of solar radiation. This could be behind what happened on Easter Island. It's also probably the reason why there've been all these strong auroras, and could be why our mobiles packed up in Orkney. It's very odd that these things you've been seeing are coinciding with the weakening of the magnetic field. Maybe it's affecting the electrical activity in your brain."

"But why just me?" said Rebecca bleakly.

"Not just you. Possibly redheads in general. Perhaps people with red hair have something a bit different in the make-up of their brains," said Jim, warming to the theme. "Something that makes you more susceptible to changes in the magnetic field." He stroked his chin as he thought. "Have you heard of fMR imaging? Sorry – functional magnetic resonance?"

"Oh, do me a favour," groaned Rebecca.

"No, I'm trying to help you – really. I'd like to know what's going on. fMR imaging is a way of monitoring brain activity. We could give it a try, if you like. I know someone who could do it. We would just try to put you into a trance, in a controlled experiment. You're definitely seeing things we're not seeing. And this might show us why."

Rebecca reacted immediately. "No thank you. Definitely not. You're mad. I've just about had enough of weird and wonderful happenings. Anyway, suppose your friend Neferatu appears again and tries to finish me off."

"Perhaps we can find out why Neferatu wants to kill you. And we'd be there, with an expert clinical team. You'd be completely safe – I can definitely assure you of that."

"I'm sorry. I really don't like the idea of people messing about with my brain," said Rebecca.

"Well, look at it this way," said Jim. "You say that people's lives are in danger, as well as your own. And what about the story you're doing? Think how much it could add to it."

In fact, Rebecca's thoughts had already been racing in the same direction. "Okay, what exactly does it involve?"

"It's completely painless and won't do you any harm. Loads of people have it done. It's like a body scan, but only looking at the head. You can see in the scan which parts of the brain are active, because they light up."

"I still don't see how that's going to help."

"It could tell us which parts of the brain are involved when you see things. How you can see things that we can't see."

Rebecca turned to Larry for reassurance. "What do you think, Larry?

"It could be worth a try, Rebecca," Larry replied. "I don't see any harm in it."

Rebecca looked hard at Larry, but he seemed to have no doubts. "Well, if you're absolutely sure. But I can't say I'm happy – I've had just about as many horrible experiences as I can take for the time being." She turned back to Jim. "Okay then. Let's get it over and done with. What do I have to do?"

"We can do it at the Medical School in Strathclyde. An old uni friend of mine, Rambo, works in the Neurobiology Department. I'm sure he could arrange it."

Rebecca instantly turned red. "Rambo! You've got to be joking!"

"He's actually called Professor Rameshwar Chalapathi Rao," said Jim.

"Well, that's all right then, isn't it," said Rebecca. She calmed down and sighed. "Can we just get on with it then."

"I'll try and fix it for tomorrow. It should be quite fun. We're going to have to reproduce in the lab the same conditions that were present when you started seeing things."

"I'm glad *you* think it should be fun," said Rebecca. "Anyway, you're going to have a job to reproduce Easter Island and the Newton Stones here."

"I think that there was something special about the wooden carving the old lady had, and even this serpent here," Jim went on enthusiastically.

"What about them?" said Rebecca.

"They could have acted like an icon, a powerful symbol that can activate certain parts of the brain. Looking at an icon can put some people into a trance. They can be used as aids for prayer. Like the Russian icons. Larry, have you got a picture of the serpent?"

"I'll take one now," said Larry, taking out his camera.

"Well, I think I'll just go back to the MacGregors," Rebecca said. "I want to pick up the papers there, and I want to see if they've found Tam yet."

"Will you be okay?" said Jim. "If so, I'll go back with Larry in his car. You can hang on to mine, but don't be too long. We'll start getting worried about you!"

"Thanks. See you later," Rebecca said, picking up her bag.

As he watched her go, Jim fetched out his mobile. "Rambo. Jim Cavendish here…"

CHAPTER 48

Mrs MacGregor was alone in the shop when Rebecca arrived.

"Has Tam come back yet?" Rebecca asked, but she could already read the answer on Mrs MacGregor's face.

"Keith's still out looking for him."

"I expect he's found a friend, or just gone on an adventure. It's bound to be something simple like that."

"He's never done it before. He's never failed to come back in the morning, demanding his breakfast."

Rebecca was drawn to the piles of newspapers on the counter. Copies of the *Metropolitan* were still tied up with string.

"I haven't had time to sort them out yet," said Mrs MacGregor.

"Do you mind if I just have a look at the *Metropolitan*?"

"I'll get some scissors for you."

Even as she cut the string around the bundle of papers, Rebecca could make out the headlines. They were totally dominated by the magnetic field story. But across the very top of the page was something that made her rip a paper from the bundle:

'POLE SWITCH CRISIS:

Exclusive interview with top scientist. Page 5'

Her hands shook as she fumbled to find the right page. Then she swore so loudly that Mrs MacGregor, startled, stopped dead in her tracks. Prominently displayed was a picture of Syreeta Dasgupta, with her name in bold letters. The interview was with Dr James Cavendish.

Stony-faced, Rebecca was scrutinising the piece in all its details, when the shop door opened and the bell tinkled. An ashen-faced Keith MacGregor walked in slowly, his head bowed, with something in his hand.

He went up to his mother with tears in his eyes. "I'm so sorry,

Mother. I found this over the way, on the bank of the burn." He placed a cat's collar with a nametag on it on the counter. Mrs MacGregor looked distraught.

Her son put his arm around her. "Something took him. I thought at first it was a fox, but, you know, the collar isn't chewed up at all, like it would be with a fox. I can't be sure, but I have a bad feeling about it. Look at what I found wrapped round the collar. I have a terrible fear that someone has done this deliberately. But who would want to? You see, no animal could have done this."

He held up a long piece of red cord, letting it dangle from his hand.

CHAPTER 49

Professor Rameshwar Chalapathi Rao was rapidly gaining a worldwide reputation, along with a growing exposure in the media, for his work on the human brain and human consciousness. His main research area was the mechanisms of mystic experiences, an interest sparked in part by his Indian background and familiarity with Hinduism.

He and his postgraduate student, Wally Campbell, were very different. Professor Chalapathi Rao was short, slight and proud of his collection of bow ties. Wally Campbell was big and built for tossing cabers. He was scruffy, happiest in jeans and frequently took to wearing a T-shirt with 'Braveheart' emblazoned on it. Now the two of them were preparing Rebecca for the scan.

The magnetic resonance imaging unit, or MRI, was in the middle of the room. It consisted largely of a huge cylinder, which looked like a gigantic doughnut, with a hole in the middle into which the patient's head was inserted.

Rebecca was lying in a green hospital gown on a narrow bed and was beginning to have second thoughts as her head was fixed into a brace, so that it would not move during the experiment.

"Can I just put this over your head, Rebecca?" said Rambo, fitting what appeared to be a large mask over her eyes. "Right, we'll test it now. If anyone's got a mobile phone, just make sure it's switched off, please."

"Mine's off already," said Rebecca.

Jim went to switch his off. "If the solar radiation increases any more, there'll be far bigger problems to worry about than just mobile phones," he said, glancing at the scanner.

Wally raised an eyebrow and pressed a button on a small digital camera which was linked to a computer. This was connected to the mask on Rebecca's face, and the effect was immediate.

She found herself looking at a scene of spring woodland, with a carpet of bluebells and green-leaved trees.

"Can you see the image yet, Rebecca?" Rambo asked.

"Yes, it's lovely. As long as it's all like this, I won't feel so nervous."

Larry and Jim were setting up a camcorder to record Rebecca's reactions in the experiment.

"One thing, Rambo," asked Larry. "There's a massive magnet in the scanner, isn't there? Doesn't the electromagnetic field have some effect on the brain?"

"Not that I know of. At least, nothing like that has been reported, and millions of scans have been done," said Rambo. "Still, this experiment is new territory," he admitted.

"We're set up now, Rambo," said Jim.

"Nearly there," Rambo replied, as Rebecca slid towards the machine, so that her head was in the hole. "I can assure you, Rebecca, you won't feel a thing," he said.

She felt that Rambo at least acknowledged her presence in the room as a human being, and not merely a passive object in an experiment.

"This is really cutting-edge stuff, Rambo," said Larry, visibly impressed with the experimental set-up. "I'm afraid I've got rather out of date."

"Yes. Things have moved fast in this area. My particular field is looking at how human consciousness is different to that of animals. Nowadays this is all much sexier than astrophysics." He glanced, smiling at Jim.

"Why's that?" asked Larry.

"The speed at which we're finding out how the human brain works. We have learned a lot by studying people with neurological disorders caused by head injuries, strokes and the like. And that's now taking us into the big philosophical questions. What really is consciousness? What is free will? Who am I?"

"I'm still Rebecca! At least I hope so," said a voice from the machine.

"Sorry, Rebecca," said Rambo. "Just getting a bit carried away. We're ready to go now. Are you quite comfortable?"

"As comfortable as I'm ever going to be in this contraption. Can I move around?"

"To some extent. But you won't be able to move your head. First, we're going to show Rebecca a picture of the serpent. Ready, Wally?"

Wally pressed the button on the camera again.

"Can you see it, Rebecca?" asked Rambo.

"Yes, very clearly. It's the carving of the serpent on the Moon-Stone."

"That's good," said Rambo. "The serpent is one of the most potent ancient symbols."

"Concentrate hard on the serpent, Rebecca," said Jim. "Try and let your mind focus on the image."

"If you really want to know what I'm concentrating on, it's that interview you gave to Syreeta," Rebecca hissed. "That was so sneaky."

"Don't worry. Everybody'll be doing stories on the magnetic field, now," Jim said. "But this one here could be much more interesting."

"Please try to be quiet, everybody," said Rambo.

Rebecca tried again to concentrate on the picture.

"Anything happening, Rebecca?" asked Jim, after a minute.

"No – but I don't feel exactly relaxed. What am I supposed to do? Hypnotise myself or something? All you lot are making me feel nervous."

"Anything unusual on the monitor, Rambo?" Jim asked.

"No – just normal."

"Rebecca, you could try to memorise the image. Then close your eyes," suggested Jim.

Rebecca studied the picture and closed her eyes.

"Anything yet?" asked Jim, after about thirty seconds.

"No – I just can't concentrate."

"Right, let's start again," Jim said. "Larry and I will sit quietly in the corner of the room and shut up. Just pretend we're not here."

"Some hope," said Rebecca.

"Just a thought," Larry said. "Can you remember anything that happened at the Stones, before the things you told us about?"

"Nothing really. It was very quiet – only the rooks cawing and water dripping. It had just stopped raining."

"I don't think we can do much about the rooks," said Jim.

"But the water – was it near you?" asked Larry.

"I suppose so. There was water dripping somewhere near the Stones."

"Is there a tap here, Rambo?" Larry called over.

"Over there. Put a tray in the sink if you want to make it louder."

Larry set the tap dripping steadily. Then he started the camcorder again and sat down with Jim at the back of the lab.

"Ready? Let's go again," said Rambo, pressing buttons.

Rebecca gazed at the serpent and closed her eyes. She began to breathe deeply and regularly.

Rambo looked puzzled and moved closer to the monitor. An area towards the back of the brain was rapidly changing colour, as it was becoming active.

"My God. This is a bit of a first," Rambo whispered. "The cerebellum is lighting up."

CHAPTER 50

The image of the serpent began to fade slowly, and Rebecca felt her mind drifting, as if into a waking dream.

The figure of a woman, in her early thirties, was walking towards her, dressed flamboyantly in bright blue trousers and a smock in a colourful floral design. Her eyes, which peered through a fringe of ginger hair, were heavily made up with green eye shadow, and she had a blob of yellow paint on her cheek.

She leaned over Rebecca affectionately. "You will drink your milk, won't you, Rebecca, dear. You know Daddy would like that," she said softly, in a Scottish accent.

"Yes, Mummy," replied Rebecca, in the voice of a little girl.

Rambo looked over to Jim and Larry, clearly puzzled at hearing the different voices. Jim crept over to the camcorder and checked that it was functioning correctly.

Still smiling, Rebecca's mother gradually disappeared, and another figure took her place. He was an elderly man, bald but with a fox-red clipped moustache and dressed in a brown tweed suit. He was flushed and clearly very irritated.

"I always said that Mr Blair was a charlatan," he told her, clenching his fists.

Jim and Larry sat there, stunned at hearing Rebecca speak in a man's voice. Rambo studied the monitor closely.

The man in turn was swiftly replaced by a Highlander, in full nineteenth century dress tartan, complete with plaid slung over his shoulders, kilt and sporran. She recognised the tartan of deep blues and greens as clan Campbell, the clan to which the Burns belonged. It was the tartan she had worn as a kilt, when learning Scottish dancing at school. He spoke in what Rebecca thought was Gaelic, although she could not understand what he was saying. "*Na biodh sgàth ort.*"

"That was Gaelic she was speaking," said Wally quietly.

As this vision, too, faded, Rebecca lay there, breathing deeply. But suddenly, her calm was interrupted and she became agitated. A powerfully built and forbiddingly stern figure was striding towards her, in what appeared to be a bleak desert landscape, a sword strapped to his side. He seemed determined to say something to her.

She recognised him instantly. It was the extraordinary figure that Neferatu had called Ptolemy. He came closer and closer, until his head was next to hers, and said something to her in a tongue she did not understand. But there was no doubting the authoritative tone. He stepped back and looked at her, a hint of concern in his expression, before turning to walk back across the rough terrain.

The feelings of terror she had felt at the Newton Stones now came flooding back to her. As he, in turn, faded from her vision, she was still twitching with fear. She lay there, trembling, wondering if she were in some way losing control of her mind.

"I don't believe it," said Larry. "That was a man's voice again. And it sounded like he was speaking some form of classical Greek."

A grey mist seemed to swirl around Rebecca, only to melt away as another scene unfolded. It was as if she were watching a film in 3D, and yet a film so realistic that she was somehow part of it. The air around her was growing warmer and, hearing the gentle sounds of waves breaking on a shore, she knew she was near the sea.

It was a moonless night, but the sky was clear and the stars were bright enough to light up low buildings in a town. A few dim lights flickered behind glassless windows, but otherwise there was no evidence of anyone around. Then there came the sound of urgent footsteps, faint at first, but rapidly growing louder. Four figures came into view, walking quickly down a cobbled street, towards the sounds of the sea. Rebecca could see that two of them were women, one older than the other, her titian hair sprinkled with grey and tied in a bun behind her head. The younger woman, a girl in her late teens, bore a distinct resemblance to the older woman. She had deep red long hair, worn loose under a gold band. Both wore cloaks wrapped around them, but she could see that their dresses reached down to their slippered feet. The other two figures were clearly soldiers, who she could see were attired Roman-style and, judging by the plumes in their helmets, high-ranking.

As the party swept round a corner, a harbour came into view, with a group of men waiting anxiously on the quayside. One was holding a rope attached to a small dinghy and, among the fishing boats anchored in the harbour, she could see the outline of a far larger boat. A Roman galley.

Reaching the quayside and the dinghy, the two soldiers stepped back and looked around warily. The woman and the girl stopped and embraced each other. Rebecca heard them talking to each other in low, passionate tones, and managed to recognise several words of the language they were speaking as Latin. But it was being spoken so fast and in such an accent that it was impossible for her to decipher what they were saying.

Then she heard the older woman mention the name 'Cleopatra'. One of the soldiers called out "Selene", urging her to release the girl.

A large group of people approached, running and shouting. The soldiers moved to separate the women, still embracing and then holding outstretched hands to each other. One soldier swiftly half-lifted the girl into the dinghy. It was moving even as she fell into it.

The dinghy headed towards the galley while the older woman stood waving, tears pouring down her cheeks. Flanked by the two soldiers, she turned slowly to defiantly face the crowd of people that had poured on to the quay.

The newcomers stopped in their tracks, realising they had arrived too late. At the head of the crowd, fuming with silent rage, stood a man. Rebecca gasped as she recognised his face. It was unmistakably Neferatu, dressed in a Roman toga.

"It's him again! What's happening?" she cried out. Before she could react, a dense darkness and profound silence fell around her.

Jim moved to the edge of his seat. "What does she mean, 'It's him again'?"

Rambo put a finger to his lips.

"I think I know," said Larry under his breath, visibly alarmed. "Rambo – be ready to stop this experiment. I don't like the way it's going."

CHAPTER 51

Rebecca was now conscious only of her own breathing and the blood pumping through her ears. The air around her chilled slightly, and she shivered, feeling goose-pimples form on her arms.

A pinpoint of light appeared. It grew slowly at first, and then so rapidly that she was dazzled. Strange symbols: zigzags, spirals, concentric circles and moving dots, formed at the periphery of her vision. They danced around, changing colour and shape, and then faded.

The light shrank back again to a small bright ball, which started to flicker at its edges. Slowly, it became a dancing flame. As she watched it, a man's face became visible to one side, followed by his crouching body, lit up by the glow.

There was a certain sensitivity about his face. His eyes were pale blue and twinkled with intelligence. He was fine-featured and, with his luxuriant red beard, he had the look of a bohemian artist. But for his extraordinary attire, he would not have drawn a second glance in a modern city.

He was wearing a leather cap, tied under his chin by leather straps. A pair of antlers was fixed to the top of the cap. As he stood up, she saw that his body was covered by a long sack-like garment, made up of a patchwork of various fur pelts crudely stitched together in a checkerboard fashion. Odder still, sea shells were tied on to the longer pieces of fur, so that they rattled when he moved. Long leather strips hung in profusion from the pelts, to form a fringe around his legs below the knees. Around his neck, he wore a necklace of pierced shells strung on a leather thong.

The flame came from a small bowl, perched on a rock-mound, which contained a greasy looking liquid, together with a wick made of twisted strands of fur. The light fell on to a rough wall, which stretched away on either side into the darkness. Occasionally, the flame sputtered and flared momentarily to light up other walls and part of a rock ceiling. Rebecca realised she was in a cave. As the man moved, the sounds from the shells echoed, and she sensed the cave was very large.

The man reached for a leather flagon and drank from it. Next, he picked up another small bowl, this one full of red liquid. He dipped his finger into it and stood, staring at the wall for a full minute.

Then, he started to paint on the wall with his forefinger. He drew an outline first, quickly and intuitively, stopping only to dip his finger into the pigment. Sometimes, he changed to another bowl containing a black liquid and switched colours. He alternated between them, occasionally wiping his finger on a piece of fur next to the bowls.

Gradually the figure of a stag took shape, heavily stylised, but easily recognisable. A natural bump in the rock became its swollen flank, and cracks in the wall became parts of the antlers, so that the living rock and the paint combined to become the stag.

The form of the animal completed, he took a step back, studied it and closed his eyes as if meditating. Opening them again, he stepped forwards, picked up the bowl of black pigment and marked a series of small dots inside and outside the form of the animal.

A happy expression spread over his face, as if he were satisfied with his finished work. Dipping his whole hand into the red liquid, he smeared it on his face, before picking up the bowl and pouring the remaining contents into his mouth. He then placed his hand palm-down on to an unpainted part of the rock close to the painting and blew the contents of his mouth in a spray on to and around his hand. When he took his hand away, the outline of it was clearly imprinted on the bare rock.

Stepping backwards again to view his work, he studied it for several minutes, wiping his hand on the piece of fur. He then lifted his head, sniffing the air, and pawed the ground, first with one foot, then with the other. Finally, he gently shook his antlers and, leaving the lamp on the floor of the cave, turned and disappeared into the darkness.

Jim crept silently over to Rambo, who was glued to the screen.

"What's going on? Why's she gone so quiet?" whispered Jim.

"I don't know," said Rambo, glancing up. "But the cerebellum's still very active."

CHAPTER 52

As Rebecca gazed at the lamp, hypnotised, the white light stopped flickering and grew in size, until the image of a full moon appeared, the features of the lunar landscape clearly discernable. Below the moon, she could see the sea, glittering with reflected moonlight.

From the shoreline, a dark forest stretched sharply upwards, eventually thinning to a barren landscape of rocks and boulders, strewn over a hillside.

High above, the moon lit up a range of snow-covered mountains, which soared dramatically into a crystal-clear sky. Never before had she seen stars shining so brightly.

She felt her senses intensely heightened as the sweet, distinctive scent of pines drifted around her and a warm breeze brushed her cheeks. It was as if some long lost primordial sense had been switched on in her brain, so that she was omnipresent, part of everything, yet independent of it, like a visiting spirit.

About two hundred yards up the hill was a cliff-face, cut by deep gullies and gorges, which disappeared into blackness. At the base of the cliff, she could make out dark areas, where quick little movements caught her attention. She realised these were the entrances to caves, from which human figures were emerging, picking their way through the boulders. Rebecca knew instinctively that they must be prehistoric cavemen.

They arrived in small groups; dark-haired men and women of all ages, although children were noticeably absent. With their long unkempt hair, the men exuded a sense of brute animal strength. Although barefoot, they seemed quite untroubled by the rough terrain.

Threading their way through the trees, they headed towards a glade in the forest where moonlight filtered through the surrounding woodland, casting shadows on the rough grass. And there, in the centre of the glade, Rebecca could see the focus of all this activity: a roughly-hewn pillar of rock, about ten foot high and leaning slightly to one side. The pillar was covered in swirling, labyrinthine carvings.

The cavemen were chattering excitedly, their voices high-pitched, obviously anticipating a major event. Their number swelled rapidly, and crude animal-skin flagons appeared, evidently full of some kind of liquor, since everyone drank enthusiastically as they were passed around.

She involuntarily tensed when the drumming started, as the memory of events on Easter Island flitted through her mind.

A group of men was seated next to the monolith, with drums made out of hollowed tree-trunks between their knees. The rhythms of the drumbeats soon became intricate and subtle, and Rebecca, as before, began to feel her pulse quickening.

Then, as if at a predetermined signal, the gathering split into two, with the women forming a large circle around the men. In time with the drumming, the women started clapping and chanting, so that layers of different sounds floated over the clearing.

Spreading out, the men chose individual patches of grass. Slowly at first, and then rapidly, they started whirling on the spot in an anti-clockwise direction. Like clumsy dervishes, they turned at an identical speed, one arm pointing to the ground, the other held aloft. There was little elegance involved, but the desired effect soon became apparent as their eyes glazed over.

It was only when the tempo of the drumming and clapping slowed that they came a halt and drifted out of the circle. As each man moved away, they gradually formed another circle to enclose the women. Then the men took up the clapping, and the drumming became more urgent.

The women were not dancing so much as jumping. Forming a long line, they put their hands on each other's hips and snaked around inside the circle. With each jump, they thudded their heels into the ground, setting up a solid beat under the clapping and drumming. Initially, the line of women moved like a primitive conga dance, their hips swaying and brushing provocatively against the men. Then a pattern emerged. One woman took the lead and danced in ever-decreasing circles, the others following her, so that they formed a spiral. Reaching the monolith in the centre of the glade, the woman changed direction and led the line back out in the same spiral, until they were again brushing up against the men.

Now, a long unearthly howl drifted through the glade. At the entrance to one of the caves, Rebecca recognised the antler-headed caveman who had been doing the painting. Raising his head to the moon, he howled again, pawing the ground with his feet. He bounded with gazelle-like grace from boulder to boulder, through the trees towards the glade. Reaching it, he ran around the outside, leaping high into the air. Then he howled once again, and the clapping and dancing stopped abruptly. Moving towards each other, the men and women started to pair off and embrace, with various couples drifting towards the privacy of the deep forest.

Rebecca found herself unaccountably drawn to these happenings. She became flushed and dry-mouthed with excitement. She instinctively wanted, and yet was unable, to join in.

But, in one swift instant, any deep feelings of physical desire turned quickly to sheer horror. There in the laboratory, she let out a scream. "No! no!" Her arms by her side started shaking.

Larry rushed over to Rambo. "I really think we should end this."

Rambo's hand hovered over the switches.

Rebecca was frantic. In the heat of the ritual, nobody had noticed the rustling of the leaves, or the watchful faces peering through parted branches in the surrounding forest.

At some signal, the intruders burst into the glade. They were clearly a different race, tall athletic men. They were also armed, some with long wooden clubs, others carrying sharply-pointed spears.

The resistance of the cavemen was token. A few men quickly took stock, lowered their heads and charged bull-like in an attempt to butt their opponents. Some succeeded but, without weapons, were either speared in the back or were simply clubbed to the ground and brutally beaten about the head.

The antler-headed man himself did not even attempt to escape, but stood at the edge of the clearing, almost camouflaged by the trees. Then he, too, was seen and offered no resistance when he was grabbed by two of the invaders and dragged into the centre of the clearing. They tore off his headgear, exposing his long red hair, and forced him on to his knees next to the monolith.

Rebecca had already sensed who would appear next. A figure she knew only too well emerged from the forest. Dressed in just a loincloth made out of a fur pelt, the man had the head of a bird.

Without ceremony, he quickly wrapped a leather thong around the red-haired man's neck and started to pull.

CHAPTER 53

"Right – that's it," said Rambo, shutting down the scanner and taking the mask-like device from her face.

For Rebecca, the visions were only just beginning to fade. She stopped screaming. Opening her eyes a little, she was dreading what she might see next. What she actually saw were the faces of Rambo, Larry and Jim, filled with anxious concern as they leaned over her.

"It's all right, Rebecca, it's all right now. You're here with Jim and me, Larry. You're quite safe here."

As if after a particularly powerful nightmare, Rebecca was still not sure which world she was in, or whether the terror-laden world of her visions had really vanished.

"What happened, Rebecca?" asked Jim. "Can you talk to us? It was amazing. Did you know you were speaking in all sorts of different voices? Really different voices, and different languages even. There were men's voices coming out of your mouth. It was extraordinary. But then what happened? You started to scream just now."

"Jim – she's in shock. Give her time," said Rambo, checking Rebecca's pulse.

Rebecca, still half in her other world, could not speak. She looked around, trying to adjust to the fact that she was once again in the safety and quietness of the laboratory. The visions were beginning to fade, and she was struggling to recall precisely what she had just seen. Then her eyes opened wide and once again filled with terror.

"It was him!" she gasped. "It was the bird-man. The priest. And it was Neferatu! I know it was Neferatu." She looked at the three of them in turn. Did they understand what she was saying?

"And he was strangling someone. Another man. It was another sacrifice."

"Who was he strangling?" asked Larry gently.

"A man with antlers on his head. I've seen him before. He was the man doing a painting in a cave, painting a deer. And then it was as if he became the deer himself – he was moving like a deer. And he had red hair."

"He sounds like some sort of prehistoric shaman," interjected Jim.

Rebecca looked up at him. "I don't know who he was, but I know Neferatu killed him."

"What else did you see?" asked Rambo.

"There were people like cavemen dancing around, clapping and chanting. The deer-man was leaping about. It looked as if they were all about to have some sort of orgy. They were starting to pair off and go into the forest.

Then it happened. But I couldn't do anything – it was all so fast. Another group of men rushed out of the forest and started attacking the cavemen. I could see them coming, but I just couldn't warn them. I tried to shout to them, but they couldn't hear me. The attackers just speared them and really laid into them with clubs. It was so horrible – there was blood everywhere. Everyone was screaming. There were bodies all over the place."

She put her hands up to her head in a futile attempt to blot out the memories.

"It's okay, Rebecca. You're safe. It's all over now," said Larry, putting his hand on her shoulder.

She shook her head slowly. "At the beginning it was so lovely. I saw my mother. You know, both my parents are dead now, and it was quite reassuring. Then I saw my grandfather. He died, too, five years ago."

"Wasn't there someone speaking Gaelic?" asked Jim, his eyes alive with excitement.

"Yes, I think so. There was a Highlander with straggly red hair in a kilt and tam-o'-shanter. It could have been Gaelic I suppose, but I have no idea what he was saying."

"Yes, he *was* speaking Gaelic," Wally called over. Wally was busy disconnecting the digital camera. "He was saying, 'Don't be afraid.'"

"You went quiet for a bit after that," said Jim. "We weren't sure what was going on."

"Hang on," said Rambo. "Let's just help Rebecca sit up."

They listened as Rebecca described the town and the harbour. "I think I was watching a girl escape in a boat. A woman was helping her, maybe her mother. They both had the same red hair. They seemed quite important, and they were beautifully dressed, like they were royalty. Two soldiers were with them, Roman soldiers, I think. Then this horrible mob appeared! And guess who was leading them! Neferatu again! What *is* this man? It was definitely Neferatu. But he was wearing a toga."

"Surprise, surprise," said Larry. "You know, you were speaking Latin yourself at that point, in two different female voices. You had a funny accent and you were speaking too fast for me to pick up much. But I could make out the name 'Cleopatra' and 'go now' and 'the gods be with you'. I'll have to listen to it again."

"Well, I did Latin at school," said Rebecca. "Everybody seemed to be speaking Latin. I heard the older woman say 'Cleopatra'. And one of the soldiers called the older woman 'Selene'."

Larry and Jim looked at each other, bewildered at hearing the names 'Cleopatra' and 'Selene'.

"The girl only just managed to escape," Rebecca went on. "And Neferatu was in a fury. The girl was in a small boat, but it was heading towards a larger one, with masses of oars sticking out of it. I suppose it was a galley."

"What about this Cleopatra and Selene?" said Larry. "It seems all wrong to me. The Cleopatra we all know about had a daughter called Selene. Now in Rebecca's vision, it was the other way around. Cleopatra was the girl, and Selene was the older woman, possibly her mother, and they both had red hair. And what was Cleopatra escaping from? Where was she going? If it was Neferatu, why would he be after her? It's all quite intriguing."

"But before all that, you were speaking in another strange man's voice!" said Jim. "Who was he? And what was he saying?"

"I think I recognised him," said Rebecca. "He was the one who rescued me at the Stones. The one called Ptolemy. I knew he was trying to tell me something, but I couldn't understand what he was saying."

"I should have managed to record it," said Jim. "Hang on." He went back through the recording and pressed 'Play'.

Rebecca listened, looked at Jim and then shook her head in disbelief. "But that's not me," she said.

"Actually, it is," said Jim. "That was you speaking a few minutes ago, Rebecca."

"No, no. It can't be," she said. "I don't believe it."

"Larry – didn't you say it was classical Greek, Rebecca was speaking?" said Jim.

"But I don't know any Greek!" she protested.

"It's definitely classical Greek," Larry replied. "But this must be the first time, for hundreds of years, that anyone has heard it spoken like that."

"It's just not possible," said Rebecca, shaking her head. She looked bewildered and horrified.

"Don't worry, Rebecca," said Larry. "It doesn't make any difference to the person you are here and now."

"Your brain will be functioning now in its normal way," said Rambo. "If you like, I can show you the images on the screen. You'll see nothing has changed permanently. But I can honestly say I've never seen anything like it before during a scan. The changes in brain activity were amazing. First of all, the brain activity in the parietal lobes almost stopped. That does sometimes happen when people meditate. But then the cerebellum became active, and that's plain weird. That's a first."

"What do you mean, the cerebellum?" asked Rebecca.

"It's the part of the brain at the back of the head," said Rambo. "Normally it's associated with very finely co-ordinated movement, like playing a piano or driving a car. But you were just lying still. It was as if the cerebellum had another function, as if some kind of sixth sense were switched on in your brain."

"Now I feel like some sort of freak," said Rebecca.

"No, no, you're fine," said Rambo. "There'll be a perfectly good explanation, you'll see."

"You know," said Jim, "if that really was Ptolemy, it would be interesting to know what he was saying. It sounded urgent, as if he were trying to give a warning."

"It was certainly ancient Greek," said Larry. "Ptolemy was most likely to have been taught by Aristotle, like Alexander the Great. I'll work on it. And maybe we should take another look at the inscription on the Sun-Stone. We might find out who Ikar was, apart from being Neferatu's accomplice who fought with Ptolemy at the Newton Stones. He seems in some way to be associated with the Sun-Stone."

"That inscription?" said Rebecca. "It's been translated already. The lady in the shop near the Stones told me a Dr Waddell had worked it out. She said he was some sort of expert."

"Dr Waddell? Have you heard of him, Larry?" asked Jim.

"No, but we can look him up. I'll call in at the university library when we get back to Aberdeen. Then let's meet up in the hotel – at around six."

Rebecca made up her mind quickly. "Could I have a lift back to Aberdeen, Larry?"

"Sure," he said. "I'm leaving right now." He thanked Rambo.

"I have a hunch we've fallen on something very big here," said Rambo. "Let me know how you get on."

CHAPTER 54

Miles Harris, the news editor of the *Metropolitan*, hit the roof when he read Syreeta's interview with Jim Cavendish. The magnetic field story was now too big for the team to be headed up by the science correspondent. Harris wanted control of it himself. He summoned Geoff Evans to his office.

"Geoff. I want you on this magnetic field thing."

"It's not exactly my type of story…"

"You've got a bloody science degree, haven't you?"

"Psychology, actually."

"Well use it, whatever it is. Get on to the government and find out what they are going to do about it. And get a damn move on. I want to run with it for tomorrow."

Evans, who had been on his way to having lunch with the mayor, raised his eyes to the ceiling and went back to his desk. He picked up the phone and tried the press office at DEFRA. Syreeta, seated opposite him, was busy on a local story. When she heard him say the words 'magnetic field', she stopped typing and casually pretended to leaf through some papers while she listened.

As soon as Evans had finished the conversation, she made for Charles' office. He jumped as she swept in.

"Charles. This magnetic field story." She didn't give him a chance to respond. "Why is Geoff Evans on it?"

"That'll be Harris," snorted Charles. "Evans is the last person who should be on this story." He invited Syreeta to sit down. "Tell you what. Stay with it. Sounds like you've got a good rapport going with Cavendish. Use it. Get back to him and find out what's going on. Don't worry, I'll back you up."

She had almost reached the door when he called out half-heartedly, "You could just try ringing him this time. No need to fly anywhere at this point."

Syreeta swung around. "Don't you get it yet? This *is* a big story," she said, and flounced out of the office.

When she got back to her desk, Evans was still on the phone and sounding increasingly frustrated. "Well, who can I talk to about it?" he fumed. "I've just tried DEFRA. They said try the Home Office. You're the spokesman – you must know something. Someone in the government must be able to say what's going on. What are you going to do? Why the secrecy? What are you trying to cover up?" He paused. "What do you mean – 'Try Downing Street'? I thought you were supposed to be joined-up government these days."

Syreeta packed up her laptop. As she left the office, Evans was still on the phone.

"If the Prime Minister can't issue a statement, who can? People have a right to know..."

CHAPTER 55

Jim switched his mobile back on as he walked down the main steps in front of the Medical School. It rang immediately. He recognised the US number. "Hi, Greg. I was just about to phone you."

"Jim, we think it's bad. The Earth's magnetic field is still weakening, and we think it's going to get worse."

"So do we," said Jim, quietly. "I just hope our government can get its act together."

"Well, all hell's been let loose here, that's for sure."

"Why? What's happening?"

"It's the solar radiation we're worried about at the moment. If it gets any higher, we think transformers will be knocked out by power surges. We've started a crash programme to build more, but that'll take time – so we need generators. They're being made in a big way right now. What's more, we're assuming satellites will be hit and planes will be grounded, so we're planning alternative road and rail emergency transport systems." He was silent for a moment. "But it's always the unexpected, isn't it?"

"What do you mean?"

"Put it this way. People with red hair? Are they in the news over there? Doing funny things? Like having visions?"

"Red hair? Funny you should say that. But what about them? Is it important?"

"It's getting quite serious here. Some of them are having visions, but some of them are being picked on. People are starting fights in bars, calling them names, ganging up on them. Even ginger kids are being picked on. Sounds funny, I know, but it's getting nasty. Some people are being driven to change their hair-colour – dying it, or wearing wigs. But it doesn't seem to make much difference.

People are still attacking them. Listen, I've got to go. I'll keep you posted."

Jim was wondering what to do next, when his phone rang again.

"Jim? It's Syreeta. I've been trying to get through to you for hours! Your phone's been switched off."

"I'm sorry – I've been busy with quite an important experiment."

"Did you see my piece in the *Metropolitan*?"

"Yes, I certainly saw it," answered Jim, without enthusiasm.

"What's the matter? Were there mistakes in it?"

"No, no, it was all quite correct. But it did rather drop me in it with Rebecca. I've had a bloody earful from her about giving you all the info on the pole switch. She accused me of doing you special favours. Putting it frankly, it's between you two to sort it out. You're both working for the same paper, aren't you?"

"Listen, Jim, I'm officially doing the magnetic field story. Rebecca's supposed to be working on the redheads story. But, Jim, she's really worrying me – she's acting very odd. Do you think she's okay? She still seems obsessed with this Neferatu man. She still thinks he wants to kill her."

"I know. Something's going on in her mind, but I'm sure there's no danger here. He's just a bit weird, that's all. But this is the peculiar thing! It's all coinciding with this drop in the magnetic field – and it's getting worse."

"What do you mean?"

"I'm probably asking for trouble telling you, but I've just been speaking to Greg in the States. He says there are a lot of redheads acting strangely. And people are picking on them – attacking them. Nobody knows why, and nobody knows what to do about it."

"Tell me more. Do you think Rebecca is involved? I am her friend, you know."

"Well, that experiment I mentioned. It was with Rebecca."

"What! What the hell have you been doing to her?"

"It's okay – she's all right. We set her up to have more visions – we scanned her brain – but she got a bit frightened. Well, terrified actually. But she's okay now."

"Jim, what exactly happened?"

After Jim had outlined what had happened, he was taken aback to hear Syreeta take Rebecca's side.

"Poor thing. Did you have to do that? You must have made her feel a hundred times worse. Is she around?"

"Yes. We're about to head back to Aberdeen."

"Tell her I'll see her later."

"But we'll be in Aberdeen."

"Talk later, Jim. I'm on my way to Heathrow. See you this evening." As she rang off, Jim groaned.

CHAPTER 56

Larry dodged impatiently past a couple of students dawdling outside the entrance to the university library and pushed hard against the swing-door. He flashed his pass as he strode past the security guard and made his way to a computer in an alcove near the entrance to check the online catalogue. He was pleased to see that the book he was after was in the history stacks.

He knew the layout of the library well and, within minutes, established that the book he needed was not actually there. The odd thing was, there was a distinct and fresh gap, entirely dust free, on the shelf where the book should have been, as if someone had only very recently taken it out. Quickly noting the long queue at the checkout desk, Larry cursed and headed instead for the two students at the 'Returns'.

As he approached them, he drew in his breath and did something completely alien to his nature. Muttering apologies, he smiled grimly and promptly and uncharacteristically jumped the queue.

The librarian, an attractive middle-aged lady, looked up and gave him a questioning smile. She didn't know Larry by name but had seen him around enough to guess he was on the university staff.

He impatiently pushed over a slip of paper. "The computer catalogue says this book's in. I've checked the shelves, but it's not there. It looks as if someone has just taken it out. Any idea where it might be?"

The librarian studied the piece of paper. "Just a moment," she said, and tapped into her computer. She located the book in the records immediately. "It should be on the shelf. It hasn't been taken out since 1997."

"Well, it's not where it should be."

The librarian's assistant looked over from the checkout desk. "Excuse me, but I saw it yesterday. Somebody who wasn't a member of the university tried to take it out. He said he thought he could use the library because he was a delegate at a conference here." She frowned. "Strictly speaking, he shouldn't have been allowed in."

Larry marched over to her, ignoring the queue of waiting students laden with books. "What did he look like?"

She thought for a second. "Sort of dark-haired – maybe Middle Eastern. Strange bright green eyes. Quite unusual."

"And what happened about the book, exactly?"

The assistant shrugged her shoulders. "Nothing really. I told him he could take out temporary membership, but that we'd have to check out his credentials first."

"And?" said Larry.

She shrugged her shoulders again. "He said that in that case, he'd just consult it. He's probably put it back in the wrong place."

"Oh yes, I'm sure he has," said Larry under his breath. "Thanks. Thank you very much." He walked towards the exit, thinking hard. Then, quickening his step, he pushed the exit door open and set off smartly across the campus to the university conference centre.

He strode up to the registration desk, but with the conference well underway, nobody was on duty. He rapped a table impatiently. "Anybody around?" he called. A young girl emerged from an office. "Get me a copy of the delegates list, please," he demanded.

The girl looked slightly affronted but disappeared back into the office and returned with the list.

"Thanks," said Larry, already flicking through the pages.

He found the names beginning with 'N' and ran his finger down the list. "Dr Neferatu," he said to himself. "Affiliation – Private. Residence – St Andrew's Hall."

He knew St Andrew's Hall well. It was a new hall of residence on the edge of the campus. He had attended formal dinners there often enough as a guest of the warden, a fellow archaeologist. Like most of the halls of residence, St. Andrew's Hall was used for accommodating delegates attending various meetings and conferences during the vacations.

"Have you got a plastic bag, please?" he asked.

"Yes," replied the girl. "You can have an official conference bag."

"I'll take a few of these as well if you don't mind," he said, and picked up a bundle of leaflets outlining the conference programme. He put them in the bag. "Thanks," he said, and walked briskly out of the building towards St Andrew's Hall.

With the students away, the hall was quiet. The porter at the main entrance was halfway up a ladder fixing a light bulb.

"John – do you know which room Dr Neferatu is staying in?" Larry called up to him.

The porter looked down. "Number 24, Professor Burton," he said. "Strange man that Dr Neferatu. Never turns his lights off." He unscrewed a light fixing and looked down again. "I don't think he's in at the moment. He's probably at the conference." He took out the old bulb and looked at it. "He's leaving tonight as soon as it finishes."

"I only wanted to return some papers," said Larry, holding up the bag.

"Just put them on the desk. I'll see he gets them," replied the porter, putting the old bulb in his pocket and taking out a new one.

"They're very important. Can I put them in his room?" asked Larry.

"Hang on a sec," said the porter, trying unsuccessfully to fit the bulb in.

"Don't come down. I can see you're busy," Larry called up again. "Is there a spare key?"

The porter managed to insert the bulb into the socket and reached for the lamp cover to refit it. "On the hook behind my desk."

Larry darted behind the desk and grabbed the key. "Thanks – I won't be long," he said.

Number 24 was on the ground floor. Larry knocked on the door and waited. There was no answer. He put his ear to the door and listened. He thought he detected a faint noise inside, then realised he was holding a plastic bag full of leaflets and assumed it was those that were rustling.

Inserting the key, he unlocked the door and went to open it. The door didn't budge. Puzzled, Larry knocked again. He stood there for a full minute, but it was deadly quiet. Checking that nobody was coming down the corridor, he turned the door handle and put his full weight against the door. Again, it wouldn't open. He stood there, made a decision and steeled himself. Stepping back, he took a deep breath and rammed the door with his shoulder. The door burst open and he fell inside.

The light from the naked bulb in the room was so dazzling that he had to shield his eyes. To his intense relief, there was no sign of Neferatu. He checked the door and saw that a bolt on the inside had ripped away from the wood, but that little damage had been done. Only then did he notice the open window.

Apart from the light and a pile of books on the desk, there was no evidence of Neferatu's stay in the room. He picked up the books one by one and looked at the titles. He noted 'Prehistoric Orkney' by Anna Ritchie and 'Field Guide to Pictish Symbol Stones' by Duncan Mack and put them to one side.

The last book in the pile was the one he had been looking for: 'The Phoenician Origin of Britons, Scots and Anglo-Saxons' by L A Waddell. He tapped the book lightly, slipped it into the carrier bag and left the room, carefully locking the door behind him.

The porter was behind his desk, the maintenance work completed. Larry thanked him, handed back the key and ambled out of the building.

Finding a bench by the lake in the campus grounds, he settled down to look through the book. After a few minutes, he smiled, closed the book and fished out his phone.

"I've found what we're looking for," Larry said to Jim. "I just need to check a few more things in the library and then I'll meet you back at the hotel. Still about six, okay?"

He didn't notice the large bird eyeing him from the top of the tree behind the seat.

CHAPTER 57

Rebecca checked her messages as she sat by herself in the hotel lounge, waiting for the others. There was a voicemail as well as a text from Syreeta, who said she was worried about her and announced that she was now on her way to Aberdeen, herself. She switched off her phone when she saw Jim arriving back in the hotel, clutching the camcorder.

He caught sight of her and came straight over. "I've had your friend Syreeta on the phone," he said, sitting down. "She's coming to Aberdeen. Did you know?"

"Did she say what she wanted?"

"I guess she's concerned about you."

"Maybe. On the other hand, it could be she's after my story."

"She struck me as being genuinely worried about you. And she told me she's doing the magnetic field story, not the redheads."

"Well, if you believe that."

"You certainly have a decidedly odd side, Rebecca," he said bluntly.

"What do you mean?"

"I mean every time you're around, weird things start happening. The need to get a story out of all this, whatever it takes. Sometimes it seems as if the story is more important than real people. Don't you go anywhere without causing trouble?" He looked at her coldly. "Sometimes, you almost frighten me," he said, lowering his voice.

Rebecca looked at him in amazement at what he had just said. "You think *you're* frightened. You were the one who suggested putting me through all that experiment stuff, weren't you? It was horrible. Try thinking about what I'm going through."

Then her tone changed. "Anyway, how could it remotely be

my fault 'weird things start happening'? What on earth has it all got to do with me? Maybe it's you. Maybe you're just too stuck in your own world to see what's going on."

She glared at him again, and then exploded. "Christ! Don't you realise what I've been through? I narrowly escaped being sacrificed – twice. I've been haunted and stalked by that evil Neferatu. Not that you believe any of that, of course."

"I don't know that anyone in their right mind would believe it," he countered.

"What about poor Señor Nata? He was real enough, wasn't he? Or was that all in my imagination as well? That piece of red cord Mr MacGregor found was real enough, wasn't it? How much more proof do you need?"

"Well, you do seem to have it in for Syreeta a bit. Have you two had a row?"

Rebecca's eyes narrowed. "Why the sudden interest in Syreeta?"

"No sudden interest. I just think she seems a great girl. And she's worried about you, as I said."

Rebecca flared again. "You really don't get it, do you? Well, let me tell you. Syreeta is after my redheads story – she's desperate to take it over. There's nothing she'd like more than for me to drop out."

"I thought you two were friends," Jim replied.

Rebecca looked at him defiantly. "Listen. It might sound corny to you, but this is a big story. It could make my name. Just accept it, okay?"

"You're beginning to sound quite paranoid," Jim retorted.

Rebecca was about to respond, when Larry bounced over. He sat down and looked at each of them in turn. "Is everything all right?" he ventured brightly. He didn't wait for an answer. "Look what I've just found in Dr Neferatu's room. He actually had the nerve to steal it from the library."

Rebecca and Jim both looked puzzled.

Larry held up the book to show them. "L A Waddell, published

1924. Just don't ask me how I got hold of it."

Jim took the book and flicked through it. "Why would Dr Neferatu want this?" he asked.

"At a guess, he wanted to find out about the Newton Stones. There was a book on Pictish symbol stones in his room as well. And there was another one about prehistoric Orkney. Why on earth would he be interested in prehistoric Orkney, I wonder?"

"There's a lot about the Newton Stones here," said Jim. "And I think I'm beginning to see a connection."

"How's that?" said Larry.

"It's funny. I mentioned the Newton Stones as a possible research project in the paper I prepared for him. I knew you were interested in them as well."

"Perhaps this is all part of Neferatu's plan. Could he have been using us to draw Rebecca there – into a trap?" asked Larry.

But Jim was absorbed in reading the book.

"It does come over as a bit wacky to say the least," said Larry. "Must be why Waddell was never taken seriously. Mind you, there's one thing that's really fascinating. He's suggesting the Phoenicians landed here in Scotland, and even settled for a while."

"You've read it already?" said Jim, surprised.

"Oh, I've only skimmed through it," replied Larry. "He seems to stretch things a bit, but then he was once Professor of Chemistry and Pathology at Calcutta Medical School. So I suppose he must have had some credibility."

"But what does it say about the inscription?" interjected Rebecca.

Larry took the book back and leafed through until he found the page he wanted. "This is the translation as he worked it out," he said.

Larry held the book up so that they could see, and quoted: 'This Sun-Cross was raised to the God of Sun-Fire by the Phoenician, Ikar of Cilicia.'"

"Can I have a look at it?" said Rebecca, reaching for the book. She avoided looking at Jim.

"And where might Cilicia be?" Jim asked Larry.

"It's in modern Turkey now," he said. "It used to be the coastal strip around Tarsus in the ancient Greek world. You remember Paul of Tarsus?"

"So let's say that Ikar of Cilicia had a fight with Ptolemy," said Jim. "How does that help us?"

Larry smiled smugly. "Well, I've been doing some more reading in the library, and it's all very interesting.

The Cleopatra we all know had a daughter, also called Cleopatra – Cleopatra Selene, often known just as Selene. Selene means 'moon' in Greek. After Cleopatra's death, Selene was married to King Juba II of Numidia, in North Africa. They ended up in a town called Caesaria in Mauretania, which was part of the Roman Empire. It's now in Algeria, on the Mediterranean coast."

Larry smiled at them both. "It's highly likely that Selene also had a first-born daughter named Cleopatra. They went in for that sort of thing. She would have been the last Cleopatra. The end of the Ptolemaic line. We can't know for certain that she existed, or what happened to her. But one thing is certain – Cleopatra's ancestors came from Macedonia. She was a descendant of Ptolemy Soter – and red hair was not uncommon in Macedonia. There's even a bust of Cleopatra with reddish hair in the Altes Museum in Berlin."

Jim looked unimpressed. "So are you saying that *if*, and I mean *if*, Rebecca's vision was of something that actually happened, then what Rebecca was seeing was the famous Cleopatra's granddaughter escaping somewhere? And that she was escaping from the very same Dr Neferatu? Come on! A bit far-fetched, don't you think?"

"Try and keep an open mind, Jim," said Larry.

"All right, trying to keep an open mind," said Jim, "on top of all that, you expect me to believe that Dr Neferatu tried to kill

Rebecca, that he was also the enemy of a general in Alexander the Great's army, that he had it in for Cleopatra's granddaughter and that he also didn't like shamans?"

"Don't you see?" said Larry, exasperated. "Every single person who spoke through Rebecca happened to have red hair. For some reason, Neferatu has clearly got something against redheads."

"But why? And why me, especially?" asked Rebecca.

"I don't know," said Larry. "But we'll get to the bottom of this. I promise."

"Okay," said Jim. "You know classical Greek don't you, Larry? How about the so-called warning Ptolemy gave to Rebecca? Did you manage to work out what he was saying?"

"My Greek's a bit rusty, I'm afraid. Can you play it back for me?"

Jim ran through the recording, found the 'warning' and pressed 'Play'.

Larry listened. "It's not that easy to understand. I could make out a few words though. The word for 'red' is there, and 'hair'. So it's clearly to do with 'red hair'. And 'ring' – 'a ring'. He mentioned 'Horus', too, the ancient Egyptian god."

"Well?" said Jim.

"Right," said Larry. "I'll give you my best guess. What I think he's saying is, 'When Horus comes, people with red hair will fear his ring.'"

Jim shrugged his shoulders. "Doesn't exactly reveal much, does it?"

"Red hair again, though," Larry answered. "And definitely some sort of warning." He looked at the others. "It seems quite relevant in view of what's been going on. But goodness knows what his 'ring' has got to do with it. And what's all this about Horus coming? I'll have to look him up again – see if I can find any clues about him or his ring."

"I don't see what difference it'll make. Bit of a waste of time if you ask me," said Jim.

Larry didn't quite know what to make of Jim's negativity. He looked over at Rebecca. She seemed so vulnerable. He felt almost overwhelmed by a wave of sympathy for her, as he realised that she reminded him of his own daughter Kate, whom he had lost so many years ago.

He went over to her and put his arm around her shoulder. "Don't worry, Rebecca. We'll get there. You're going to be okay," he said, trying to sound confident and reassuring.

CHAPTER 58

As she sat on the bed in her hotel room, Rebecca felt puzzled and upset by Jim's attitude towards her. Only a couple of days before, he had been so warm and had shown real affection. Now he seemed cold and withdrawn and she felt as if she had annoyed him in some way. Why had he changed? Was it her fault? Or maybe he'd had second thoughts about getting involved?

It seemed something was holding him back from giving more of himself. She wondered if he still felt hurt by his failed marriage. It seemed as if his American wife had been mainly attracted by the idea of marrying into an aristocratic family and hadn't really been in love with him at all.

But surely he had got over that by now. Marriages fail. It doesn't have to stop you feeling something for somebody else. What she could not understand was his lack of appreciation about all she had gone through. As if it had all irritated him. She could see no evidence of protective love in him.

He was a scientist, of course. She accepted that a scientist had to be rational and always needed proof of everything. But she had expected a little measure of loving sympathy after all she had gone through.

At first he had seemed sympathetic and had wanted to help her. Now he seemed to mock her and treat her as if she were making it all up. And then today, she felt she meant nothing to him, as if she were merely the subject of an interesting scientific experiment. He had seemed so positive and full of life when they had first met. Now he seemed somehow deadened and negative, especially towards her.

She knew her own behaviour had not always helped. She had been short-tempered, even hysterical, at times. But then so would anybody else, surely. These were not normal days.

Syreeta was another problem on her mind. She really didn't feel she could trust Syreeta anymore. All this concern for her welfare was just a cover. All she seemed really interested in was taking over on her redheads story. Maybe taking over Jim, too, in the process. And if Syreeta thought she could talk her round, she was mistaken. Tough. Rebecca certainly wasn't going to make it easy for her.

But then she cut all these destructive comments short. *What am I doing? Am I becoming completely paranoid or something?*

At least Larry was kind. He alone seemed to understand exactly what she was going through.

She went online and checked her emails. As expected, there was one from Charles, asking how she was progressing with the story. She replied, promising to send him a piece shortly. Then there was another message from Syreeta, saying she was worried about her and was coming to Aberdeen that evening. Rebecca deleted it.

Turning on the television, she checked the 24 hour news. It was now dominated by stories about the Earth's failing magnetic field, the likely effects of increased solar radiation and the possibility of a pole switchover. Nothing about attacks on redheads. Had it all stopped and gone away? She checked the media websites. Basically the same. There was the odd piece about people with red hair continuing to disappear, but no more. The whole redhead story seemed no longer worthy of news headlines.

Frustrated, she checked 'Red Aloud', a website dedicated to redheads. Now she could almost hear the cries for help. The blogs were all jammed full of stories about redheads having visions and strange experiences, many of them terrifying. They were being mocked, despised or, at worst, physically abused. There were even cases where non-redhead members of their own families were turning against them.

And again, in some of the comments, she noted a distinct lack of sympathy for them. People were being critical, cruel even. What was happening? And yet the world at large seemed to have other things to worry about.

She checked her watch. It was seven o'clock. She managed to get through to the press officer at the Home Office, and asked her straight out whether there were reports coming in about redheads being persecuted.

She didn't expect much help, and indeed she didn't get much. "Yes, there are a few reports coming in from the police of them being called out to disputes involving redheads. But, putting it frankly, we're more concerned about the effects of the solar radiation. It's beginning to affect electricity supplies, and that is serious. We're working flat out here, trying to get emergency generators in place. Phone reception is going down in some places. You are lucky you got through. What's more, if the poles do switch over, we've got a real problem on our hands. Frankly, it's all tying up most of the government. Sorry, but the redhead situation will just have to wait."

For a while, Rebecca sat there fuming. Then she decided to do something positive and write up the story of the missing redheads in Scotland. This was serious and important and could not be ignored.

She had barely started typing when there was a knock on her door. She heard Syreeta's voice. "Rebecca? Are you there? It's me – Sy." She sat there in silence until she heard Syreeta's footsteps fade, as she walked back down the corridor.

CHAPTER 59

The television newsreader on the evening news looked distinctly distracted as she leafed through her papers and turned to face the camera.

Jim turned up the volume on the television in his hotel room.

"There are now reports coming in that solar radiation is becoming a serious problem, as the intensity of the Earth's magnetic field continues to fall. It now seems likely that the North Pole and the South Pole are on track to switch over completely.

Some energy suppliers are warning that electricity supplies will almost certainly be disrupted. Internet and phone network providers are also warning customers that their services could be affected. We invited the government to speak to us about emergency plans, but no one is available for comment. However, we have received the following written statement from the government:

'The government is still awaiting key information that will indicate the speed of the magnetic field change. In the meantime, we are preparing the necessary emergency measures that may be required. Further information will be given as the situation develops...'"

Jim was concerned. Clearly the government was getting worried about the drop in the Earth's magnetic field, and it was at last dawning on them what the consequences might be. Yet they had not announced even the most basic plan of action. And there was still no mention of harassed redheads, either from the government or on the national television news. He assumed that the cosmic events were taking precedence over anything else.

Switching off the television, he was relieved to get through to Greg straightaway. "Hi. What's going on with you? Our government hasn't started to get its act together yet."

"They're probably panicking. Things are happening very quickly now, and they're probably caught out," said Greg. "Did you know it's started already? Vortices have formed in the magnetic field in different parts of the world, just as we anticipated. Even now, there are odd spots in the South Pacific where compasses are pointing south. Definitely on Easter Island, where you were. And your part of the world – Scotland – is very unstable as well. Amongst other places."

"Yes, I checked with my department. We're picking up the same."

"It's certainly happening very fast," said Greg. "I've just been on to Shinzo Yoshino at Tokyo University, and he's confirmed what we're seeing. Let's hope people are getting their emergency plans together.

Sorry, Jim, gotta go. We have to revise the official statement we were just about to put out. I'll keep you posted. Bye."

Jim wondered if he should be helping in some way, or speaking to someone. The Cambridge University authorities had already firmly reminded him that any contact with the Press or government should be cleared through them first. His mind was in a whirl and he was finding it difficult to concentrate. He sat down on the bed to think.

There was an almost immediate tap on his door. He opened the door to find Syreeta standing there.

"Jim – hello! Can I have a word, please?"

"Of course," he said, surprised to see her so soon, and held the door open to let her in.

She sat down on the bed, crossed her long brown legs and brushed her hair away from her face.

"Rebecca doesn't seem to be around," she said. "Either that, or she's not wanting to see me."

"She does seem to be behaving rather erratically, I know that." Without prompting, he started to tell her about the experiment with Rebecca, while Syreeta listened.

"So these stories about redheads? Something is really happening then?" she said.

"It certainly looks like it. Look at Rebecca, for example. Her behaviour has been downright weird."

"To me, she sounded very scared," said Syreeta.

"I know – but she doesn't need to be. I'm convinced there's a perfectly good scientific explanation for it all."

Syreeta looked at him in silence for a moment, as if unsure what to think. "But about the pole switch? What's the latest?" she asked.

"You'll have to talk to the official spokesmen about that," Jim said. "I got a bit of an earful from the university after you did that interview with me."

"How about your friend in the States?" she asked. "Could he help? Could you give me his phone number?"

Jim couldn't see any objection. She could easily track down Greg if she really wanted to. He wrote it down for her and was handing it over when there was another tap at the door. He opened it to find Rebecca standing there, smiling.

"Jim, are you busy? I just wanted to say I'm so sorry for being difficult. This…"

She tailed off as she noticed a movement in the room and peered over his shoulder to see Syreeta sitting on the bed.

Rebecca pushed past Jim as Syreeta stood up. "Oh, I see you *are* busy. Syreeta! What on earth are you doing here?"

"I tried your room, but there was no answer," said Syreeta. "I didn't know where you were. I was worried about you."

"Looks like it," snorted Rebecca, glaring at her. Then she turned to Jim. "You can forget what I just said."

"I think it's time I went," said Syreeta. "I was on my way out, anyway. I've got some calls to make – and a story to write. Call me when you're feeling better, Rebecca." She went to the door. "Thanks for everything, Jim," she said, closing it behind her.

Jim looked at Rebecca and shook his head in dismay. "What's up with you? As if I haven't got enough on my plate without all the histrionics," he said. "This is turning into some bloody awful farce."

"Maybe it is to you," retorted Rebecca. "Are you completely insensitive? To me, it's deadly serious."

"Listen, Rebecca," he said, "irrespective of your feelings and my feelings, something *really* serious is happening in the world. It may not mean much to you, but this poles situation looks like causing complete chaos, not just here but all over the world. No power, no internet, no phones. And meanwhile, you choose this moment to have a tantrum. You may not admit it, but you are behaving rather strangely. Not your usual cool self, let's say."

"A tantrum! Me behaving strangely! And what about you!" exploded Rebecca. "Well, if that's how things are," she said, turning on her heels, and strode out of the door, slamming it shut behind her.

Jim threw his hands in the air, went to the mini-bar, took out two small bottles of red wine and poured himself a generous glass. Lying down on the bed, he propped himself up against the pillow and drained the glass.

Then he lay back and ran the extraordinary events of the day through his mind. Something very odd seemed to be happening to Rebecca. She was clearly mentally disturbed. But could it all really be connected to the cosmic changes going on? That seemed to be the rational explanation. Even Greg had said that redheads all over the States were acting oddly and having visions. It could all be part of the same phenomenon. Could it be true, after all, that she had been receiving messages from the dead? Surely that was going too far. Then there was Dr Neferatu. How did he fit into it all this, if indeed he did?

And what about his own feelings towards Rebecca? They seemed to be all over the place. He acknowledged that he had been strongly attracted to her on Easter Island. At least until *that dinner*.

It must have been after that weird evening that their relationship had changed. It was as if she had become different person. He couldn't help thinking about the way she kept losing her temper. She seemed to have become quite wild. Frighteningly so, like someone possessed. He didn't know if he could handle her, or even if he wanted to. One minute he was drawn to her, the next he was almost repelled.

Then perhaps it was *his* attitude towards Rebecca that had been affected. Maybe the cosmic changes were affecting *him*. It was all very confusing. And yet, deep down, he found he still had strong feelings for her. He was even beginning to feel sorry she had walked out.

He half-heartedly watched a bit of television, then, after finishing off the second bottle of wine, switched the television off. He was tired, so he got ready for bed.

As he lay there, his head in a pleasant haze and waiting for sleep to come, he found he could not stop his mind returning to Rebecca.

He must have drifted off and yet, if what happened next was just a dream, it nevertheless seemed very real. He was suddenly aware that Rebecca was lying next to him in the bed. As she lay on her side, he could actually feel the warmth of her body and smell the fragrance of her skin. He gently turned her on to her back and kissed her, passionately. Yet, when he opened his eyes, still half-asleep, he was bitterly disappointed to find that he was hugging a pillow.

He lay there for a while, gazing at the blinking fire-detector above. From that moment he knew that, despite everything, he was indeed very much in love with Rebecca.

CHAPTER 60

Stromness was the second main town of Orkney after Kirkwall. A place with a romantic feel, it had always had associations with voyages of exploration, and it was the last port of call where Captain Cook took on food and water, before crossing the Atlantic to survey the coast of Canada.

In the clear, bright early morning, the town was getting ready for the day, and the first ferry for Scrabster on mainland Scotland was already leaving the port.

A postman was approaching a house at the end of a terrace, overlooking the sea. Reaching the front door, he appeared, to any casual onlooker from the street, to be taking letters from his bag and slipping them through the letterbox.

Inside, a little red-haired girl of about six years old was sitting at the kitchen table with her teddy bear in her lap.

Her mother heard the flap on the door rattle, as she was serving breakfast. "Shona – will you go and get the post, darling?" she asked her daughter.

Shona obediently went to the front door, but there were no letters on the mat. She opened the door, hesitated for a moment and then came running back. "Mummy, somebody has painted a funny picture on the door," she cried.

"I'll go and have a look. Just start your breakfast, or you'll be late for school," her mother said, as she went to look at the door. The child was right. There was a freshly-daubed sign on the door. It was similar to a swastika but painted bright red. She couldn't help the chill of fear and foreboding that ran through her.

Stepping into the street, she looked up and down. No postman to be seen. Otherwise, everything seemed perfectly normal and she could see a neighbour going into the corner shop. Going back inside, she was still alarmed, but felt inclined to blame it on the local young lads.

The back door stood ominously open but, as she stepped into the garden, there was no sign of her daughter. She called her name again and again and then, with gathering panic, she ran inside and checked upstairs. No Shona. Running back downstairs and into the kitchen, a sudden terror gripped her. There was no escape from the dreadful truth that Shona had gone, and could have been taken by someone or something connected to the horrible red daubing on the front door.

"Oh, no! Shona, no!" she cried.

CHAPTER 61

The disappearance of Shona on its own would normally have constituted a major event in Orkney, but she was not the only child to disappear that day. During the previous night and early that morning, identical signs had appeared on numerous front doors where red-haired children happened to be living. It soon transpired that red-haired children had been disappearing all over the islands.

Rebecca heard about the abductions on the radio and immediately set off for Aberdeen airport to catch the first available flight to Kirkwall.

When she arrived, she found the police had already commissioned a public meeting room in Kirkwall for a press briefing, and so she sat herself down in the front row.

The spokesman, pending the arrival of the Chief of Police for Scotland, was Chief Constable Douglas MacKenzie, the most senior officer in Orkney, and he was already having a hard time. One Glaswegian reporter was haranguing him for more details.

"I've told you already," said the exasperated policeman, "we simply don't know anything. We have nothing to go on. Nothing remotely like this has happened before. There is simply no precedent for it. All we know is that something like fifty children have disappeared since last night – and they all have red hair."

The reporter was sceptical. "What? All with red hair? And you say you haven't a clue? There are clearly some people out there with a grudge against red hair. You must have some inkling who they are? It can't just suddenly happen overnight."

The policeman gave him a level look. "Listen. I know no more than what I've just told you. Nothing remotely like this has happened before in Orkney. It could be locals, or it could be outsiders. We just don't know."

The reporter tried a different tack. "What about these red swastikas? Who exactly are we dealing with here? Some sort of sick cult, a neo-Nazi group?"

Chief Constable MacKenzie looked affronted. "Now listen here. I can assure you, there's absolutely no history of Nazis in Orkney," he said. "Occasionally, we have some funny happenings with so-called local 'covens' of witches, but this is not their sort of thing."

He waved an arm in the direction of the town. "Look at the place – it's a closed community. If anything sinister were going on here, we would know about it." He paused. "Anyway, let's be clear. This is not exactly a swastika. It is very similar, but these signs have got a tail. Like this." He turned to a flip-chart and drew a sign that Rebecca instantly recognised as similar to the 'sun-sign' she had previously seen on the Newton Stone.

While the press corps was contemplating this, Rebecca jumped in to ask, "Why do you think it's only red-haired children who have disappeared?"

He looked over to her, noting her hair colour. "I'm sorry, miss – we've no idea. It's clearly not just a coincidence. As you might have noticed, we have plenty of red-haired people living here. But precisely because red hair is so common, we don't tend to get any cases of prejudice against it. It's just normal."

At that point a policeman handed him a sheet of paper and whispered something in his ear. Chief Constable MacKenzie read the message carefully then pulled himself up straight and looked hard at his audience. He waited for silence before making his announcement.

"I've just received a directive from the Home Secretary that will affect you all. I'm sorry to tell you, we are having to operate a total shutdown in Orkney. I'm afraid no one will be allowed to come in, or leave, until this has been sorted out. No exceptions, apart from the emergency services, of course."

The place predictably erupted to cries of "What!" "Why?" "You can't do that!" "You've got no right!"

Chief Constable MacKenzie held his ground. "You all came here to get a story. Well, when we do sort this out, you'll be the first to know. Now, I must ask you all to leave the hall and find accommodation, if you haven't already found somewhere." He waited until the outbursts had finished, before continuing. "From now on, Orkney is officially in a state of emergency. Anyone who does not cooperate will be confined to a secure place where we can keep an eye on you."

Again uproar ensued, but the appearance of uniformed officers at the doors soon reinforced the sincerity of his intentions.

CHAPTER 62

The morning ferry from Kirkwall was nearing its destination of the island of Norstray. The sky was grey and overcast, threatening rain, but a few passengers were braving the weather and standing outside at the stern of the ship. Most of them were idly watching the white foam wake as it streamed out into the distance.

A middle-aged lady, well-dressed for the winter weather in an anorak, stood by herself. A swarthy-looking man, dressed only in a completely unsuitable business suit, came on deck, eyed the passengers for a minute, then casually went and stood alongside the lady.

He watched the coastline passing by for a short while, before turning to her. "Are you visiting Norstray as a tourist?" he asked.

Within a minute, the lady was excitedly explaining that she was visiting the place of her birth after twenty years of living and working as a civil servant in London.

Neferatu listened to her intently.

As the sea breeze gusted, she let go of the rail, pulled her brightly-coloured woollen hat hard on to her head and adjusted her glasses.

"I don't know that anyone will remember me now," she said. "My family moved to Mainland a long time ago. I thought I'd come and visit the place for old times' sake."

Neferatu's striped blue tie was fluttering like a flag, and his greasy hair was completely dishevelled by the wind.

"But what about you?" she said, eyeing his suit. "Are you here on business?"

"I suppose I am," he replied. "I am an archaeologist. I came here for a meeting in Kirkwall to talk about the excavations at Brodgar. So I thought to myself, why not have a look at the prehistoric burial site on the north of Norstray. In fact, I think I am not wearing the right clothes, but, you see, it was not in my plan to come here." He tried to tuck his tie back into his jacket and turned to face her. "Are you planning to stay long in Norstray?"

"Just a couple of days. I'm staying at the pub in Sandy Ness. There's not a lot of choice. And you?"

"Oh, I am only here for one day. I need to take the bus to the north of the island. Do you know if there is a bus which goes from the ferry terminal?"

"Bus! You'll be lucky, I think. You might get one from Sandy Ness, I suppose. Do you want a lift to Sandy Ness? I've hired a car which I have here on the ferry."

An instant smile spread over Neferatu's face. "Thank you so much," he said, smoothing back his hair.

As they entered the port, Neferatu squeezed himself into the small car and talked nonchalantly about the weather as they drove off the ship.

"Perhaps you will allow me to turn the heating on," he said, reaching for the controls and turning them to maximum.

The lady took of her hat and put it on the back seat. Her mousy, lightly-permed hair showed grey at the roots.

"I wonder if I could ask a great favour of you?" asked Neferatu, as they climbed away from the terminal.

"Of course."

"I have read about the Devil's Clawmarks – they are at a ruined kirk. I would very much like to see them, and I think the kirk is very close to Sandy Ness."

"Yes, it's just outside the village. In fact, we go right past it."

"You are too kind."

They drove on in silence until the car slowed down for a road junction.

"Did you hear the news?" Neferatu asked, without looking at his companion.

"What news?"

"About the children disappearing – the children with red hair."

The lady grimaced. "It wouldn't surprise me if the gingers set it all up themselves. Nasty people. It's probably all about witchcraft."

Neferatu did not reply, but nodded his head and smiled.

Driving along a quiet, uninhabited stretch of road, it took no longer than fifteen minutes before the kirk came into view as they approached Sandy Ness. Long abandoned, and now a shell devoid of any ornamentation, the old kirk maintained its grim reputation in local folklore for being associated with the Devil. A few tourists still liked to climb the stone stairway to inspect the enigmatic gouges, which people said resembled some diabolic hand or the claw of some gigantic bird. But at this time of year there were no visitors.

Neferatu opened the gate to the churchyard and stood aside for his companion to pass through. The dark winter clouds overhead, the grey stone walls and the cold added to the sombre atmosphere.

"Creepy, isn't it?" she said. "When we were kids, we used to dare each other to climb the stairs and put our hands into the clawmarks. Up there." She pointed to the stone stairway on the outside of the building.

Neferatu climbed up and inspected the six grooves in the stonework. He ran his long fingernail along each one in turn and then came back down.

The lady looked at her watch, the darkening sky and then at Neferatu. "It looks like rain," she said. "Perhaps we'd better move on."

"With your permission, I would like to look inside," he said.

He went through an open doorway. The interior of the kirk was open to the sky, and the ground was covered with a mass of nettles. He leaned against the wall next to the doorway, so that he couldn't be seen from outside, and rubbed his hands together to warm them.

When he did not reappear, his companion called out, "Hello?" There was no reply. She looked through the doorway but could see nobody. "Hello!" she called out again. No sound came from within. She looked up the sky. It was even darker now, and she felt a spot of rain. She called out once more and then walked through the doorway. She still could not see anyone.

Then he quickly came up behind her. She didn't have time to scream. His hands went round her neck and squeezed. Her glasses fell off as he forced her down into the nettles. A gurgle came from her throat, and her face started to turn blue. For a short time she flailed her arms wildly, trying to grab his hands, and kicked her legs at him. Then her eyeballs started to bulge and gradually glazed over. For a few seconds more her limbs twitched and then she lay still.

Neferatu slowly released his grip and stood up. Her bag was still wrapped around her shoulder. He freed it and tipped out the contents. Finding her purse, he pocketed all the contents and then threw it to one side. He went back through the doorway and looked around. It was still completely deserted. Returning to the body, he took it by the hands and dragged it against a wall in a dense patch of nettles.

Without even a backward glance, he went on through the gateway, abandoning the car despite the light drizzle that had set in, and started walking at a fast pace in the direction of Sandy Ness.

The bar of the Fisherman's Rest was crowded with men. They were lean and tough, men who fished the sea and worked the land. Many of them were in overalls.

Neferatu walked up to the bar. His hair was windblown, and his smart suit was crumpled and sodden. The landlord, a large, burly man, seeing that he was clearly an outsider, welcomed him cautiously.

"How can I help you?" he enquired.

"My car ran out of petrol just outside the village by the old kirk," Neferatu said. "I just need to get some petrol and take it back there."

"The garage is just a bit further up the road. They'll soon sort you out." He looked at Neferatu's damp clothes. "Can I offer you anything while you're here?" he said, pointing to the menu for the day written up on a blackboard behind the bar.

"Perhaps later," said Neferatu. He glanced at the men standing around him at the bar. Many had beer glasses in their hands. "I'll have what they are drinking," he said.

"That'll be a pint of our best bitter, then."

Neferatu took a small bundle of notes from his pocket and, without looking at them, put two on the bar. The landlord took one and gave him his change. Neferatu left his beer on the bar, turned round and listened to the conversation. It was animated and voices were raised.

"Why should we waste our time looking for them? They're outsiders anyway. Always live by their own rules."

"Thieving sods. You can't even leave a bike unlocked now."

"And watch out for your women. Load of lechers, they are. I could easily see the way that ginger sod Jock Lewis was eyeing up my wife."

"And the women aren't any better. Sluts they are. Go with anybody."

"We don't need them here."

"Notice the way they keep to themselves. Bugger anybody else."

Neferatu suddenly raised his arms in the air. The conversation petered to a halt and the men looked at him, puzzled.

"In my country we used to deal with them properly," he said.

"And where might you be from, then?" asked a short, dark-haired man in blue overalls.

"Egypt. I'm an archaeologist."

"So what are you doing here?" the same man continued, eyeing Neferatu's dishevelled appearance distrustfully.

"Just visiting. I want to look at the chambered cairn at Quoyness."

The man looked around at the others and then faced Neferatu. "So, all right then, how exactly did you deal with them? The gingers?"

"Let us just say it was not pleasant," Neferatu said. Then he started walking towards the main door. "Now, I must get my car." He turned and left without another word, and without looking back.

The men looked at the swinging door. "So, what do you make of that?" said the landlord to nobody in particular.

"It would have been interesting to know how they dealt with the gingers," said the short, dark-haired man.

At the local garage Neferatu bought a can of petrol and politely turned down the proffered lift back to the car. Taking the can, he walked casually out of the village, apparently indifferent to the rain. Well clear of the last house, he threw the can over a hedge and turned back.

At the edge of the village, he broke into a run towards the pub and burst in through the entrance. The men crowded around the bar were now again talking furiously and gesticulating.

"Call the police! Call the police!" shouted Neferatu. "A murder has been committed!"

There was instant silence. Everybody stared at him.

"What do mean? Where?" said the landlord.

"There's a body – a woman's body. In the old kirk."

"Is she dead? Are you sure?" asked a man in jeans.

"She's dead, absolutely. She has been strangled," said Neferatu grimly.

"There's not even a bloody copper to call," said the landlord. "They've both gone to Kirkwall. Some bloody meeting about those ginger brats disappearing."

The men looked at each other. Then the landlord came from behind the bar. "You'd better come with us," he said to Neferatu.

The men stormed out of the pub. Some ran off to get cars, while others started to run out of the village towards the kirk.

Neferatu got into the front seat of the landlord's car parked outside the pub, and three men jammed into the back.

The car lurched to a halt by the gate outside the kirk. The landlord ran to the gate and then stopped, waiting for Neferatu.

Neferatu pushed past him. "Over here," he said. The others followed, not saying a word.

The woman was lying on her back among the nettles where Neferatu had left her, her dead eyes staring at the sky. Her bag was lying alongside her, the various contents strewn around in the nettles. The landlord picked up a pen, a make-up case, a brush, a small mirror and finally an empty purse. Then he went through the bag. "I can't find any identification. No money, no cards. They must have been in her purse."

"She's not from around here," said somebody.

"Whatever murderous bastard did this must still be on the island," the landlord said.

Neferatu took a quick step backwards from the body. "I think I may have seen who did it," he said quietly. All eyes turned in his direction. "I saw a man running away. That's why I came to look. I don't think he saw me."

"Which direction did he go in?" asked the landlord.

"Towards the village. He was walking very fast."

"What did he look like?"

"Blue overalls. Big. In middle age. He had ginger hair. Very ginger hair."

The men looked at other.

"Sounds like Jock Lewis," said the young man in jeans.

"Could be."

"Or Walter Cowan."

"What about Dave Mathieson? He's a nasty piece of work. Capable of anything."

"Bloody police," exclaimed the landlord. "Why aren't they damn well here – where they should be?"

"If there's no police, it looks as if we'll have to sort it out ourselves," said a man with a beard. "Before he gets away." There were murmurs of agreement.

"Let's find Jock Lewis first," said the man in jeans. "I'd bet anything it was Jock Lewis."

"Listen! Listen to me!" said Neferatu loudly.

The men stopped talking and angry eyes looked at him.

"You cannot know who did it. It could have been anyone with red hair. Maybe he does not come from Sandy Ness.

"What are you saying?"

"There is only one way to be sure. You must deal with them all. Find everybody with red hair. There is no alternative. Every single person on the island who has red hair."

There was an uneasy silence.

"You must see this," said Neferatu. "Their little children have gone. This is your chance. Get rid of them all. Finish off the rest. No exceptions to be made."

"What do you mean, finish off the rest?" asked the landlord.

"If you want my help, you must bring them here tonight. We can deal with them, like we dealt with them in my country."

"And just how did you deal with them?"

"How they deserved to be dealt with."

Neferatu stood by the body. "Perhaps the next time it will be somebody you know. Your wife. Your daughter. I am telling you – do it now. I shall help you – I can arrange everything."

At first there was silence. Then the man in jeans said, "Let's get Jock Lewis first. Rob, Hamish – come with me."

"I'm going to Hardwick to get my brother," said the man with a beard. "He hates the bastards as much as I do. Especially when he hears about this…"

"Bring them all here at nine o'clock tonight. This place," said Neferatu. "Make sure you get them all and bring them here."

"And you? What are you going to do?" asked the landlord.

"Leave it to me. You will see tonight what I can do."

Neferatu stood and watched them all as they hurried away.

When the last car had disappeared from sight, he went back to the kirk and climbed the stairway to the Devil's Clawmarks. He placed his long fingers over the grooves in the stone.

Seconds later, an eagle spiralled upwards above the ruins in the twilight and headed due south. There was no longer any sign of Neferatu.

CHAPTER 63

Very early that morning at the university, Larry had been working alone in the room allocated to him as a visiting professor. There was a knock at the door and he swung round, surprised at being interrupted. It was Jim who walked in.

He thrust a copy of the *Metropolitan* in front of Larry. "Have you seen this?" he said.

Larry glanced at the headline on the front page:

'POLE SWITCH STARTS'

The story was by-lined Syreeta Dasgupta.

"Yes, I've seen it already. I had assumed that it was you behind it like last time, Jim."

Jim didn't deny it. "All I did was give Syreeta Greg's phone number. I didn't talk to her myself. But this pole switch is getting a bit serious – and I get the feeling that the government's just not prepared."

Jim took the paper back and handed Larry the *Beacon*, the Edinburgh daily. He laid the paper on Larry's desk so that he could read the headline:

'POWER CRISIS: SOLAR RADIATION CAUSES EMERGENCY'

Larry read the story. "If this is right, there could be electricity breakdowns all over Christmas. Let's hope there's enough power to cope."

"I knew they should have announced emergency plans earlier," Jim said. "People are going to panic now, and they'll blame the government."

Larry nodded in agreement, but he looked as if he had other things on his mind. "Do you know where Rebecca is? I tried her mobile but she was on voicemail. I left a message asking her to phone back, and I was just about to ring you about her."

"She's probably in Orkney, following up the redheads story," Jim said. "My guess is she probably shot off as soon as she heard about the red-haired kids disappearing. According to the hotel, she checked out very early this morning and went to the airport."

"Well, I'm wondering if even you are convinced now?" said Larry.

"Convinced about what?"

"Convinced that there's something very peculiar going on, and that Rebecca's bang in the middle of it. Something we may not even understand."

"Look, Larry. It's my belief that there's a perfectly rational explanation for all of this. But, okay – let's test your approach and see where it gets us. For a start – what have we got to go on?"

Larry sighed. "People with red hair. So many of them are being attacked. Murders, kidnappings, disappearances – and it's happening all over the world. Other redheads say they have suddenly been having visions. And then there's Neferatu – he seems to be cropping up all over the place."

"Oh, no, not Neferatu again," said Jim. "What on earth could he possibly have to do with all of this?"

"For one thing, you know there was an attempt on Rebecca's life on Easter Island – by a man supposed to have the head of a bird. Poor Señor Nata's family was witness to that – and Neferatu just happened to be there, too. Then you and Rebecca were both attacked by an eagle on Orkney. And Rebecca says she saw a large bird of prey at the Newton Stones a moment before, guess who, old Neferatu just happens to turn up again. And what does he do? In fact, he pretty well nearly kills her."

"What are you getting at?" asked Jim.

"I'm beginning to think Neferatu might be the key to all this. And what's more, there always seems to be some sort of connection with large birds of prey."

Jim burst out laughing. "Ah, well, yes, I'll give you that.

Neferatu's nose is distinctly hawk-like. But, to be serious, Larry, you're not really suggesting, are you, that Neferatu somehow grows wings and flits around the world?"

"I'm not pretending I know all the answers," said Larry, "but there are a lot of strange coincidences going on. I really do believe Neferatu wants Rebecca dead. But why? What could he possibly have against Rebecca? She had never even met him before she came to Easter Island. I really do think we have to keep an open mind about Neferatu, Jim."

"Okay, okay," Jim said. "But, personally, I prefer the more rational explanations. Birds of prey are not that uncommon, you know."

"All right then," Larry continued. "What about Rebecca and these apparent visions?"

"So, it looks like a redhead thing. We saw the effect on Rebecca's cerebellum ourselves. Basically, she's one of those people who can, if the conditions are right, go into some sort of trance. There are quite a number of people like that. Sometimes there can be some sort of trigger – a certain symbol, or an icon. Or repetitive sounds, such as drums beating, water dripping – classic conditions for bringing on a trance-like state. But it seems all these occurrences are exacerbated in redheads by the effects of the changes in the magnetic field."

"What, the changes in the magnetic field are just affecting people with red hair?" said Larry.

"It's quite possible. Science has shown that quite often people with red hair are hypersensitive to certain things, such as pain caused by heat and cold. They can respond unusually to anaesthetics as well. It's almost as if they have a different physical and mental make-up to non-redheads."

"But they're not just any old visions, are they?" said Larry. "There's a pattern, isn't there? In the experiment, all the key characters seemed to have red hair, starting with her mother, then her grandfather, and then the Highlander, Ptolemy Soter, Cleopatra,

Selene… Even the prehistoric shaman was red-haired. On Easter Island, the living corpse she described had a red beard, and the figure in a loincloth which appeared at the same time had some kind of red headdress."

"Well, it could be that her own red hair has become part of her psyche. She could be ultra-sensitive about it, which could affect her mental state."

"There's something else I must tell you," Larry continued. "I've been listening to the exchange in Latin between those women, Selene and Cleopatra. I couldn't make it all out, but it sounded as if Selene was talking about Cleopatra being sent to safety in Scotland." He took in breath. "Now, don't slam into me, Jim, but as you know, at least two of the people she saw in the scanner were definitely her ancestors. Her mother and her grandfather. Now, I have a feeling she could be communicating with her red-haired ancestors through these visions."

Jim looked at him as if he were mad. "Are you really, seriously suggesting that some rotting corpse of an Easter Islander, or some mad Macedonian general, are both Rebecca's long-lost ancestors? And that Rebecca is descended from Cleopatra? That Cleopatra's granddaughter was sent to Scotland, just so she could carry on her dynasty over here? You'll be telling me next that Rebecca is some sort of flame-haired queen!" he laughed. "Well, I suppose, now you come to think of it, that does kind of sum up something about Rebecca!"

Larry shrugged his shoulders and smiled.

Jim shook his head. "You're a rational man, Larry. I can't believe that you believe in all this. You know, what really gets me about all this past-lives stuff is that people always seem to be descended from someone well known or glamorous. Never some peasant in China – or a eunuch in a Turkish harem."

"Okay, okay, I know what you mean," said Larry. "Of course, Ptolemy Soter must have a huge number of descendants by now. But Rebecca was speaking ancient Greek, however you look at it –

and it's a fact that she doesn't know a single word of Greek."

"Yes, difficult one, that," conceded Jim. "Perhaps she's heard the language on the radio or in some Greek theatre production, and it somehow stayed in her memory."

"Oh, come on," said Larry. "That's a desperate argument."

"What I will say," said Jim, "is that, just possibly, we could be talking about a case of dissociative identity disorder – what people used to call multiple personality disorder. That could be one explanation."

"Yes, but in that case, isn't it a bit of a coincidence that all the multiple aspects of her personality happen to have red hair?" said Larry.

"Seems fair enough to me. They could all be different aspects of her personality, of which the experience of red hair is an integral part."

"But in that case, her mother, her grandfather, some unknown Highlander and the others, right back to the shaman, would all be different aspects of Rebecca's personality. Surely her mother was real enough? And her grandfather? And anyway, surely they would all have to be women, wouldn't they?"

"But if they are all supposed to be Rebecca's ancestors, Rebecca might be descended from some prehistoric shaman? Are you saying she's inherited shamanic powers? Is that what you're getting at?" said Jim.

"Shamans are actually well known for their ability to communicate with their ancestors. Their spirit helpers are often their own ancestors," replied Larry.

Jim's face set hard. "No. No, I don't buy all that. Rebecca simply saw the shaman in a vision. Just like all the other characters. He was simply a figment of Rebecca's imagination."

Larry decided to play his trump card. "But there you are. There's the difference. Both the living corpse and Ptolemy – they were real. Rebecca insists they were real people. She said they were *physically* there – that they *physically* fought to save her life. She said Ptolemy *physically* fought with Ikar at the Newton Stones. I don't really know how to explain this, but I believe that, when she was in great danger, she somehow managed to raise the dead, by which I mean raise them bodily, here into our own dimension."

Ignoring Jim's gesture of disbelief, he continued, "Now assuming that is what happened, that people who were dead were brought back to life, just imagine! What if other red-haired people are starting to show these same powers? The ability to resurrect the dead? Señor Nata's family, for instance? Other people, that's to say non-redheads, are not going to like it very much. Could this be a motive behind all these murders and disappearances around the world?"

"I'm still not with you," said Jim.

"Don't you see? Visions are one thing – raising the dead is another. It's an enormous power – and it raises enormous problems. Just think – for example, whenever redheads are threatened, they could raise an army of warrior ancestors to protect themselves. It could be that somebody or something is desperate to stop redheads' powers getting out of control. Maybe, to that end, whomever or whatever it is, is taking advantage of the prejudice against redheads.

Putting it frankly, Jim, even you seem to have been a bit irrational when it comes to redheads. You sometimes come across as distinctly having something against them."

"Oh, come on now. Don't drag me into this," protested Jim.

"Look, I know you are not going to accept any old theory without some logical proof," said Larry, "but, at times, you are a bit lacking in imagination. And there are occasions when a little imagination is exactly what you need.

Now, if you want proof that something very odd is going on, just have a look at this."

He reached to the back of his desk and pushed that morning's edition of the *Hibernian* in front of Jim. On the front page was a picture of someone's front door in Orkney, heavily daubed with a large red 'sun-sign'.

Larry stabbed at the picture with his finger. "See the upturned bar? That's exactly the same sign that's on the Sun-Stone at Newton." He waited, keen to see Jim's reaction.

Jim looked at it without speaking. Then he said, "Okay. I suppose I can see what you're getting at. Everything is getting so strange. I'm beginning to think anything is possible, now. I suppose there is some truth in what you were saying just now. There have been times recently when I've felt quite an aversion to redheads. But only very recently." He looked mystified. "I really can't explain why. It's quite 'irrational', as you put it."

Larry looked at him, waiting for him to say more.

But Jim seemed embarrassed. "You must have noticed what's been happening between Rebecca and me. I think I've quite fallen for her, Larry. And I know she likes me. But recently it's just as if we really hate each other. Then I don't know what I feel. It's as if something has come between us. Holding us apart like magnets repelling each other. And she's the same. She's always flaring up, having tantrums. Sometimes she can be like a parody of a redhead."

Larry looked at him sympathetically. "Don't you see? I don't understand it myself yet, but you can feel that a real contempt for redheads is building up, all around the world. And it's being reciprocated. Except that the redheads are in a minority. You told me yourself the same thing was happening in the States, according to your friend Greg. That it was linked to the changes in the magnetic field. Now we've got Orkney."

"But how do you feel? You don't seem affected at all by all this," observed Jim. "You seem to be genuinely fond of Rebecca, all the time. You don't seem irritated by her. No repelling magnets with you!"

Larry took out his wallet, produced a crumpled photograph and showed it to Jim. "Maybe this has got something to do with it."

Jim looked at it. The photograph showed an attractive woman with short, red hair in a 1950s' perm.

"My mother," said Larry. "A redhead who carried the gene for red hair in its dominant form. I'm beginning to think I could be carrying the gene in the recessive form, because I've been having some visions myself, recently. No, don't worry! Nothing like Rebecca's. Just very powerful dreams, the same as I used to have years ago. I thought they had gone. Now they're back." Turning away from Jim, he gazed out of the window across the campus. "Also, I have a daughter myself, and I suppose I have a lot of sympathy for Rebecca."

He stood up and started collecting up the papers on his desk. "And there's something else. Tomorrow's the winter solstice."

"And what's that supposed to mean?" said Jim. "Hordes of druids on the march? A load of old hippies banging drums and chanting 'Hari Krishna'?"

"I'm being serious, Jim. As you know, in the ancient world, this was when people celebrated the return of the strength of the sun. I really believe it's no coincidence that all those red-haired children have disappeared in Orkney right now. I think this might be a time when the children, Rebecca and other red-haired people could be in great danger. I may be wrong but I really think we should be in Orkney. And I think we should go right away. This could be the moment when Neferatu strikes again."

Jim looked at Larry, half smiling. "You're really serious?"

"Look, Jim. I know all this is hard to accept for you as a scientist, but you should see it could be the biggest breakthrough since quantum mechanics. I just need you to try and go along with this. Come with me to Orkney. You're not going to pass up an opportunity like this, are you? We have to go now." He stood up. "Let's go."

"Okay, okay," said Jim. "But if you want my opinion, I think it's madness."

Larry grabbed his briefcase, stuffed the papers in it and opened the door for Jim. Within a few moments, they were in Jim's car on their way to the hotel.

CHAPTER 64

Coming to a straight stretch of road, Jim turned to Larry. "By the way, did you find out anything about Horus? Did he wear a ring that was special or something?"

"Couldn't find any evidence of a ring, but I did find out something." Larry produced some sheets of paper from his briefcase and showed one to Jim, pointing to an illustration. "Look at this. There's a small statue of him, called Horus of Pe, on display in the Egyptian section of the British Museum. And guess what? It has the head of a falcon."

Jim glanced at it. "Go on."

"Horus was the son of Osiris and Isis, the brother and sister gods of ancient Egypt. He started off as a sky god, and then became a sun god. And here's the interesting bit. In one temple in ancient Egypt – Edfu – he took the form of a bird. A peregrine." He tapped another illustration with his finger. "Not only that, but at another temple, he was worshipped as a man with the head of a hawk."

Jim swore and pulled up abruptly at some traffic lights as they turned red. Larry sorted out another sheet of paper.

"It gets even more interesting. Listen to this. Osiris was killed by his brother, Seth. According to one version, this happened before Horus was born – Horus was conceived miraculously by his mother, Isis, *after* Osiris was murdered. Isis was the sister of Seth and Osiris. It was quite a family feud." Larry looked pleased with himself. "Still with me?" He leafed through the sheets of paper until he found another illustration and held it in front of Jim.

"Not the sort of character you'd like to meet on a dark night," said Jim.

"The Seth animal," said Larry. "A dog-like body, a long tail – sometimes forked at the end – pricked-up ears and, here we go…" His voice rose in ill-concealed excitement. "*He had red hair*. And he was also identified with the serpent."

"The serpent…" said Jim, as he accelerated away from the lights. "I thought it was supposed to be a serpent on the Newton Stone that put Rebecca into a trance."

"There's more," said Larry. "Myth has it that Geb, the Earth-God, divided Egypt into two halves. Horus was given the northern part, Seth the southern. Maybe the myth reflects historical reality, because north and south battled and the conflict may have been represented by Horus and Seth. Eventually, the north conquered the south and Egypt was united. Horus was the winner and the first state-god of a united Egypt."

"And what in heaven's name has all this got to do with Rebecca and red-haired kids in twenty-first century Scotland, not to mention the inhabitants of Easter Island?"

"Don't worry, I'm getting there," said Larry. "Horus became identified with the sun, with day, with light and the fertility of the Nile. With all things good."

"And Seth?" asked Jim.

"Poor old Seth. He became god of the desert, its red colour and all the nasty things associated with the desert. All the things the ancient Egyptians feared – storms, thunder, wind, rain, destruction – things strange and unknown. The dark – the night. That was how he became the embodiment of all things evil. In effect, Seth became the bad god – and as a result, all red-haired people began to be feared, hated. Even sacrificed."

"I had noticed that things tend to get stormy whenever Rebecca's around," said Jim dryly. "Come to think of it, there is distinctly something of the Red Queen about her, isn't there? And you say she's supposed to be descended from Cleopatra. No surprise there, then – Cleopatra certainly caused plenty of trouble."

"Hey! You'd better be careful what you say, Jim," laughed Larry. "If you offend a Red Queen, 'Off with his head!' are the words that come to mind."

"I'm quaking in my boots," said Jim. "But what were you saying about Seth and Horus? You're not actually suggesting they're battling it out now in the twenty-first century, are you?"

"That's exactly what I'm thinking," replied Larry. "And I'm serious about our old friend Neferatu. I'm convinced he's involved."

"Involved in what, exactly?"

"That's what we've got to find out," said Larry.

Jim drew up outside the hotel reception and parked the car. They hurried off to their rooms.

Larry was still squeezing things into a suitcase as Jim stood behind him, already packed. The television was on.

"Ready?" Jim asked.

"Just about," Larry replied. Just then a news flash on the television made them stop in their tracks.

"It now looks certain that the Earth is about to undergo a dramatic pole switch. According to scientific advisers, this could happen at any moment, as the Earth's magnetic field continues to weaken. Electricity supplies have already been disrupted in some parts of the country, and some electronic communications are breaking down.

The government has put out the following statement: 'Due to the increase in solar radiation, some people may suffer power failure. However, we are installing emergency systems in major population centres, to ensure key services are maintained. The resulting solar radiation may affect electronic communication systems such as satellite navigation, global positioning systems, television, radio and mobile phone networks. The government wishes to assure everyone..."

At that moment, the announcer himself was interrupted by a loud hiss of interference. Then the picture disintegrated, leaving only a loud crackling noise.

Larry checked the radio and the hotel phone; neither was working. However, just as he put back the receiver, the television sprang back into life.

The newsreader, caught off-guard, was looking to the side and seemed to be receiving a message from off-camera. He turned back to the camera. "We apologise for the break in transmission. Here is the rest of the news. Orkney has cut off all transport communications, while the disappearance of around fifty children is being investigated. The police authorities are not allowing anybody to enter or leave the islands, except in the case of emergencies.

There are reports coming in of widespread intimidation and bullying in Scotland. So far the victims have been people with red hair. The Home Office has put out a statement that any red-haired person who feels concerned about his or her safety should report to the nearest police station. As soon as we receive more…" At that point, the television picture and sound disappeared completely.

"What on earth is going on?" said Larry.

"The government has just made sure that there's going to be a general panic. You'll see," said Jim. "Do they really think redheads are going to report to police stations? It'll only make them more paranoid than ever."

"Great," said Larry. "And how the hell do we get to Orkney, now? Try Rebecca's mobile again."

Jim keyed in and listened. "No signal – and we don't even know where she is."

"Well, we'd better do something, and fast," said Larry. "Rebecca's obviously in danger now. We have to get to her before Neferatu does – if he hasn't already, that is."

"I don't think we're going to get much help from the police," said Jim. "I really can't see them swallowing your Neferatu story."

"Just let me think," said Larry. "How about if we were to deliver something?"

Jim looked blank.

"Emergency equipment, for instance," said Larry.

"Such as what?"

"Electrical equipment, for example. Generators. The government is talking about power cuts, and I don't see Orkney being spared."

"Great idea," said Jim. "But where do you propose getting a load of generators from?"

"How about the Archaeology Department? The generators we use on digs? There's a shed full of them – they won't notice if we borrow a few for a while. We could go via the Scrabster-Stromness ferry – that one's the quietest. But we must hurry. Before there's a complete shutdown."

"We should take a compass as well," said Jim. "I have a feeling we're going to need one."

CHAPTER 65

The white van loaded with mobile generators headed out of Aberdeen for the long haul to Scrabster at the extreme north of the Scottish mainland, and the ferry port for Orkney. Jim took the first part of the drive, with Larry opting to navigate.

"There'll probably be a big exodus of people with red hair," said Jim. "I imagine they'll want to get together for safety, when they see what's happening. And there'll probably be plenty of other people on the move, too. They'll be heading for the big cities, – Glasgow, Edinburgh and the like – in the hope they'll be power supplies there, especially over Christmas. It could be chaos soon, with a big demand for any sort of transport."

Steady lines of cars were streaming south, laden with passengers and luggage. "Looks as if it's started already," said Jim.

Heading north, Larry and Jim found they were virtually alone. Jim checked the fuel gauge. "We're okay at the moment. But, you'll see – there'll be a run on petrol soon." His prediction proved true. As they passed north of the town of Keith, there were cars queuing at a garage on the opposite side of the road.

"And just look at the price. It's twice normal already," exclaimed Larry.

"Hey, just look at the man guarding the pumps," replied Jim. The man was holding a double-barrelled shotgun.

They both fell into a troubled silence. It was broken by Jim. "If the power's going down, we may even need the generators for ourselves."

"Could be," answered Larry, deep in thought.

They drove on through the afternoon, taking it in turns at the wheel. The roads south were becoming quieter, and they felt strangely isolated. It was not until evening that Jim pointed out the dim outline of buildings in the distance and the sea beyond.

"Okay, that's Scrabster ahead. We should make straight for the ferry – if it's running, that is. And even if there is one, we're going to have to sound pretty convincing to get on it."

"Just let me do the talking," said Larry.

"So, somehow we get on it and we get to Orkney," Jim continued. "Then what? How do we find Rebecca?"

"We don't," said Larry. "We find Neferatu first."

"What! And how do you propose to find Neferatu? Not only do we not know where he'll be, we don't even know *how* he's got there. Unless, of course, he's managed to *fly* there in his own mysterious way, so to speak." Jim fluttered his arms in a sardonic gesture.

"Well, I believe he's somehow managed to get to Orkney," said Larry, making an effort to ignore Jim's negative attitude. "The evidence is too strong now. How he got there, I have no idea. Though I'm beginning to have a theory about it. You're perhaps going to find this difficult to accept – but I believe he's somehow managing to transport himself using certain icons, through which he can appear or disappear. In which case, the best thing we can do is hunt for possible icons and hope to find him that way."

"Icons?" said Jim, taken aback. "What do you mean – icons? What the hell are you talking about?"

"Don't you see?" said Larry. "They've been a constant in all this. Whenever Neferatu appears, there's always a symbol of Horus close by. He could be using symbols of Horus as icons in order to move around. That bird-man carving on Easter Island, for instance. And it was next to a sun observatory."

He caught Jim rolling his eyes heavenwards. "No, no – hear me out, Jim. As far as I can see, this is the only possible explanation. If you remember, there was something very odd about Neferatu's arrival on Easter Island. It was a Friday when we had that dinner. Neferatu said he'd arrived there on the Wednesday before. But Pablo said there had not been any flights that day. Neferatu then said it could have been the day before. But Rebecca told me later that there had been no flights that day, either. Neferatu actually had no idea when he had arrived."

Larry paused for a moment for Jim to take the idea on board. "And then there was the Sun-Stone at Newton with the actual 'sun-sign' on it," he continued. "That whole monument is dedicated to the God of Sun-Fire. In other words, Horus."

He turned to Jim. "Can you remember exactly where you saw the eagle that attacked you in Orkney?" he asked.

"On Birsay," said Jim. "We had just been looking at a symbol stone there. Okay – so there is an eagle carved on it."

"Well, well, I think we could be on to something," said Larry triumphantly. "Somehow, Neferatu is using icons to travel around physically. He must be using them like a portal to transport himself into another dimension." He disregarded Jim's look of incredulity. "Don't you see? It's the same as with Rebecca. She used icons as well, but to *communicate* with her ancestors in another dimension. Icons like the *moai kava-kava* figure on Easter Island and then, when we did the experiment, the picture of the serpent. Without actually knowing what she was doing, in all probability."

"No, I don't *see* at all," said Jim. "It all sounds like mumbo-jumbo to me, highly unlikely, not to say impossible."

"But there's more," said Larry. "The *physical* manifestations of Rebecca's ancestors occurred close to ancestor stones, which were all associated with redheads – like the *moai* statue at Orongo and the Moon-Stone at Newton. Those manifestations needed the right portals as well."

"Well, I'll just take your word for it," said Jim. "But – okay, okay – let's go to Birsay and have a look. If we actually manage to get to Orkney, that is."

CHAPTER 66

They caught sight of the ferry as they approached the docks. There were none of the usual queues of cars and Jim drove cautiously right down on to the quayside, expecting to be challenged. They could see a lorry driving up the ramp ahead of them. As it disappeared on to the boat, an official made to shut the gates.

"Leave this to me," said Larry, and jumped out of the van. He strode confidently over to the official. "Sorry we're late," he said.

The official looked surprised. "Sorry, sir, emergency supplies only."

"Special request from the Chief of Police in Kirkwall. Generators. He wants them installed at the police station immediately."

"Can't say I was expecting anything else. Have you got the paperwork?"

"No. We were told it was an emergency. We've just rushed up all the way from Aberdeen," said Larry.

The official hesitated. "Well, I don't know about that."

"Well, do you want to tell the Chief of Police you wouldn't let me on board, or shall I?" said Larry tersely, as he reached for his phone. He then realised it probably wouldn't work, anyway.

At that moment, a deckhand on the boat leaned over the rail. "Ready when you are."

The official relented. "Okay. But I'll have to check what you've got in there."

Jim drove the van over and opened up the doors. The official checked the generators. "All right," he said. "Drive on."

As the van was secured into position, Larry smiled with satisfaction at Jim. "Coffee – food. Let's see what we can get."

The boat, not surprisingly, was almost deserted, and the only food and drink on offer was from vending machines. Going on deck as the boat left port, they leaned against the rail, coffees and snacks in hand.

Darkness had fallen, but the sky was already starting to glow with a strong green light. Once again, the Northern Lights were flickering in the heavens.

A deckhand wandered over to join them and gazed up at the sky. "Pretty, isn't it? We see this all the time now," he said. "Where are you going, anyway? I thought no one was allowed to travel here any more."

"The main police station in Kirkwall. To install some emergency generators," answered Larry.

"Look after themselves first, don't they?" said the deckhand. "We've got power cuts all the time now. Pretty sure this'll be our last trip. The radar's down and the radio's down – all the communication systems. We're only doing this trip because it's emergency supplies."

Larry turned to Jim. "Try your mobile again. Try Rebecca."

Jim stabbed in the number and listened. "It's completely dead," he said.

The deckhand seemed unsurprised. "You'd better be careful," he said. "Strangers are not exactly very welcome at the moment. Since those kids disappeared, people are a bit edgy. They're starting to blame each other and there's been some fights – quite nasty. The police are having a job to keep control."

"Thanks. We'll be careful," said Larry.

CHAPTER 67

As Larry drove the van off the ferry, the lorry in front of him was stopped by a uniformed officer, who stepped out of the darkness and went round to speak to the driver. It seemed to take an eternity as they chatted together amiably. Eventually the officer stepped back with a big smile and waved the driver on.

"This could be a bit more difficult," said Larry, moving the van forwards and opening the side window. "Good evening, officer," he said.

The officer seemed barely beyond boyhood. In fact, he was not a full policeman at all. A badge on his cap stated 'Community Warden'. "Papers, please," he said.

"Oh dear, we gave them to an officer in Scrabster," said Larry. "He took them from us before he allowed us on board." The officer looked unsure what to do.

"All on your own tonight?" asked Larry sympathetically, looking around the deserted quay.

"Yes. Everyone is out trying to deal with the riots. That's why I'm here. It's getting a bit rough, tonight. People fighting all over the place. A lot of injuries – and the hospital is getting short of medical supplies. What with the power being cut off as well – it's mayhem. It's not usually like this."

"Did the lorry driver have all his papers?" ventured Larry.

"Er, actually, no he didn't. But I know he's okay. He's a mate of mine. He's been to get emergency drugs from Scrabster. The hospital's running out."

"Same as us," said Larry. "We've been to get emergency generators for the hospital. Have a look if you like." He got out of the van and opened up the back. The officer peered in. "You know, we should be pressing on," Larry said. "Don't want anybody dying just because we didn't get there fast enough." He closed the van doors and jumped back in the cab. The officer stepped back and, with some hesitation, waved him on.

"You should have been a politician, the way you told that pack of lies," observed Jim, as they drove off straight into the town.

Stromness was in total darkness and seemed to be deserted. The only light came from the waving green curtain of the Northern Lights, which cast an eerie glow over the buildings.

Jim was peering out, looking for any signposts. "God, it's dark in this place."

"Let's just head straight for Birsay," said Larry impatiently. "Which way is it?"

Jim continued to search for roadsigns but could only make out a deserted road. "Just turn left. This is a small place – there must be a signpost soon."

After five minutes driving around the town, Larry pulled over so that Jim could look at the map. I've found Stromness and Birsay," he said. "But all I can say is, we've got to head north."

"That's a great help. I know that – but which road do I take? We could be going in any direction. The irritating thing is, I remember getting lost in this place once before."

Jim became exasperated. "Dammit. We just need to head north by any means, wherever we are."

At that moment, the Northern Lights flickered a few times, then faded away altogether. "I think I know what's going on," said Jim. "Where's the compass?"

"On my key ring," said Larry.

Jim slipped the compass off the key ring and put it flat on his knee. He tapped it, then tapped it again. The needle was going round in circles.

Larry looked over at the compass, a puzzled expression on his face.

"You realise what this means, don't you?" said Jim. "It's finally happened – the Earth's magnetic field has totally disappeared. At least around here."

Larry picked up the compass and inspected it. "Maybe it's because we're inside the van." He opened the door to get out.

"Come back! Quick! Shut the door," shouted Jim, pulling him back.

A tangled throng of fighting, shouting men, armed with metal bars and wooden cudgels had suddenly emerged from the darkness. Jim instantly locked the van doors, but as the violent group surged towards them, it quickly became evident that these men were completely oblivious to the presence of both the van and its occupants.

As they moved into the beam of their headlights, it appeared that four or five men were being savagely beaten up. Each time one of them managed to break free, he was pulled back into the crowd, as if being forced to run a never-ending gauntlet. Within a minute or two, the frenzied mob had passed out of their view back into the darkness, their cries fading in the distance.

"Jesus!" said Jim, shocked and astonished. "What's that all about?"

"My guess, wrong colour hair," said Larry simply. "Let's just get out of here."

Jim pointed to a road ahead. "Over there. Let's just hope it's in the right direction."

It was not. But after a mile or so, they passed a single signpost to Birsay.

CHAPTER 68

The abduction of Rebecca was carried out quickly and efficiently. She had barely left the police station, when a large black car drew up behind her. Unseen by Rebecca, the rear door of the car opened and Neferatu slid out. He was dressed in the same damp suit that he had been wearing on Norstray. As the car crawled slowly alongside, he caught up with her, clasped a hand over her mouth, dragged her back to the car and forced her into the back seat before she had time to realise what was happening. Neferatu pushed her head down on to the seat as the car accelerated away.

He released her only as they were crossing the causeway that led out of Kirkwall, over the Bay of Weyland. She sat up, shocked and dazed.

Neferatu turned towards her, with his familiar sneer. "So, you just couldn't resist coming here, could you?" he snarled, in a guttural accent she hadn't heard before. "And you walked right into my trap. Your friends will follow you. But there'll be no escape this time."

She found it difficult to find her voice. "Why do you want to kill me? What have I done?" she whispered.

Neferatu face was impassive. "You have to die," he said, "because you are the Queen."

Rebecca sat there, stunned. "The Queen? What Queen? What do you mean?" she asked.

"You must know that you are the leader of the tribe – the Queen of the Redheads."

Rebecca struggled to make sense of what was happening. "I still don't understand," she said. "I don't know what you're talking about. I'm not a Queen of anything. I'm just a journalist writing a story. I don't understand why you want me dead."

"You don't need to understand," was all he would answer.

Then why doesn't he just kill me right now? she thought.

It was as if he had read her mind. "You could have had a quick and easy death. Now we have something very special for you."

"Let me go! I don't belong to any tribe."

"Oh yes, but you do," he said.

"What are you on about? Where are you taking me?"

"Somewhere where nobody will find you," he answered coldly.

The driver turned around. His face was Middle Eastern. "We are getting very near," he said, his accent similar to Neferatu's.

Rebecca looked outside the car. It lurched as they swept around a roundabout and headed down a road signposted to Stromness. Neferatu was now staring straight ahead impassively, indifferent to the passing landscape.

Suddenly, feeling she had nothing to lose and infuriated by his arrogance and stupidity, she shouted, "What have you done with all the children? Where are they? What are you planning to do with them? They're just innocent children, for heaven's sake!"

He slowly turned to face her, his green eyes burning into hers. "They are quite safe enough – until tomorrow. We have taken them to many secret places – similar to where we are taking you. They are scattered all over the island. But you will be kept completely alone – and you will suffer."

Rebecca looked at him with contempt. "You sick bastard," she said, and raised her hand to hit his face.

Neferatu grabbed her wrist and twisted her arm so that she squealed with pain. He let go of her and raised his fist as a warning. She sat there, shaking.

"How far is it now?" he said to the driver, as they drove slowly along the side of a loch.

"We're here," said the driver. He turned off the road and headed down a track towards the water.

Rebecca thought she couldn't feel more wretched, until she saw the large, grass-covered mound in front of them. It looked like a smaller version of the tomb of Maeshowe.

As the car pulled up abruptly into a parking space, Neferatu sprang into action. He jumped out of the car, grabbed Rebecca, forced her arm behind her back and frog-marched her towards the entrance. She caught a glimpse of the name of the tomb on a sign: 'Unstan Chambered Tomb', as the driver knelt down and opened a low iron grill-gate.

Saying nothing now, Neferatu forced her on to her knees and pushed her roughly into the entrance passage. Before she could turn, she heard the gate clang shut and the click of the key in a padlock.

Neferatu turned and walked back to the car, calling to Rebecca over his shoulder, "You can shout and scream all you like. They're all dead there. Enjoy their company – you'll be joining them soon." The car reversed, turned around and sped back towards the road.

Rebecca crawled the four feet through the passage into the tomb, took one look and quickly headed back to the gate. She shook it violently, but it was firmly locked. "Help! Help! Get me out of here!" she screamed.

She went on screaming until her voice became weak and hoarse. Nobody appeared. Not even a bird. Only a cold winter breeze blew intermittently from the loch.

She tried stabbing the keys on her phone and putting it to her ear. It was completely dead.

Finally, slumping against the cold iron of the gate, she found herself weeping uncontrollably. Realising the futility of her situation, she backed away from the gate and made her way back into the gloom of the tomb.

Standing up, all she could initially make out were large slabs of cold, grey stone covered in patches of green lichen. On closer inspection, she could see that some of the slabs were set vertically to create dark chambers around a central space. She wondered how long the Neolithic dead had lain in these chambers, before their bones had finally been cleared.

In the dim light of the tomb, she noticed two windows in the roof, but they were impossible to reach.

Defeated and dejected, she sat down on a stone sill at the entrance to a chamber and tried to keep calm. The atmosphere was cold and damp and even in her winter coat she started to shiver. She clasped her arms around her and began to go over what Neferatu had said. But it did not make any sense to her. Trying to imagine what Neferatu could have been talking about, she got up and walked around, checking to see if there were any means of escape through the chambers. There were not. She was effectively sealed in.

She was about to sit down again, when a small carving on a stone at the entrance to a chamber caught her eye. It was like a child's drawing of a bird, about three inches long and etched into the rock. She could not help wondering who had done it. Like her, the bird seemed trapped inside the tomb.

She remembered Jim telling her that Orkney was dotted with remote tombs like this. She realised it could be weeks before anybody trapped in them would be found. They were the ideal places to keep captives in. She thought about the small children now imprisoned inside them. Imagining what they must be going through, she was overwhelmed with desperate concern for them.

She crawled back to the gate and called out – but to no avail. Feeling completely desolate, she returned to the inside of the tomb and sat down again on the cold stone sill with her head in her hands.

It was beginning to get dark, and with the darkness it was becoming colder. She put her arms around her knees, making herself as small as possible in an attempt to keep warm, watching the skylights and the entrance-gate, dreading what she might see.

As the darkness grew, she wondered desperately whether anybody would guess what had happened to her, or whether they might organise a rescue mission. Any animosity she had felt towards Jim and Syreeta had long dissipated, and she now yearned for them to appear.

Who might miss her on Orkney? In reality, nobody would notice her absence. Besides, the people of Orkney had other things on their minds.

Her mind was beginning to switch off when something flashed past her head, zigzagged around her and disappeared inside a chamber. She shrieked and waved her hands around her hair in panic. Shaking, she looked around, trying to convince herself that it was only a harmless bat.

She was very thirsty and would have done anything for a glass of water. She checked her watch. It was nearly seven o'clock and she had had nothing to eat or drink since early that morning. She was now desperate for someone, anyone, to appear.

Then, a freezing mist seemed to come up out of the floor, swirling around her ankles. She jumped up, but it rose rapidly up her body, until she couldn't see anything around her.

Edging back against an upright stone slab, she stood there, frozen. In one chamber, a pile of gleaming white bones shone through the mist, as if they had an inner light. The mist eddied, and she caught glimpses of dark, shadowy figures in it. Dead, glazed eyes seemed to pop out of nowhere, stared at her and then disappeared, only to reappear somewhere else.

A hand suddenly grasped her shoulder, and she almost fainted. A hairy face appeared in front of hers, followed by a body which seemed to materialise as she watched. The face bore a kindly expression. It was that of a middle-aged man with a fiery beard and unkempt red hair down to his shoulders. He was wearing a belted jacket and trousers, crudely stitched together out of some rough brown woollen material.

What transfixed her and strangely reassured her were his clear blue eyes. He said something to her in an urgent tone, but she couldn't comprehend what it was. It sounded a little like Gaelic. He waited for her response, but all she could say was, "I don't understand." Clearly impatient, he repeated the message. Rebecca shook her head. "I don't know what you're saying."

Then there was another voice, yet no body this time. It was the voice of a woman. A mixture of wonder and relief surged through Rebecca. She recognised the voice of her own mother. But the tone was earnest.

"He is telling you to put back the Odin Stone. It is urgent. It is true what he said. You are the Queen. You must put back the Odin Stone."

At that moment, there was a *clank* from the direction of the entrance. Instantly, the apparition, the voices and the mist all disappeared. Two huge swarthy men emerged, one after the other, from the entrance passage into the central chamber and stood up. Together, they grabbed her arms. Dazed and exhausted, she was unable to struggle this time, though she was bewildered by their strange appearance. Apart from loincloths, they were completely naked.

CHAPTER 69

The two hefty men forced Rebecca through the entrance to the tomb. One was taller and stronger-looking than the other, and his air of authority seemed to denote that he was in charge. Seizing two spears which they had left outside, they prodded her towards the track without a word. With one on either side, she was briskly marched towards the road and shoved along roughly if she tried to slow down.

As they reached the road, she caught sight of a group of terrified, wailing children, all with red hair, emerging out of the gloom. Some were holding hands, most of them crying, one girl carrying a howling baby. Only one guard accompanied the children, and he hit them occasionally on their sides with a spear, as if shepherding a flock of sheep. Rebecca desperately wanted to console them, but she was hastily pushed into line behind them and swept along, unable to do anything to help.

It seemed only a short time before they reached the path that led up to the Ring of Brodgar. From the opposite direction of Stenness appeared another group of miserable red-haired captives, emerging out of the darkness. It became clear that they were mostly children, exhausted and barely able to walk. Among them were one or two women, usually carrying an infant, and the occasional man with a guard close by, spear at the ready.

More guards stood at the junction of the road and the path, directing the throng up towards the stone circle. This was lit by flares set on top of the stones, so that it looked like a ring of fire.

There, standing at the entrance, was Neferatu, hands on his hips and a thin satisfied smile on his face. He was now dressed in fine white robes, apparently indifferent to the cold. He surveyed the crowd carefully, as if looking for somebody. As Rebecca came into sight, his eyes lit up and he made his way towards her.

"So pleased you could join us," he said, with a mocking half bow.

Rebecca broke away from the group and stumbled over to him. "Why are you doing this?" she asked, angry and bewildered. "What is this all about?"

"It's about getting rid of the lot of you, once and for all," Neferatu replied.

He beckoned the taller of the guards who had brought Rebecca out of the tomb. "You know your orders, Inherkhau. Move her on."

Rebecca stood her ground, even when a guard held a spear to her leg. "Look at these children. They're freezing cold."

Neferatu smiled again. "Don't worry yourself about that. They'll soon be warm." He laughed. "Very warm."

Inherkhau stuck his spear into Rebecca's back, making her cry out with pain, and forced her into the Ring.

Neferatu stopped two of the guards. "Get the scum to prepare their own pit," he commanded them.

Within minutes, the captives were all handed a variety of digging implements: shovels and spades for the adults, and trowels and even sticks for the smallest children. Inherkhau thrust a spade into Rebecca's hands.

The guards ordered them to start digging in the middle of the Ring. At first they only removed the thin turf, but as the pit slowly deepened, a pile of dirt grew alongside. As the smallest and weakest of the children soon grew weary, guards marched over, seized them and threw them out of the pit. They huddled together, cowering whenever the guards approached them.

Neferatu strode over towards them. "Take the biggest to find wood," he ordered. "Anything, as long as it will burn."

After an hour or so, the pit was about twenty foot square and two foot deep. By this time, those digging consisted mainly of the few men, the rest ordered to level out the pile of soil and rocks. The only woman now left digging was Rebecca, the others having been dragged away as they collapsed with exhaustion, to be dumped with the children. Her back ached as it had never ached before, and her hands were now bleeding.

A tough-looking, middle-aged man edged towards her. She recognised him immediately; it was Sandy Lewis, the man she and Jim had met at the Stones of Stenness.

Unobtrusively, he pulled his shirt out of his trousers, ripped off a strip of it and handed it to her. "Use this," he said quietly.

Rebecca took it, tore it into two, wrapped the pieces around her hands and stayed close to him while she dug her spade again into the stony subsoil.

"Listen, I have to tell you something. You'll think I've gone mad, but it's absolutely true," she whispered, trying not to draw attention. "You've got to believe me."

"What is it, lass?" he replied, throwing a shovelful of rubble out of the pit.

"They threw me into the tomb at Unstan just now. It sounds crazy, I know, but I had a vision there of a strange man. He looked like some kind of wild hippie, but his clothes were made out of some sort of rough material. He could have been one of the people who lived around here in ancient times. Anyway, he spoke to me. I couldn't understand what he was saying – but I could tell it was important and urgent." Sandy carried on digging as he listened. "Then I heard my mother's voice – I know it was my mother. She said this man was telling me I had to put back the Odin Stone. As quickly as possible. I was thinking – what if it's true? Maybe it could save us?"

Sandy looked astonished. "What? The Odin Stone at Stenness?"

"Yes. The one that was destroyed years ago. That was his message."

Sandy was quiet for a moment. "A lot of us have been having visions – I have seen my grandparents. But the Odin Stone? How on earth can that be put back?"

"There must be a way," insisted Rebecca. "And it may be our only hope."

At that moment, Neferatu, who was standing some way away, noticed them talking. He stormed over. "Keep digging," he shouted at Rebecca. "There is no time for talking. Soon, the sun will come up, and you and your wretched people will meet your fate. You will be gone. Forever."

Then he marched over to Inherkhau. "It's time for you to go now. They will be waiting for you on the island. Be back by dawn."

Inherkhau nodded and went to talk to a group of guards. Minutes later, unnoticed by those below, a flock of birds hovered over the Ring, before heading due north, led by a peregrine falcon.

Rebecca and Sandy watched Neferatu stride away purposefully towards the entrance to the Ring and disappear out of sight.

"Who is that?" asked Sandy. "Is he in charge of all this? Is he responsible?"

"His name is Neferatu," she said, under her breath. "I don't know why, but he wants to kill us all. He seems to think I'm special. He tried to kill me before – said I was some sort of queen. I know he means to kill me, and probably you, too. And everyone one else here who's been rounded up." A guard came up quickly and hit Rebecca's leg with his spear.

Just then, there was a loud noise at the entrance to the Ring; a heavy clanking noise that echoed around the stones. At the entrance to the Ring, Rebecca and Sandy could see that the guards had become visibly excited, raising their spears and cheering, as something seemed to be making its laborious, clumsy way towards the Ring.

Everybody seemed to be mesmerised, captors and captives alike, their eyes straining for a glimpse of whatever it was coming ever closer.

Sandy grabbed Rebecca's arm, forcing her to turn round and look at him. "I'm going to try and make a dash for it. I know about the Odin Stone – and I think I know what they were on about in the tomb. Listen, I don't know what's happening right now, but this could be our only chance. No time to tell you. I just hope I can put it back. I'm sorry, I'll have to leave you here – but if I get away now, I may be able to help. Before it's too late. Bye!"

He checked around. The guards were becoming increasingly excited by events outside the entrance, and the captives stood silently, all looking in the same direction, as if spellbound by whatever fate had in store for them.

Sandy now crept slowly sideways until he reached the darkest corner of the pit. Then he climbed out, crouching close to the ground. Moving cautiously toward a huge upright stone, he caught sight of a fiery glow and the gleam of hot metal, slowly approaching the entrance like an old steam engine. The guards seemed overjoyed. Seizing his chance, Sandy slipped away into the darkness and sprinted down the hill towards the loch.

At first, it was impossible to discern what it was. Then the guards roared with excitement. As the huge, flaming monster was hauled into the Ring, the children started whimpering, and the men and women gasped in horror.

CHAPTER 70

It took two blows with a sledgehammer to break through the front door of the fisherman's cottage on the Orkney island of Norstray.

At the time, Jock Lewis, Sandy's only brother, was working on his car by the light of a hurricane lamp in the garage to the rear.

Duncan, Jock's fourteen-year old son, was in the tiny front room doing his homework by the light of a candle. The boy started with fright when he heard the front door crash in, and cowered against the wall as the three men burst in on him. One grabbed him by the arm, twisting it behind his back. The boy howled in pain as he was marched out of the house and into the street.

Hearing his screams, Duncan's mother ran in from the kitchen. A second man cuffed her around the head and bundled her past the smashed-in door. She screamed for her husband, but as Jock rushed in from the garage, he barely made it to the back door. A blow to the face broke his nose. With blood streaming down his face, he was kicked and beaten and then shoved outside to join his wife and son.

Wiping the blood from his face, Jock looked aghast at his bloodied hand and at his brutal attackers. As if in some sort of nightmare, where everything is topsy-turvy, they were not, as he had first imagined, some unknown gang of hooligans. He was horrified to find that these were people he knew. These were his neighbours, people he had known for twenty years.

"Hamish! Malcolm! What in hell's name is going on? What's up with you all? What have we done?" he cried, trying to find some reason behind the situation.

Malcolm threatened him with his fist. "Just shut it, ginger scum." He made as if to kick Jock, but pulled back and turned to Hamish and Rob, another neighbour, who had armed himself with a wooden chair-leg. "Okay. Let's go! Let's take them to the Devil's House."

Jock's wife was clutching her son, sobbing quietly with shock. When Rob laid a hand on Mary's shoulder and started to shove her forwards, it was too much for Jock. "Get your bloody hands off her," he bellowed, and charged forwards, knocking the lump of wood out of Rob's hands. Malcolm leapt to grab the cudgel, raised it above his head and brought it down on Jock's skull as hard as he could. Jock slumped to the ground, groaning.

"Pick him up," growled Malcolm. "Look, this is only just the beginning. Get moving! No time for talking."

Jock was hauled up and stood there, totally shocked and bewildered, nursing his swelling bruise and shaking his head in disbelief at Rob.

The three of them were herded along the main village street by the three men. Neighbours, who up until today had apparently been their friends, now stood silently in doorways. Curtains twitched as shadowy faces watched the procession from behind their windows. Jock put his arms around his wife and son, looking at each man in turn, still searching for some sort of meaning behind it all.

At the main road junction just outside the village, they caught sight of another bedraggled group of red-haired men, women and adolescent children; this time accompanied by a gang of about fifty men armed with pitchforks, lumps of wood and even shotguns. Norstray's population was small, and Jock and his family were able to recognise almost everyone there, captors and captives alike.

Some of the armed men conferred together and then, with more curses and threats, moved their captives along a narrow lane.

The ruins of the kirk appeared on the horizon, standing out bleakly against the night sky. About a hundred yards before it, the group came to a halt. In the gloom, the austere building seemed to have taken on an even more forbidding aspect than usual, and the graveyard tombstones stood proudly erect, like grim and impartial observers.

As Jock and his family watched, a large peregrine falcon flew in and perched on the highest point of a wall at one end of the ruin. Then two sparrowhawks, smaller than the falcon, arrived out of the darkness and joined it, taking up position slightly below, as if in deference to the falcon. The birds seemed to be eyeing the crowd below expectantly, their heads twisting from side to side.

When they were followed by a flock of six kestrels, which landed at the opposite end of the building, the landlord of the Fisherman's Rest raised a pitchfork in the air.

"Christ Almighty, is this what he meant, that weird stranger?" he said. "How did he manage this? It's super-human, that's what it is!" He gestured to the others with the pitchfork to move the captives along through a broken doorway, into the nettle-covered interior. Jock raised his fist, only to have the pitchfork thrust brutally against his chest.

The captors took up position at the doorway, while their prisoners watched with unease as a flock of hen harriers swooped in and landed, strutting menacingly along the top of the broken walls.

As more and more birds arrived, the air became thick and threatening with feathered activity. A terror-struck young girl turned to her parents. "What's happening? Why are all these birds here?" she cried, echoing the primeval fear of the evil they seemed to represent, felt by all the captives.

The fear made them restless. Then it turned to rage. One young man, unable to contain his fury, made a desperate dash for freedom through the doorway, but was viciously beaten back inside.

Yet more flocks of birds – kites, buzzards and ospreys – continued to circle and then settle, forming a continuous, thick, black band around the top of the walls. As the birds became more agitated, the sound of their rustling feathers grew louder. Intermittently, there would be a flap of wings, as two or three birds flew from one side of the ruins to the other.

A light rain was now beginning to fall, adding to the misery of those within the walls, where there was a growing sense of impending doom. There were shouted appeals for explanations and calls for mercy but, apart from the odd curse, they went unheeded. A boy of fifteen, a friend of Duncan from the next village, started to complain that he was hungry and was rapidly hushed by his father. But other men, unable to contain themselves, started to force their way towards the doorway, shouting angrily for their release and threatening their captors with revenge.

Then, suddenly, as if some unknown force were being unleashed in protest against what was going to happen next, a blast of wind knocked the birds off balance, so that they fluttered around and settled again wherever they could. A flash of lightning lit up the whole landscape and was followed by a clap of thunder so violent that it shook the ruins. As the echoes of the thunder faded away, small pieces of masonry rattled down. Then there was silence.

It was as if the birds had received an invisible signal. They rose up as one into the air and circled menacingly above the ruins. The falcon flew up higher than the rest, as if it were somehow in command, and hovered, scarcely visible now in the night sky.

But it was the falcon that was the first to dive down on to the throng below. It swooped down, slicing the face of a woman who was looking up, leaving a thin line across her cheek from which blood started to well.

As the captives instinctively lowered their heads to protect themselves, a pair of harriers landed on the shoulders of a man who had covered his head with his hands. One of them caught hold of his ear and, with a few jerky movements, pulled at the ear until the lobe tore away in its beak. The man screamed in pain and beat the birds off. They flew up above the building, wheeled tightly and swooped down to attack again.

For a brief moment, the bulk of the birds held back. Then, as if sensing blood, they fell together like huge black hailstones on to the terrified crowd below. The captors instantly retreated from the building to avoid the fate of those inside, but quickly moved back, taking up position in the doorway and under the open windows, so that no one could escape.

Terrible screams filled the night air as the birds landed on their prey, flapping their wings and stabbing with their beaks. Any attempt to fight them off was futile. Occasionally, someone might beat a bird off, but it always returned to attack again, pecking savagely at the hands trying to protect the face.

As the captives withdrew their badly injured hands, one after another the birds dived in to peck at the exposed eyes. Only then did some of the birds, with chunks of flesh or part of an eyeball held firmly in their beaks, leave the fray to flap triumphantly up and on to the walls. There they perched, consuming their gains.

Clothes were ripped and torn away, exposing areas of flesh into which their beaks were sunk. The almost inhuman screams of terror and pain were half-drowned by the beating of wings.

It took no more than five minutes or so for the carnage to be complete. The birds' intent seemed to be to maim, to blind, rather than to kill. Those blinded started to move around, fumbling, tripping over, colliding with each other in their attempts to escape the horror. Too distraught to speak, they wailed and moaned, nursing gashed cheeks, bloodied arms and legs or ripped ears.

The birds and the captors began to drift off. The birds circled for a while, as if inspecting the bloodbath below. But the captors melted away into the darkness without speaking, some with faces bearing an expression of grim satisfaction, while others were expressionless, as if unable to comprehend the grotesque climax that had resulted from their dreadful actions.

CHAPTER 71

Sandy Lewis had managed to escape from the Ring of Brodgar unnoticed, with Rebecca's words still ringing in his ears. He knew enough about the Odin Stone and its magic from local folklore to understand what she had been talking about. He had also had his own visions. One after another, his grandparents had appeared to him in dreams, so real that he had thought they were in the room with him, and had told him not to fear for his future. He didn't know what they had meant exactly, but the experience had powerfully affected him.

Even so, he found it hard to believe that putting back the Odin Stone could help the poor wretches he had left behind, and yet what choice did he have? It was the faintest of hopes, but the only alternative was to accept without a fight the massacre of innocent people under circumstances of almost unbelievable barbarity.

Having escaped the immediate danger, he planned to make for his brother Jock's dinghy, moored in the Bay of Ireland nearby. If he used the engine, he could easily make the short distance to his fishing boat at Stromness. From there, it would take an hour or so to reach his family and friends on the island of Norstray and get some help.

He was in sight of Sandy Ness on the island of Norstray when the wind caught his little fishing boat sideways on. A powerful gust whipped across the bay and swung the boat around. Grabbing the wheel, he caught a glimpse of a strange black cloud of circling birds rising into the night sky and hovering above the ruins of the kirk. Seconds later, blood-curdling screams and cries of pain cut through the air towards him.

He froze for a second, then slammed the engine into full-ahead, made for the shore and beached his boat. Even as he clambered out of it and splashed through the shallow sea, he could see birds wheeling haphazardly above him, one or two swooping down menacingly in his direction.

Stumbling over the shingle, he made his way towards the kirk and climbed over the wall into the graveyard. A solitary kestrel dived towards him, missing his head by inches, before disappearing up into the darkness.

At the entrance to the kirk, he came to an abrupt stop and almost retched. There in front of him was a scene from hell, a re-enactment of a medieval painting of Judgment Day. Men and women, with gaping blood-streaked hollows for eyes, staggered around, hands held out in front of them, tripping over fallen bodies and bumping into the walls. Some were lying on the ground, sobbing hysterically, shrieking in pain. Others lay there, twitching uncontrollably. One or two were lying completely motionless among the nettles.

For a moment, Sandy was too shocked to move. Then, bewildered, he began to walk around, stepping carefully over bodies. Some faces seemed familiar, and yet so mutilated that it took him a while to identify them. They were all people he knew; local friends and neighbours, and others from nearby villages.

Among them in the darkness, he suddenly recognised the face of his brother, Jock, who was stumbling in his direction. Sandy caught hold of him. Jock had no eyes. Only bleeding sockets. "Oh, my God, my God," he kept repeating to himself.

"Jock, it's me – Sandy. What's the hell's been happening? What happened, Jock?"

Jock ran his bloodied hand over Sandy's face. "Sandy? Is it really you?"

"Yes, it's me," Sandy said.

Jock grabbed Sandy's arm. "Where are Mary and Duncan? Have you seen them? Are they all right? I tried to stay with them, but the birds got my eyes. What's it about, Sandy? What have we done? This is hell, isn't it?"

"Stay here," said Sandy. "Sit down on this stone. I'll go and look for them."

He found Jock's wife and son, lying on the ground together, Mary half on top of Duncan. Sandy knelt down beside them. Ribbons of bleeding flesh hung down from their faces, but they were alive, breathing and moaning. "Mary – it's Sandy," he whispered. She stirred and stretched out a hand towards him. "Jock's okay," he said. "I'll bring him over."

Sandy went back to Jock, took his arm and guided him over to his wife and son. Jock knelt down besides Mary and lovingly ran his hands over her.

Sandy put his hand on Jock's shoulder. "Who or what in the name of God did this?"

Jock turned towards Sandy. "You won't believe it. It was the birds. They just fell on us and tore us to pieces, like something out of a horror film. But someone, or something, must have set them up. We couldn't get away, because we'd been driven up here like criminals and outlaws.

And who drove us here? Unbelievable! *Our own neighbours*, people from the village. They suddenly turned on us – they were so violent! Don't ask me why. We've done *nothing* to justify this. *Nothing*. They picked on anyone with red hair. Anybody with red hair was rounded up and dragged up here. Men, women, lads and lassies. They'd have got you, too, if they'd found you. It was like an organised war."

Sandy shook his head in disbelief. "*Exactly* which neighbours did this to you?"

"Malcolm. Rob. Hamish. *Our friends*. Rob and I were actually out fishing together a couple of days ago. It was as if they didn't recognise us. They turned on us – like they suddenly hated us. And the language. They swore and insulted us – 'ginger bollocks' – 'fire crotch' – 'blood nuts'. They've never used that sort of language before.

Some children disappeared first, and now this. But why? What have we done to them? One moment they're normal – then they do this!"

Jock put his hands to his face as blood-filled tears rolled down. He tried to wipe his face with his hand, but only succeeded in smearing it.

Sandy looked around at the carnage and took his arm away from his brother's shoulder. "Look, I'm going to have to get help. We need doctors."

"Not from here, Sandy. Not doctors from here. There's something very foul going on here. You've got to get us away from Norstray."

"Okay, I'll go to another island, perhaps Stronsay. I've got the boat on the beach."

"For Christ's sake, be quick. They could come back."

Sandy squeezed Jock's arm. "I'll be quick, but I have to do something else first. Something very urgent. I'm so sorry, but there's no time to explain. I'll be as quick as I can." He stepped carefully over the bodies, before sprinting back to the beach.

Heaving the boat back into the water, he leapt into it just as the prow cleared the sand. Starting the engine, he swung the boat around and headed at full speed over the now calm sea towards the island of Stronsay.

CHAPTER 72

The atmosphere in Kirkwall police station was electric. Chief Constable Douglas MacKenzie was addressing about forty assembled staff. He took off his cap and passed his hand over his wiry grey hair.

"It's essential that we maintain some sort of order here. I don't understand what's happening any more than you do. But here are the facts. Fifty red-haired children have gone missing. We have no idea where they are. It seems that people with red hair are being picked on for some unknown reason. And the power's down. We've had reports of looting already. I can't emphasise it enough – we're in a very serious situation here. And we have to stay calm. Things could easily get violent."

One of the officers, Iain Buchan, was standing at the back. "Let's not kid ourselves. It's utter chaos out there. I've just driven down from Settiscarth. Anyone with red hair has been savagely beaten up and hounded out of town. I didn't even dare to stop to investigate. I kept my cap pulled down and my car doors locked. If anybody had seen me, I could have been a target, too. And my hair is not even that red – just a bit sandy. The trouble is, you don't know if you're going to be another target."

"Well, as far as we're concerned, you're just another bloody ginger," a dark-haired sergeant said loudly.

Buchan exchanged furtive glances with a few of his colleagues who happened to have hair of varying shades of red. They all looked uneasy.

But it was too much for a hefty constable named Chuck Ramsay. "And who the hell do you think you're talking to?" he blazed at the sergeant.

"You, if you like, you bloody freak," retorted the sergeant, turning towards him.

The Chief Constable raised his hands in the air. "Please, please. Come on. Don't start that here. We don't want any of this here. We are the police. The professionals, remember. We're above all that sort of thing."

Ramsay and the sergeant continued to glare at each other, each hardly containing his anger.

Another officer from Stromness turned to the red-haired man who was standing beside him. "What about you, then? What does your wife call you? Ginger nuts, does she?" he said in a loud whisper. The reply was a blow to the nose that sent blood streaming down his face on to his white shirt.

Constable Ramsay, taking instant advantage of the situation, marched straight over to the offending sergeant and kneed him hard in the groin. There was immediate mayhem. The Chief Constable called for calm, but his voice was drowned by catcalls and shouting. He hesitated for a few moments before quietly edging his way towards the exit.

Four men simultaneously turned on Ramsay. He swung around, catching two of them with thumps to the head, before he himself was felled by a blow from a truncheon. The four aggressors started to kick him as he lay curled up on the floor, his arms raised in a vain attempt to protect himself.

Iain Buchan made a dash for the door but was brought down by a rugby tackle well before he reached it.

Another russet-haired officer attempted to slip unobtrusively out of the fire exit at the back of the room. He made it as far as the car park outside before the others caught up with him. They beat him to the ground and kicked him savagely and repeatedly, until he showed no more sign of life.

CHAPTER 73

There was not a single light to be seen on the island, as Sandy approached the ferry terminal on Stronsay. It was in complete darkness. About fifty yards from land, he cut the engine, pulled his hat down to his ears and drifted silently to the embarkation point for the ferry.

As he warily made his way to the terminal building, the whole area seemed deserted. Yet when he peered into the entrance, he was startled to see a group of men running out of the darkness towards him. He tried to run for cover, but too late, and he was thrown to the ground by a blow to the head which knocked his hat off. As he tried to get up, a tough-looking man went to kick him.

"Stop! He's one of us," he heard someone say.

Sandy staggered to his feet and looked around. Four men, with hair ranging in colour from bright red to pepper and salt, were eyeing him warily.

"For Christ's sake," said Sandy, "I want some bloody help. Not to be beaten up. People are being murdered out there – people like us."

"You'll not get any help here," said the tough-looking man. "We have to get away. We were looking for a boat. Then we saw yours."

A man in his twenties, with long hair tied in a ponytail, spoke up. "They're all out hunting for us, like animals. It's been going on since midday. They're rounding up anybody with red hair."

"I know," said Sandy. "It's happening all over the place. I've just escaped from Brodgar. They've collected up all the red-haired kids there. It's beyond belief, I know, but I'm sure there's some sort of huge sacrifice about to take place.

It's a total nightmare. It's already started on Norstray. They've

300

herded up all the people with red hair and driven them into the ruined kirk – and then set a load of man-eating birds on to them. It's bloody carnage. We have to do something to help."

"I suggest we look after ourselves," said a middle-aged man with greying red hair. "I tell you, if we stay here any longer, we'll all be killed."

Sandy looked at him hard, before replying. "Listen to me. I've just left my brother on Norstray with his eyes literally pecked out. There are lads and lassies there, with their faces ripped open. There are women with flesh hanging from their arms. And there are people who are beyond any help."

He clenched his fists, scarcely able to contain himself. "Perhaps you'll find this difficult to believe, but there are children out there at Brodgar, who I believe are going to be sacrificed at sunrise. Right now, they're being made to dig their own grave." He looked at each of them in turn, grim and determined. "We have to help."

There was a long pause before the man in a ponytail spoke up. "Okay then, so what are we supposed to do?"

Sandy paused for a moment. "I don't know if any of you have been having visions lately?" he said, eventually. The men looked at each other for an instant and nodded. "Then you might believe this," said Sandy, and he explained what Rebecca had said about the Odin Stone.

However, before anybody could respond, there was an angry shout nearby as a mob of islanders swept round the terminal and rushed towards them.

"Quick," barked Sandy. "Get into the boat."

The angry cries were closing in on them as he swung the wheel around. Clearing the port, Sandy shut down the engine to half-throttle and headed round the island, keeping well away from the darkened shoreline to avoid attracting attention.

"And just where are we going?" asked the middle-aged man.

"We're going to put the Odin Stone back," Sandy replied. "Anybody got a better idea?"

He looked hard at them all in turn, but nobody demurred. "Good," he said, and held out his hand, first of all to the middle-aged man. "My name's Sandy Lewis…"

CHAPTER 74

At eight o'clock the previous morning, Syreeta had creaked open the door of her hotel room, still in her nightclothes, and grabbed the copy of the *Metropolitan* she had ordered to be delivered to her room. And there it was. Right on the front page. Her pole switch story gleaned from Greg and Jim had made it, complete with bold headline and prominent by-line. She'd hardly dared hope for this size of coverage, and she couldn't help smiling with pleasure as she read her own words.

Then, switching on the television news, she caught her breath in shock as the grim-faced presenter announced the news about the disappearance of red-haired children on Orkney.

She phoned Rebecca. No answer from her hotel phone, and when she tried her mobile, just a strange buzzing sound. Within minutes, Syreeta established that Rebecca had checked out of the hotel at seven o'clock that morning. She tried Jim, but his mobile was on voicemail. Irritated, she tried Larry. No answer from his room phone, and his mobile, too, was switched off.

Eventually she found out from the hotel receptionist that both Jim and Larry had checked out half an hour earlier. "No, I'm sorry they didn't leave a message," said the girl. "They seemed to be in a hurry."

The university couldn't help. "I'm sorry, Professor Burton doesn't appear to be in his office," said a woman's voice after a while.

Throwing her mobile on to the bed, Syreeta sat there, trying to work out what to do next. She switched the news back on. The presenter was now talking about the swastika-like signs that had been daubed on the front doors in Orkney. Deciding that Rebecca and the others must be trying to get to Orkney, she phoned British Airways.

"What do you mean, all flights have just been cancelled?" she asked in exasperation. "What breakdown in electronic communications? What caused it?"

She listened for a while and then turned the sound on the television back up. The isolation of Orkney was now the main item.

Syreeta swore to herself and switched on her laptop. Not knowing quite where to start, she searched 'orkney solar'. It just came up with a string of references to solar panels. Then, halfway down the page, she read, 'Maeshowe and the Winter Solstice'. She checked the date on the newspaper. It was December 20th. When she entered 'orkney winter solstice', 'Maeshowe' was top of the list.

She instantly made the decision that somehow she had to get to Orkney, even if it meant driving to Scrabster. Within thirty minutes she was in her car heading north.

The roads were almost empty, and when she arrived in the evening, the town was deathly quiet. The streets were in darkness with the dull flickering glow of lamps and candles from within the houses supplying the only light.

She drove anxiously to the ferry terminal, stopped the car and slumped over the steering wheel, exhausted. Not a ferry in sight. This is what she had feared. The quay was completely deserted and a large notice on the door of the ferry company office announced: 'All ferries cancelled until further notice'. Pulling herself together, she got out of the car and made her way to a pub adjacent to the quay.

The pub was almost empty, but finding a fisherman willing to take her to Orkney was surprisingly easy. The publican had raised his eyebrows at the sum of money she had offered, but it was only a couple of minutes before a man in a thick jersey and a full beard tapped her on the shoulder.

They made Mainland late in the evening. Even from a distance, she could see that Kirkwall was like a ghost town. Only the outline of the buildings stood out against the night sky.

The fisherman drew the line at taking her into the actual port of Kirkwall, for fear of being picked up by the police. Instead, he dropped anchor in the Bay of Weyland and rowed her in his dinghy to the outskirts of town. He pointed out the road to the centre of Kirkwall and slipped back unobtrusively to his boat.

The first thing Syreeta noticed, outside an administration building above the harbour, was the abandoned yellow car. The door had been left open, as if the driver had left in a great hurry. Nervously looking inside it, she saw that the key was still in the ignition. The car started instantly.

It was peculiarly quiet as she drove into the town. There was the odd pedestrian, but on hearing her approach, each one slipped into the shadows, as if unwilling to be seen.

Eventually, she found the police station and pulled up outside. It seemed the obvious place to make enquiries, even if it meant posing as a stranded tourist. It was when she went to close the car door that she caught sight of the crumpled body lying in the car park. She edged nervously towards it and then recoiled in horror when she saw its staring eyes and red hair.

Her heart pounding, she looked around for help, but there was nobody to be seen. She got back into the car and quickly drove out of Kirkwall. Well clear of the town, she pulled up in a lay-by and searched the door pocket. Finding a map, she checked the route to Maeshowe.

CHAPTER 75

Sandy had fished the Orkney waters all his adult life, and even on a moonless night had no need to consult a chart to find his way to Mainland. He motored past Stromness and steered up an inlet called The Bush to get as close as possible to the Stones of Stenness. Shutting down the engine, he drifted silently for a while, until he bumped up against the bank.

He passed his tool box to the middle-aged man. "John – take this. We're going to need it later." He turned to the others. "MacDonald, Angus, Rob – help me moor the boat."

They walked quickly down the empty road for about two miles. Even at a distance, they could see the light of the flares at the Ring of Brodgar, and the sounds of human activity, shouts and children crying drifted over to them. Keeping to the shadows, they crept down the road until they reached the causeway, where they could just make out the four Standing Stones of Stenness.

"And how do we know where the Odin Stone used to be?" whispered MacDonald.

Rob, who was barely out of his teens, replied. "It was about one hundred and fifty yards north of the Stones. Towards that house over there – it's called Odin House. We came here once on a school trip."

Sandy opened his tool box. "First, we take down the fences – I've got some cutters. Then, at that last stone over there, we spread out in a line about three feet apart and take one hundred and fifty good strides towards the house. That's where we stop and look around for the hole. All right, let's go."

Just as they counted to one hundred and forty nine, it was Rob who tripped, and stumbled in the hole where the Odin Stone used to stand. "I think I've just found it," he said.

"Right," said Sandy, "let's mark the position." He took off his yellow oilskin and laid it over the hole. "We should be able to see that okay."

"Are we really going to try and put the Odin Stone back again?" asked John.

"This could be the key to it all," replied Sandy. "We don't have many other options – unless anyone has any better ideas?"

"No, apart from just getting out of Orkney," said MacDonald, flicking his ponytail away from his collar.

"Don't even think about getting away from Orkney," Sandy said. "For one thing, we'd be leaving all the others to their fate! And for another, we don't have enough fuel. So, we at least try. Agreed?" The others nodded.

"What do we use for the Stone?" asked Angus, a burly builder. "We can't use any of the Standing Stones – they're too big and heavy. Even if we did manage to dislodge one, we'd never be able to move it over here."

Sandy looked back to the Standing Stones. "There is one smaller stone that's lying down flat."

"I can't see one," said Angus.

"The 'table-top' slab. It's lying on the ground between the uprights over there. It was supposed to have been the sacrificial slab of an altar. Until about forty years ago, its proper place was up on top of those uprights. Let's go and have a look."

As they stood over it, Angus still looked doubtful. "It's enormous. I don't see how we're going to lift it, let alone move it a hundred and fifty yards."

"God man, use your initiative," said Sandy. "What we do is try levering it up and shuffling it along. In fact, that's probably how it was moved in the first place."

"You make it sound easy," said Angus.

Sandy eyeballed him. "And what else would you suggest, Angus?" Angus shrugged his shoulders.

"We're going to need some levers. Angus – go with MacDonald

and try and get hold of some fence posts. But be careful – other people could be looking for wood for burning. We mustn't be seen."

"This could take ages," said Angus.

"Well, we've got to be quick," said Sandy. "John, Rob and I will try to dig this slab out."

He found two screwdrivers and a chisel in his tool box and passed a screwdriver to Rob. "Here. Start digging the dirt away so we can get some purchase with a lever."

"If we're going to use that slab for the Odin Stone, you'd better remember to put a hole in it," said Angus over his shoulder, as he disappeared into the blackness.

"He's got a point," said John.

Sandy passed him the chisel and a hammer. "Start chipping," he said. "By the time they get back, we'll have a hole. It's only got to be big enough to get a hand through." A sliver of rock flew into the air as John struck the slab.

After twenty minutes, Angus and MacDonald were back, dragging four fence posts between them.

"You're right, there's not much wood around. It's all been taken already," said MacDonald, throwing his two posts on to the ground.

Angus grunted with approval on seeing that John had chipped his way through the slab, making a hole big enough to pass his hand through. Sandy and Rob had cleared as much soil away as possible from under the edges of the slab.

Sandy got up off his knees. "Shall we give it a go then?"

Together, they wedged the ends of the posts under the slab. There was an ominous crack from one post, but the slab shifted.

"Right, now – do the same again and get a post right under the slab. Angus – get yours under."

As the slab began to shift, Angus rammed his post under it. They stood back, smiling with satisfaction.

"We're going to do it," said Rob.

"Now we try to get it upright," instructed Sandy. Between

them, half-levering, half-lifting, they stood the slab upright on its edge. Rob stuck his arm through the hole and wriggled his fingers, laughing.

Sandy stopped smiling. "That was the easy bit."

He grabbed the side of the slab. "Are we ready? Two on each side." He waited until they were in place. "Now – Rob, Angus. Move it forward on your side by about a foot."

"One, two, three… lift," said Rob.

Together they edged the slab forwards by a foot.

"I guess we can do it then," said Sandy.

It took them an hour to get back to the oilskin and the hole in the ground. Slowly, they eased the slab into place. Suddenly, it fell into the hole with a dull thud.

"Okay. Stand away," said Sandy, praying that the heavy stone wouldn't topple over.

They all moved away from the slab together, Sandy gingerly taking his hand away at the very last moment. The slab didn't move.

"We've done it!" cried Rob, hitting the air with his fist.

"Shush," said Sandy. "We don't want to attract attention.

John looked in amazement at the Stone. "I would never have believed it possible."

"Well, we've managed to return the Stone," said Sandy. "Now we'll see what happens next."

It was the last thing he said before he felt the searing pain of a razor-sharp talon ripping open the top of his head. All the others saw was a flash of the bird's white under-feathers as it disappeared back into the gloom. The other birds struck immediately afterwards.

CHAPTER 76

Larry and Jim arrived at Birsay shortly before dawn. The van shuddered as Larry pulled on the handbrake in the car park and slumped back.

Jim got out and stretched his arms. "Come on," he said to Larry, and held the door open for him. Reaching the top of the steps down to the causeway, they were relieved to see that the tide was out.

"Okay, let's go and find the symbol stone," said Larry.

"I'm still not quite sure what you expect to find there," said Jim. "Neferatu standing by it, perhaps, hands in the air and saying, 'It's a fair cop'?"

"We'll see," said Larry.

Jim led the way over the causeway and went straight up to the symbol stone. "This is it. See the carved eagle."

At that moment, a peregrine falcon swooped down threateningly from the indigo northern sky, as if in warning, but veered off just before it reached them, flapping its way upwards into the distance.

Larry watched it. "Well, well," he said. "Try telling me that's nothing to do with Neferatu. Which way is it heading?"

"Judging by the glow where the sun is going to come up, it's going due south," said Jim. "But hey! Quick, look behind you! I think you mean which direction are *they* flying in?"

As Larry turned, a pair of birds flew over from the north, high in the sky. In the sky further to the north, they could just make out faint black specks that were rapidly getting closer and larger. Then the birds, large and small, flew over in what was roughly a straight line, as if united by design.

Larry and Jim watched, fascinated, like boys at an air display.

Some birds flew singly, some in pairs, others in small groups. Apparently indifferent to the two spectators, they all seemed to be heading in the same direction, south, following the first falcon.

"Look at them! They're all birds of prey," said Jim in amazement.

"I know it's fanciful," said Larry, "but it looks as if Neferatu's got some help. I wonder what they're up to. We should try to follow them. Let's go."

They ran back over the causeway to the van, while a few straggling birds continued overhead. In no time, the flock had become specks again, a jagged black line against the brightening horizon.

"Get a move on," said Larry, as Jim unlocked the door. Larry grabbed the map, opened it up and studied it. "There are two roads south. One to Stromness. That's the one we came up on. The other goes to Stenness and Brodgar."

"What?" said Jim. "What did you say?"

"Stromness or Stenness and Brodgar."

"Of course! That's it!" exclaimed Jim, banging the steering wheel with his fist. "Brodgar. The Ring of Brodgar. That's what was meant by 'the ring', of course! That's the ring of Horus! It's supposed to have been a sun observatory, and today's the day of the winter solstice."

"'When Horus comes people with red hair will fear his ring'," intoned Larry. "I think that's where we're going to find Rebecca, and we'd better hurry. I can't think of a more powerful icon Neferatu could use. And my guess is, he's up to something pretty appalling this time."

Jim skidded the van around and slammed through the gears as they headed south.

Fifteen minutes later, they pulled up by the Stones of Stenness, parking the van behind a small yellow car. Getting out of the van, Jim stopped short, the door halfway open, and peered through the pre-dawn half-light into the distance.

"Just look at that! I don't believe it. Over there – you can just make it out, there's a stone with a hole in it. They've put it back! Someone's put the Odin Stone back!" Then he noticed a movement by the Stone. "And there's someone there – I think it's a woman."

Syreeta didn't see them until they had almost reached her. She was feeling sick at the gruesome scene in front of her; four mangled bodies lay around the base of the Stone. They were barely recognisable as human beings. Every exposed part of their bodies was a grotesque mass of ripped flesh, blood and bone, with flaps of skin hanging away from their faces and hands. Their clothes were torn to shreds, as if whatever had attacked them had been in some sort of crazed frenzy to get at the flesh beneath. Worst of all, all their eyes had been torn out.

Syreeta turned round slowly, in deep shock, to face Larry and Jim. All three stood there in silence, stunned, finding it difficult to comprehend what they were seeing.

Jim put his arm around Syreeta's shoulder and turned her away. "What are you doing here?" he asked, gently.

"I was worried about Rebecca."

"But why here? Why did you come to this place?"

"I am supposed to be an investigative journalist. But I didn't quite get it right. I thought you two might be at Maeshowe."

"Was it like this when you arrived?"

"Yes. But I could see the birds even from Maeshowe. I could see a whole flock of them dive-bombing something, so I drove over here to see what was going on. They were already flying off by the time I arrived. But this is what they did – I know it was the birds that did it."

Jim looked at the Stone, and again at the mangled bodies. "It must have been these men who managed to put the Stone back. But why? Why was it so important? And why did the birds attack them for doing it?" He stood there, shaking his head in disbelief.

CHAPTER 77

As they walked back to the two cars in silence, the sun was just rising above the horizon, and the Ring of Brodgar could be seen on the hillside on the other side of the causeway. Larry peered into the distance towards the Ring. Though he couldn't make out details, he could see that it was swarming with people.

"That looks like trouble if I ever saw it," he said.

Jim held the van door open for Syreeta. "If you're going to come with us, leave your car here. It stands out like a sore thumb."

He drove the van slowly past the Stones of Stenness and over the causeway, occasionally going on to the grass to make sure that they could not be seen. Parking behind a barn some distance away from the Ring and well out of sight, he switched off the engine.

Then he turned to Larry. "What now? You seem to have all the answers."

Larry threw him a questioning glance, wondering at Jim's sudden irritability. "I don't know that I do have all the answers. Why do you say that?" he said.

Jim now looked sullen. "I just don't understand why we are getting mixed up in all this," he said. "It's nothing to do with us, and it's just walking into trouble. It's seriously grim stuff going on in this place."

"Are you suggesting we just walk away?" asked Larry.

"But what exactly can we do to help?"

Larry looked at Syreeta. "I don't know what to do either – I just wanted to help Rebecca," she said.

"For Christ's sake, what's up with you two?" Larry said, climbing out of the van. "Let's at least try and see what's going on."

Jim shrugged his shoulders dismissively but opened the door, got out and, without a word, held it open for Syreeta.

As they made their way slowly up the steep hillside, keeping their heads well down, they could hear the sound of children crying.

"Make for the large rock over there," said Larry. The rock was the Comet Stone.

They crouched, hidden behind the Stone, while they got their breath back. Finally, all three peered uneasily around the sides.

The sight that greeted them would have been shocking enough if it had been some sort of theatrical performance. But this was no performance art, this was all too real. The whole area was milling with swarthy, Eastern-looking, black-haired men who, despite the cold, were wearing only loincloths.

"God, it's like a return to pagan times," whispered Larry. "And look at all those poor children – some are just toddlers. They must be the children who disappeared – there must be at least fifty of them. And see those women over there? Some of them are holding babies."

Huddled together in the cold and visibly distressed, every captive was now attired in a white shift and thin slippers. Without exception, all had red hair. Some of the children were hugging each other protectively. Others were crying and screaming for their mothers.

Their cries were partly drowned out by the sound of drumming and the loud, discordant sounds of some kind of horn, which came from the centre of the Ring. Black smoke was pouring upwards, and heat waves shimmered in the air.

"Get down and stay here a moment," Larry said. He cautiously crept up the hill to get a better view. The pit was now visible, filled with glowing, red-hot embers and flickering flames.

He edged back to the others and sank down on his haunches. "They're planning a huge massacre here," he whispered.

He eased upright again, to see something emerging through the smoke; something huge and golden. Slowly, it trundled into sight. A gigantic statue on four huge wheels was being hauled to the centre of the Ring.

"My God, this is unbelievable. They've even got a Moloch here! They've even brought a bloody Moloch!" he said. "This is absolutely terrifying. They're actually going to make sacrifices to Moloch. You have to see this – but for heaven's sake keep your heads down."

The statue must have been a massive forty feet high. It was surmounted by the large head of a bull, the mouth and eyes of which belched forth smoke. The bull's head was set on a human torso, cut off so that it had no legs.

The head seemed to be carved from solid metal. It was superbly executed, with long horns curving upwards, like those of a Spanish fighting bull. Even the folds of skin hanging around the neck seemed realistic.

But it was impossible to miss the eyes. They were inset with jet-black stones that flashed through the smoke with reflected red light from the sun.

Its long arms hung down, so low that the huge metal hands scraped the ground. Connected to its wrists were golden chains which passed upwards and over the shoulders, the ends dangling behind the statue's back.

"What are they going to do with it?" asked Syreeta.

"Oh, they don't intend to just throw their victims into the fire," said Larry. "They intend to use that thing to actually drop those poor people into the pit. It's a foul ritual, probably tied up with bull worship."

Jim looked perplexed. "How on earth could they have got a thing like that here, unnoticed? Who got it here?"

"Neferatu," said Larry. "He must have used the Ring of Brodgar as a massive portal to bring it through to our dimension. That must be how he got all those people helping him here as well."

Propelled by a mixture of sheer shock, disbelief and morbid curiosity, the three of them took advantage of the commotion and crept cautiously up towards the Ring.

A number of red-haired men and women in white shifts could

be seen among the crowd, leaning forwards in two files. They were dragging the statue along with ropes. Shortly before the pit, they stopped.

As the Moloch ground to a halt, a number of swarthy, near-naked men armed with whips and spears manoeuvred some of the redheads behind it. It seemed that they were being made to push the heavy Moloch the remaining few yards to the edge of the pit.

With the final heave, a woman slipped and fell. A man in a white costume stood over her shouting, until she staggered to her feet. She looked around, her face pale and gaunt.

Larry shook Jim's shoulder in horror, pointing to the woman. "Oh, no, it can't be! Over there! That's Rebecca. We must do something! And look, right next to her! That man shouting orders – it's Neferatu! He looks like an ancient Egyptian priest. In fact, the whole lot of them look like Egyptians. I just knew it – I knew he was the one behind all this."

The Moloch finally approached the edge of the pit, the front wheels perched perilously near the edge. There was a signal from Neferatu, and four or five of the Egyptian guards hauled on the chains behind the statue. The hands cranked up, finally joining together to form a platform in front of the head, as if the Moloch were about to eat.

The guards locked the chains to secure the platform, and wooden steps were carried over and placed at the side of the monstrous machine.

When Neferatu raised his hand, the crowd in the Ring suddenly fell silent, except for the whining and haunting crying of the children. The red-haired captives huddled together, now apparently quietly awaiting their fate.

CHAPTER 78

Neferatu stood, resplendent in his ceremonial robes, as High Priest of the Temple of Edfu. He now wore a high white headdress, with a dazzling green stone set in the front. All eyes were irresistibly drawn towards him. He was standing, facing the sun, watching it as it started to rise above the horizon, bathing the Ring in the thin light of a northern dawn. The Egyptian guards stood in line, awaiting his command.

"Bring the first one!" cried Neferatu. He eyed the male prisoners with disdain and pointed to one man with thick, wavy, red hair, who was surreptitiously working his way back to the centre of the group, trying to avoid attention. "That man!" Neferatu barked.

The man panicked and tried to run for it, but three guards caught him and soon hauled him on to the steps. They pushed him roughly up to the platform and forced him on to it at spear-point. He struggled wildly to get back to the steps, but Inherkhau climbed up and thrust a spear into his chest, drawing blood.

Neferatu now raised his arms towards the sun, while the cacophony of drums and horns increased to a crescendo. "For Moloch!" he shouted.

Two guards stepped forwards and loosened the golden chains, which rattled upwards. Simultaneously, the hands of the Moloch parted and dropped, like the trapdoor beneath a gibbet. The man frantically tried to grab the body of the Moloch but missed and fell screaming into the pit, his arms waving like windmills. As he was devoured by the flames, a cloud of hissing smoke and steam poured out, and the guards went wild with joy.

Larry watched in disbelief and horror. Yet, turning towards Jim, he was shocked to see his friend's eyes glistening with excitement, bordering on pleasure. His fists were clenched, and his whole body seemed tense with the sheer effort of trying to control some powerful inner emotion.

"God man! What's the matter with you?" Larry growled. He grabbed Jim's shoulders. "Do you realise what's going on here? It's not some dog-fight. It's human slaughter! Dammit, get a grip, will you." But Jim's eyes were dancing wildly, as if he had been taken over by some invisible force.

Larry shook him hard. "You can't let yourself be dragged into this! You can't take their side! Can't you see, something's happening to you. Something is taking control of you. Use your intelligence, man! You're not one of them!" Jim didn't respond, as if completely unaware of Larry.

Larry brought his face up level with Jim's, so that their noses were practically touching. "Okay, okay, but what about Rebecca?" he shouted. "Rebecca! Think about Rebecca!"

Jim's eyes finally stopped flashing and began to focus on Larry's face in front of him. His hands unclenched, and his whole body seemed to relax and calm. He closed his eyes, opened them again and sighed deeply.

Larry turned to Syreeta. He was surprised to find she was hardly reacting at all. No horror in her expression. No revulsion. She seemed to be in an almost trance-like state, as if she were indifferent to what was going on. Larry shook her gently. Her eyes flickered, and her face seemed to come back to life.

"I'm sorry," she said. "It's all so horrible. It's like a terrible dream. I had the feeling something – something hideous – was trying to take over my mind, blinding me to what's going on. It just doesn't seem real."

Larry looked at her, baffled. "Come on, Syreeta, you've got to pull yourself together. We're going to need your help." Yet he could see Syreeta was still not her usual inquisitive self, still not quite switched back to reality.

"It's all too much, Larry," she said. "It's all too big. It's no good, is it? There's nothing here we're going to be able to do to help anybody. We just have to let it be."

"That's just what we're bloody well not going to do," said Larry, through gritted teeth. "Pinch yourself, Syreeta – wake yourself up."

He turned to Jim. "First things first – let's get you two away from this place."

As the three of them looked towards the Ring again, the next victim was already being dragged towards the Moloch.

"Okay, let's go," Larry said.

They crouched and almost had to crawl back down the hill, until they were out of sight of the guards. Then they ran back to the van. Larry climbed into the passenger seat, slumped back and got his breath back.

"What on earth happened to you both back there?" he said. "You seemed to get caught up in it all. You almost seemed to be enjoying it, Jim. And you, Syreeta, you just looked switched off – as if this sort of thing happens every day."

Jim looked uncomfortable. "I can't explain it, and I feel very bad about it. I don't like to admit this – but I seemed to feel in sympathy with the mob. I felt a sort of wave of hate against red-haired people. God knows where the feeling came from – I've honestly never felt that way before."

Syreeta looked embarrassed. "It was the same for me. I just didn't feel any sympathy for all those people. I don't know what it was, but I couldn't shake it off until we got down the hill and right away from that place."

"What about right now? Do you get the situation now?" asked Larry. "Are you ready to help?"

Jim seemed to make a massive effort to pull himself together. "Oh, my God," he said. "We've just left them all up there. We have to stop it! Where can we get help? If anything happens to Rebecca… if that bastard Neferatu…"

"We won't get any help around here, that's for sure. Anyway, we'd need an army to tackle that lot," said Larry. "And there's no time – we can't even use the phone."

He thought for an instant. "Okay, let's see what the compass is doing."

He laid it in the palm of his hand. The needle swung one way and then in the opposite direction, without settling.

"It's still fluctuating," Jim said.

"What's going on?" asked Syreeta. "Would you mind explaining what's happening?"

"The earth has lost its magnetic field – it's completely disappeared," replied Jim. "And you know what that means? That means the solar radiation must be pouring in – and there's nothing to stop it."

"That's it!" cried Larry, his eyes suddenly glinting. "Of course! That must be where Neferatu's power is coming from! Solar radiation! He's somehow using it to do whatever he wants!" He banged the dashboard repeatedly with his fist. "There must be something we can do!"

"If it is the solar radiation," said Jim, "the only way to stop it would be to create another magnetic field – at least around here."

Then a look of determination spread over his face. "Do you know, Larry, I think I've got an idea."

CHAPTER 79

Jim clicked open the glove box and fumbled inside. "Where's the map? Where's the map?" he demanded, scattering most of the contents.

Larry calmly took the map out of the door pocket and passed it to him.

Jim tore it open. "We need to find a stream." He stabbed at the map. "Here, here. Just by Maeshowe."

"Why do we need a stream?" asked Syreeta.

"To try and create and a magnetic field around it," said Jim. "If we can pass enough electricity through the water, it should set up a magnetic field around the stream. You know – like passing electricity through a copper wire. I just hope it'll be strong enough to cut down the solar radiation at Brodgar – and stop Neferatu."

Larry and Syreeta gave each other worried glances.

"Electricity? Where do get electricity from?" said Syreeta.

"The generators," replied Jim. "We've got generators in the back of the van. Look – I know it's a long shot, but we have to try it. There's no alternative I can think of."

He started the van, sped away from the Ring and, three minutes later, skidded to a halt on a grass verge next to a small stream. It was largely overgrown with grass, but water tumbled through it.

Jim jumped out of the van. "We need to get the generators out and link them up," he shouted, opening up the back of the van.

Larry helped him get the first generator out. "But surely the electricity will just earth into the ground?" he said.

Jim climbed into the van to get the second generator.

"Not if we can increase the conductivity of the water enough. If we can manage that, the electricity will run through the water rather than the soil."

"And how do we do that?" asked Syreeta, looking mystified.

"We put salt in the water," said Jim, pulling the next generator to the door of the van. "We've just passed a bin of road-salt further down the road. Can you two go and fill the van up? But before you go – I need help getting these last generators out." Together the three of them lifted the remaining generators out and on to the grass.

"We'll need some shovels from somewhere," said Larry.

"I think I saw a gravedigger's hut at the kirk, just by Maeshowe," said Syreeta. "We could try there."

"Good idea. We'll see you in a minute, Jim," said Larry, as he got into the driver's seat.

Now alone, Jim looked at the six generators for a moment, then hauled them together in a line, the last one next to the stream. After what seemed an eternity to him, the van swerved to a halt back at the stream, and Larry and Syreeta jumped out.

"I was right," said Syeeta. "We found a couple of spades in the hut."

"Then can you two start shovelling the stuff into the stream?" said Jim. "I just need to connect the generators together, then we're ready."

Larry moved the van upstream from the generators and as close to the stream as he dared. Syreeta handed him a spade, and together they began shovelling the salt into the water.

"I'm going to start the generators," called over Jim. One by one, they roared into life. He carefully picked up the live wire attached to the generator nearest to the stream, slid down the bank and stuck it into the water. "Keep an eye on the compass," he shouted.

Larry stopped shovelling and checked the compass. "Nothing yet," he called out.

"Try more salt," yelled back Jim.

Larry dumped another large load of salt into the water, and leaned on his shovel to get his breath back. He checked the compass again and shook his head. "Still nothing, Jim."

"Let's try something else," said Jim, picking up a cable attached to the generator furthest from the stream. "Larry – take this and stick it in the water downstream. That should complete a circuit. Just don't electrocute yourself!"

"Hold this a minute, Syreeta," said Larry, handing the compass to her, and he ran down to the last generator. He carefully picked up the cable, holding it well away from himself, and pushed it into the water.

As Larry stood back, Syreeta studied the compass.

CHAPTER 80

Neferatu was wild-eyed as he continued to shout his commands. Not a single red-haired man now remained; every single one had been sacrificed. Dark smoke and steam billowed from the pit, the fire overwhelmed by so many bodies. Neferatu paused as he peered into the pit.

"Keep the women until last. They can suffer. We'll take a child now, a nice fat child to get the fire going again."

The guards picked a plump boy, aged about eight. In a frenzy of fear and panic, the child grappled wildly with his captors, kicking out and biting the hand of one guard, who yelped and momentarily let him go. In the confusion, the boy twisted round, freed himself and hurtled towards the edge of the Ring before the other guards could stop him.

But he never made it out of the Ring. Inherkhau caught him by the arm, and half-carried him back, squirming, to the Moloch, to be dumped at the bottom of the ladder.

For Rebecca, this was too much to bear. She ran to the boy and swiped Inherkhau's face when he tried to stop her. The guard's face contorted with rage. Grabbing the boy and wrapping her arms around him, Rebecca turned to face the rest of the oncoming guards.

Neferatu was unfazed. "How convenient. I was coming to you next, anyway," he said.

Poking the two of them with their spears, the guards forced first the boy, and then Rebecca, up the ladder towards the platform.

Neferatu looked up at them. "Ah yes, I've waited so long for this moment," he gloated.

Then Inherkhau clambered halfway up the ladder and jabbed his spear into Rebecca's leg, forcing them both on to the platform.

Rebecca screamed at him and stood defiantly, teetering at the edge of the platform, her arms once again around the terrified boy. Neferatu ordered Inherkhau to use his spear again and force them both into the middle.

As she turned to face the mob beneath, the boy cowered behind her, clutching her legs and hiding his face in her shift so that he did not have to look down.

Taut with sheer terror, Rebecca felt all the fight in her ebbing away. She looked around desperately, faintly hoping that someone might suddenly come to their rescue. But there was no one.

The guards were now gathering in front of the pit and starting to relentlessly chant, raising their spears up and down in time to the drumming. The ear-piercing, tuneless screeching from the horns was deafening.

Uncontrollably, her mind started to race backwards. How had she had got into this mess? Why did she have to get involved? Neferatu had already tried to kill her twice before – so why hadn't she tried to protect herself? Was this it? She didn't want to die – she longed to live the life she would never have. She felt powerless, as if her life had been taken over and driven by strange events and emotions outside her control.

Then she looked down and saw Neferatu standing there, a sneering, scornful smile on his face, relishing his moment of triumph.

A flood of pure contempt surged through her. Who was he to treat her in this way, with her royal blood, the blood of Cleopatra running through her veins?

She no longer wished to look at him. A sense of exultation took over from her contempt. Lifting her chin, she gazed defiantly and imperiously over the waters of the loch and into the distance.

CHAPTER 81

Larry went over to Syreeta and eyed the compass in her hand. "It's just floundering, Jim," he called out. "Is there anything else we can do?"

But Jim didn't respond. He was staring into the distance at the Odin Stone. Larry and Syreeta turned together to follow Jim's gaze and stood dumbstruck, rooted to the ground. The Stone was starting to glow a delicate blue colour.

At first, Jim thought he was imagining it, but then the blue light started pulsating. After a few seconds, it grew strong enough to bathe the whole area around the Stones in blue light.

It was Larry who broke the silence. "My God, the stream must be running under the Stone. The electricity has energised it, somehow."

"It could be the silicon in the rock making it act like a light-emitting diode," said Jim. "The electricity must be dissociating the silicon from the silica – the quartz crystals."

"If you say so," said Larry.

As they watched, the Stone grew steadily brighter and brighter, and the pulsating increased.

CHAPTER 82

Behind Rebecca, the boy buried his head deeper into her shift, and she held his hands tightly as they stood on the scorching platform. The heat was starting to penetrate her thin slippers, and she shifted from foot to foot.

Below them, Neferatu turned to face the sun, stretched out his arms and closed his eyes. The noise of the drumming and ancient instruments became ear-splitting. He took in breath, ready to make the command that would complete his task.

Then, suddenly, the noise faded. A horn squeaked, and there was silence. Neferatu opened his eyes. Everybody was looking in the same direction, towards the Odin Stone.

The pulsating light became more and more dazzling, until it grew into a huge sphere of brilliance, turning into what seemed like a gigantic light bulb. The light was so strong that new dark shadows formed behind the other four Stones, obliterating the long shadows caused by the sun.

As the throbbing light rose higher and higher into the sky, Neferatu's outstretched arms dropped to his sides and he, too, watched, transfixed, with the others.

The ball of light now seemed to become alive. While everybody watched, darker areas formed inside it, only to dissolve away and reappear in other parts of the ball. The darker areas formed indistinct shapes, which momentarily became solid. Then the shape of, what looked like, a leg formed, only to become a bone which changed into a pumping heart. Blood vessels formed like spaghetti, a staring eyeball floated around for a second and became a set of teeth. It was as if the components of a body were being created haphazardly, without any relationship to each other. Slowly, the various body parts fell into place and appeared to solidify, eventually forming the shape of an animal.

The head was the first part to be recognisable. It had a long, curved, pointed snout, and the ears stood upwards, with little tufts at the ends. The eyes were slanted in the Egyptian style and glowed like red neon lights. Behind the ears, its lank red hair hung back over the shoulders. Next, the trunk, arms and legs became distinguishable; but it stood upright and was attired in a white loincloth. The skin was a murky white and covered with orange-coloured down. The last thing to form was the fork-ended tail, jutting from beneath the loincloth and thrashing about in the air, like a serpent with a life of its own.

The grotesque apparition began to look around and take in the scene. It then turned its giant form to face the Ring of Brodgar.

At the sight of the monstrous figure, Neferatu's expression changed completely. His face darkened, and he shook with a mixture of abject fear and pure hate. "Damn you, Seth!" he cried.

As if in response, the god opened its gigantic mouth and roared. A blast of wind swept over Brodgar, rocking the stones in their foundations.

At this, Neferatu fell to his knees and raised his head to the sun. "Horus! Horus! Where are you? Where *are* you?" he pleaded.

Immediately, a black dot appeared in the centre of the sun. It grew rapidly in size, taking shape as it did so. Within seconds, as if projected down by the sun, a dark cloud of ever-changing shadows enveloped the Ring of Brodgar. The shadows grew in intensity, taking the form of a colossal human body, standing with its feet on either side of the Ring. But its head was that of a falcon. It was Horus, god of the sun, and it stared with contempt at the Seth animal.

Seth put his head back and roared again into the sky. High above Stenness, large black rain clouds formed and swept across the heavens, blocking out the sun. Lightning flashed across the darkening sky. The rain fell as a few light drops at first. Then it seemed as if celestial floodgates had opened, and the rain cascaded down.

Neferatu looked around forlornly. His followers had fallen silent, water dripping from their bodies, their hair plastered to their heads. Rebecca and the boy stood drenched on the platform, the Moloch cooling rapidly. Below them, the embers in the pit hissed and turned black. Clouds of steam billowed up around the two lonely figures.

Almost imperceptibly at first, like a rainbow when the sun goes in, the figures of Seth and Horus faded. Within a few seconds they were gone. The brilliant light around the Odin Stone became weaker and shrank, until only the Stone itself continued to glow. Finally, it turned back to dull grey, and an eerie silence settled over the landscape.

It was Larry who first noticed the Odin Stone starting to come back to life.

CHAPTER 83

Larry pointed a shaky arm towards the hole in the Odin Stone.

On one side of the hole, a pair of hands had appeared. The hands were soon followed by a pair of arms. The hands then seemed to grab the Stone from the inside, like someone trying to pull his whole body through. After a struggle, the figure of a Highland warrior gradually emerged through the hole and stood next to the Stone. Dressed in rough tartan, his straggly red hair hung down to his shoulders from under a tam-o'-shanter. In one hand he held a broadsword, and in the other a small wooden shield, decorated with metal studs. He faced towards Brodgar, raised the sword high in the air and shook it. His wild battle cry resounded around the Stones.

As he moved to one side, another similar figure pulled himself through, followed by another and another; until a whole army of about forty, flame-haired Highlanders was gathered around the Stone. They were all fully armed with a variety of swords of different shapes and sizes, and even the odd musket.

Forming themselves into a rough line facing Brodgar, they stormed towards the causeway, blood-curdling battle cries filling the air.

Meanwhile, more and more red-haired warriors poured through the hole. After the Highlanders came Norsemen, with horned helmets and battle-axes. They formed a tight group, bellowed oaths to Odin and Thor and chased after the Highlanders.

Larry, Jim and Syreeta watched, spellbound. Larry was the first to speak. "They're the ancestor warriors," was all he said.

Still more warriors were arriving through the hole: Phoenicians in white tunics, cone-shaped helmets and bronze swords; and the Peleset, the ancient Sea People, with their red-plumed headdresses.

Larry pointed to the Peleset coming towards them, barely able to contain his excitement. "Look! They're the same as the man with the red-feathered headdress who Rebecca saw on Easter Island."

A horde of Carthaginians came next in their glinting bronze cuirasses, marching three abreast in precise formation, their spears held upright. They were followed by red-haired South Pacific islanders, heavily tattooed and carrying huge wooden clubs, performing brief war dances before leaping and bounding across the rough grass.

As the horde charged towards them from Stenness, Jim and Syreeta watched, still totally astonished. Larry, though, could now scarcely contain himself.

"Go on! Get them!" he yelled, as they neared Brodgar.

Then, without warning, a lone horse and rider, resplendent in golden armour, leapt through the hole, the rider's breastplate reflecting a flash of sunlight. The bay stallion reared as the rider stuck his spurs into its flanks. With superb horsemanship, he wheeled his horse around and came galloping along the causeway.

CHAPTER 84

At Brodgar, even as the Highlanders came nearer, steam billowed out of the pit. It blended with the soft mist that enveloped the hillside, becoming ever thicker and taking on a faint red tint; like a premonition of the bloody carnage that was about to occur.

In the Ring itself, there was complete confusion and chaos. The Egyptian guards were lost in the haze and wandered around aimlessly, waiting for orders that never came. Mothers searched desperately for their children, their spirits leaping whenever they caught a glimpse of a lone child, only to be dashed when they realised it wasn't their own. Others, who were luckier, clasped their children, praying they would come to no harm.

The guards heard the battle cries of the Highlanders before they caught sight of them. The warriors emerged through the mist and were upon them before they could react. The guards, caught by surprise, hesitated for a moment. Then, as if by common assent, they took to their heels and ran for their lives.

They fell over each other, trying to flee in all directions, closely pursued by a motley collection of red-haired fighters. Some of them made it to the edge of the Ring, only to be met by yet more warriors, and were slaughtered as they backed up against the stones. A few stumbled and slid down the hillside to the loch, to be hacked down in the water. Some even tried to swim to safety but could not escape the thick hail of well-aimed spears thrown by the Carthaginians.

Only Inherkhau stood his ground, grimly facing the horde with his spear pointing out in front of him. A Highlander staggered to a halt then boldly strode towards him, swung his sword almost casually and cleaved the spear in two. As Inherkhau dropped the stump to the ground, the Highlander swung his sword back in an arc towards Inherkhau's neck. Inherkhau stood there motionless, his eyes fixed straight ahead. The Highlander studied him for a moment and then prodded Inherkhau's head with the point of his weapon. The head toppled from the still-standing body and rolled away.

Before Jim, Larry and Syreeta reached the Ring, they could already sense the havoc that had been wreaked. A dreadful aura of death hung over the place, and they found themselves tripping over the bodies of the Egyptian guards that lay scattered around, some hacked to pieces.

Through the mist, they could make out the dim outline of the Moloch, with its arms hanging down and its blackened hands scraping the scorched soil. Puffs of steam spluttered out of the pit to merge with the mist.

The captive group of women and children had simply looked on in bewilderment as the battle raged before their eyes. Now they seemed paralysed and lost, unable to comprehend what was happening.

Jim, ahead of Larry and Syreeta, ran into the Ring towards the Moloch. Rebecca and the boy were standing motionless at its base.

As Syreeta came up and took the boy's hand, steering him away from the pit, Rebecca fell into Jim's arms. They didn't say a word, but stood there, holding each other. Even as he clasped her tightly, Jim could feel her still shaking.

Larry, meanwhile, was peering into the mist, as if looking for somebody. Occasionally, the odd ghostly figure of a warrior appeared, only to be swallowed up again by the fog.

Neferatu sprang from behind the Moloch without warning. Brandishing a dagger above his head, he seemed to be running straight for Rebecca. Larry instantly leapt into action and tried to grab him, but Neferatu effortlessly knocked him aside, sending him floundering to the ground.

Jim, catching sight of Neferatu, instinctively moved in front of Rebecca to protect her.

Neferatu came to a stop and pointed the dagger at Jim's throat. "Move!" he ordered. Jim looked at him defiantly and shifted slightly to shield Rebecca better.

In a flash, Neferatu lunged towards them. Still protecting Rebecca behind him, Jim swung both of them to one side, so that Neferatu almost fell past them, lurching to a halt.

Neferatu turned and edged back around the pit towards them, his eyes glinting like emeralds. He jabbed the dagger at them, skilfully manoeuvring them both back along the brim of the smouldering pit, until they came up against the gigantic wheel of the Moloch, unable to go any further. Moving closer to them, Neferatu once again raised the dagger, a twisted sneer of triumph on his face.

Only Syreeta saw clearly what happened next. Some sort of ethereal figure was emerging through the mist behind Neferatu, silently closing in on him. The figure, clad in a golden breastplate, was holding a short sword, which it slowly pulled back, ready to strike.

Neferatu, clearly unaware of the approaching figure, still bore an expression on malevolent gloating. His foul expression instantly changed to shock and horror, as he received a sharp blow to the back and saw the bronze blade of a sword appear out of his chest. He screamed in agonised pain as the blade twisted only once and disappeared back through his body.

Neferatu staggered round to see the magnificent figure of Ptolemy Soter standing there, holding a bloodied sword.

Turning back, Neferatu looked up at the Moloch. His face betrayed no emotion, as if his mind were already far away. Then his eyes lost their brightness, changing to a dull brown and finally turning to black, like a light being switched off. Slowly, he toppled over into the pit. There was a long, loud hiss and a cloud of steam as he disappeared into the ashes.

Ptolemy Soter looked at Rebecca, a faint smile playing on his face. Smartly bowing his head towards her, he raised his arm in a salute, before striding away to fade into the mist. Moments later they heard the sound of a galloping horse, growing ever fainter, until it was gone.

CHAPTER 85

Like a herald of change, a sudden breeze blew through the Ring of Brodgar, so that the mist swirled and slowly lifted.

As it drifted away, it became clear that the Moloch was no longer there. It had disappeared, vanished into the vaporous air, as if it had never existed. Gone, too, were the red-haired warriors, and gone the countless bodies of dead Egyptian guards.

As the four onlookers looked around the Ring, stunned into silence, Jim instinctively held Rebecca close. Apart from the women and children, the scene was now deserted. Some of the women were running to claim their children, or to comfort those who were still left alone.

Jim slowly shook his head, trying to verify the reality of what he knew he had just witnessed with his own eyes.

"And where is Neferatu now?" he said.

"Gone. Never to return, I hope," said Rebecca.

Larry nodded in agreement. "He's lost his power. Redheads have taken over now," he said.

Syreeta turned to him. "What do you mean?" she asked.

"You'll see," said Larry. "Rebecca has her full powers now. She brought Ptolemy Soter back to life. It was Ptolemy, himself, who just saved her."

"Hang on a minute," said Syreeta. "What powers? And what do you mean, 'She brought Ptolemy Soter back to life'?"

Larry smiled. "The man you just saw really was Ptolemy Soter. He is her ancestor. What's more, he is also the ancestor of Cleopatra. It was he who founded the whole Ptolemaic line of rulers in ancient Egypt. Cleopatra's father was a Ptolemy, too. What very few people know is that Cleopatra's granddaughter escaped persecution by fleeing to Scotland and settling here. Rebecca is only the latest of a royal line of redheads. She really is 'Queen of the Redheads', and that's why Neferatu wanted her dead."

"Are you trying to tell me Rebecca has royal blood?" asked Syreeta.

Rebecca smiled but said nothing, still looking around the Ring.

Larry passed the compass to Syreeta. "Look at this," he said. "Do you remember what happened before?"

Syreeta held the compass flat in her hand. The needle wavered and then settled. She shook her head. "But it's not pointing to the north any more."

"It's pointing south," said Jim. "That is just incredible."

"Check your phone," Larry said to Syreeta.

She switched it on. "It's working," she said.

"Can you get the news," instructed Larry.

Her fingers flicked over the pad. "World in chaos as poles switch," she read out aloud.

"Well, would you believe it?" said Larry. "There's been a full reversal of the North and South Poles. The Earth's magnetic field has completely switched over."

Jim looked around Brodgar and over to Stenness. "The poles must have been poised, almost ready to reverse."

Then he looked shocked. "My God – was it us? Were *we* responsible for this? Seriously – I wonder if it was us who gave the poles the final push – when we electrified the stream? Heaven forbid! It was just an accident. I never meant to do that. All I wanted to do was create a local magnetic field – to stop the solar radiation from getting through around here."

"But how does all this affect me?" asked Rebecca.

"Not just you, but all other redheads," said Larry. "As Jim will tell you, there was a major deviation of the magnetic North Pole around here, 30,000 years ago. It only lasted a short while, but I believe, for that time, it had a profound effect on red-haired people."

"How do you mean?" asked Syreeta.

"I believe that, just like what happened to Rebecca, they found they could communicate telepathically with their ancestors in another dimension. And then, just like now, when they were in danger, their ancestors appeared to them in bodily form to help them. But you can just imagine how the non-redheads would have reacted towards 'super' redheads with their newfound powers. They must have held them in awe. Some tribes would have begun to worship them. For a time, the redheads ruled the non-redheads."

"Hey, that sounds familiar," said Jim. "A bit like Easter Island, I suppose."

"Exactly," said Larry. "And, like on Easter Island, when the redheads displayed their powers, there would have been a lot of jealousy as well – and even hatred towards them. Now it's my theory that there exists a folk memory of these distant events which has always affected people's attitude towards redheads, right up to the present day. And in a way, it's true. They really are a different breed."

"You are talking about me," said Rebecca. "Don't forget what I've been through. You can't imagine how much all these people here have suffered."

Jim took her hand and held it tightly.

"But if the North Pole went back to its old position after it changed 30,000 years ago, what happened then?" asked Syreeta. "The redheads must have lost their magic powers again?"

"That's precisely what happened, and it was at that moment that the others exacted their revenge. They wanted to annihilate the redheads, who had had such power over them. But not all were killed. Many escaped, of course. And yet, they and their descendants were pursued all over the world..."

"Even to Easter Island," said Jim.

"All sorts of places," said Larry. "You can find this in mythology everywhere. Of course, eventually there was a lot of interbreeding. So, you could say that the genes for the hidden powers of redheads continued to be passed on – alongside the genes for red hair."

Syreeta was looking confused. "But who were those gigantic Egyptian-like monsters that appeared?"

"They were the Egyptian gods, Horus and Seth," said Larry. "They existed, or you could say, still exist, in a further, more distant dimension, even than the ancestors."

"For crying out loud, I'm still trying to get my head round the idea of ancestors appearing from another dimension," gasped Syreeta.

"There are ten dimensions, actually, according to the latest theory," volunteered Jim.

Syreeta ignored him. "But what made Seth and Horus appear just now?"

"It was the disappearance of the magnetic field that enabled them to cross over into our dimension," said Larry. "Seth is the god of the redheads. He is associated with the moon – as is Stenness. Horus is the god of the non-redheads, and associated with the sun – as is Brodgar. Together, Horus and Neferatu were on a mission to eliminate all redheads – before the poles switched. And that's exactly what they were trying to do just now. But in the end they failed."

"The Earth's magnetic field has returned, and at full power. It's protecting us from the solar radiation again," said Jim.

"Yes, but not only that," said Larry. "It'll be protecting us from Horus and Neferatu, as well. But they very nearly made it – the poles finally switched only just in time." He looked over to the Standing Stones of Stenness. "You know, Seth may have won the battle, but he's not necessarily won the war."

"You mean this so–called war is still going on?" said Syreeta.

"Well, sometime, the poles are going to switch back again," replied Larry.

"So, Neferatu could come back again, in theory?"

Larry nodded.

"Tell me Larry, how do you know about all this?" Syreeta asked.

"He has a vested interest," cut in Jim. "He's a bit of a closet redhead himself."

Larry and Rebecca exchanged glances and smiled with just a hint of self-satisfaction.

CHAPTER 86

Syreeta was startled when her phone rang. "Syreeta? Charles here. Where the hell are you? I asked you to get back here! There's a lot going on…"

Syreeta held the phone away from her ear while Charles ranted on.

"Syreeta – are you there?" he asked, after a pause.

"Yes – I'm still here, Charles. Listen, I think I'm on to something here you might be interested in…"

Rebecca, still holding Jim tight, looked over to Syreeta, smiled and then caught sight again of the boy who had faced death with her. He was standing by himself, alone and forlorn in the centre of the Ring. She squeezed Jim's hand before hurrying away towards the boy. But before she could reach him, she saw that there was another woman also running towards the boy, arms outstretched, who swept him up into her arms, hugging him tightly. Rebecca watched as the mother turned, looked around anxiously and ran from the scene, clutching the boy's hand.

Elsewhere, there were several groups of tearful children, still terror-struck, being comforted by mothers and friends. As Jim walked over to her, Rebecca noticed a small girl all on her own. She crouched and asked the girl her name.

"Shona," the girl whispered.

Larry, watching Rebecca with the little girl, then caught sight of a bedraggled, middle-aged man, who came staggering through the entrance to the Ring, as if badly injured. His jacket, jeans and shirt were all ripped to shreds.

It had taken all Sandy's physical and mental strength to get to Brodgar from the garden shed where he had sheltered, until the birds had finally given up their pursuit. He had seen the white van slewed on to the grass verge, and had prayed there might be somebody around who could help him. Hearing only a quiet murmur of human voices from the Ring, and totally bewildered by the apparent peace of the scene after the commotion of the night before, he had cautiously crept up the hillside. It was with overwhelming relief that, just as he collapsed to the ground, he saw Larry hurrying towards him.

Larry helped him to sit up. Sandy's hair was now matted with dried blood from a deep gash on the top of his head. He was distraught.

"Thank God! Thank God! At last! I tried to get help. I banged on doors, but nobody would open up. No one would help…"

Larry winced as he inspected the wound. "What happened to you? Where have you come from?"

"It was the birds. They were evil, like something out of a horror film."

"Birds? You mean birds did this?" asked Larry.

"Yes. Great big birds. They came out of nowhere and just came at us. You wouldn't believe it…"

"Take your time. It's all okay now," said Larry. "You mean the attack at the Odin Stone? I saw what they had done."

Sandy looked up. "We had just put the Stone back, when they came and swooped on us. They knocked us to the ground. We didn't stand a chance…"

"I think I know who was behind all this," said Larry. "It doesn't sound possible, I know, but I believe someone called Neferatu and his followers had the power to take the form of birds and attack people. I can tell you some quite incredible things have been happening around here…"

"Neferatu? I know about Neferatu," said Sandy bitterly.

"Well, the good news is that Neferatu is gone, and with him, I imagine, the birds as well," said Larry. "But right now, we should do something about this gash of yours."

At that moment Rebecca and Jim arrived, Rebecca still holding

Shona's hand. When she caught sight of Sandy, she hurried towards him. "Oh, my God, what on earth has happened to you?"

"It was the birds," said Sandy. Then he looked at them all in turn. "But that's not all, I haven't told you everything. Terrible things have been happening on Norstray. There's been a massacre…"

Struggling to hold back tears, he began to tell them about the appalling events that had taken place there. "I'll tell you one thing," he said. "I am very lucky just to be alive."

"Right, we should get some doctors over there as fast as possible," said Larry.

He looked at Rebecca and Jim, and then at Sandy and Shona, the distraught women and children. "I think I'm going to have to stay in Orkney a while. These people are going to need some help."

"Thank you, Larry," said Rebecca.

Larry looked up at the sky. The sun had broken through the clouds, which glowed red on the horizon. The waters of the Loch of Harray shimmered in the early morning light.

"'Red sky in the morning – shepherd's warning'. Things are going to be very different now," he said.

As if in reply, a rainbow, symbol of promise, began to appear, brilliant and clear, arching high in the sky over the loch. Everybody in the Ring stopped what they were doing, and stood and watched, entranced.

At one end, the rainbow lit up the Standing Stones of Stenness. The other end reached down into the sunlit water, and the whole loch seemed to explode into a million glittering, brightly coloured lights.